D0340265

Glenda Leznoff

HEARTACHE AND OTHER NATURAL SHOCKS

TUNDRA BOOKS

Copyright © 2015 by Glenda Leznoff

Published in Canada and the United States of America by Tundra Books,
a division of Random House of Canada Limited, a Penguin Random House Company

Library of Congress Control Number: 2014951823

Library and Archives Canada Cataloguing in Publication

Leznoff, Glenda Barbara, 1956-, author
Heartache and other natural shocks / written by Glenda Leznoff.

Issued in print and electronic formats.
ISBN 978-1-77049-836-5 (bound).—ISBN 978-1-77049-837-2 (epub)

I. Title.

PS8573.E995H42 2015   jC813'.54   C2014-905503-X
                                                 C2014-905504-8

Edited by Sue Tate
Designed by Five Seventeen
The text was set in New Caledonia.

www.penguinrandomhouse.ca

Printed and bound in the United States of America

1 2 3 4 5 6   20 19 18 17 16 15

Penguin
Random
House

TUNDRA BOOKS

For my parents, Ruth and Arthur Leznoff

JULES

"Subterranean Homesick Blues"

I'm halfway between Montreal and Toronto in one of those awful gas/food stations off the 401. If purgatory were a real place, it would look like this: lots of people, lots of plastic, bad food and toilet lineups. Right now, I'm sitting in an orange plastic chair, attached to a brown plastic table, bolted to the floor—so no one will steal it? Who designs these places? Ugly Inc.?

Bobby is picking at his french fries, Mom is sipping coffee and I'm pretending to read so I won't have to talk to them, but I can feel Mom's blue hawk eyes zooming in on me. She says, "Julia, you should eat something."

Is she kidding? I'm so nervous I could throw up. Besides, if eating would make her happy, I'd go on a hunger strike.

If I went on a hunger strike, would she let me go home? What would happen if, instead of going to the bathroom, I snuck out the exit, ran across the highway and stuck out my thumb? Would anyone pick up a desperate-looking teenager? Anyone other than a pervert, I mean. And where would I go if I had the guts to make a run for it?

I think about my escape options:

1. I could fly to Paris, get a job waitressing in the Latin Quarter and become an artist. But unlike Vincent van Gogh, who sold only one painting in his entire life and died penniless, I'd get discovered and become rich and famous, at which point I may or may *not* forgive my parents for ruining my life.

2. I could take a vow of silence and join a Benedictine monastery. Except I don't believe in God, and they probably don't accept fifteen-year-old Jewish girls. Scratch that.

3. I could go to Tibet and visit those temples with the bronze bells and golden Buddhas. I'd spin prayer wheels—the ones that look like Purim gregors—and my prayers would be carried off into the wind. Or maybe I'd spend weeks making an intricate mandala from brightly colored grains of sand, and in the end, I'd sweep it all away into a pile of thin gray dust, a symbol of the impermanence of life.

Because everything *is* impermanent. I know that now. I didn't know it a year ago. A year ago, I was just a normal teenager living in a three-bedroom, semidetached house in the Town of Mount Royal, thinking my life was a straight road. I walked to T.M.R. High every day with my best friend, Mollie

Fineberg, and twice a week I took jazz dancing classes with Eva von Gencsy from Les Ballets Jazz at the Saidye Bronfman Centre. I was happy and I didn't even know it. And why didn't I know it? Because I didn't understand that things change. Someone should warn you about that when you're growing up. Someone should inform you that living in a nice house, in a beautiful city like Montreal, doesn't mean that your life is going to be that way forever.

Bobby shoves his french fries in my face. They're drenched in ketchup. He says, "Jules, you can have one if you want." He squints at me. He has big brown eyes and thick lashes, just like Dad. Why do boys always get the great lashes? He's being unusually considerate for a nine-year-old brat, but I shake my head. My stomach is bubbling like a witch's cauldron.

Mom drains her coffee, and we head back to the station wagon. In three hours we'll be in a rented house in Willowdale, Toronto. I've never been to Toronto. If I had to make a list of all the places I'd like to visit in my lifetime, Toronto wouldn't even be on it. I try to imagine what my life will be like there, but I can't. All I can think about is everything I've left behind.

Last night I slept at Mollie's, and we stayed up till four in the morning talking and listening to music. All the songs seemed to be about us: "You've Got a Friend," "Fire and Rain," "Bridge over Troubled Water." Every time a song started up, we'd look at each other and burst into tears. Our eyes got so red and puffy, we had to put slices of cucumber on them, like they tell you to do in *Vogue*'s beauty tips. The cucumber was cold and a bit sticky. We lay on our backs on Mollie's bed and listened to Simon & Garfunkel's *Bookends* album all the way to the end, where it's just Paul Simon's lone guitar and their two beautiful voices singing about "a time of innocence, a time of confidences."

When the song finished, neither of us spoke. I listened to the scratchy sound of the needle skimming across the record and the steady ticking of the grandfather clock at the end of the hall. I thought about all the nights I've slept at Mollie's and how I've always loved the sound of that clock, but now it was just counting down the seconds till I had to leave town, like some evil death-clock in a Dalí painting or a Bergman film.

We crawled under the covers, and I whispered, "Mollie, I can't do this."

She said, "Jules, it will be really hard at the beginning, but then you'll get used to it. People get used to anything. And after a while, new things will happen. Good things."

I wanted to ask her *What good things could possibly happen to me in a strange high school, in a new city where I knew no one?* But I couldn't speak because it felt like there was a dry stone stuck at the bottom of my throat, and it's still there.

In the car, my mother listens to the CBC news: more about Nixon, the bombings in Cambodia, the floods in Bangladesh. Disaster everywhere. I tune out. I lean my head against the window and stare at the farms and fields, with their brittle stacks of hay and their endless rows of corn. Who lives here? I wonder. Who lives in these sad, crooked farmhouses in the middle of nowhere, with views of the highway and of cars speeding past carrying strangers to the big city, far, far away?

CARLA

"No Time"

Debbie's at the wheel of her mom's Buick LeSabre, Marlene's in the passenger seat and I'm in the back, peeking out the window. Steve lives in Forest Hill: quiet street, big house. The first time we drive past, no one's around. I make Debbie circle the block. The second time we cruise by—oh my God—there he is, coming out of the house.

"Shit!" I say, ducking down. Steve knows Marlene and me from Camp Minawaka, but he doesn't know Deb.

Marlene says, "Uh-oh, he sees me."

I can't look, but I hear his voice. "Hey, Marlene?"

Debbie stops the car.

"Drive!" I whisper.

Marlene puts on her fake-surprised voice and says, "Oh, hi, Steve, how's it hangin'?"

Steve's voice gets closer. "Hey, Mar, what are you doing here?"

"Drive! Drive!" I hiss, flattening myself to the floor.

Marlene says, "Gotta go. See ya around, Steve."

Debbie guns it, and we leave Steve in the dust. As soon as

we get around the corner, Debbie pulls over, and she and Marlene burst out laughing. I pop up and scream, "What the hell did you think you were doing back there? He almost saw me!" But Deb and Mar are practically peeing themselves laughing, and soon I'm laughing too.

After that, we go to Sam the Record Man because Marlene wants to buy the Doors' *L.A. Woman* album—which I already have. Then we go back to Marlene's to listen to it and eat jujubes. Marlene read that jujubes have almost no calories, so we eat them all the time, but they sit in your stomach like rocks.

The song "L.A. Woman" is seven minutes and forty-nine seconds long, with Jim Morrison singing "Mr. Mojo risin'" over and over, like he's going to come right on the spot. Deb says that his "mojo" is his dick and it's rising because he's horny, but Steve told me that "Mr. Mojo risin'" is an anagram for Jim Morrison's name—like when you mix up the letters into a different order—which is so cool! I love knowing things like that. Of course, I still can't believe that Jim Morrison is dead. Marlene and I were at camp when it happened. July 3. When Mar heard that they found his body in a bathtub in Paris, she bawled her eyes out. He was only twenty-seven, the exact same age as Jimi Hendrix and Janis Joplin when they overdosed last fall. Spooky, eh?

Anyway, after we talk about Jim Morrison and his stupid heroin-addict girlfriend, Debbie grills me about Steve. She thinks he's a real hunk and I should definitely give him a call, but I won't. The thing is, he said he'd call me, and it's been two days since camp ended.

"Hey, Carla, I'll call you as soon I get home," he said on the bus.

Yeah, right. I should've known better. Camp romances never last, because once the guy is back in the city, it's O-V-E-R. It's like camp never happened. It's like suddenly he's living on a different planet, in a different galaxy, and there's no fucking way he can pick up the phone. Well, I couldn't care less. It's not like I'm in love with him or anything. But if we're going to break up, I want to call the shots. It's one of my rules: Dump him before he dumps you. I'm not a girl who gets dumped. It's a good thing we didn't fool around that much. Well, we necked and he felt me up, but that's all. And he was sooo pushy. What a jerk.

Marlene invites Debbie and me to sleep over, but Ma says no because I've been at camp all summer and she wants me home for dinner. Besides, the family from Montreal, the one renting the McDuff house next door, is supposed to show up today. Ma says they have two kids just like us, a boy and a girl. I wonder if they're French. I wonder if the boy is my age—a cute boy with a sexy French accent. Now that would be something to look forward to.

"It Don't Come Easy"

Telegram to self: Have arrived in hell. Worse than expected.

When Mom pulls up to the McDuff house and says "We're here," my heart sinks. The house is a new fake Tudor, like all the other new fake Tudors on the block. There are no graceful, leafy maples on this street like there are at home, only spindly, pathetic tree-twigs sticking out of empty lawns like undernourished orphans. It makes you sad just looking at them. And that's just the outside. Inside, everything is modern—in a bad way. The kitchen is so white, it hurts my eyes. The den is all glass and chrome. Bobby's room is done in red, white and blue geometrics (yuck), and over the desk is a poster of Dave Keon. Not Henri Richard, not Jean Béliveau, but Dave Keon of the Toronto Maple Leafs. Bobby stares at it, stunned, like someone who's been stabbed in the neck. We hate the Leafs! We're Habs fans.

But worst of all is my room. If you think hell is red, think again: it's pink. Yes, everything in eight-year-old Karen McDuff's bedroom is pink: the dresser, the curtains, the frilly bedspread, even the walls. They're the color of bubblegum, of Barbie's toy Corvette, of Pepto-Bismol. It's a color that has a very short shelf life in a girl's fairy tale world, and after that, it makes you want to puke.

Mom yells for us to come help with the bags. We're unloading the station wagon when a dark-haired woman bursts out of the house next door and rushes at us with a plate of muffins. She calls out, "Hello-ooo! You must be the new neighbors. I'm Gina Cabrielli, and this is Buzz." A boy Bobby's age races up behind her. Introductions are made. My mother gushes over the muffins.

Buzz looks at Bobby and says, "I have a basketball hoop in my backyard."

Bobby says, "Cool."

Buzz says, "You wanna play?"

Bobby says, "Sure." And they're off.

The moms beam at each other. It's like watching people pair up at a party. I grab my suitcase from the trunk and take it upstairs to the pink inferno. When I get back outside, a brown Buick is pulling into the Cabriellis' driveway. The driver is a girl with whitish-blonde hair parted straight down the middle and mean snake eyes. The other girl, the one who steps out of the passenger seat, wears silver hoop earrings, a halter top and tight cutoff jeans. She has pouty lips, thick, glossy black hair like Mrs. Cabrielli's and curves in all the right places.

Mrs. Cabrielli says, "Carla! Come here and meet our new neighbors."

Snake Eyes backs the Buick out of the driveway. Carla trudges over, and I can feel her eyes scanning my body for features and flaws. She knows my vital statistics within seconds: too tall, too skinny, gangly legs, small breasts, long chestnut hair and brown eyes. My mother introduces me as Julia, which I hate.

"Jules," I say.

"Julia will be going to Tom Thomson Secondary School," my mother says to Carla in that way mothers have when they're trying to set you up.

"Oh yeah," Carla says, tossing her hair over her shoulder.

"Carla can show you around," Mrs. Cabrielli offers.

"Sure," Carla says, but she's just being polite. I can tell. She doesn't want to show me around any more than I want to hang out with her. You either like people right from the start, or you don't. That's what I think. Take me and Mollie, for example. We met on the first day of grade one. I was milling around the playground when the bell rang. The teacher told everyone to partner up. I looked around and saw a girl with frizzy hair, a round face and serious, dark eyes staring straight at me. She said, "Do you want to be my partner?" I said yes. It was friends at first sight.

Meeting Carla is the opposite of that. After a few awkward moments, I say, "I better unpack. See ya."

Carla says yeah in a voice as flat and dry as cardboard.

I carry my box of records to my room and shut the door. If I were in Montreal, Mollie and I would bike over to Kane's Drugstore to buy orange Popsicles, or we'd hang out at the pool and see if Mike Cameron and his friends were showing off their dives on the high board. Mollie has a crush on Mike. Right now, Mollie's probably practicing her cello. She practices three hours a day because she's gifted. One day, she's going to be a world-famous concert cellist, and she's still going to be my best friend.

Around six, Mom calls me for dinner. I tell her I'm not hungry, and for once she doesn't bug me. Later, Dad calls from Montreal to see how we're settling in. I pick up the phone in Mom's bedroom. When I get on the line, Dad's voice sounds far away, like he could be in Paris or Moscow. He says, "How's my favorite girl?" It's our little joke because, of course, I'm his only girl.

I say, "I'm okay," but my voice warbles.

"Hey, kiddo, tough day?" he asks.

I hear a click and Bobby's voice comes on the phone from downstairs. "Dad, when you come, can you bring my hockey stick?"

I put the phone in my lap and listen to their voices filter through the receiver like static. I feel like an astronaut drifting through space, tied to my spaceship by a long, thin telephone cord. I hear Dad's voice saying, "Jules, poopsie? Are you there?"

My tongue scrapes across the inside of my mouth, but no sound comes out. My words tumble down into the dark oily pit of my stomach. I hang up and walk back to Karen McDuff's bedroom. I sink onto her ruffled bedspread and lie there like a corpse in a pink, satin-lined coffin. I stare at the ceiling. This is all my mother's fault. Sure, she tells everyone that "We're moving to Toronto to provide a better future for the children," but that's bullshit. Just because thousands of Anglophones are leaving Quebec doesn't mean we had to.

I should have seen this coming last October, when things in Quebec started to unravel, but back then, I didn't even know what the *Front de libération du Québec* was. When the FLQ kidnapped James Cross and Pierre Laporte, I didn't get it. I mean, kidnappings happen in other countries, but not in Canada. It didn't feel real. Even when Pierre Trudeau brought in the War Measures Act and the tanks rolled down Saint Catherine Street, it was like watching a play from the front row. I didn't think it had anything to do with *me personally*. It wasn't until I opened the *Gazette* and saw that photo of Pierre Laporte's dead body stuffed into the trunk of a Chevrolet that it actually hit me: A man had been murdered in my own city, and this story was not going to have a happy ending for anyone.

I remember the evening after the FLQ killed Laporte. It was a Sunday, and the Epsteins were gathered for our weekly dinner at my grandparents' big old house in Outremont. Bubby and Zadie's dining room table was loaded with the usual platters of food: meatballs, kugel, stewed peppers, smoked meat, eggplant. There are eighteen of us, so we always eat in shifts: first the kids, then the adults. Usually Joe, my oldest cousin, and I watch TV after dinner, but that night was different. When the adults gathered at the table, Joe and I stuck around, and there was none of the usual jokes and laughter. Somewhere in the city, James Cross, the British trade commissioner, was being held hostage, and Pierre Laporte, the Quebec immigration and labor minister, was dead.

"This is the beginning of the end," my mother said. "There's no future for the English in Quebec."

Dad scoffed. "You don't know what you're talking about, Natalie. I work with the French. The staff in my store are Québécois. They don't want to separate."

"That's what they say to your face, but what do they say behind your back?" asked Uncle Seymour.

Aunt Rose turned to my dad. "Irving, wake up and smell the coffee. Just look at the French universities and the trade unions. They're crawling with separatists. They hate the English, and even worse, they hate the Jews."

Aunt Connie, who everyone calls Aunt Commie because of her socialist leanings, thumped her fist on the table. "The FLQ are separatists, Rose, not Nazis!"

"This isn't about anti-Semitism," added Uncle Seymour.

"That's right," said Aunt Connie. "This is about French rights. The French have been treated like second-class citizens in their own province for over a hundred years. And they've had enough. I don't blame them for getting upset."

"Upset!" shrieked Aunt Rose. "They murdered Laporte! You call that 'upset'?"

At this point, everyone jumped in. Aunt Rose called Aunt Connie a communist. Aunt Connie called Aunt Rose a fascist. Zadie said they were blowing everything out of proportion. Dad said that there was nothing wrong with everyone in the province being bilingual. After all, he was bilingual. French is a beautiful language.

"Not the way you speak it," joked Uncle Seymour.

Aunt Rose tried to get in the last word, as always. "Irving," she said, "you may work on Saint Hubert with the Frenchmen, but let me tell you something: In the end, you're still one of *les maudits anglais*. The pendulum is swinging, and if we're smart, we'll get out of this province before things get worse."

"But where would you go?" Bubby asked, her voice quavering.

Dad patted Bubby's wrinkled hand. "Don't worry, Ma," he said. "The Epsteins have lived in Montreal for four generations. This is our home. We're not going anywhere." And that was that. Or so I thought.

Then in February, Aunt Rose and Uncle Seymour announced that they were moving to Florida and Joe would go to university in Gainesville. It was like the map of Joe's life had been snatched up and shredded.

And finally, on a warm spring evening last May, Mom and Dad broke the news about our own move. Mom did all the talking. She said, "We're moving to Toronto. The house and the store are going up for sale. We're leaving at the end of the summer." For a moment, no one spoke. Bobby and I just stared at her like she was an alien speaking in a garbled alien language that we couldn't possibly understand. She had to repeat herself. Her words came at me in slow motion, hovering in the air like little Scrabble tiles dancing on a cartoon cloud and then exploding around my ears like grenades.

Bobby yelled, "I'm not going!"

I turned to Dad, waiting for him to rescue me. "Dad, you said this is our home," I pleaded. "You said—"

"Julia, we have to be realistic," Mom said, cutting me off. "The French don't want us here. Why should we stay where we're not wanted?"

"Because we *live* here," I said. "This is a free country. We can live wherever we want. This is so stupid!" I could hardly breathe. It felt like a monster had just clawed into my chest and ripped my heart out of my body. I could almost feel the muscle fibers popping and twanging like broken guitar strings. *Snap. Snap. Snap.*

Bobby started crying. Mom looked over at Dad like she expected him to help her handle things. She said, "Irving . . ." But he just stared at the backs of his hands. And that's when I knew this was all her idea. He didn't want to leave Montreal.

So why wasn't he fighting her on this? They fought about everything else. Why was he caving in?

I stopped talking to my parents after that. I really didn't see the point in conversing. I had nothing left to say to them. After all, what could I possibly say to make them change their minds?

CARLA

"Babe I'm Gonna Leave You"

Over dinner, Ma gives us the scoop on the Epsteins. She and "Natalie" are already buddy-buddy. That's the kind of mother I have. Mrs. Welcome Wagon herself. If she makes muffins, she takes some next door. And their kid Bobby has been in and out of our house all day long.

"The poor woman knows no one in Toronto," Ma explains. "Imagine starting over in a new city with two kids."

Papa hears the words *starting over* and—presto—he launches into his "when I was a poor immigrant" story. "When I moved from Napoli, I had two bucks in my pocket, and I didn't speak a word of English."

"You didn't have two kids," Ma points out.

"I was practically a kid myself," Pa insists.

Already it's a contest about who's worse off. I've heard Papa's hard-luck story about a million times, so I change the topic. I ask, "Where's Mr. Epstein?"

"Ah," says Ma. "Mr. Epstein owns a women's clothing store, and no one wants to buy the business because so many people are leaving Montreal, so he's stuck there till he finds a buyer."

Papa frowns. "He let his wife move without him?"

"They had no choice. He'll come later," Ma says.

Buzz asks Papa if Bobby can join his hockey team because Bobby plays left wing, and last year he scored the most goals for his team.

Ma tries to give me more cannelloni, but I pass, even though I love her cannelloni, because I don't want to get fat. I lost seven pounds at camp—the food was so shitty!—and I just bought this pair of Howick wide-legged jeans, size 27. They are so cool. But if I eat cannelloni, it's going to go straight to my ass, and nothing looks worse than a fat ass on a pair of wide-legged jeans. I mentally flip through my wardrobe, trying to decide what to wear on the first day of school, because, as *Cosmo* says, first impressions are very important.

Suddenly I realize Ma is talking to me. "What?" I ask.

"I said it would be nice if you introduced Julia to your friends."

I groan. "Look, Ma, just 'cause you like Mrs. Epstein doesn't mean I have to like her daughter, okay? Julia is not my type."

"You don't even know her," Ma says. "Would it hurt you to be nice to that girl?"

"Do you mind if I pick my own friends?"

"She doesn't know anybody, Carla."

"Ma, will you lay off," I say.

But my mother doesn't know how to lay off. No, she's like a dog with a bone. So, first we fight in English. Then she switches to Italian—which I hate because she talks twice as fast in Italian—and the louder she gets, the louder I get, till we're yelling at each other across the table, me in English and her in Italian. Finally, Papa smacks the table with his hand and bellows, "*Basta!*" and Ma and I both shut up. Then he glares at me with those beady brown eyes. "Carla," he says in his deep, don't-mess-with-me voice, "you invite her over once, and you don't ever have to do it again." I open my mouth to argue, but what's the point. God has spoken.

Later, I'm in my bedroom, about to do my nails, when guess who finally phones three and a half days late—but who's counting? Steve. He's been thinking about me. He misses me. I want to reach through the telephone and strangle him with my bare hands, but I'm cool. We gossip about people at camp. I picture him on the water-ski dock: sun-bleached hair, boyish smile, muscular body—California beach boy. Nice snapshot, but hey, winter's coming, and then what? He's not what you'd call a great conversationalist. And who cares if he's the captain of his hockey team. I'm not the kind of girl who freezes her butt off sitting on some splintered wooden bench in a hockey arena, yelling, "Go, Steve, go." I'm nobody's cheerleader. So, when he asks if I want to go to a movie, I say, "Steve, the summer was really fun, but I just don't have time for a long-distance relationship"—as if

Willowdale to Forest Hill is long distance. Steve sputters a bit. I tell him I have to go.

I'm glad I broke up with him. In fact, I'm going to take a break from guys for a while, especially high school guys. They're so immature. Besides, I have goals. This year, I want a lead in the school musical. Last year, Mr. Gabor directed *Hello, Dolly* and I was in the chorus, but no one notices you when you're in the chorus. And what's the point of being in a play if no one notices you? And it's not like I don't have talent. I'm the best actress in my class. Probably in my grade. In fact, I would have made a much better Dolly than Pauline Heppleworth, who has a good voice but cannot act. I mean, all she does is throw her hands around and toss her hair. She's a hair actress! And I'm way better looking than she is. Everyone says so. But Pauline was in grade thirteen and I was only in grade ten, and grade tens never get the leads. But now I'm in grade eleven, and Mr. Gabor likes me. He gave me 88 percent in drama last year, and he is *not* an easy marker. When I did my monologue, he told me I have "a strong onstage presence," and he wouldn't say it if he didn't mean it. A compliment from Mr. Gabor is worth about a million compliments from anyone else.

I sort through my nail polish colors. I pick Pearly Pink. It goes really well with my tan. And a girl has to look her best, even when she's not dating.

JULES

"The Times They Are A-Changin'"

My mother doesn't waste any time. The morning after our move, four days before classes start, Mom leads me down the empty hallways of Tom Thomson Secondary School and into the guidance office. The guidance counselor is a chubby, balding man stuffed into a pale yellow shirt and a greenish suit. He reminds me of a ripe squash. Mr. Squash. He welcomes us and says, "You know, Julia, this school is named after one of the Group of Seven painters, Tom Thomson. Have you heard of him?"

Before I can squeak out an answer, my mother replies, "Of course she has. Julia took an art class at the Redpath Museum with Arthur Lismer, who said she has a gift for color."

Mr. Squash raises an indulgent eyebrow. He's probably thinking that if he had a buck for every child whose parents think their kid is a genius, he'd be living on a yacht in the Caribbean. My mother ignores Mr. Squash's smarmy smile and points out that not only am I artistically gifted, but my marks are excellent, which is why I should skip grade ten and be placed in grade eleven.

This is news to me. I stare at my feet.

Mr. Squash says, "We don't encourage skipping grades."

My mother looks at Mr. Squash with cold, unblinking eyes. Her blonde hair is swept up into a chignon that shows off her long neck and high cheekbones. The words *not possible* are not in my mother's vocabulary. She says, "I think we both realize that the Ontario school system has thirteen grades, whereas Quebec's has only eleven. The two systems do not mesh." The way she says "mesh" sounds accusatory. "The point is, Julia has a 94 percent average, and it would be a mistake not to move her forward."

Mr. Squash flicks his pen against his clipboard and shifts his attention to me. "What do you think, Julia?" he asks in a condescending voice.

I glance at him. What do *I* think? Is he joking? Nobody gives a damn what I think. If what I thought counted for anything, I wouldn't be sitting here, in this new school, in this suburban wasteland. This meeting is just a game, a power struggle between Mr. Squash and my mother. I am like Vietnam, stuck between China and the United States. A pawn. A battle zone. No one gives a shit about what Vietnam wants. Vietnam and me, we're just territory.

I have a sudden flash of my face, photographed, like an Andy Warhol print, against the flag of Vietnam. It's a funny image. It almost makes me laugh out loud. And at the same time as I'm thinking about that, I'm noticing Mr. Squash's ugly, brown ribbed socks and how my mother is glaring at me, as if she could will me to say something intelligent instead of sitting on my chair like a sullen lump.

In the end, I just shrug. Mr. Squash must think I'm an idiot. "Do you think you could handle grade eleven?" he asks. "The rest of the kids would be a year older than you," he adds, as if I can't do the math.

"I'll be fine," I say.

Mr. Squash purses his lips. "I suppose we could give it a try," he says. My mother smiles triumphantly. We discuss my electives. I choose drama and art. It's over quickly. When I shake Mr. Squash's pulpy hand, he says, "You know, Julia, skipping a grade can be difficult. Don't expect to get the same high marks you got last year."

I stare at him with a deadpan face. I may be a social misfit, I may have the confidence of a gnat, but one thing I *do* know is how to get good marks in school. School is not my problem.

In the lobby, we pass Mr. Squash's next appointment: a thin, elegant woman and her son. The woman has a willowy, fragile kind of beauty. Her son slouches in his chair: lean, angular, all legs, black T-shirt and long black hair. As we walk by, he flicks his hair out of his eyes and looks at me. His face changes everything about him. His body is loose and lazy, but his expression has an unsettling intensity. His face is narrow with high cheekbones, a nose that looks like it's been broken at least once, lips that are too wide and sharp predatory eyes. Those eyes are unnatural: pale gray-blue, cold like a winter moon ringed in black. Wolf eyes. Eyes that know their own power. Our eyes meet. Neither of us smiles.

I spend the rest of the day in my room reading *The Drifters*, a book about six young people from different countries who, unlike me, have the guts to run away from home. They end up in Torremolinos, Spain, swimming, meeting cool people in the bar, having sex and basically living out my romantic fantasy life. The book is thick, but I have plenty of time.

After dinner, the doorbell rings and my mom calls out in a way-too-cheery voice, "Julia, it's for you." For a minute, I'm confused because I don't know anyone in Toronto, but there, standing in the front hall, is Carla Cabrielli. She's flanked by two friends: Snake Eyes, the string-bean blonde, and a short, wiry girl with a mouth full of braces who reminds me of a terrier. Carla introduces Debbie and Marlene and says, "Do you want to come over to my place?" She couldn't sound less enthusiastic. Personally, I'd rather stay home and pick lint off an old sweater, but it's obvious to everyone that my social calendar is wide open.

The Cabriellis' basement is a dark room with high windows, pine-paneled walls and an orange shag carpet. Carla tosses a bag of chips onto a vinyl card table while Marlene flips through the records on the stereo stand. Debbie flops onto a corduroy beanbag chair and checks her hair for split ends. "So, you're from Montreal," she says without looking up.

"Yeah."

"So, what's it like there?" she asks.

"It's great," I say.

"What's so great about it?"

I shrug. "Beaver Lake, the restaurants, the old city . . ." I remember my uncle Seymour's latest joke about Toronto: *What's the difference between yogurt and Toronto?* Answer: *Yogurt has culture.* It's not a joke Debbie would appreciate.

"Why did you move here?" Marlene asks.

"Because of the FLQ," I say. Marlene stares blankly at me. "The separatists. The FLQ?" I repeat. Silence. Does she even know what I'm talking about? Are these girls living in the same country as me?

Marlene says, "Oh, right. They kidnapped that French guy last year."

"They kidnapped two guys," I say. "James Cross and Pierre Laporte."

"And they shot the French one," Carla says, like she knows.

"They didn't shoot him," I say. "They didn't use a gun." Carla gives me a cold stare; she obviously doesn't like being contradicted. "They locked him up for a week and then strangled him with the chain he wore around his neck. After that, they dumped his body in the trunk of a car and left it in an airport parking lot."

"What happened to the other guy?" Marlene asks, interested now. There's nothing like a few gory details to get people hooked.

"James Cross? He's the one they kidnapped first," I explain. "It was October 5th, his birthday. He was in his bathroom getting ready for work when three guys from the FLQ burst into his house. They had an M1 rifle, a .22 Beretta and a Luger pistol. They ripped out the phone wires, handcuffed him and took him to their hideout. Then they sent a list of demands to a radio station. Five days later, a different FLQ cell group kidnapped Pierre Laporte."

The girls stare at me. I know I'm talking way too fast, but I can't stop. I'm like a runaway train. I say, "Pierre Laporte was playing football with his nephew on his front lawn when four men with machine guns pulled up to his house. They dragged him into their car. He had a wife and children. They made him write a letter to Premier Bourassa begging for his life. They threatened to execute him. No one believed they'd do it, but they did. They killed him!" I screech to a halt. You can practically smell the burning rubber. The girls gawk at me like I'm some kind of weirdo.

Finally, Marlene says, "Uh . . . did you know him? Like, personally?"

"No," I say.

There's an awkward pause. Carla and Debbie exchange looks, eyebrows raised. Carla drawls, "O-kay, then. Sooo, are we playing cards or what?"

I feel my face flush. I'm being way too intense. This is supposed to be a "fun" night and I'm blowing it.

Carla plunks a game on the table and turns to me. "Do you know how to play Rummoli?" she asks. I shake my head. "It's like poker on a board game. You *do* know how to play poker, don't you?"

"Sort of," I say.

"Well, you'll pick it up. You must be smart if you're skipping a grade." The way she says it is like a challenge. Or an insult. My mother must have told her mother.

Marlene puts on a record: Tina Turner singing "Proud Mary." Carla grins, and the girls instantly launch into a backup singer dance routine, rolling their arms and bobbing their heads as they sing along. I sit there while they roll on over to the table and take packs of cigarettes and bags of coins from their purses. Carla and Marlene smoke du Mauriers. Debbie smokes Player's menthol.

Debbie looks at the empty table in front of me. "She doesn't have money," she says to Carla, talking about me like I'm not even here.

"We'll have to lend her some," Carla says.

"Well, I don't have that much," Debbie says.

"You're so cheap," Carla says.

"I can pay you back," I say.

"But what if she wins?" Debbie says, still ignoring me.

"Sooo . . . ," Carla says, "she'll pay us back and she'll keep what she wins. Jeez. Never mind. I'll lend her the money."

Marlene stacks her nickels and dimes in neat piles, singing along with Tina. Debbie stuffs a piece of Juicy Fruit gum in her mouth and doesn't offer any to the rest of us. Carla counts out three dollars in change and pushes it toward me. She tells me the rules, and we begin. I don't care if I win or lose; the game is just something to do while the girls talk about people I don't know. The name Steve comes up a lot.

"Carla was dating him at camp," Marlene explains. "He's a real stud, but he doesn't understand about women's clothes." Marlene bursts out laughing.

"Shut up," Carla says.

Marlene keeps laughing.

"What's so funny?" Debbie asks, cracking her gum.

"The wedgie!" Marlene gasps. "Tell them about the wedgie." Carla smirks. "Tell them!" Marlene insists.

"Okay, okay," Carla says. "It was after a campfire. Steve was walking me back to my cabin, and we were necking in the woods, and he kept trying to pull up my shirt, which looks like a halter top, but really it's a one-piece with snaps at the crotch. So there he is, yanking away, and there I am getting a goddamn wedgie!" Carla laughs. "I mean, all he can think about is his hard-on and how horny he is."

"So, what happened?" Debbie asks.

"I told him to stop, obviously," Carla says. She opens her du Mauriers and places a cigarette between her lips. "I am so tired of dating jerks," she mutters, striking a match. "They spend all day yakking about sports and music, and then all night trying to get into your pants. It's so predictable."

"So, did he?" Debbie asks.

"What?" Carla says.

"Did he get into your pants?"

"Fuck off," Carla says.

"I'm just joking," Debbie says.

"Yeah, well, it's none of your business," Carla snaps.

I can't tell if Carla is angry at Debbie for prying or if she just doesn't want to talk about her personal life in front of me. We ante up and play the hand. Marlene pushes her cigarette box toward me. "You want a ciggie?" she asks.

"No, thanks," I say, trying to make it sound like I don't want to smoke at this particular moment, but I guess it's obvious that I don't smoke at all because suddenly the girls swivel their heads like sharks catching the scent of blood.

Carla props her elbow on the table and dangles her cigarette between her fingers. She says, "So, Julia, tell us about yourself. What do you do for fun? Do you have a boyfriend?" She smirks, like she already knows the answer.

"Not really," I fumble. And then, for some stupid reason, I add, "Not now."

"But did you in Montreal?" Carla persists.

I grope for something that might satisfy her curiosity without making me seem like a total loser. What can I say? That I had a crush on Jon Mendleson but the only thing we ever did together was dissect a frog in science class? I think my hand touched his when I passed him the scalpel. I'm desperate, so I lie. "I sort of had a thing going with a guy from my science class, but it didn't really go anywhere." Pathetic.

Carla looks at me with dark, alert eyes. "How long did you go out for?" she asks.

"Not long."

"What does he look like?" Marlene asks.

"Tall. He plays basketball. He has curly hair."

"An Afro?" Carla asks.

"No, just curly."

"Is he hot?" Debbie asks.

I gulp.

"Debbie, you're embarrassing her," Marlene snickers.

"I'm just asking a question," Debbie drawls. "Like is he a good kisser? Is he sexy? I'm not asking how *big* he is or anything."

Carla grins and throws a handful of chips at Debbie. "Debbie, you're such a slut!" she says. The girls laugh. Suddenly they're all in a good mood again.

Marlene explains that the "big thing" is an inside joke because "In school, this girl, Sherrie Cumberland, told us that her boyfriend's dick is nine inches long, and she knows because he measured it with a ruler." Marlene giggles.

Carla laughs and turns back to me. She takes a long drag on her cigarette and says, "I bet you're the type who likes to have deep, meaningful conversations with guys." She blows smoke in my direction. I stare at my cards and fold. Marlene raises a nickel. Debbie puts in. Carla calls it. She wins with a full house and scoops the change toward her. I look at my watch. It's only 8:08. I wonder how long I'll have to stay in the game.

We play for another hour. Debbie and I lose our money to Carla and Marlene. Finally, I say, "I have to go home. I still have things to unpack." We all know I'm lying.

At the front door, Marlene says, "See you at school."

Debbie says, "Yeah."

Carla says, "Thanks for coming."

The door slams behind me. As I walk across the dark lawn, crickets shriek in a piercing chorus, and I know that in the Cabriellis' basement, the girls are already talking about me.

It's too early to go back to the McDuff house—my mother will just interrogate me—so I cut along the hedge to the backyard and then down the hill into the ravine. Ravines are a strange feature of the Toronto landscape. It's like the city is built on a grid of straight lines, but below street level, like giant cracks in the earth's surface, are these ravines. Some are tame, little gorges with streams and parks, but others extend for miles, with cycle paths and walking trails. It's like a sub-city zone. Mom told me not to walk in the ravine at night, so that's exactly where I go.

I stride down the cement path into the forest. I listen to the sounds of the night: the rustling of leaves, the scrabbling of small animals in the bush, the fast, angry clacking of my sandals on the cement. I like the hardness of the path hitting my heels. I even like the rush of fear I get when I imagine that I'm lost, or that someone's following me, or that the trees are whispering warnings in an ancient druidic language that I cannot understand. I walk, and walk, and walk. I wonder how long it would take a person to walk all the way from Toronto to Montreal.

When my legs feel like lead pipes, I head back to the house, but I don't go inside. Instead, I lie down on the back deck underneath the birch tree and stare up at the stars. The birch is the only nice thing about the McDuff house. It has white papery bark and long elegant branches like the smooth, bare arms of ballerinas. The leaves are heart-shaped, and some are turning canary yellow, but at night you can't see color. Everything is shadow upon shadow.

As I lie there, the wind picks up and dark clouds scuttle across the sky, blocking out the stars. The air gets that heavy feeling that comes before a rain. Down in the ravine, the forest whooshes and rattles in a junglelike voodoo ritual.

It takes a long time for the rain to come, and when it does, it falls in fat, heavy droplets, one on my elbow, one on my eyelid. It's cold, but I don't mind; in fact, I like it. Soon the rain is pelting down, and the wind is tossing twigs and leaves across the deck, against my body. My clothes stick to my wet skin. I shut my eyes, feeling the scratchy, tearing wildness of it all; I'm really grooving on it. And then the screen door squeaks open, and there's my mother, looming over me, like some scowling giantess.

"What do you think you're doing?" she asks, enunciating each word.

I don't want to break my monk's vow of silence, but mothers need answers. "Just lying here," I say.

"It's raining."

"I know."

"You're lying in the rain."

Obviously.

"Why would you want to lie outside, in the rain, in the dark?"

How can I explain it, especially now that she's ruined it?

"I asked you a question," she says.

"I just felt like it," I reply.

"You just felt like it," she repeats. She presses her fingertips to her forehead. "I don't get it. You felt like lying in the rain?"

I jump up and lurch past her into the kitchen, but she grabs my arm and digs her fingers into my flesh. "Julia!" she says, spinning me around.

"Why are you always on my case?" I shout.

"Because this is not normal behavior!"

I want to scream *It's rain, just rain. It's not pot. It's not speed. I'm not having sex with old weird men. I'm not selling my body on the street. It's just plain, ordinary rain. And what the hell is normal anyway? Do you actually think I'm losing my mind? Do you always have to stare at me like I'm out of my mind?*

But I can't say that, because it would only make it worse, so I stand there and we glare at each other in a contest of contempt. Her blue eyes bore into mine, but she can't break me. She can wait till hell freezes over before I'll speak a word to her.

She says, "Julia, we are not moving back to Montreal. So cut the melodrama and get on with your life." Then she swoops out of the room like a witch on a broomstick.

I continue my role as the Ice Queen. The ground chills beneath my feet, and everything I touch turns to frost and snaps off. I return to my ugly pink cell and throw myself on my ugly pink bed. I feel like I'm living in exile—which somehow reminds me of Alice, the live-in maid we used to have when I was little. She was from Jamaica. She used to tell me that she was always cold, even when she wore a sweater, and that people in Montreal didn't share a laugh the way her folks did back home. She said that if it wasn't for the money, she wouldn't stay a day in this mean country. She used to drag herself around the house, and eventually my mother "let her go" and hired a French Canadian girl from a family of thirteen kids who was lots of fun. I never liked Alice, but now I understand that she was homesick, which is a real kind of sickness, and that maybe in Jamaica she was a different, happier person.

CARLA

"Watcha See Is Watcha Get"

According to *Cosmo*, a girl has to make the most of her assets, and I don't like to brag, but I have more to work with than most girls at my school. Take Marlene, for example. She's way too short, especially in the legs, but what can she do? Get stretched on a rack? I tell her: Don't worry, there's lots of short guys looking for short girls. And I'm sure her teeth will look really great when her braces come off.

And then there's Deb. Debbie's boobs are like two pebbles on a highway. Bummer! Debbie wants to get those silicone implants, but her mom says no. Deb hates her boobs (who wouldn't?). When I was in grade six and my boobs suddenly popped out, I was so embarrassed, especially when Ron Kachinsky used to run into me on purpose and pretend to bounce off my chest like it was a trampoline—until I finally kicked him in the shin so hard, he limped for a week. And it still bugs me the way I'll be walking down the street and some guy will twist his neck around like a pretzel to stare at my boobs. Jeez! Men are such pigs. But, on the other hand, as I get older, I've learned to work with what I've got, if you catch my drift.

Which brings me to the question of the day: *What to wear to school?* At first, I was thinking my Hash jeans with the star on the butt and the rainbow stitching because they really hug my bum and they're comfy, but now I'm thinking my white miniskirt because my legs are really tanned and soon the tan is going to fade, so I might as well show off my legs while they're at their best.

And then there's my top. My yellow tank top is so cute and it shows a lot of cleavage, but if Papa sees it, he's going to have a big hairy fit about what's appropriate to wear to school. Or there's my black, stretchy, tie-dye T-shirt, which sort of makes me look like a leopard. I try on both and turn sideways to check myself out in the mirror. I look great. I pick up the phone and poll Marlene and Debbie. Mar votes for my black top; Deb votes for the yellow one. A tie! Ugh! I can't decide, so I flip through *Cosmo* and do a quiz about what kind of guy I'm attracted to.

1. When you go out for dinner, your date should
   a) Split the cost with you
   b) Let you pay
   c) Pay for everything

Definitely c). If he likes me, he can bloody well pay. I mean, sure, I believe in equal rights for women and all that shit, but when it comes to dates, guys should pay. Besides, like my grandma Nonna Cabrielli says, "It's just as easy to love a rich man as a poor man."

2. On your first date, the guy should expect
   a) No kiss
   b) A brief kiss
   c) French-kissing

God, I hate those questions. It depends on the guy, obviously. I mean, if I like him, I'll want to kiss him, and if I don't, forget it. I skip to the next question.

3. The thing I value most in a guy is
   a) Conversation
   b) Humor
   c) Physical appearance

Well, I'd like to choose "all of the above," but since that isn't an option, I circle c). At least I'm being honest. The truth is, if a guy has a face like a toad, no girl's going to look twice. Besides, when you're a ten out of ten like I am, you don't want to dip into the single digits.

"Smiling Faces Sometimes"

Light washes into the early morning sky like water into a metal pail—cold and gray. The numbers on my alarm clock click over. 4:48. 5:32. 6:24. At seven o'clock, I go down to the kitchen and sprinkle cereal into a bowl so it will look like I've eaten. At 8:15, I leave for school. I take the shortcut: down the ravine, across the wooden bridge that arches over the stream and up the paved trail through the trees to the school.

From the outside, Tom Thomson Secondary looks like an ugly concrete slab, but inside, it's new and modern, with open-plan areas and Lego-colored lockers. Students gather in the corridors, joking around and comparing summer stories. I keep my head down. I could be a time traveler disguised as a student, an alien from a parallel universe or a mutant with strange telepathic powers, like Sophie in *The Chrysalids*, and no one would have a clue.

My homeroom is in the English area. I grab a seat against the wall, in the third row, and doodle in my notebook as students file in: keeners in the front, rebels at the back. It's important to get a good desk on the first day because once people choose their spots, they hardly ever change them. It's just one of those things.

Mrs. Llewellyn, the English teacher, takes attendance. She's in the middle of explaining about lockers and schedules when Wolf Eyes slips into the room. There are empty seats in the center of the room, but he doesn't go there. He sits in the back corner, in no-man's-land, in the seat closest to the door.

Mrs. Llewellyn looks up at him. "And your name is . . . ?"

"Ian. Slater."

So that's his name. He slouches in his chair and sticks his long bony legs into the aisle. I don't look at him, but I see him out of the corner of my eye, in his jeans and black T-shirt, his knees jiggling, his eerie, gray-blue eyes staring at nothing. He's like a coiled spring. He's like an accident on the highway that you know you shouldn't look at. Maybe I notice him because he's the only familiar face in the class, but I don't think so. There's something about him; it's like I already know him. I can't shake the feeling that we're two meteors hurtling through space, in arcing trajectories, on an inevitable collision course.

At noon, I avoid the noisy lunchroom and push through the main doors into the bright sunlight. Kids hang out near the entrance, smoking. I hesitate, trying to decide if I should go for a walk in the ravine or hang out in the bleachers with my nose in a book. Then the doors swing open, and Ian Slater steps outside. He has an unlit cigarette dangling from his mouth. He squints into the sun, spots me and lopes over in my direction. I freeze. When he's about a foot away from me, he removes his cigarette, holds it lazily between his thumb and forefinger and says, "Hi."

"Hi," I say. I can't believe this is happening. Am I psychic?

"You're in my homeroom," he says in a low voice.

"Yeah." He noticed.

He sticks his cigarette back in his mouth, tilts his head, and his wolf eyes hook into mine. One look is all it takes and I'm hypnotized, consumed by every detail of his face: the long cords of his neck, the hollowed-out space between his cheekbones and his jaw, the whiteness of his forehead beneath his long black bangs, the way his wide, sloping lips hug his cigarette. There's a small scar at the crease of his mouth—a thin white stitch. It's impossible not to stare. Ian reaches into his pockets, and his hands come out empty. "Do you have a light?" he asks.

"Oh," I say. How had I not noticed he'd been hunting for a light? "Uh, no," I say. I blush. I wish desperately that I smoked. Why don't I smoke?

Ian smirks. I wonder if he can read my mind. We both look over our shoulders, searching for someone with a match, and that's when I see Carla, Marlene and Debbie staring at us from across the courtyard. They're whispering. Carla has a stunned expression on her face, like she's thinking, I can't believe *he's* talking to *her*. I pretend not to see her, but within seconds, she's elbowing through the crowd of smokers, flashing me a big, fake, high-beam smile. Debbie and Marlene follow in her wake.

"Hi, Julia," Carla says, barging in between Ian and me. "I see you have a new friend. Aren't you going to introduce us?" She tosses her hair over her shoulder and thrusts out her chest. She's wearing a tight yellow tank top and an ankh pendant on a leather string that hangs just above her cleavage. She smiles at Ian. The smile says *Go ahead, have a look.*

Ian grins. He says, "Does anyone have a light?"

Carla and her maids-in-waiting dive into their purses for smokes and matches. Carla wins the race and strikes a match. Ian cups his hand around hers, guides the flame to his cigarette and leans over. He inhales and the tip of his cigarette glows red. He exhales a long smooth wreath of smoke, and we watch in awe, as if we've never seen anyone smoke so beautifully in our entire lives. Ian releases Carla's hand and says, "Thanks."

Carla is speechless. Marlene edges over to Ian. Her braces glitter in the sun. "You're new, aren't you?" she says in a perky voice.

Carla shoots her a back-off-bitch look and proceeds to run the conversation. She quizzes Ian. He's from North Bay. His father is a mining executive who got transferred to head office. He lives on Hawthorne Crescent. I can tell from Carla's expression that Hawthorne Crescent is a nice address.

I stand there for a while listening in, watching Carla pose her body this way and that, like a model at a photo shoot. Ian smokes and doesn't say much. Finally, I say, "I think I'll get some lunch." Carla glances at me as if to say *Are you still here?*

Ian says, "See ya."

I go for a walk in the ravine. If Mollie were here, she'd laugh and tell me to forget about Ian Slater because he's trouble. She'd say that Carla and Ian deserve each other. Mollie always tries to look on the bright side of things. Last month, Mollie told me, "Moving to a new city is an opportunity to reinvent yourself." Then she spun out a fantasy, like we do sometimes to entertain each other. She said, "Maybe, on the first day of school, you'll be looking for a classroom and a handsome guy, some Adonis with golden locks and a great body, will say *Hey, I'm going to that class*. And the next thing you know, you'll be studying together, and he'll ask you out to a movie. A good movie, like a Fellini. And he'll pay for your ticket *and* your popcorn. And afterward, when he drives you home, you'll talk for an hour in the car with the motor running, and then he'll lean over and kiss you. And the kiss will be so passionate and hot that you'll practically wet your pants!"

We both burst out laughing.

I wonder who Mollie's having lunch with right now. Is she sitting on the hill where we always used to sit? Did she get a good locker? Is she in any classes with Mike Cameron?

When I walk back to the main entrance, Carla, Ian and the girls are gone. I think about Ian and his strange crystalline eyes that pull you in like gravity. If he wanted to, he could be anything: a rock star, a gigolo, a thief, a psychic, a rodeo rider, a lion tamer, a movie star, anything—and he wouldn't even have to try.

CARLA

"Chick-A-Boom"

Oh yes! Oh yes! I believe in karma! And here's why: I did not want to invite that boring Julia Epstein to my house the other night, but I did it to get Ma off my back. So—and here's the karma part—today, I'm standing in the smoking area, checking out the action, and who do I see? Julia, talking to this guy who could be Mick Jagger's twin brother. No joke! Same body type, cheekbones, sex appeal, charisma, the whole package. And there he is, shooting the shit with Julia! Well, I cannot believe my eyes, but when opportunity knocks, I answer. So, I strut my stuff right on over, and, oh my God, he's even better looking up close! His eyes are like diamonds on black velvet. And he has that lean, tough, sexy thing going on that makes me want to pounce. And yeah, I said I was off guys, but that was before I met Ian. Even Deb and Mar can't believe how hot he is. And here's the best part: he's in my drama class with Mr. Gabor, which is fantastic because Mr. Gabor is the best teacher in the entire school, Ian and I will get to do improvs together (ooh, can't wait), and Ian will get to see how incredibly talented I am.

Unfortunately, Julia is also in the class, but I seriously doubt she can act. She doesn't strike me as the theater type. Most theater types, like me, have outgoing personalities and are *fun*, but Julia is one of those sensitive, straight, intellectual girls who listens to Bob Dylan all day long. Bob Dylan and Joni Mitchell. Puh-lease! I can just picture her doing one of those existentialist plays—Beckett or someone like that—something so deep and symbolic, no one understands what the hell it means anyway.

But who cares. Ian Slater is in my drama class, and Mr. Gabor is so cool. I love the way he walks into a room like he's king of the castle. And there's something about him that makes you *really*, *really* want him to like you.

Ian liked him too. I made sure to sit beside Ian in class, and I stuck to him like glue because all the girls were checking him out, even Sherrie Cumberland, who already has a boyfriend. She was practically gobbling him up with her eyes. Mind you, I can't blame her. Ian is definitely the best-looking guy in grade eleven, maybe even in the entire school. Of course, he's not a big talker, so I still don't know what lies underneath that sexy, rugged veneer, but I'm going to find out. Ian Slater is a mystery, and I love mysteries. I am going to read him from cover to cover.

JULES

"Desolation Row"

I'm sitting against the black-curtained wall of the theater studio, listening to a guy named Benjamin Osborne tell me that he has a photographic memory and top marks in physics, when who walks into the room but Carla Cabrielli and Ian Slater. Both of them. In my drama class. Just when I thought my courses were Carla-free. I immediately consider switching electives. The history of Inuit ice fishing? The mating habits of the earthworm? I'm about to slink out of the class and go straight to Mr. Squash's office when Mr. Gabor walks in, and suddenly all thoughts of dropping this course vanish.

Mr. Gabor is a large man dressed in black, built like a bull. He has powerful shoulders, a thick neck, a pitted face and dark wizard eyes. When he strides into the studio, he's like a general taking command of his troops. When he takes attendance, chanting our names, it's like he's reciting poetry. "Julia Epstein" never sounded so good.

Mr. Gabor gives us an overview of the course. He tells us that this year, we'll be focusing on character development, monologue and scene work, and—as part of our physical training—we'll be learning the art of stage fighting, primarily fencing. When he mentions *fencing*, there's a rumble of excitement from the guys, and Ian sits up straight.

Across the room, two lanky boys in red lumber jackets whisper to each other. They both have long frizzy hair and remind me of Dr. Seuss's Thing One and Thing Two. One of them raises his hand and says, "Mr. Gabor, Mr. Gabor . . ."

Mr. Gabor turns to face the boys. He arches an eyebrow. "Ah yes, I see we have the two *J*s with us again, in their handsome matching attire." The class chuckles.

"Jason and Jeremy," Benjamin whispers.

The *J*s grin goofily.

Mr. Gabor says, "Yes, Mr. Titlebaum, you have a pressing question?"

"Uh, yeah, what musical are we doing this year?" Jason asks.

"There will be two theater productions this year," Mr. Gabor announces. "A musical and a Shakespeare play. The musical, *Oklahoma*, will be directed by Mrs. Farnell."

Carla looks stricken. Several people gasp. Mr. Gabor silences them with a sharp stare. "As for myself, I will have the pleasure of directing *Hamlet*."

There's a collective groan. Benjamin says, "Mr. Gabor, with all due respect, aren't we all too immature and unskilled to tackle one of the greatest plays ever written in the history of theater?"

"Yeah, we're too stupid to do *Hamlet*," Jeremy says.

"You may be lazy, Mr. Ginsberg, but you are not stupid," Mr. Gabor says firmly.

"I'm stupid," Jason calls out, "'cause when I read Shakespeare, my eyes glazeth over. All those thees and thous . . ."

"Yeah, man, it's so outdated. It's, like, irrelevant," Jeremy says.

"Ooh, big word," Jason says. "*Irrelevant*. Wow. Style points, man." They high-five each other and the class laughs.

Mr. Gabor glowers at the *J*s. "For your information," he says icily, "I have not chosen to produce *Hamlet* because it is *easy*, but because it is *compelling*." His gaze sweeps across our faces like the harsh white beam of a searchlight, and our laughter fizzles into an uncomfortable silence. "Do you want to become actors?" he asks in a scathing voice. "Because there is no better tutor than William Shakespeare. Do you want to try on the skin of a man who faces adversity? Meet Hamlet. Imagine that your father has been murdered by your uncle, your mother is behaving like a whore, your girlfriend is being used as a pawn against you, the people you thought were your friends have betrayed you, and the society you live in is seething with corruption. Watch Hamlet wrestle with this, and then discover how, even in the most desperate of times, a man can act with dignity and courage."

Mr. Gabor glares at us, and we sit cowering in our chairs, a bunch of blundering initiates yearning to join his secret society, if only he will find us worthy. We bow our heads and wait for judgment. Mr. Gabor's eyes come to rest on Jeremy Ginsberg's sheepish face. "And is this *relevant*, Mr. Ginsberg?" he asks. "I believe that Shakespeare has more to say about alienation, madness and morality in 175 eloquent pages than you or I could cobble together in a lifetime."

Jeremy gulps.

Mr. Gabor marches into his office and returns with a stack of *Hamlet* paperbacks. "I was going to give these out next month," he says briskly, "but I think some of you need an early start." He passes out the books, one by one, placing them in our hands like precious gifts.

After school, I sit on the back deck and crack open the play. I figure that if Mr. Gabor loves *Hamlet*, so will I. I'm hoping that *Hamlet* will hit my soul like a bolt of lightning. But it doesn't. Instead, I struggle with the language, looking up the meaning of old English words and obscure sexual puns. Finally, I skim through the hard parts to the climax—and I don't get it at all. Why does Hamlet agree to fight a "friendly" duel with Laertes when he suspects that something is fishy? He even tells his best friend, Horatio, that he has a really bad feeling about the fight, and Horatio says, "*If your mind dislike any thing, obey it.*" In other words, *Listen to your instincts and don't do it*. It's good advice, but Hamlet ignores it. He says: *"There is a / special providence in the fall of a sparrow. If it be / now, 'tis not to come; if it be not to come, it will be / now; if it be not now, yet it will come. The / readiness is all."*

What does that mean? Is Hamlet resigning himself to fate or the will of God? Why would he willingly walk into a trap? I mean, all through the play, he agonizes about doing the right thing, and then, in the end, he goes and does the wrong thing. The fight is a setup. Laertes's sword is dipped in poison and Hamlet is killed. So is Laertes, and the queen and king. It's a blood bath. And, yeah, I know this is a tragedy, but what's the point? What is Shakespeare trying to say?

I'm reading the scene for the second time when I see Carla, Debbie and Marlene slogging up the hill toward Carla's house. Carla peers through the hedge that separates our two yards and stares at my book. "Doing homework already?" she sneers. I shrug. Carla says, "I hate Shakespeare. It puts me to sleep. If it wasn't for *Coles Notes*, I wouldn't know what the hell is going on." She laughs sharply and then looks at me. "I bet you don't use *Coles Notes*."

"Well, no," I admit. My English teacher at T.M.R. High said that using *Coles Notes* was cheating.

Carla juts her chin toward my copy of *Hamlet* and asks, "So, are there any good parts for girls?"

"Well, there's Ophelia, Hamlet's girlfriend, and Gertrude, Hamlet's mother, the queen."

"That's all?" Carla exclaims. I nod. "Jeez! What kind of play is that?"

"You should audition for the girlfriend," Debbie says to Carla.

"Yeah, you should," Marlene says.

"What's the girlfriend like?" Carla demands.

I begin to explain that Ophelia is a girl who gets dumped by Hamlet and goes insane, but before I can finish, Carla waves her hand dismissively. "Forget it. I don't do girls who get dumped. What about the queen?"

"I'm not sure about her," I say. "Either she's so in love with Claudius that she doesn't suspect that he murdered her husband or she's trying to secure her position as the queen of Denmark."

Carla nods. "I'm going for the queen. At least she's not a wimp."

Marlene asks me, "Are you auditioning?"

"I don't know," I say. But as soon as I say it, I realize that actually I do want to audition because if I'm going to learn anything while I'm stuck in this awful school, it's going to be from Mr. Gabor. If he's directing *Hamlet*, I want to be in it.

Carla's eyes narrow. She says, "Well, Julia, whatever you do, don't try out for the queen, 'cause that part has my name on it." She laughs like it's a joke, but it's no joke. It's a warning.

CARLA

"Baby I'm-A Want You"

I'm walking down Hawthorne Crescent with Debbie and Marlene, looking for Ian's house, and I'm in a bad mood. It's hot and humid, and I should not have to be doing this.

Is this nuts?

Yes, it is.

Do I hate myself?

Yes, I do.

So why can't I stop myself?

Because for the last ten days, I've been hunting Ian down in school, finding out where his locker is, learning his schedule by heart, and he still hasn't asked me out! I mean, what's a girl supposed to do? What *is* his problem? I've never had to wait this long for a date. Never. Debbie says that if I dangle myself in front of his face long enough, he'll bite. Marlene thinks he's psycho. Ian's in her chemistry class, and last week he was sent down to the principal's office for lighting his cigarette with a Bunsen burner. She thinks he's dangerous. I don't know what to think.

Marlene says, "There it is," and we look over at number 47.

Ian's parents must be loaded because the place looks like a mansion: white pillars, wrought iron gates, formal landscaping, the works. Ian's motorcycle's in the driveway. It's a Honda 750 Four. It's black, and he rides it to school wearing his scuffed-up black leather jacket with the buckles and zippers, or just a plain white T-shirt flapping up his back. He always parks his bike beside Jim Malone's bike. They've become friends, probably because of their bikes. Jim Malone is in grade thirteen, and he's a pig. He thinks he's hot shit because last year his band had a gig as a warm-up band at the El Mocambo. I've been to the El Mocambo twice, even though I'm underage, and I say *Big deal!* It doesn't make him a rock star.

Debbie lights a ciggie and says, "Now what?"

"You want to ring the doorbell?" Marlene asks.

"No."

"Then what?" Deb asks.

"I don't know," I say.

"Well, you're the one who wanted to come here," Debbie says.

"I know, I know. Just give me a second, okay?" I say. It's not like I'm nervous or anything; I just want to play this right. Marlene taps her foot. Debbie smokes. A bead of sweat trickles down my back. Damn. Sweat is so unattractive.

A car cruises down the street. A silver Mercedes-Benz. We watch as it pulls into Ian's driveway. A slim dark-haired woman in a soft green dress and matching heels steps out of the car. She opens the trunk, takes out a couple of bags from Holt's and glances over her shoulder at us. "Hello," she says.

"Hi," we say.

"Are you friends of Ian's?" she asks. Her voice has a lilt to it. We nod. She spots Ian's bike in the driveway. "Would you like to come in? I'm sure he'd enjoy a visit from three pretty girls."

Marlene and Debbie look at me. I think *What the hell — she's asking.* "Sure, thanks," I say politely. I follow Mrs. Slater up the front steps. As she puts her key into the lock, I can't help but notice her diamond ring—a rock that could knock your eyetooth out, as Ma would say. Mrs. Slater smiles at me. She has the same delicate skin and gray-blue eyes as Ian, but her eyes are more dreamy. I wonder if Ian's eyes ever look dreamy. Maybe in the bedroom . . .

Mrs. Slater opens the door, and we step into a stunning marble foyer. There's a vase of roses on a table, a spiral staircase leading upstairs, a crystal chandelier hanging from a second-floor ceiling and, off to the side, a living room full of puffy sofas and billowing drapes, all done in pinks and creams like the inside of a seashell.

"Classy!" Debbie whispers. Marlene's eyes bug out of her head.

Mrs. Slater opens the door to the basement and calls down to Ian. I hope he'll be excited to see me. I notice the way he checks me out at school, like I'm a hot car he wants to test drive. Maybe he just needs someone to pass him the keys. I think about how nice it will be when we're dating and I'm popping by the mansion all the time.

And then the basement door flies open, and instantly I know I've made a big mistake. Ian stands rooted to the floor like a guard dog. He practically has his teeth bared. "What are you doing here?" he growls.

"We just dropped by," I say.

"Shall I make some tea?" his mom asks.

"They're not staying," Ian snarls.

Deb and Mar exchange looks. Mrs. Slater laughs, as if Ian's bad manners are just a joke, but it's the kind of tinkly horror-movie laugh that sends chills up your spine.

I say, "We really have to go." Mar and Deb are already at the door.

Mrs. Slater says, "Perhaps another time." She holds out a thin limp hand, and as I lean in to shake it, I catch a whiff of perfume mixed with booze. And bingo, I get it. No wonder Ian doesn't want us here. I can feel his eyes drilling holes into the back of my skull, but what am I supposed to do? I don't even bother saying good-bye. I rush out the door, and Ian slams it on my heels. Shit! Shit! Shit!

On the street, Debbie and Marlene are already in full gossip mode about how nasty Ian is and how Mrs. Slater is so upper crust.

"I think I detected an accent," says Mar.

"Yeah, British. Like royalty," Deb agrees.

"Maybe Ian is heir to the throne, 112 times removed," Mar snickers.

I don't say a word about how Mrs. Slater stunk of booze at three-thirty in the afternoon.

Debbie says, "I guess you can cross him off your list."

"Why would I do that?" I say.

"Carla! He practically threw us out of the house!" Mar says.

"Yeah," Deb says. "Why would you want to go out with a guy like that?"

"I don't know. I just do," I snap.

Debbie and Marlene look at me, disgusted. But I don't blame Ian for this; I blame myself. Why did I have to barge in like that? I can hear Nonna Cabrielli's voice in my head saying, *"Chi prima non pensa, dopo sospira"*—he who doesn't think ahead will suffer. Yeah. I'm so mad, I could kick myself.

All night long, I roll around in bed, twisting in my sheets, having imaginary conversations with Ian that go nowhere. Finally, at three in the morning, I decide there's only one thing to do: pretend the whole thing never happened. If I can't fix it, I'll wait it out.

So, at school, when Ian avoids me, I'm not surprised. In class, when he sits beside the two *J*s instead of me, I shrug it off. I sit with Sherrie Cumberland. After school, when he hangs out with Jim Malone, I pretend I couldn't care less. I hang out with Deb and Mar. I have plenty of other things to do.

In drama, for our first assignment, Mr. Gabor asks us to create a monologue based on a fairy tale or nursery rhyme, and I focus on that. I decide to do a vampy version of a skipping song about a Girl Guide and her date. I borrow Ma's clingy, yellow satin gown and black spiked heels. I sweep up my hair and paint my lips with Raging Red, and when I step into that studio, ooh baby, I sizzle. Jaws drop. Even the *J*s are speechless for once. Yessiree, when you're hot, you're hot. I sashay into the spotlight like a pro, and I sing-talk that skipping song in my low, sultry, Mae West voice:

I'm a little Girl Guide dressed in yellow.
This is the way I treat my fellow:
I hug him, I kiss him, I kick him in the pants,
And that's the end of our romance.

I move on to the next verse and slink around the studio with a bump and grind. I get laughs exactly where I want them. Mr. Gabor chuckles, and the guys hoot and whistle. But best of all, without even looking, I know Ian is hooked. He slouches in his seat, the corners of his lips curl into a smirk, and his eyes track my every move. Oh yeah! Gotcha!

JULES

"You've Got a Friend"

The only subject I'm behind in is math, so after school, I get help from my teacher. By the time I leave his office, the math area is empty. I'm about to turn the corner to go to my locker when I spot Carla and Ian in the hallway. She's reaching up to get her binder from the top shelf of her locker while his eyes slide up her bare legs, over her bum and across to her chest. If eyes were fingers, he'd have his hands full. This is *not* the kind of moment I want to walk in on, so I hang back.

"Where're you going now?" Carla asks Ian.

"I'm coming to your house," he says, flirting.

I can't believe he's coming on to her. Last week they didn't even sit together in drama, and now this.

Carla smirks and slams her locker door. "Who says you're invited?" she teases.

Ian puts his hands on either side of her, so that her back is flat against the locker, her body caged by his. "Don't you want to invite me to your house for some milk and cookies?" he purrs in a low, rumbling voice that reminds me of the Big

Bad Wolf when he licks his chops and says *All the better to eat you with, my dear*.

"I'll give you a ride on my bike," he says.

The fluorescent lights hum. Ian leans in closer and they're about to kiss, but then the back of Carla's head clunks against her locker and they pull apart.

"Okay," she says. "Let's go."

They turn in my direction. I don't want them to see me, so I dash down the hall toward the stairwell, but I know I'm not going to make it in time. In a panic, I try two doors. The second one opens, and I slip inside just as Ian and Carla turn the corner. I crouch behind the door and listen to Carla's loud laughter as they pass. I'm so intent on eavesdropping that I don't notice I'm in a small room with a glowing red light until a male voice behind me says, "Excuse me."

I nearly jump out of my skin. I whip around to see a ghoulish face looking at me with a very annoyed expression.

"Don't you know you're not supposed to walk into a dark-room when the red light is on?" he says sternly.

"Oh! I'm sorry," I blurt. "Did I ruin anything?"

His eyes widen. "Well, if you'd burst into this room two seconds earlier, my entire roll would've been *tabula rasa*. Hours and hours of posing and shooting. Clarissa would've had my head on a platter, and I could've kissed good-bye my big chance of becoming Richard Avedon's personal assistant."

He looks vaguely familiar. My eyes begin to adjust to the darkness. "Who's Richard Avedon?" I ask.

He frowns and rattles off: "Famous photographer. *Harper's Bazaar*. *Vogue*. Marilyn Monroe. The Parisienne Collection . . ."

"Oh yes," I say, pretending I know what he's talking about. "Do you know him?"

He sighs. "No, but it is one of my many ambitions to be a famous portrait photographer and work for *Vogue*." He crosses his arms in front of his chest and assesses me. "I suppose you're more of an Imogen Cunningham type. Or—wait. Wait. Diane Arbus. Black and white. Raw. Naked. Dwarfs. Freaks. Am I right?"

I gawk. What is he talking about? I want to ask who Diane Arbus is, but I sense this may be a stupid question.

He says, "Oh, please don't take that the wrong way. I'm not saying you're only interested in dwarfs and naked people. I'm just saying that you strike me as someone who's . . . intellectually artistic."

"Really?" I ask.

"Yes."

"But you don't know me."

"Yes, I do. You're Jules, the new girl in my drama class."

And then I recognize him. Geoff Jones. "I didn't recognize you in this light."

He grins. He has an eager puppy-dog smile that doesn't

quite fit with his scrubbed-clean, handsome looks, but it's the kind of smile that makes you want to smile right back. Geoff is one of the stars of the drama class. His monologue this week was brilliant. We had to do character monologues based on fairy tales and nursery rhymes. I did Rapunzel in her tower, waiting for the prince to return, wondering if his visit had been just a figment of her imagination. The crazy-isolation thing kind of appealed to me, but I think it made some students uncomfortable because after I finished, there was dead silence before people started clapping. Mr. Gabor said that I was "theatrically unnerving, in the best sense."

Carla did a spoof of a skipping poem about a Girl Guide who dumps her date. Typecasting? Still, I have to admit, she has great comic timing, and she sure knows how to flaunt what she's got.

But the funniest monologue was Geoff's. He dressed up as Little Bo Peep, in a fluffy hat and flouncy crinoline. His Bo Beep was an alcoholic transvestite who had fallen asleep and lost her sheep, and now she was threatening to turn them into lamb chops if they didn't come out of the forest wagging their tails behind them. Even Mr. Gabor cracked up.

"I loved your Bo Peep. It was hilarious," I tell him.

"Thank you," Geoff says with a crisp bow. "And I liked your Rapunzel. It made my skin crawl. That's why I thought of Diane Arbus and those photos she took of freaks. Do you know what she said about freaks?" I shake my head. "She said,

'Most people go through life dreading they'll have a traumatic experience. Freaks were born with their trauma. They've already passed their test in life. They're aristocrats.'"

We stand face-to-face under the red light as those words wash over us, and I know, in that moment, that I've stumbled upon someone who belongs to the same tribe as me. "That's very profound," I say.

"I know," Geoff says. "Do you want to stay and see what I'm working on? Or do you have to go?"

I stay. In the red light, everything has a clinical laboratory calmness. The chemicals in the air smell acrid and metallic. Geoff has one roll of film hanging up, drying, and some negatives ready to be printed. He sets up the enlarger and times the exposure. Next he submerges the shiny exposed paper into a pan of liquid, swishing it back and forth with a pair of tongs, lifting it up so that the solution drips off and then dipping it into a second pan and a third. We listen to the splash of liquid and the clink of tongs on the metal pans. It's oddly peaceful, like being in a murky underwater world.

I watch over Geoff's shoulder as smoky shapes spread across the slick paper and form into a black-and-white photo of a woman's face. She looks like Cleopatra with her high forehead, prominent nose and luminous cat eyes. "What do you think?" Geoff asks.

"She's stunning!" I say.

Geoff laughs. "I'll tell her."

"Who is she?" I ask.

"My mother."

I gasp. "*That* is your mother?"

"She's an actress. She needs a new head shot."

"Is she famous?"

"Not yet. When she lived in New York, she did off-Broadway. But then she got married and moved here, and they got divorced. And now she does plays, and occasionally commercials—just for the money. Have you seen the soap commercial where a cowgirl uses a bullwhip to flick the dirt off clothes?"

"No."

"She was the cowgirl."

"Oh," I say. "It must be great to have a mother who's an actress."

"It has its perks," Geoff says. "She's helping me practice my monologues for the *Hamlet* auditions."

"Already?"

"Sure. You should try out."

"I might." I pause. "Carla Cabrielli is trying out for Gertrude."

Geoff rolls his eyes. "She thinks she's so hot."

"She's my neighbor. We're renting the house next door."

Geoff freezes. "Oh my God! Jules, be careful! Carla's the queen bitch of the entire school. And Debbie and Marlene are her skinny mean dogs who snap at you when you walk by. In junior high, she made a hobby out of making girls cry. And last year, she broke up with her boyfriend—on his birthday!"

"I think she has her eye on Ian Slater," I say offhandedly.

Geoff nods. "Yeah. They're in my French class. Whenever she leans over his desk to 'borrow a pencil,' she almost has her cleavage in his face. *Quelle* trollop!" I laugh. Geoff grins back at me. "Listen," he says, "keep away from that girl. Don't talk to her. Don't even look in her direction. You don't want anything to do with Carla Cabrielli."

CARLA

"Motorcycle Mama"

Two days after I do my Mae West number in drama, Ian slides into the seat beside me, just like that, like his cold-shoulder treatment never happened. I act nice, but not too nice. After class, he follows me to my locker and practically kisses me right there in the hall. Inside, I'm shrieking, "Yes! Yes!" But I've learned my lesson. I play it cool. When he offers me a ride home on his motorcycle, I say, "Okay," like I have nothing better to do.

In the parking lot, he climbs onto his bike and waits while I stuff my books into my fringed leather purse, sling it over my shoulder and throw my leg over the back of the bike—which isn't easy when you're wearing a miniskirt and you have to tuck everything in and arrange your hair all at the same time, but I manage.

The truth is, I've never been on a motorcycle before and I'm not sure what to do with my hands. I mean, do I hug his waist or just place them on his hips? I must look like a total idiot because finally Ian glances over his shoulder and says, "Have you ever been on a bike before?" It's like he's asking if

I've ever had sex before, and I blush like the motorcycle virgin I am! He says, "Just hold on tight and lean with the bike."

"No problem," I say. And I'm about to tell him where I live—'cause he's supposed to be giving me a ride home—when he guns it and we're flying. I fling my arms around his waist and scream. The wind rushes down my throat like an arctic blizzard, and my hair whips all over the place. Ian leans into the corner, and it feels like we're going to wipe out. It takes all my willpower not to lean in the other direction. I keep thinking *Holy shit, I'm going to die without ever having sex*.

I duck behind his back to hide from the wind, and when I look up again, we're zipping down Leslie at 100 miles an hour. Is this his idea of a fun date? Does he think I get a kick out of playing chicken in traffic? I push my boobs up against his back to see if that might get his attention and slow him down, but no, he just keeps zigzagging around like a crazy lunatic. I want to throw up. Meanwhile, my miniskirt keeps flapping around my bum, like Marilyn Monroe over the air vent, only I can't use my hands to hold it down because I have Ian in a death grip!

By the time we get to my house, my whole body is cold and stiff. I try to pretend that I'm Ann-Margret when she slides off her motorcycle and shakes her long beautiful hair out of her helmet, only Ian didn't give me a helmet, so my hair looks like a rat's nest. When my feet touch the cement, my legs almost buckle. Ian smirks and says, "So, what'd ya think?"

"That was . . . great," I lie through my teeth. "Do you want to come in?" He flicks his hair off his face and grins.

Fortunately, Ma and Buzz are out. I lead Ian into the kitchen, and we sit at the table near the French doors, facing out onto the ravine. Ian helps himself to Ma's chocolate chip cookies. I do most of the talking because Ian is one of those guys who doesn't offer up anything unless you ask him a direct question. I find out that he's an only child; that he had (notice "had," *past* tense) a girlfriend in North Bay named Kimmy (sucky name, if you ask me); and he hates school 'cause it's all "meaningless bullshit," which is mostly true. I mean, am I ever going to use a trigonometric function after I leave high school? Uh . . . no.

I'm just putting the kettle on for coffee when Ian says, "Hey, there's Jules." I look out the window and see Julia Epstein walking up the hill.

"She lives next door," I explain. "She gives me the creeps."

Ian leans back in his chair. "Why?"

"She's so prissy."

"Her Rapunzel was good."

"Sure, if you like that weird, sicko kind of thing."

Ian laughs. I spoon coffee into our cups. Julia disappears behind the hedge. Ian says, "I heard she skipped a grade."

"So? Big deal. It doesn't make her a genius," I say. "To be a genius, you have to skip at least two grades. To skip one grade, all you need is high marks and a pushy mother. Which she has."

"So, what do you care?"

"Who said I care? She just bugs me, that's all. I don't see why you have to defend her."

"I wasn't defending her," Ian says.

"Yes, you were."

"Look, I don't even want to talk about her."

"Neither do I," I say. "You're the one who brought her up."

Ian takes out his cigarettes. Export "A"s. "Do you have a light?" he asks.

I don't know why he can't carry matches like everybody else. I toss a pack onto the table and say, "You know she likes you."

"Who?"

I roll my eyes. He knows exactly who I'm talking about. "Julia," I say. Ian turns his head away, like he's bored with the topic. "She has a crush on you."

"Is that what she told you?" Ian asks.

"I don't talk to her."

Ian lights up and takes a drag. "If she has a crush on me, how come she's never my partner in drama?"

"Because she's avoiding you," I explain.

"Because she likes me so much," he says sarcastically.

"No, because of me, you dork. Because most of the time, you're partners with me. But if you weren't with me, she'd be on you like a fly on shit."

Ian laughs. I sigh. Guys are so dumb. They don't have a clue about the way the female mind works, which is far more complicated than the male mind. It's why male birds are more colorful than female birds. Because, basically, they're stupider, and if it wasn't for their flashy looks, the females would probably peck them to death. I stare at Ian and wonder why I even bother. Finally, I say, "In case you haven't noticed, Julia watches you all the time, but she pretends she's doesn't. She's sneaky. She's one of those uppity, brainy, goody-two-shoes girls who thinks she's better than everyone else. And she probably walks by your house late at night."

"Like she's spying on me."

"Yeah. Exactly."

"But not like you, when you showed up at my house," Ian says, smirking.

"I wasn't spying," I snap. "I just happened to be in the neighborhood, that's all."

Ian throws his head back and laughs.

"Fuck you," I say. I know he's playing with me, but this thing with Julia really pisses me off. I walk over to the table and help myself to one of Ian's cigarettes. He stands up. I think he's going to light it for me, but instead, he takes it out of my mouth, tosses it onto the table and kisses me. Just like that. In the middle of an argument. He just leans in and gives me this long, slow, sensual kiss. His mouth tastes like cigarettes, but I don't care because I've never been with a guy who's this sexy. I don't even have time to think before his hands are traveling down my back, sliding over my bum, pulling me in tight, tangling me up into his body. And he's kissing me the whole time, devouring me like a pastry. When his tongue slips into my mouth, my thighs squeeze together and my mind turns to mush. I feel the heat of his body through his T-shirt and his hard-on through his jeans. When we finally pull apart, we're both panting, like we've been running a long-distance marathon.

I stare into his crazy ice-blue eyes and say, "You wanna go down to the basement?" I can't believe I'm saying that, because I'm not usually so . . . slutty, but the way Ian kisses, I can't help myself. I want to make out till our lips get raw.

Ian smiles and stubs out his cigarette, and we're about to go downstairs when the front door opens and Buzz blasts into the kitchen holding a shopping bag. Damn!

"Guess what I got," Buzz says, ripping into his bag. He yanks out a pair of hockey skates and thrusts them at Ian, not even fazed by the fact that he's never met Ian before. "Bauers," he says proudly.

"Cool," Ian says.

Ma says, "Hello. Is that your motorcycle in the driveway?" She's doesn't sound too thrilled. I make introductions. Ma offers Ian a snack, but he says he has to go. I walk him outside, and we share a secret smile because we both know what we'd rather be doing. I say, "See you in school." Ian grins, climbs onto his bike and zooms down the street. I watch until he turns the corner, and I'm like a pressure cooker, with the steam bubbling up in my body and then screaming out the top of my head because—oh my God—he kissed me! He actually kissed me! And he's the hottest kisser ever!

I close my eyes and sigh, and then I hear music coming from Julia's open window next door. "Only Love Can Break Your Heart." Neil Young. Deb, Mar and I saw Neil Young last January at Massey Hall—a solo acoustic guitar. What a great concert! I bet Julia's never seen Neil Young. She's probably never even been to a concert. I wonder if she saw Ian's motorcycle parked in my driveway. I hope she did.

Friday night, Deb, Mar and I sit at my kitchen table making diet strawberry milkshakes in my mom's blender with frozen strawberries, Sweet'N Low and ice milk. Deb and Mar are arguing about how many calories are in the milkshake, but all I can think about is Ian. "I am in love," I announce.

Debbie sucks on the straw of her milkshake and says, "Carla, you're not in love, you're in lust."

"It *is* love," I insist, "because when we kiss, I melt into a big wet puddle."

Mar and Deb roll their eyes. Maybe after a week of hearing me describe what it's like making out with Ian, they're bored. Or jealous. It's not like *they've* ever gone out with anyone. But of course, it would be rude of me to bring that up. They simply don't understand what it's like to feel a man's lips on yours and his hands on your body. I sip my milkshake, which would taste a lot better with real ice cream, and say, "I've never felt like this about a guy before."

Marlene says, "You said that last year about Tim Fraser."

"Yeah, well, this is different," I explain. "Tim was a boy; Ian is a man. And he's older."

Deb and Mar's eyes pop wide open. "Like how old?" Deb asks.

Oops. I wasn't going to tell them that part—about Ian being eighteen and still in grade eleven—but since the cat is out of the bag, I fill them in on how Ian got suspended for fighting last year and flunked out.

Marlene gasps. "I told you he had a temper."

"Yeah, but it wasn't his fault," I explain. "There was this jerk who kept bugging him, and one day they got into a fight, and then he got expelled."

"You said 'suspended,'" Deb says, narrowing her eyes.

"That was the first time. The second time, he got expelled."

Deb and Mar exchange looks. "Wow," Deb says. "And you want to *date* this guy?"

"Debbie, you don't know anything about him," I say.

"Yeah, well, neither do you," Deb says.

"Yes, I do," I say. "We spent three afternoons together."

"And half the time you were necking," Marlene snickers.

"So what? You guys are so judgmental." I push my milk-shake away. "Look, if you're going to sit here and run him down, don't bother staying."

"We're not running him down," Debbie says.

"He failed his chemistry test," Marlene says.

"So? Lots of people fail chemistry," I say. "It's a hard course."

"It's not that hard," Mar says. "It was just the periodic table. Straight memorization."

"Just because he doesn't like school doesn't mean he's stupid," I say.

"I'm not saying he's stupid," Marlene says. "He probably didn't even crack open his book. That's the point. He doesn't even bother trying."

"He's just a little bit wild," Deb says in that condescending tone she has.

"Yeah, well, maybe I like 'wild,'" I snap. "Maybe I want to do something really wild and crazy, like go downtown to a disco and dance all night, or even have passionate, sweaty sex with a hot and horny eighteen-year-old guy!"

Deb's and Mar's jaws drop. "Really?" Marlene asks.

"Yeah," I say, although I'm not totally sure.

"Wow," Deb says.

"But we're only sixteen," Mar says. "We're not even legal for anything, except driving."

"Are you actually going to?" Deb asks, and we all know she means *sex*.

I shrug and light a cigarette.

Marlene says, "I didn't realize you were such a feminist."

I hadn't really thought about whether I'm a feminist or not, but now I'm liking the idea. "Well, of course I'm a feminist," I say. "I believe in equal rights for women, and freedom, and sex, and all that stuff."

"Are you going to burn your bra?" Deb asks, smirking.

"No! I'm not Germaine Greer," I say. "Maybe she can go braless, but you won't find me flopping around like some breast-feeding hippie."

Debbie laughs so hard that she practically snorts her milkshake. Marlene says, "Deb, remember the time we found that book under your mom's pillow—*The Sensuous Woman* by 'J'—and it had those chapters about masturbation and oral sex?"

Deb grins. "Yeah, maybe Carla wants to borrow it."

"Fuck off," I say, laughing. "I'm not jumping his bones yet. We haven't even gone out on a real date."

"What about tomorrow night?" Mar asks.

"I think he's hanging out with Jim Malone."

Mar gawks. "On a Saturday night? What about your Saturday night rule?"

And yeah, it's true, I have this Saturday night rule: boyfriends have to save Saturday nights for me. "I haven't told Ian about the Saturday night rule yet," I explain.

"So, call him up and ask him out," Marlene suggests.

"I can't do that," I say. "He has to call me."

"I thought you were a feminist," Mar says.

"I am!"

"Are you afraid he'll say no?" Debbie snickers.

"No!" I say. I grab the phone. "Fine. I'll call him." I dial. I know his number by heart, even though I've never actually phoned before. Debbie and Marlene light cigarettes and watch me. "Quit staring," I say. Marlene giggles.

A man—Mr. Slater, I presume?—picks up the phone, and I ask for Ian. There's a long pause. I practice blowing smoke rings while I wait. Finally, Ian picks up.

"Hi," I say in a very upbeat voice.

"Hi," he says flatly.

"So, what're doing?"

"Nothing."

"Oh. Well, I'm having a strawberry milkshake and thinking about you." I suck loudly on my straw so Ian can hear. It makes a rude slurping noise. Deb and Mar smother their laughter with their hands. There's silence on the other end of the line. "So, do you miss me?" I ask, teasing.

"I can't talk now," Ian says.

"Why?" I ask. "Are your parents there?"

"No. Look, don't call me at home, okay?"

"What?"

"I gotta go," he says.

"But what if I want to talk to you?"

"We'll talk at school."

"But—"

Click. He hangs up. What the hell? I put down the phone.

"What happened?" Marlene asks.

"Nothing," I say.

"Is he going to call back?" Deb asks.

I shrug. I reach for my cigarette and take a long, slow drag. Deb and Mar watch me like a couple of vultures. "But what did he say?" Marlene asks.

"Nothing, so just back off," I snap. I drop my cigarette into my strawberry shake. It sizzles and sinks, looking really gross. I toss the whole thing into the sink and watch it ooze down the drain. Nobody hangs up on me. Ian Slater better learn that.

JULES

"With a Little Help from My Friends"

Dad is supposed to come to Toronto for the weekend, but he cancels. Stomach flu. Last weekend, he was short-staffed at the store. Bobby and I are really bummed. It's the third week of September, and he hasn't come once. We sit at the kitchen table and no one talks. I pick at my food and think about Ian. All week, Carla has been clinging to him like a limpet to a rock. In homeroom, when she's not around, Ian tugs on my hair and says, "Hey, Rapunzel, how's it going?" That's what he calls me; it's like this thing between us. But in drama, he sits with Carla draped over him, and we act like total strangers.

I look across the table at Bobby, who's smooshing his spaghetti into his meat sauce. Mom is the only one smiling. In fact, she's looking positively perky. She says, "Guess what? I have some exciting news."

Bobby and I eye her suspiciously. *Exciting* is one of those dangerous words that parents use to try and con you into thinking that something crappy, like moving to Toronto, is going to be fun. For a moment, I wonder if our house has sold and I prepare for the worst, but Mom says, "Today, I got a job."

Bobby stops slurping his spaghetti. "What?"

Mom grins. "I'm taking a job as a nurse in a doctor's office. After all, I was an Emergency nurse when I met your dad, and I still remember a thing or two." Mom explains that the job is three days a week, in a medical/dental building on Leslie Street. The plan is that Bobby will come home with Buzz after school, and if I'm not back, he'll stay with the Cabriellis till Mom returns at six o'clock. She's already cleared it with Gina Cabrielli.

"Mrs. Cabrielli doesn't work," Bobby sulks.

"I don't have to be like everyone else's mother," Mom says.

"But why are you working if you don't have to?" Bobby asks.

"Well, I don't know a lot of people in Toronto," Mom says, looking directly at me—like we're both in the same boat, which we are *not*—"and I saw an ad in the paper, so I applied. I had the interview this morning with Dr. Katzenberg, and he offered me a job right on the spot. He said if I wanted the position, it was mine, and I couldn't think of a single reason to turn it down." She beams, like her lucky number just got plucked out of a hat.

"What did Dad say?" Bobby asks.

"I haven't told him yet."

"He's not going to like it," Bobby warns.

"It's not his decision," Mom says lightly. "Perhaps I'm becoming a women's libber." She laughs. "Well, Julia, what do you think?"

I stare at her with flat, cold eyes. Does she expect me to be overjoyed just because *her* life is falling into place? Sorry. I don't care how she fills her days.

Mom says, "You could at least wish me good luck."

"Good luck," I say, sticking my fork into my spaghetti and twirling it around as if this requires my complete and devoted attention.

Saturday morning, I'm at the North York Public Library doing research for my English essay on T.S. Eliot's poem "The Love Song of J. Alfred Prufrock." The poem is about this guy, Prufrock, who keeps wishing he had the courage to do something meaningful with his life, but instead, he just grows old and cynical. He says, "I have measured out my life with coffee spoons," and he calls himself Hamlet's "attendant lord" because, like Hamlet, he can't act on anything. It's the kind of poem that haunts you. I decide to write an essay comparing Prufrock and Hamlet. Mrs. Llewellyn is going to be really impressed.

I'm heading over to the stacks to grab some books when I remember Diane Arbus's quote about the freaks. I'm curious to see her photos, so I nip into the photography section. When I can't find anything, I ask the librarian, Mrs. Sarkissian, for help. She knows exactly who I'm talking about. She steeples her red fingernails and says, "Maybe there's something in our clipping files." She leads me around the corner and down an aisle. She says, "I think MOMA is planning a retrospective of her work next year."

"MOMA?"

"Museum of Modern Art, in New York."

"Oh."

She purses her red lips together. "Such a shame she won't be there to see it."

"Why not?" I ask.

Mrs. Sarkissian blinks at me. "She committed suicide in July."

"Oh," I say again. I feel kind of stunned. A week ago, I didn't know Diane Arbus existed, and now I find out she's already dead. Mrs. Sarkissian passes me a clipping file, and I take it to a table and open it up. Right on top is an article about her suicide. On July 26, 1971, at the age of forty-eight, she took an overdose of barbiturates, climbed into the bathtub and slit her wrists. She'd been suffering from depression. Next year, in 1972, she will be the first American photographer to be exhibited at the Venice Biennale.

I find a quote from Lisette Model, one of Diane Arbus's teachers: "The camera is an instrument of detection. We photograph not only what we know, but also what we don't know." I scribble this down in my notebook. Then I spread the photos across the table. They're black-and-white portraits, and every single one of them is odd and unsettling. I find the freaks Geoff was talking about: Eddie Carmel, "the Jewish Giant," standing in his parents' Bronx apartment, his head almost scraping against the ceiling; and a dark-eyed Mexican dwarf, sitting on a bed in a shabby hotel room, stark naked except for a fedora.

Even the normal-looking people aren't really "normal." In one photograph, a skinny boy with a strung-out expression on his face stands in Central Park clutching a toy grenade in his clawlike hand. In another photo, a happy housewife sits on a floral couch cradling a baby in her lap. But on second glance, you notice that the thing in her lap is *not* a baby; it's a monkey in white baby clothes.

That's how Diane Arbus gets you. That's how she lets you know that people are not what they seem to be. Freaks can be ordinary, and regular folks can be totally bizarre. And the thing I like best about Diane Arbus is that no matter who her subject is, she doesn't pity them. She doesn't judge them, either—because she's one of them. And I'm one of them too.

On impulse, I steal the picture of the lady with the monkey-baby. I slide it into my purse. I can practically feel it pulsating at the bottom of my bag as I return the clipping file. Then I go over to the pay phone and call Geoff Jones. When he answers, I say, "I didn't know Diane Arbus killed herself."

"Last summer," Geoff says. "So tragic."

"Yeah."

"What are you doing now?" Geoff asks.

"I'm at the North York library doing research."

"Get your stuff and meet me out front in ten minutes."

"I'm writing an essay," I say.

"Not today, shweetheart," Geoff says in a Humphrey Bogart voice. "Today is your lucky day, 'cause I'm gonna be your personal tour guide to Toronto."

Ten minutes later, we're chugging down Yonge Street in Geoff's mom's 1961 beat-up Volkswagen Bug: "Baby Blue"—named for the color, not the Bob Dylan song. It's an old rust bucket. The shocks are gone, the heater is temperamental, and there's a crack in the windshield, but Geoff says, "If we put five dollars into the tank, it can take us anywhere we want to go."

It's sunny and warm, so we roll down the windows and Geoff belts out show tunes all the way downtown to Yorkville, which, he explains, is like the Greenwich Village of Toronto: hippie hangouts, coffeehouses, music clubs and candle stores. Geoff buys us chocolate-dipped ice cream cones at the Dairy Queen. Then we jump back in the car and zip off to his favorite destination: The Beaches.

The Beaches is a funky old neighborhood of brick row houses built along the shoreline of Lake Ontario. Geoff parks Baby Blue on a side street in front of a quaint stone house with a wide veranda and a pretty garden. He tells me that, one day, he's going to buy that house, when he becomes "a famous photographer or actor, whichever comes first." We wander down the street, and at the end of the block, Lake

Ontario stretches out before us like a vast, rumpled, blue silk sheet. It looks more like an ocean than the country lakes I'm used to. "It's so big!" I exclaim.

"Aye, lassie. That's why they're known as the *Great* Lakes," Geoff says, putting on a Scottish accent. He has his camera with him, and he snaps action shots of toddlers running in and out of the water, screeching and getting soaked. "Can you remember being that young?" Geoff asks.

I think back, and a memory comes into focus, like a photo from a childhood album. I'm four years old at Granby Zoo. I'm holding a peanut in my chubby hand, and Dad is hoisting me up in his arms as I lean toward the elephant cage. The elephant spots me and lumbers across the cement. I'm terrified, but also mesmerized, as his long gray trunk curls through the iron bars. It undulates—this dusty, wrinkled, muscular thing—and then it swoops down and delicately plucks the peanut from my fingertips. I can still remember that moment of contact when its moist, hairy, snout-like trunk touched my fingers and I felt the dampness of elephant breath on my skin. The image reminds me of Michelangelo's Sistine Chapel, where God reaches out to touch Adam's extended finger, only in this case, God was an elephant and Adam was me.

But what happened to the rest of that day?

I turn to Geoff. I say, "Isn't it odd the way we remember some things, and other things completely disappear? We forget whole chunks of our own lives."

"Well, if we remembered everything, our heads would explode," Geoff says.

"I guess so."

"Or maybe we don't want to remember everything," Geoff says.

I think about the Diane Arbus photo in my purse and take it out. I don't want my only friend in Toronto to think I'm a kleptomaniac, but I don't want to lie about it either. "I stole it, from the clipping files," I confess. "I don't usually steal things."

"Maybe the woman reminds you of someone," Geoff says.

"No one in my family is that weird," I say, laughing. And suddenly I'm telling him all about my family, and how I miss my dad and hate my mom. I tell him about Mollie and the FLQ. Geoff doesn't know anything about Quebec politics, but it doesn't bug me the way it did with Carla.

"Were you scared?" Geoff asks.

"Not really," I say. "The only terrifying part was moving here. Moving here is the worst thing that ever happened to me."

Geoff studies me with wide hazel eyes. He says, "Jules, you know what I think? I think you've suffered a traumatic experience, which is why you're feeling so pessimistic."

"I'm not pessimistic," I say. "I'm realistic. Life isn't fair, and there's no point in pretending it is."

"But maybe you're just not seeing the bigger picture," Geoff says, his face lighting up. "Maybe you were meant to move here, so you and I could meet and we could both be in *Hamlet*. I will be Hamlet, and you will be Ophelia. Or Gertrude. And on opening night, we'll bring down the house. With my talent and your good looks . . . or my good looks and your talent . . . who knows what lies ahead. Maybe a scout from Hollywood will be in the audience, and next thing you know, we'll be signed up for a three-picture deal with Paramount and living in the Alan Ladd mansion. Of course, you might have to change your name to something a little more catchy, but that's a small price to pay for fame and fortune." Geoff grins.

I burst out laughing. It's just like Geoff to take any topic and turn it into a Broadway musical. I wonder if he actually believes this stuff, if he thinks that we're just in our ugly caterpillar stage of life, waiting for the inevitable gorgeous transformation to unfold.

Later, at home, I take out the monkey-baby photo and look at it again. I want to pin it above the bed, on Karen McDuff's ugly pink wall, as a kind of talisman against all the fake, fluffy pink-ness, but I can't do that because my mother would ask about it, so I tuck the photo into the album jacket of Bob Dylan's *Highway 61 Revisited*, which somehow seems appropriate.

CARLA

"Rainy Days and Mondays"

Monday morning, I leap out of bed because, as Nonna Cabrielli says, *"Chi dorme non piglia pesci"*—he who sleeps in doesn't catch the fish. And I'm fishing for a date, which is why my hair and makeup are perfect. Today, my eyes look dark and mysterious, and my lips look wet and shimmery. I happen to have very sexy eyes and sensuous lips, like Raquel Welch. Lots of people say I look just like her, only shorter.

At breakfast, Papa glances at my face and asks if I'm going to school or to the circus. Ha-ha. Very funny. Then he asks if my "raccoon eyes" have anything to do with my "new boy-friend." I glare at Ma. Did she *have* to mention Ian to Pa? I wonder if she told him about Ian's motorcycle. Papa calls motorcycles death traps. Papa makes fun of boys with long hair. If he didn't like Tim Fraser, who's basically a preppy jock, what's he going to say when he meets Ian?

Fortunately, Ma changes the topic. She says that on Saturday night, she and Pa are invited to the Epsteins' for dinner. "So I'll need you to babysit."

"Ma, I already have plans," I say (hoping I actually *will* have plans).

"Your plan is to babysit," Pa says.

"But, Papa, I have a date," I lie.

"So, invite your date over to the house," he says.

Buzz gives me an evil grin. Little brat. "Why do I always have to take care of Buzz!" I yell.

Papa clutches his bread knife in his fist and says, "Carla, boyfriends come and go. Family is forever."

It's a pissy, windy, rainy day, and by the time I get to school, the hems of my bell-bottom jeans are sopping wet, and my perfectly ironed hair is frizzled. I spot Ian in the smoking area with Jim Malone. I don't feel like hanging out in the cold, but I do anyway. We huddle against the wall, smoking. I don't say a word about Ian's rude phone manners Friday night.

At lunch, we meet in the cafeteria, and I drop hints about the movie *Klute*, with Jane Fonda and Donald Sutherland, because it's the perfect date flick. Action and romance. Something for everyone. But Ian doesn't bite.

By the time we get to drama, I'm in a bad mood, and to make matters worse, Mr. Gabor announces that we're doing trust exercises. I hate trust exercises. They're so touchy-feely. And who does he put in my group? Ian, Jeremy, Benjamin, Geoff and Julia. I don't even like looking at Julia, and I don't like the way Ian looks at her either.

To do trust exercises, you stand in a circle and the person in the middle has to close their eyes, cross their arms over their chest like a corpse and fall backward. Someone always catches them before they hit the floor. Easy-peasy. But wouldn't you know, Little Miss Sensitive can't do it. Every time Julia's about to fall, she stops herself at the last second. Scene-stealer.

Geoff says, "Don't think about it, Jules, just do it."

"I can't," Julia says.

What a suck. "Look," I say, "it's so simple." I demonstrate, swooning right into Ian's arms. I bat my lashes at him, but he's already looking at Julia.

He says, "Come on, Rapunzel." I hate it when he calls her that. "Don't you trust me?"

"Not really," Julia says dryly.

Ian laughs. "Just close your eyes and pretend you're falling out of your tower."

"And what are you, her Prince Charming?" I scoff.

"Why don't we skip me," Julia says nervously.

"There's a thought," I mutter.

But suddenly Mr. Gabor appears. "Ms. Epstein," he says, "do you know why we do this exercise?" Julia turns about twelve shades of blotchy red. "Because in theater, no man is an island. Onstage, we have to work as a team." He puts his hands on Julia's shoulders and positions her so that her back is to Ian. "Relax," he says, "I'm sure Mr. Slater will catch you." I want to give Julia a big fat shove, but instead, I stand there as she tumbles into Ian's arms. Geoff claps. Julia's eyes flutter open. Ian smiles down at her. And that's when I decide: no more beating around the bush. If I have to break my dating rule and ask Ian out myself, I'll do it.

After class, I follow him into the hall and say, "Ian, do you want to catch a movie Saturday night, or what?" My mouth is dry, and if he turns me down, I'm going to kill him.

Ian looks at me like he's mulling it over. Then he says, "Sure," and breaks into a grin because he knew what I wanted; he was just trying to make me squirm.

"Jerk, " I say.

"Come on," he says laughing. "Let's go back to your place."

In my kitchen, we grab a snack and head downstairs. Buzz and Bobby have turned the basement into a pillow fortress, and they're shooting Nerf balls everywhere. When we walk in, Buzz yells, "Enemy! Fire!" and they bombard us with those stupid pink and green sponge-balls.

"Quit it," I yell.

Ian pelts the balls back at the boys, but I scoop them up till they run out of ammunition.

"Gimme the balls, you lousy traitor," Buzz says, leaping out of his fortress, gun raised.

"In a minute," I say. "First, I need you to do me a favor." Buzz eyes me suspiciously. "Look, Saturday night, when Ma and Pa go to the Epsteins', why don't you two hang out there and watch the hockey game together?"

"Sure," Bobby says.

Buzz narrows his eyes. "Why do you want to get rid of me?"

"Look, I don't want to babysit," I say. "Ian and I have plans, okay?"

"What if I don't want to go?" Buzz asks. The kid's no dummy. He senses an advantage.

So, I do what I always do when the going gets tough: I resort to bribery. I pull a dollar bill out of my pocket and wave it in the air. "Listen, pip-squeak," I say, "you go to Bobby's, and this dollar is yours." The boys eye the money greedily. A buck buys a lot of chocolate.

"Deal," Buzz says, snatching the money.

Bobby pumps his arm. "'Hockey Night in Canada'!"

"Leafs versus Habs," Buzz says.

"Your team's gonna get creamed," Bobby taunts.

I drop the Nerf balls, and the boys scramble after them. "Clear out. We need some privacy," I say. Ian puts Joe Cocker on the stereo.

As the boys scamper up the stairs, Buzz wags his bum like a girl and chants, "Carla and Ian sitting in a tree, *K-I-S-S-I-N-G . . .*"

Finally, the basement door shuts. Mission accomplished! I turn to Ian. I sidle up to him, real close, and say, "I guess we can go to that movie now."

Ian wraps his arms around me and says, "Let's just stay here."

"What?" I squawk. "What about *Klute*?"

Ian nuzzles his face into my cheek. "But, Carla, we'll have the whole house to ourselves. Saturday night, you and me, alone." The way he whispers it—oh my God!—I practically wet my pants on the spot. He pulls me down onto the pillow fort. Joe Cocker sings "Feelin' Alright," and I'm feelin' pretty good myself. Ian and I make out like mad. He's so much hotter than my other boyfriends. Those guys were so predictable. It's like they were plodding through the salad course, killing time till they got to the main dish. Not Ian. With him, every course is gourmet. When we're making out, I feel like I'm Jacques Cousteau exploring an unknown tributary of the Amazon River, wondering what exotic surprise is waiting for me just around the bend.

JULES

"A Case of You"

Dad arrives on Friday night, and Bobby tackles him as soon as he walks through the door. Dad throws Bobby up in the air and then gives me a big bear hug. "How's my favorite girl?" he asks.

"I'm your only girl," I say, smiling.

Dad winks at me. He kisses Mom. We all start talking at the same time, and suddenly we feel like a family again. In the kitchen, Dad unpacks food from Montreal: smoked meat, Fairmount Bagels (you can't get good bagels in Toronto) and Bubby Epstein's homemade blintzes. While we eat, he fills us in on the family news. Bubby and Zadie are planning to visit Uncle Seymour and Aunt Rose in North Palm Beach in November. Aunt Connie is working with a Zionist organization to free Soviet Jews. Dad tells us his latest jokes, and even though they're real groaners, we grin because when he delivers the punch line, he laughs louder than everyone.

Bobby has a hockey game on Saturday morning, and I go along just to hang out with Dad. Bobby and Buzz's team is called the Hornets, and Mr. Cabrielli is their coach. Dad goes into the locker room to help Bobby suit up, and by the time he comes out, he and Mr. Cabrielli are acting like old pals, slapping each other on the back and joking around. Dad gives me money for hot chocolate and doughnuts (Mom never lets us buy junk food), and Dad and I sit in the stands and cheer with the other Hornet families.

Bobby plays left wing and Buzz plays defense. Eight minutes into the game, Bobby fakes out the defenseman and flicks the puck into the upper right corner of the net with a neat wrist shot. He pumps his arm in the air and grins at Dad in the stands because Dad has a deal with Bobby that if he scores a goal, or catches a pop fly in baseball season, he gets an ice cream. The Hornets win 4–3, and Dad springs for Orange Crush and Coke for the team.

After the game, the three of us get a booth at the Pickle Barrel for lunch. Bobby sits beside Dad, and his eyes are glued to Dad's face. It's like he's trying to make up for weeks of missing him. "When are you moving here?" Bobby asks.

"Well, hotshot, the house hasn't sold yet. Too many houses on the market," Dad explains.

Bobby slumps against Dad's arm. "How long's it gonna take?" he asks. Dad ruffles Bobby's hair.

"Maybe we'll have to move back to Montreal," I say. Dad shakes his head, but I don't back down. "Mom's the only one who wants to live here," I say.

"Jules, don't be so hard on your mom," he says. "I know it isn't easy for you, but it's not easy for her either."

"Yeah, well, she chose it. I didn't."

Dad sighs. "I hear you, kiddo. Let's just wait and see how things pan out, okay?"

At least he doesn't shut me down.

Saturday evening, Mr. and Mrs. Cabrielli and Buzz arrive for dinner, and they're hardly through the front door before the two dads are talking hockey and complimenting each other on their talented boys.

"That Buzz sure is a smart player," my dad says. "Clean checks. Not afraid to dig into the corners."

"And look at Bobby, our best winger," Mr. Cabrielli says. "That kid gives 110 percent every second he's on the ice."

Buzz and Bobby go to the basement to watch hockey. Mom serves her coq au vin, and Dad entertains his guests with jokes and stories. I stay in my bedroom and write to Mollie about Ian. This week in drama, we did trust exercises, and I had to fall backward into his arms. When I looked up, his eyes were mauve-blue, the color of snow shadows. A girl could get lost in those eyes and never want to come back.

Around eight o'clock, I sneak downstairs to grab a bite. I sit at the kitchen table, and from the dining room I hear Mrs. Cabrielli say, "I told Carla to invite her over."

"Julia's just going through a rough stage," Mom says.

"Maybe she needs a boyfriend," Mrs. Cabrielli says.

Mr. Cabrielli interrupts. "Carla has a boyfriend and I don't like him."

I stop eating. Does he mean Ian?

"Tony never likes her boyfriends," Mrs. Cabrielli says.

"This one has no manners," Mr. Cabrielli says. "Hair in his eyes. Drives a motorcycle, like a thug. What kind of boy is that, eh?"

"The same kind you were," says Mrs. Cabrielli.

"What do you mean?" Mr. Cabrielli protests. "When I was his age, I took the bus. I had respect for your parents. And I always got you home on time."

"And you never laid a hand on me," Mrs. Cabrielli teases.

"*Carissima*, you were a knockout!"

"Tony!"

"And she still is!"

They all laugh.

Mom walks into the kitchen carrying a stack of dirty plates and doesn't notice me at the table. She puts the dishes into the sink and holds her hands under the steaming water, eyes closed, just standing there letting the water flow between her fingers. She looks tired. When she turns and sees me, she practically jumps out of her skin.

Mrs. Cabrielli bustles into the kitchen carrying platters of leftovers. "Jules, there you are," she says. "Why don't you go over to the house? Carla and Ian are watching a movie on TV."

My heart jolts. Ian is there?

Dad and Mr. Cabrielli walk into the kitchen. Dad says, "Poopsie, take the evening off. That's an order."

Mr. Cabrielli jumps in. "And make sure that boy is keeping his hands to himself."

There's no point in protesting; they all seem intent on sending me off. I say good-night and leave through the back door. For a moment, I linger in the shadow of the birch tree, watching through the dining room window as they return to the table. Mom slices her amaretto cheesecake. Dad pours more wine for himself and Mr. Cabrielli. Mom declines with a shake of her head. Maybe she thinks Dad's drinking too much. They sit across from each other, Dad sprawled in his chair like a king at a banquet, and Mom sitting with her back straight, like a queen, keeping her dark thoughts to herself.

Of course, I have no intention of going to Carla's, but it's a cold night and I'm not in the mood for a walk, so I decide to try Geoff's apartment. I've never been there before, but I have his address.

As I cut along the side of the house, I see a flickering light coming from the Cabriellis' basement window. I peek through the hedge. Carla and Ian are sitting on the couch eating chips. The room is dark, except for the glow from the TV screen. In the shadows, Ian's face looks carved and smooth like marble. As I watch, he walks over to the TV, flips the channel and then flops back onto the couch. Carla gives him an exasperated look. She heads for the TV, but Ian grabs her wrist and yanks her into his lap.

I don't intend to spy on them, I really don't, but when they start to wrestle on the couch and then tumble onto the shag carpet, I don't move. Soon Ian is sitting on top of Carla, pinning her arms above her head. She sticks out her tongue at him. He waggles his tongue back at her. She laughs and squirms, but he holds her down, licking her cheek like a puppy, first teasing and then meaning it. They kiss and kiss, deep, hungry kisses that make my legs feel all rubbery. I hold my breath. I know I shouldn't be watching this, but I do.

Ian curls his leg around Carla's, and his fingers slide under her shirt. He whispers something into her ear. What? What does he whisper? He yanks off his T-shirt, and she pulls her top over her head. I see the vertebrae of his spine and the silvery gleam of her bare skin. He unhooks her bra, tossing it aside. Their bodies are both half naked now, and their torsos slither against each other like wet seals, shiny and blue in the TV light. Ian's mouth closes over her nipple. Carla shuts her eyes and arches her back. He licks a line from one breast to the other. And then, he looks straight up at the window, at me.

I gasp. Ian's wolf eyes glitter in the darkness. I jerk back into the hedge. Branches slap against my face. I swat them away and bolt into the street. Did he see me? Oh God! Did he see me? Can a person inside a house see a person outside in the night? And what if he did? What would he do? If he tells Carla, my life is over.

I run. I race through the streets as if Carla herself is hunting me down. I cringe with shame. What a stupid, sick pervert! What the hell did I think I was doing? How could I watch them? Oh God! Did he actually see me? Please, no!

I stagger up to Geoff's apartment and press my face against the cool glass door. My chest is heaving. I don't know what to do. I can't go home. Geoff is my only friend.

I push the buzzer beside *C. Jones* and wait. Geoff's voice crackles across the intercom. "Who is it?"

I take a deep breath. "Jules."

"Jules!" he exclaims. The buzzer trills. I step into the lobby and, seconds later, Geoff flings open the stairwell door.

"Hi," I say. "I should've phoned first—"

"No," Geoff says. "Come on up. Clarissa can't wait to meet you." He leads the way, bounding up the stairs. "We're on the third floor, but I never take the elevator. I have a phobia about elevators, as well as tunnels, bridges, heights, knives and women with moles and facial hair." Geoff grins, and I laugh. Coming here was a good idea. I banish all thoughts of Carla and Ian, forcing those pictures out of my mind.

Geoff leads me into his apartment through an orange beaded curtain that clinks and clatters, and there, stretched out on a blue velvet divan, like a gypsy movie star from the 1920s, is Clarissa Jones. She's eating Chinese takeout from a cardboard carton, and she's even more striking in person than she is in her photo.

"Momma, look who dropped by for a visit," Geoff says, putting on a Southern accent.

"Why, this must be your new friend, Jules," Clarissa purrs, sounding like a Southern belle straight out of a Tennessee Williams play. She tilts her head coquettishly. She's wearing a Japanese silk kimono in pale lemon, which darkens to blazing gold at the bottom of the sleeves and gown. Chrysanthemum blossoms in shades of persimmon and green melon twine upward from the hem. Her bare feet dangle over the edge of the divan, and an anklet of tiny silver bells tinkles when she moves.

"Hi," I say, suddenly feeling gawky and shy.

Clarissa slides off the divan and sails toward me, arms extended. I'm not sure if she's going to hug me or shake my hand. Instead, she cups my face in her long, slender fingers and says, "Pisces?"

"No."

"Wait, don't tell me." She peers into my eyes. Her own eyes are jade flecked with black. Looking into her eyes is like staring into the depths of a green pond, where fish dart along the bottom through cold water. Those eyes must have broken a thousand hearts.

"Cancer?" she asks.

"Yes," I answer.

"Aha!" she says triumphantly. "I knew it. A water sign. Compassionate and mysterious, ruled by the moon."

Geoff rolls his eyes. "She does this with everyone."

Clarissa laughs. "And I'm always right." She smiles at me. "Jules, you look absolutely pale. Come, sit down. I hope you're hungry." She ushers me to a threadbare crimson couch with wooden claw feet, and I feel like a child being led onto a stage where everyone performs in ad lib scenes.

Geoff passes me chopsticks and a glass of juice. He points to the cartons. "Chop suey with beef. Prawns in black bean sauce. Honey garlic ribs."

"*Cin-cin*," Clarissa says, raising her glass.

"*Cin-cin*," Geoff and I reply, clinking glasses, although I have no idea what that means.

"So, Jules," Clarissa says, "tell me about your life."

"I don't have much to tell," I answer. "I just moved here from Montreal."

"And you hate it," she announces.

"I do," I say, surprised.

"Of course you do," she says. "Torontonians have no joie de vivre. No artistic spirit. As someone who moved here from New York, I know exactly how you feel." Clarissa gives me a sympathetic smile. She has the air of a contessa who's lost her castle, pawned her jewels and ended up in some crummy apartment in the burbs of Toronto. Except the apartment isn't really crummy; it's more bohemian, filled with eclectic

knickknacks: a wooden Buddha head, peacock feathers in a
cloisonné vase, a hammered-brass lamp, a collection of blue
glass bottles.

"I love your apartment, and your kimono," I say.

Clarissa's eyes light up. "Oh, this old thing?"

"She got it from a gentleman caller," Geoff says in his
Southern drawl.

"He said it was worth thousands," Clarissa says. "I'm sure
he'd be scandalized to know I wear it around the apartment
like a housecoat, but I don't believe in saving things. Things
of beauty should be loved and used," Clarissa proclaims.
"Life—"

"—is not a museum," Geoff declares, finishing her sen-
tence. "My mother lives by that. And that's why we're broke."

"We're artists," Clarissa says with a wave of her hand. "In
this town, everything's about money, but what's truly important is doing what you love. Don't you agree?"

"Yes," I say. I imagine a gallery of Epsteins and Cohens
groaning, rolling their eyes and making sneering remarks
about flaky artists, but the truth is, I do agree with Clarissa.
Why shouldn't people do what they love? And why not use
beautiful things? I think about my mother's silver and good
china, stashed away in a cupboard, waiting for those special
occasions that never come.

Geoff taps his watch and says, "Attention, shoppers. In two
minutes, the late show is starting." He looks at me. "I hope

you're staying. Tonight, they're showing *Brief Encounter* on TV." When I confess that I don't know that movie, Clarissa and Geoff look at each other, stricken. "You've never seen *Brief Encounter*?" Geoff gasps. "Oh, Jules, you're going to love it! This is Noël Coward at his best. Celia Johnson is so vulnerable, and Trevor Howard is such a gentleman." Geoff puts a Kleenex box on the table.

"Do you think one is enough?" Clarissa asks.

I call home and tell my mother that I'll be late. Geoff flicks on the TV, and we sit back and watch the story of two middle-aged people who meet in a train station tearoom, all because she gets a bit of grit in her eye, and he, a doctor, just happens to be there to wipe it out.

"Chance, or destiny?" asks Clarissa during the commercial break.

"Destiny," Geoff says.

"I'm afraid we're hopeless romantics," Clarissa sighs.

At the next break, she pours three snifters of Grand Marnier and passes them around. My parents would be shocked to know that someone's mother is serving alcohol to teenagers, but with Clarissa, it's perfectly fine. The tangy fumes tickle my nose, and the orange syrupy liqueur melts down my throat with a sweet, delicious burn.

Brief Encounter is fabulous. The story takes place in London, where Celia Johnson and Trevor Howard fall hopelessly in love. But it's an impossible love because they're both married, with families. At first, they try to fool themselves into believing that they're just friends, but eventually they confess their true feelings for each other. The problem is, they don't know what to do about it. Should they sleep together? Should they break up their families' lives? In the end, he gets a job in Johannesburg, and instead of running away with him, she returns to her dull little row house to live out her life with her kind but ordinary husband, knowing she'll never see Trevor Howard again.

Geoff, Clarissa and I sob our eyes out.

"That was so sad," I say as the credits roll. "Why couldn't they run off together?"

"Because they're too decent," Clarissa says.

"But they belong together," Geoff says. "And now she's stuck with boring Cyril Raymond in that dreary sitting room in Ketchworth."

"What if she goes through the rest of her life and never has another moment of true passion?" I ask.

Clarissa tilts her head. "That's the tragedy, isn't it? Perfect man, bad timing."

"But *you* wouldn't have stayed in Ketchworth," I say. "You would never have chosen duty over love."

Clarissa gives me a sardonic smile. "When you're young, you do anything for love, but sometimes it's not the wisest decision." Geoff sings "Falling in Love Again" in his deep Marlene Dietrich voice. Clarissa stretches. "Do you know what would've happened if she'd run off with him to Johannesburg?"

"They would've started a wonderful new life together," Geoff says emphatically.

"Yes, and she would've been happy at first, but after a year or two, she'd begin to feel lonely in her big fancy house in the white part of town, with her black servants, and her heart would ache for those two little children she'd left behind. He, the devoted doctor, would work long hours at the hospital, while she'd fill her days having tea at the bridge club, eating cucumber sandwiches and playing cards with a bunch of stuffy racist women."

"Oh, Mother, don't be such a cynic. Maybe they'd just live happily ever after," Geoff says.

"Darling, life is not a fairy tale," Clarissa says. "Fairy tales have happy endings; life has happy moments. Noël Coward knew that." She sips from her snifter, and I suddenly wonder what happened to Clarissa's marriage. Geoff said that his dad, Keith Jones, was a doctor, just like Trevor Howard. Did he run off with another woman? But he couldn't have dumped someone like Clarissa, could he? I sip my drink. Who am I to make judgments about love—I, who spy in basement windows, watching other people's private moments.

I look at the clock; it's almost midnight. Geoff gives me a ride home. The porch light is on, but the house looks dark. At first, when I step inside, I think everyone is asleep, but then, from the kitchen, I hear voices arguing in that hushed, suppressed tone adults use when they're trying to fight quietly.

Dad says, "I told you before—"

"That is *not* what you said," Mom snaps.

"Natalie, listen—"

"Irv, you promised!"

"But what's the point? It's not working—"

There's a loud crash—china smashing against the floor—and I know it's not an accident. Dad curses. Mom tells him to shut up. I reach behind me, softly open the door and then shut it loudly, as if I've just arrived home.

"Hi," I call out. They don't answer. I take my time walking to the kitchen. Mom is sweeping up slivers of china into a paper bag. Her cheeks are flushed.

"I dropped a dish," she says without looking up.

"Did you have fun?" Dad asks.

"Yeah," I say. "I guess I'll go to bed."

At the top of the stairs, I see Bobby, in his red-and-white striped pajamas, standing in the shadow of his doorway. He stares at me. "They were fighting," he whispers.

"About what?"

"Dad says he doesn't want to start over."

"He never wanted to move here in the first place," I whisper. "It's all her." Bobby nods. "If Dad gets his way, I bet we'll move back home," I say. Bobby stares at me with dark, solemn eyes. "Don't you want to move back?" I ask.

Bobby shrugs. "I just want us to be with Dad." His bottom lip quivers, and he swipes at his tears with his pajama sleeve.

"Come on," I say. "I'll put you to bed." I walk him back into his room.

Bobby climbs between his sheets and says, "Tuck me in, like a hot dog, Jules." It's something Dad used to do with us when we were little: tuck the blankets tightly around our bodies, so that we looked like two hot dogs stuffed into buns.

"Okay," I say. "Get ready." I chop the covers around Bobby's body, wedging him into a tight roll. He giggles softly. "Good?" I ask.

"Yeah."

"Sleep tight," I say, the way Dad used to.

"And don't let the bedbugs bite," Bobby whispers the refrain.

In Karen McDuff's ugly pink room, I send prayers to a god I don't believe in to please, please let Dad win this fight. If we go back to Montreal, my parents will stop arguing, Mollie and I can hang out together, and I won't ever have to see Carla Cabrielli again.

I close my eyes, trying to blot out the image of Carla's and Ian's half-naked bodies. I squeeze my eyes tight, and the scene changes, so that instead of Carla lying underneath Ian's body, it's me. Ian's mouth is kissing my mouth. Ian's hand is pushing under my shirt. Ian's eyes are looking into mine. Oh God! Did he see me? I shove my fists into my eye sockets and wish I could make it all go away.

CARLA

"I'll Take You There"

"Well?" Debbie asks Sunday morning. She and Marlene lean across the kitchen table, holding their breath, and I wish I had a camera because they look like two balloons ready to pop. I pour milk into my coffee and slowly stir.

Marlene says, "Carla, spill!"

"Okay," I say, settling back in my chair. "The thing I learned last night is that sexual attraction brings you closer together, and I don't mean just physically, I mean emotionally. It's like, when I'm near Ian, he's a magnet and I'm an iron filing, and we snap together because we're so much in sync."

"But did you do it?" Deb asks.

"You're so crude," I say.

"But did you?"

"Deb, let her tell it her way," Marlene scolds. She looks at me. "Now, start from the beginning. And don't leave *anything* out."

"Okay," I say. I light a ciggie. "Last night, Ian showed up just as Ma and Pa were leaving the house, and Pa grilled Ian like steak. The poor guy was ready to bolt."

"Yikes," Marlene says.

"Yeah," I say. "Thank God for pot." The three of us laugh.

"Did that get him in the mood?" Deb asks.

"That and *Sticky Fingers*," I say. "It's his favorite album. Did you know Andy Warhol took the cover shot with the zipper?"

"Of Mick Jagger's crotch?" Deb asks.

"It's not Mick Jagger's," I say.

"Yes, it is," Deb says.

"No, it's not," I tell her. "Ian told me that Andy Warhol took a bunch of crotch shots of different guys, and no one knows whose crotch it really is."

"I thought it was Mick's," Deb says.

"Yeah, well, I think Ian knows better than you," I say.

"Why? 'Cause he's your boyfriend?" Deb snorts.

"No, because he's a big Stones fan," I say.

"I think the crotch looks like Ian's," Mar says. We laugh 'cause it's true. Same narrow hips and tight jeans.

"So did you play with his zipper?" Debbie asks.

"Well, first we watched TV," I say. "Ian wanted to watch hockey."

"Ew," Mar groans.

"Yeah," I say, making a face. "So I kept changing the channel, and after a while, I got his undivided attention." I smirk.

"So?" Deb asks, raising an eyebrow. She's practically drooling with anticipation.

"Well, we rolled around on the floor making out for a while . . ." I pause. "And then we both took our shirts off." Mar screeches. Debbie gasps. It's a good thing Ma, Pa and Bobby are at church. "It was like making out with a rock star," I gush. "Both of us naked, except for our jeans."

"Wow!" Mar says.

"Go on," Deb says.

I take a long drag on my cigarette. "Well," I say, "he tried to get into my pants, and I wanted to, but I knew I shouldn't, 'cause once you start taking off your jeans, one thing might lead to another. Besides, we only just started dating. So I stopped it."

"How?" Debbie asks.

"I just did," I say. I shrug like I don't remember the details, but of course I remember every single sexy second of it. I think about it all the time—the way he popped the snap on my jeans and then slid his hand down my pants. I said, "Ian . . ."

He said, "Come on, baby." Not a lot of guys can call you "baby" and make it sound good, but he can. Then he tried to pull down my zipper.

I said, "Ian!"

He said, "Don't worry, I've got a condom."

I said, "Ian, we're not doing it!"

He thought I was just playing around, but when I caught his finger in my zipper, that got his attention. "Ow," he said. Then he stared at me, surprised and confused. "Are you a virgin?" he asked, like he couldn't believe it was possible.

"As a matter of fact, I am," I said. Well, Ian laughed so hard, he practically doubled over. "I don't see what's so funny," I said. Then I asked, "Are you?"

He snickered. "Are you kidding? Not since I was thirteen."

"Oh. Well, excuse me," I said. I suddenly pictured him with all the girls in North Bay, having sex in positions even *Cosmo* doesn't know about. "I guess that explains things."

"Like what?"

"Like why you're so experienced. Practice makes perfect."

Ian grinned. "There's nothing wrong with sex," he said.

"I know that," I said. "For your information, I've had plenty of boyfriends before you came along."

"So . . ."

"So, maybe I don't want to be just one in a string of girls you screw. And in five years, you won't even remember my name."

"I remember all my girlfriends' names," Ian said, smirking.

I put on my bra and snatched my shirt off the floor. Ian sat with his knees pulled up to his bare chest, watching me with an amused look on his face. "So, was Kimmy a virgin before you started going out with her?" I asked.

"No."

"Oh. So how old was she when—"

"Fourteen? Fifteen?"

What a slut, I thought.

"You think that's too young?" Ian asked.

"Kind of," I said.

"Bullshit," he said. "Who says it's too young? Your parents? The church? You think they have the right to tell you how to run your life? Sex is natural."

"I know," I said. "I'm just talking about timing, that's all."

"You're not one of those girls who wants to hold off till you get married, are you?" Ian sneered.

"Of course not," I said. "I'm a feminist."

"Great," Ian said, ready to pounce.

"Look, I want to, but not yet," I said, pushing him away. "I mean, virginity isn't something you can get back. First you have it, and then you don't have it. And there's no turning back the clock."

Ian threw his head back and howled with laughter. "That's the stupidest thing I ever heard."

"What?"

"Why would you want your virginity back? Virginity isn't like . . . an apple. If you lose an apple, you can't eat it. If you lose your virginity, it just means that you're having great sex all the time. And sex is way better than no sex. Trust me. Do you think I want my virginity back?"

"You're a guy," I said.

"So what," Ian said. "Do you think guys like sex more than girls?"

"It's different for guys," I said. "Besides, we just started going out."

"Oh, is there a timetable for this?" Ian taunted. "Is that one of your rules?"

I grabbed a pillow from the couch and threw it at Ian's head. Ian tossed the pillow onto the floor and pulled me into a deep kiss. Then he whispered, "When we have sex, I'm gonna get you off, and you're gonna love it."

When he said that, I practically had an orgasm right on the spot. I read in *Seventeen* magazine that talking dirty can make you horny, and is that ever true! No guy has ever said anything like that to me before, and I was shocked and thrilled all at the same time. But it's not like I'm going to tell *that* to Mar and Deb! I mean, a girl can't tell everything. After all, it wouldn't be fair to Ian, would it?

"So he wanted to do it, but you said no?" Debbie asks, jolting me back to the present.

I look over at her. "Of course I said no," I scoff. "If he likes me—which he does—he'll just have to wait. Besides, like my nonna Cobrelli says, forbidden fruit is the sweetest."

"Your nonna lives in the Dark Ages," Deb says.

"All guys want to do it," Mar says.

"So how long are you going to say no for?" Deb asks.

"I don't know," I say with a shrug. "I guess I'll just have to play that by ear."

~~JULES~~

"What's Going On"

I spend the weekend dreading the thousand ways Carla is going to humiliate me for spying on her, but on Monday morning, nothing happens. Carla and Ian are all over each other, and while I've been thinking about them every waking minute, clearly they haven't given me a second thought. I'm safe. I let out a long, slow breath. I should learn a lesson from this. No more daydreaming about guys like Ian, who are beautiful but unattainable.

Life goes on. Mom is preoccupied with her new job. I hang out with Clarissa and Geoff. The birch tree sheds its yellow leaves. September turns into October without missing a beat. I have lived here for over a month, but in many ways, it feels much longer than that.

Dad comes to Toronto at the beginning of October, and he's supposed to come again the following week for Bobby's tenth birthday, but he cancels because he's busy at the store. Bobby is really mad. He yells into the phone, "It's my birthday, Dad. You promised!" Then he slams down the receiver. Mom is angry too because now she has to handle Bobby's birthday party alone.

The party is on Saturday afternoon at a bowling alley. Twelve wild, obnoxious nine- and ten-year-olds bowl two games (I keep score) and then stuff their faces with hot dogs, pop and cake in the party room. After that, Bobby opens his presents. He really cleans up: Hot Wheels, Ker-Plunk and, from Mom and Dad, Creepy Crawlers. As soon as we get home, Bobby and Buzz turn into mad scientists, squeezing green and pink goop into the metal bug-shaped molds and cooking them till they turn rubbery and squiggly. Boy, are they wired!

Later, Gina and Tony Cabrielli join us for birthday cake, and just as Bobby blows out the candles, the doorbell rings. I answer it. On the front steps is a tall man wearing a navy parka and holding a long wrapped present. At first, I think he's someone's dad from the party; maybe one of the kids forgot to give Bobby his gift. Then the man says, "Hello, you must be Julia. I'm Les Katzenberg." Mom's boss. He sticks out his big hand, and I shake it. I'm kind of stunned because he isn't what I pictured. Somehow I imagined an older, wiser Marcus Welby–type doctor, but Dr. Katzenberg looks like the kind of guy who could have been a football player in his youth. He says, "Would it be all right if I spoke to your mother?"

"Sure," I say.

Mom pokes her head into the hall and her eyes widen. "Les?" she says. She calls him Les?

"I hope you don't mind . . . ," he says, holding up the present.

Mom hurries to the door, pushing her hair off her face. "Please, come in."

"I just wanted to drop this off."

"No, no. Please join us. You're just in time for cake."

Dr. Katzenberg hesitates. "Well, thank you," he says. He passes me the present, and Mom takes his parka. They're both polite and awkward, like people who aren't used to seeing each other outside of the office.

Mom introduces Dr. Katzenberg to the Cabriellis, and Bobby looks at the oddly shaped present with googly eyes. Dr. Katzenberg says, "I guess this is for you, young man."

"Gee, thanks," Bobby says and rips it open. It's a fishing rod—not the toy kind, a real one. Bobby practically quivers with excitement. "Wow! Cool!"

"Les, you shouldn't have," my mother says, obviously thrilled that he did.

Dr. Katzenberg helps Bobby and Buzz put the fishing rod together, showing them how to tie a hook on the line and explaining about bobbers and sinkers. He tells them that he fishes for smallmouth bass at his cottage on Lake of Bays. Mrs. Cabrielli asks all sorts of questions about the cottage. Dr. Katzenberg explains that it's winterized and that he has a water-ski boat and an old "tin can" for fishing, but he doesn't spend as much time on the lake as he used to because his two boys are in university now and his wife passed away a few years ago.

When he mentions his dead wife, he says it straight out, but still, it's a real conversation stopper. Mom never told us that Dr. Katzenberg was a widower. I always assumed there was a Mrs. Katzenberg at home—an elderly, stout, cookie-baking Mrs. Katzenberg. The boys look embarrassed. Mrs. Cabrielli puts a hand to her heart. Mr. Cabrielli says he's sorry for Dr. Katzenberg's loss. But Mom looks at Dr. Katzenberg with a soft expression on her face, and there's something about it I don't like. I feel a tightening in my stomach, the way you tense up just before somebody's going to hit you.

Dr. Katzenberg says he should be going, but my mom and Mrs. Cabrielli insist that he stay. They chat about politics and how Pierre Trudeau and Margaret are expecting a baby, but I'm watching the way my mother offers her boss a second piece of cake, the way he compliments her on how delicious it is and the way he tells the Cabriellis how lucky he is to have someone as talented as my mother working in his office. I know it sounds innocent, but the whole time he's talking, I hear voices in my head screaming warnings, and I have the feeling that if I looked at my mother and Dr. Katzenberg through the lens of magical X-ray glasses, I'd see flirt-rays zipping between them like tracer bullets.

When the phone rings, Bobby jumps up to answer it. It's

Dad. Mom escorts Dr. Katzenberg to the door. When it's my turn to speak to Dad, I pick up the phone in the den. I picture him lying on his bed, his shoes kicked off and the TV turned down low. "When are you coming to Toronto?" I ask.

"Well, I'm heading into the Christmas season, poopsie. It's my busiest time of the year. You know that."

I look up to see my mother watching me as she walks back down the hall. Is she waiting to see if I'll mention the widowed Dr. Kaztenberg? I give her a cold stare. I finish talking to Dad and follow Mom into the kitchen.

Mrs. Cabrielli comments on what a gentleman Dr. Katzenberg is and how it's a shame about his wife. Mr. Cabrielli gives her a sharp look and says, "Gina, it's time to go home." Suddenly I realize that Mr. Cabrielli hasn't spoken much tonight. Usually, he jokes around with everyone, but tonight he let Dr. Katzenberg do all the talking. When they say good-night, Mr. Cabrielli glances at me with dark, brooding eyes, and that's when I know I am not imagining things. Mr. Cabrielli sees what's going on. Maybe it takes a man to know what another man is up to.

I go to bed and lie awake thinking about Mom and Dr. Katzenberg. Even if they are attracted to each other, they wouldn't actually do anything, would they? After all, he knows she's married. I think about how Mom and Dad first met. It's our family fairy tale. It's a story Dad loves telling, and Bobby and I love hearing it.

Dad always starts off like this: "So, I'm putting up shelves in the store, and the stool slips and I hammer a nail right into my pointer finger, right here."

He always shows us the scar, as if it's some major war wound.

"Well, there's blood gushing all over the place, so I get the pizza delivery guy across the street to take me to the Jewish General Hospital. So, there I am, in the Emergency, and this tall gorgeous nurse walks out. A real babe."

Mom always hits him when he calls her a babe, but he does it every time.

"She calls my name and takes me into this little curtained cubicle. Then she cleans up my finger and tells me to pull down my pants and bend over!"

This part sends Bobby and me into gales of laughter, partly because of the way Dad's eyes bug out and partly at the image of my mother ordering my dad to pull down his pants.

"I tell her, 'Sweetheart, that ain't where the problem is,' and she tells me, 'If you call me sweetheart again, you're going to look worse walking out of here than you did coming in.' Well, I can tell there's no messing with this babe, so I undo my belt and drop my pants. She takes a giant needle off a tray. I take one look at that needle and say, 'There is no way you're sticking that into my *derrière*,' but she looks at me with those baby blues and says, 'Don't worry, Mr. Epstein, this won't hurt a bit.'

"Well, she jabbed that thing into my *tuchas*, and it hurt like hell, but I swear to you, that was no ordinary needle.

That, my children, was Cupid's dart. I knew right then that this was the woman I was going to marry."

The story goes on about how my mother was already dating someone else—a handsome young intern, "a Dr. Kildare type," as my father scathingly describes him—but my father kept showing up at the end of Mom's shifts, even at six in the morning in the middle of winter, and eventually she agreed to go for coffee with him and then to a movie because Dr. Kildare was too busy at the hospital—"You snooze, you lose," says my dad. Finally, she realized that even though Dr. Kildare was a smart, hardworking man, he didn't make her laugh the way my dad did, so they broke up. Grandma and Grandpa Cohen thought that Mom was crazy to dump a doctor for some schlemiel who worked in his dad's clothing store, but once my mother makes up her mind about something, it's a done deal.

All week, I wonder if I'm overreacting about Dr. Katzenberg, but on Friday after school, Mom phones from work and says she's going out to a movie, so can I please heat up the leftover meatloaf for Bobby and me. When I ask who she's going with, she says, "Just some people from the office." *Like Les*, I wonder.

While she's out, I search her room. I don't know what I expect to find. Love letters? Gift boxes? I find nothing suspicious. Her drawers smell of her perfume: Yves Saint Laurent.

I open her jewelry box. When I was little, I used to watch her put on makeup and jewelry before she and Dad went out to a dinner party. She'd let me try on her sapphire ring and her charm bracelet. I find the bracelet and clip it around my wrist. It jingles with golden charms, each one a memento for a special occasion: a ballet dancer for when I was born, a musical note for when Bobby was born and a golden heart for my mom and dad's tenth anniversary. She never wears that bracelet anymore. Is it a sign?

At around ten o'clock, Mom sweeps into the house looking relaxed and happy. She flops onto the couch and tells me that she saw *The French Connection*, a thriller starring Gene Hackman. She says it's been ages since she's been to the movies, and really, she should do this more often. I don't say anything. She may be fooling herself, but she isn't fooling me. A married woman should not be going out with her boss, especially if her boss is a single man. Even I know it's not right.

CARLA

"Wild World"

For two weeks, everything is perfect. Ian and I make out in my basement every day after school, and we finally see the movie *Klute*. Actually, Deb and Mar are pissed off about that because I was going to see it with them, but at the last minute, Ian wanted to go, so I had to cancel Deb and Mar. Debbie made some crack about "boys always coming first," but I don't see what the big deal is. You'd think she could be more flexible. Wait till she has a boyfriend; then she'll see how complicated life is.

Anyway, Sunday morning, after the movie, I get a call from Marlene and she's practically bursting at the seams with gossip.

"What's up?" I ask.

"Come over," she says.

"I'm still in my pajamas," I say.

"Then get dressed because you're really going to want to hear this," she says.

Half an hour later, Debbie and I are sitting in Marlene's kitchen. Mar makes coffee, and Deb and I get out our smokes. "So, how was your date last night?" Deb asks in a snarky voice. She's still annoyed, but I ignore that.

"It was great," I say. "But afterward, we ended up at Fran's for coffee, and this bitchy waitress flirted with Ian, right in front of me. And she was old enough to be his mother!"

"What did he do?" Debbie asks.

"He ordered the lemon meringue pie," I say. "I would've killed him if he'd smiled at her. It made me wonder if he's done it with older women, like Dustin Hoffman in *The Graduate*. He's certainly done it with younger women."

"Has he done it with you yet?" Debbie asks.

I roll my eyes. "Deb, even if I wanted to, there's no place to go. Someone's always at my house, and Ian still won't invite me over to his house."

"Well, there might be a good reason for that," Marlene says, smirking like the cat who swallowed the canary.

Deb and I both look at her. "Okay," I say. "Out with it."

Marlene perches at the edge of her chair. "Last night, I babysat for the Hendersons."

Deb raises an eyebrow. "The ones who lives on Hawthorne Crescent?"

"Yup. Right across the street from Ian," Mar says smugly.

"Go on," I say.

Mar grins. "Well, it was around nine o'clock, the kids were asleep and I was just about to turn on the TV, when suddenly I heard this loud bang! So, I ran to the front window, and there, in the Slaters' driveway, was Mrs. Slater's Mercedes with the headlights on, and it looked like she'd just slammed right into the garage!"

"How bad?" Deb asks.

"Well, not horrible. But the garage has a big dent in it."

"Wow," I say.

"There's more," Mar says. "Next thing you know, Mr. Slater storms out of the house and—"

"What does he look like?" I ask.

"Short, bald, jowly—"

"Really?" I say. "She's so stunning. You'd expect her to marry Mr. Tall-Dark-and-Handsome."

"Uh-uh," Marlene says. "The guy's no prince, and he's about fifteen years older than her."

"I guess she married for money," Deb says.

"How do you know that?" I ask.

"I'm just putting two and two together," Deb says in her know-it-all voice. "My mom always told me that whenever you see an old fart with a young babe, it means the woman's a gold digger and the man's an idiot."

I don't say anything. I pass my ciggies around and light us up. "Go on," I say to Mar. I haven't heard such good gossip since . . . forever!

Mar takes a deep drag and continues. "Well, Mr. Slater took one look at the car and went ballistic. He charged over to the Mercedes and flung open the driver's door. Mrs. Slater didn't budge. I opened the living room window to hear better, and at first, I wondered if Mrs. Slater was hurt, because I heard this gasping noise, like she was sobbing, but then Mr. Slater pulled her out of the car, and I saw that she was actually laughing. Laughing hysterically, like a madwoman!" Mar does an imitation of Mrs. Slater laughing, and she looks like a cross-eyed, shrieking psycho in a lunatic asylum.

"No shit!" Deb says.

"Yeah," Mar says. "It gave me chills just listening to her because there was *nothing* funny going on! Anyway, Mr. Slater was not amused. He grabbed Mrs. Slater and tried to steer her into the house, but she kept stopping and doubling over with laughter, which only made Mr. Slater even more furious. So he tightened his hold on her, like this." Mar grabs my shoulder and digs her fingers into my flesh like a claw.

"Ow," I say. "Okay, I get it."

"Gee," Debbie says. "I bet that left bruises."

"You know what I think?" Marlene says, leaning across the table. "I think she was drunk out of her skull!"

Deb nods. Mar can hardly sit still. I don't say anything, but I can practically hear the puzzle pieces of Ian's life snapping into place. I was right about Mrs. Slater and her drinking. No wonder the mansion is off-limits.

Deb, Mar and I chain-smoke and speculate about the Slaters' marriage. We figure that Mrs. Slater was the most beautiful girl in North Bay, and she married Mr. Slater, a rich mining executive, even though she didn't love him, because she thought he'd be her ticket to the good life. But in the end, he turned out to be a jerk and she became an alcoholic trapped in a loveless marriage with a messed-up kid and nowhere to go.

It's a smart guess, if you ask me, but I don't want Deb and Mar spreading malicious gossip about *my* boyfriend, so I say, "Well, we don't know anything for sure."

"Yes, we do," Marlene says. "We know Mrs. Slater crashed her car into her garage and Mr. Slater dragged her into the house. I saw it with my own eyes."

"What if her foot slipped?" I say.

"Carla, get real," Deb says.

"Okay." I say. "So, what if you're right? What if Mrs. Slater is an alcoholic and Mr. Slater is an asshole? What if they left North Bay because everyone in town knew about their messed-up family?"

"Yeah," Mar says, like a movie detective. "Yeah. That fits."

"Well, the point is, they're probably trying to get a fresh start. So, do we really want to be trashing them? And have you thought about what this would do to Ian if it got out?"

"I'm not trashing them," Mar says weakly.

"Marlene, you can't tell anyone," I say firmly.

Marlene looks totally deflated, and I don't blame her. With a story like this, she could have been the Tom Thomson gossip queen for at least a week. She scowls at me and slouches in her chair.

I say, "Poor Ian. I wish I could do something nice for him." And then I get this fabulous idea. "Deb, you can invite him to your party!"

"I'm not having a party this year," Deb says.

"Yes, you are. Everybody looks forward to it." Deb's birthday is on October 31, and she always has a costume party. I love costume parties. Last year, I dressed up as Pebbles from *The Flintstones*. I wore a skimpy, fake-leopard-skin, off-the-shoulder mini-dress and a bone in my hair. I was so cute! Everyone said so, even Sherrie Cumberland. And she's not the type to dish out compliments.

"I hate having my birthday on Halloween," Debbie whines. "It's like a freak show. Why couldn't my mother squeeze her legs together and hold off for another twenty-four hours?"

"Debbie, your parties are always so great!" I say, sucking up to her. "And you'd be doing me the biggest favor in the world. Pleeease," I plead. "I'll even help you clean up."

Debbie sighs and looks over at Mar.

"It would be fun," Marlene says.

"I guess," Deb says.

I give her a big hug. "You're the best!" I say. "Let's make a guest list. We'll invite everyone we know, except Julia Epstein."

JULES

"Anticipation"

On Monday, Mr. Gabor breezes into the studio and announces that in preparation for *Hamlet*, we're going to learn how to fence. Ian immediately starts asking questions like: "Will we be using real swords?" and "Will we be using rapiers or foils?"

Mr. Gabor asks, "Do you know something about fencing, Mr. Slater?"

"Yeah, I do," Ian says.

"Really?" Carla says, twisting around in her chair to gawk at Ian. "*You* know how to fence? Like Zorro? Is that your secret hobby or something?" She laughs, but as soon as the words are out of her mouth, Ian gets this cold look in his eye. It's like Carla's crossed an invisible line, and she knows it. She says, "Hey, just kidding." But it's too late. Ian's jaw is twitching like he's biting down hard on something.

Mr. Gabor barks, "Cabrielli, your attention, please," and begins talking about the different styles of sword combat. It turns out that when Mr. Gabor was in theater school in London, he studied kendo for seven years with a sensei, a martial arts master. "*Kendo* means 'the way of the sword,'" he explains.

He demonstrates some moves called *kata*, and it's like watching one of those Japanese movies where the samurai warrior leaps into action, slashing his opponent to ribbons. You'd never guess that a big man like Mr. Gabor could move so gracefully, but he does.

Jeremy says, "Whoa, man, far out!"

Ian stares at Mr. Gabor like he's just discovered God.

Mr. Gabor brings out a box of stage swords from his office, and Ian can hardly wait to get his hands on one, but when he slices his sword through the air, it wobbles and makes a tinny *wap-wap-wap* sound. "This sword is crap," Ian says, disgusted.

"It's a stage sword, Mr. Slater," Mr. Gabor says. "Stage fencing is about creating the *illusion* of danger." Mr. Gabor lines us up and teaches us the basics: how to hold the grip with our fingers instead of a fist, and how to do this scampering heel-toe shuffle that fencers use when they move back and forth. It looks easy when Mr. Gabor does it, but when we try, we sound like a herd of stampeding elephants. The only one who looks good is Ian. God, does he look good!

Mr. Gabor also shows us the salute and en garde positions and how to "beat our blades" against each other's swords. Finally, he marks out a couple of simple attack and parry exercises and asks Ian to help demonstrate. At first, they do everything slowly so we understand the technique, but then Mr. Gabor nods at Ian and they ramp it up, like a real fight. Ian is amazing. He lunges and hits in lightning bursts of speed, and I can tell by the smile on Mr. Gabor's face that he's getting the biggest kick out of the fact that Ian actually knows his stuff.

When they stop, we all applaud. Mr. Gabor gives Ian a slight bow. He says, "Well done, Mr. Slater! I'll be expecting great things from you."

When we break to practice in pairs, Carla immediately rushes over to Ian, but Ian turns his back on her and walks over to me. "Hey, Rapunzel," he says, flicking his hair off his face, "let's see what you can do with a sword." Carla looks stunned. I don't know what to say. But Ian's already facing me, raising his sword into the air.

Carla gets stuck with Geoff, whose only athletic ability is tap dancing. She's spitting mad. She keeps glaring at me. Ian ignores her and shows me how to position my body and work the sword with my wrist. He's a tough coach, and *not* patient at all, but I like the way he's so precise. "Lead with your blade, not your feet, or you'll telegraph your attack," he instructs. "Don't push the blade, follow it. Drop your back arm when you lunge." Since when did he become so articulate? I try to focus, but when Ian puts his hand on mine, shifting my fingers to hold the grip properly, all I can think about is how strong and smooth his fingers are. For a second, I flash to Carla's basement, remembering Ian's fingers sliding under her shirt, but then I shake off the thought.

I listen carefully to Ian's instructions, and we spend the whole class practicing together. At first, my cuts are feeble, nervous swipes, but after a while, I begin to get the rhythm and balance of it and it feels good. I stop thinking with my conscious mind and trust my "body-mind," as my dance teacher used to call it, letting the movement flow. Ian watches and nods his head. "Rapunzel, I never figured you for a fencer, but it looks like you're a natural," he says.

I feel myself blush. "I used to take dance classes," I say. "So it's kind of like dancing with a weapon in your hand."

"I never thought of it that way," he says. He tilts his head, assessing me. "We should spar together when you get better."

My heart thumps. "I have a lot to learn."

"That's okay," he says, smirking, "you're a fast learner." He's staring at me, kind of amused. I think he might be flirting with me.

Across the room, Geoff leaps at Carla like a swashbuckling pirate with two left feet. Carla scowls. "You're such a klutz," she sneers.

"Well, it would help if you picked up your sword and defended yourself," Geoff replies. Carla snarls. Geoff lunges again and almost stabs Carla in the leg.

"Shit!" she yells, and swats him across the arm with her sword.

"Ow!" Geoff shouts.

"Shut up," Carla says.

From across the room, Mr. Gabor roars, "Cabrielli! My office. Now!"

The buzzer goes. Geoff stares at the welt on his arm. Carla marches into Mr. Gabor's office. And Ian walks out of the studio with me.

CARLA

"Where Did the Love Go"

I'm sitting in Mr. Gabor's office, and he's giving me a lecture about swords and safety. I nod in all the right places, but inside, I'm fuming because Ian is such a prick! He knows I hate Julia. He picked her as a partner just to get back at me. And why? Because I teased him? Can't the guy take a joke? I mean, how was I supposed to know that fencing is such a big deal to him? Who does fencing? It's not like he ever talked about it. And why did he have to be pawing Julia, "correcting her technique"? How cliché!

"Cabrielli!" Mr. Gabor snaps at me.

I guess he can tell I'm not really listening. "What?" I say.

"I am not speaking for my own edification."

I hate when teachers use big words like that, but I get the gist. "I'm having a bad day," I say.

"I thought you were serious about drama," Mr. Gabor says.

"I am!" I insist. "I love drama. It's my favorite subject. I even want to do *Hamlet*." Mr. Gabor looks surprised. "What?" I say. "You don't think I can handle it?"

"I thought you'd try out for the musical," Mr. Gabor says. "I didn't think *Hamlet* was your cup of tea."

"Well it *is*," I say, annoyed because obviously he doesn't think I'm intellectual enough to do Shakespeare. "As a matter of fact, I want to be Gertrude," I say. I wasn't planning on getting into this, but once we're on the topic, I go with the flow. "I think I would make an excellent Gertrude because I happen to have a very powerful personality, and queens are strong and confident people, don't you think?"

An amused smile flickers across Mr. Gabor's lips. He says, "Just because you want the part doesn't mean you're going to get it."

"Are you saying I'm not good enough?" I ask, offended.

"No, Cabrielli, you're good enough," he says. "You have excellent timing and a strong presence, but you don't focus. Being an actor requires discipline. You can't have 'bad days.' You need to work harder, dig deeper, go beyond the obvious."

"I can," I insist. "I can be really, really deep if I want to be."

Mr. Gabor doesn't look convinced, but that only makes me want the part even more. If there's one thing I hate, it's being dismissed. "Just give me a shot at this," I say. I stare him down. I can be tough, like Papa. And maybe Mr. Gabor likes the fire in me 'cause he chuckles, and I sense this mental shift.

He leans across the desk and says, "Okay, Cabrielli, if you want to audition, you have to prepare yourself. Understand the language. Taste the words in your mouth. Find out what makes Gertrude tick—as a queen, a mother, a lover, a woman. And don't just dabble with the part, own it."

I nod my head. This is so great. He's talking to me like I really count. Like he's my mentor, director to actor. I'm so excited, I pop out of my chair. I say, "Mr. Gabor, thank you. I'm going to work so hard, it's going to blow your mind."

Mr. Gabor laughs and then gives me the Gabor glare. He says, "And if you ever hit anyone again—"

"I'm sorry about that."

"You will deliver your apology in person to Mr. Jones." He grunts and jerks his head toward the door. Case closed. I waltz out of the office. I'm so pumped up, I could fly. And maybe I don't get 90s like Julia, but I must be some kind of genius to turn a detention into a casting call. One problem down, one to go.

I race through the hall, and sure enough, who do I see hanging out at Ian's locker? Zorro and his little protégé. Ian's giving Julia fencing tips. "Your footwork's good, but your wrists are weak. You should do arm curls and push-ups every day." Blah, blah, who cares. But Julia's nodding like a doll with its head on a spring.

Damn, that girl moves in fast! I want to twist her head right off her neck. But I know I can't play it like that in front of Ian, so I saunter over, real casual, and say, "Ian, you were so cool with that sword. Who knew you had this hidden talent!" And then, just to prove I'm not threatened by that bitch, I say, "Julia, you weren't bad either for a beginner."

"Thanks," Julia says quietly.

There, done. I smile at Ian like it's time to skedaddle. "Let's go," I say. "You can teach me some of those moves in my basement." Hint, hint.

Ian swivels his head to face me. "I'm giving Jules a ride home," he says.

"What?" I squawk. I look over at Julia and her eyes fly open, like this "ride home" is news to her too.

Ian grabs his jacket from his locker. "Come on, Rapunzel, let's get out of here," he says. Julia scampers after him. And I'm left alone in the empty hall.

I can't believe this is happening to me. Ian is choosing Julia over me? Ian Slater is rejecting *me*? Is he out of his fucking mind? Anger shoots up my spine. My entire body vibrates with rage. And wham!—I kick his locker, hard! And then, oh my God, the pain! The pain! I think I just broke my big toe.

"Helplessly Hoping"

"Thanks for the ride," I say, climbing off Ian's bike.

"No problem," he says. "So are you asking me in?" He grins and looks at me with those smoky eyes, and more than anything I want to say yes.

"No," I blurt. Ian looks surprised. I glance over at Mom's car in the driveway. "I'd like to," I say, "but things are kind of weird at home." I can't imagine what my mother would say if she saw Ian in his black leather jacket, unshaven and long-haired, sitting at our kitchen table smoking cigarettes. I'd never hear the end of it.

Ian nods. "I get it," he says.

"Maybe another time?" I say desperately, hoping he doesn't think I'm not interested.

"Sure." He smiles. He glides his bike down the driveway and takes off.

In the McDuffs' garage, I find a broken hockey stick. In the kitchen, I grab two cans of soup. I bring these to the basement and begin training. First I do arm curls with the soup cans until my arms ache. Then I do push-ups, but I can barely get to eight before I collapse. I have Gumby arms—pathetic! This will have to change. To limber up, I practice my dance exercises: *pliés*, *tendus*, *battements*. I figure that a lunge in jazz is almost the same as a lunge in fencing, and extended lines are something every dancer understands. I play "Soul Makossa" on the stereo and rehearse my old dance routines. In my mind, I can hear my jazz teacher, Eva von Gencsy, counting out the beats in her deep Hungarian accent: *Von, two, sree, four, five, seex, saven, eight.*

Next I pick up the broken hockey stick, my trusty sword, and run through the attack and parry exercises. Mr. Gabor says that we have to keep our steps controlled and tight because "big moves are slow moves." He says, "Fencing is the graceful economy of movement." Ian sure has that down. He even looks like a fencer, with his slim frame and flinty eyes. I still can't believe he drove me home, the two of us leaning into the road, my body pressed against his back . . .

Carla's going to be so mad! But it's not my fault he offered me a ride. And why shouldn't I talk to him? We were just talking about fencing. He said I was a natural. He said he wanted to spar with me, *if* I ever get good enough. Sometimes I think he likes me. And I know I shouldn't read into these things, but he *did* pick me to be his partner. And, yes, he was pissed off with Carla, and I'm not saying he made a play for me, but there are twenty-three other students in drama, and he didn't pick any of them.

I really did feel the connection. But maybe it's just me, not him. Sometimes it's hard to tell what's real or to know the truth about another human being.

CARLA

"You've Got It Bad Girl"

When Ma sees me limping and wailing into the house, she takes me right to the North York General Hospital Emergency, which is the most depressing place on earth, full of old, sick, moaning people and crying, screaming children. I say, "Ma, just take me home and let me die," but Ma shushes me and puts her arm around me.

The nurse at the front desk asks what the problem is. I tell her I accidentally banged my toe on a table. Two hours later, I'm still in the waiting room and my toe is swollen like a giant sausage. Finally, I get an X-ray. The doctor says that my toe isn't broken, just sprained. They tape it up and tell me to ice it, keep it elevated and take an aspirin. Gee, thanks. I waited two hours for that?

I want to kill Julia Epstein. I want to saw off her head with a rusty blade. I want to throw her into a pit of poisonous snakes with big, sharp fangs. I want to drop her from a plane into an ocean full of thrashing, hungry sharks. I want the sharks to chomp on her flesh in a feeding frenzy until there's nothing left, not even the bones.

At home, I phone Marlene and Debbie. They rush over, and the three of us sit on my bed. They can't believe how gross my toe is. I tell them about drama class. I say, "Marlene, remember after Rummoli, when you said that Julia Epstein is boring, but harmless? Well, think again. Today, she rode off on Ian's motorcycle."

Debbie and Marlene gasp. They can't believe she had the nerve. After all, isn't it obvious that I am Ian Slater's girlfriend? What kind of person takes a ride from someone else's boyfriend? A slut, that's who. A slut disguised as Little Miss Perfect.

Of course, Debbie is quick to point out that it was Ian who asked Julia to be his partner and offered her a ride home.

"Yeah, that's true," I say. "Ian Slater is a self-centered, egotistical jerk. But he's *my* jerk, and it was up to Julia to turn him down. She's poaching."

Marlene says, "Maybe this is a sign."

Debbie says, "Yeah, like maybe you should be done with Ian."

"Oh, I am absolutely done!" I say. "I'm not going near him. He'd have to beg me on his hands and knees, and kiss my big, fat, ugly, swollen toe before I'd ever think about going out with him again."

"Don't even think about it," Mar says.

"I'll cross him off the party list," Deb says.

"Good," I say.

"There's plenty of fish in the sea," Mar says.

"Damn right," I say. But the only fish I want is Ian.

At dinnertime, Ma brings me a plate of ravioli, but I'm too bummed to eat. I can practically feel my heartbeat throbbing in my toe. When Papa gets home, he comes upstairs and sits on my bed. He stares at me with his beady, all-knowing eyes.

"It was an accident," I say.

Papa shrugs; he knows I'm lying. He says, "*Cara*, you've got to watch your temper, eh?" He hugs me, and I push my head into his shoulder. "So, what happened? Was it that boy?" I grunt. Papa squeezes me tight. "*Tesorina*, he's not worth it. Send him packing. You're the prize."

But I don't feel like the prize. I want Ian. He's perfect for me. We like the same music. He gets my jokes. I'm wild for his kisses. And he doesn't let me push him around the way most guys do. Tears well up in my eyes. Papa gives me his handkerchief. He says, "You know what Nonna Cabrielli would say?"

I glance at him and nod my head. "*A tutto c'è rimedio, fuorché alla morte*," I mumble. There's a cure for everything except death. Great.

In the morning, I can barely walk because of my sprained toe. In fact, I have to wear sandals because there's no way I can get a shoe on my foot. When I stagger into drama, Mr. Gabor does a double take. "What happened to you?"

"Sprained toe," I say, sliding into my seat and sticking out my bandaged foot so everyone can see it. "But don't worry, I can still fence," I add, trying to show Mr. Gabor what a brave little trooper I am.

Mr. Gabor raises an eyebrow. "Why don't you go read *Hamlet* in the library."

"No!" I blurt. The last thing I want to do is leave Ian and Julia alone in the studio. "I can learn a lot by watching," I say.

Mr. Gabor points to the door. Maybe he thinks he's doing me a favor. "Take your *Hamlet* and get outta here," he says sternly.

I sigh. This is horrible. I limp toward the door just as Julia walks in, and in a fit of spontaneous rage, I give her a quick hip check into the door frame. She hits it with a loud thud. I say, "Julia, would you watch where you're going! I'm injured!"

Heads turn. Julia says, "I didn't—" But by this time, everyone is staring at her, thinking she's the one who bumped into me.

Seconds later, Ian saunters around the corner. He looks at my foot and asks, "What happened to you?"

"Like you care," I snap. "Creep." I wish I had crutches so I could whack him.

In the library, I pop an aspirin and dig *Hamlet* out of my bag. I try not to think about Julia making doe eyes at Ian. I flip open the play and read the first few pages without understanding a word. It's a very *long* play. I doodle in the margin. I draw a crown. Queen Gertrude. I put down my pencil and try not to skim the pages because if I'm going to perform Shakespeare onstage for Mr. Gabor—which I am!—I should probably understand everything. Julia Epstein is not the only one with brains in this school, and she sure as hell is not getting my part!

I focus on Gertrude's speeches, but the language is practically in code. For example, when Gertrude says, "*Good Hamlet, cast thy nighted color off,/And let thine eye look like a friend on Denmark,*" what she means is *Hamlet, take off those ugly black clothes because ever since your father died, you've been moping around the castle like the world's biggest grump. Basta. Everyone dies. Be happy you're back home in Denmark, and move on with your life.*

Gertrude certainly knows how to move on. Her bed's not even cold before she's screwing her dead husband's brother! I guess Claudius must be a real stud, or a terrific liar, because Gertrude is totally taken in by him. She doesn't have a clue that he's the one who murdered her husband. I guess, as they say, love is blind—which, of course, makes me think about Julia and Ian and how she's seducing him with this fencing fixation. The thought of them darting around the studio and smashing their swords together makes me want to erupt like a volcano. I slam my book shut and head home.

I take the street route instead of the ravine because it's drizzling and I'm afraid of slipping and hurting my sausage toe. I'm about two blocks from my house when I hear a motorcycle edging up behind me. I don't even have to look to know who it is.

"Hey, what happened to your foot?" Ian calls out over the noise of his bike. I keep walking. "You want a lift?" he asks.

Is he kidding? What nerve! "What is this, musical rides?" I mutter. "Every day a different girl?"

Ian laughs. "Are you jealous?"

"Me? What gives you that idea?"

"Oh, I don't know. The big dent in my locker?" I limp faster. Ian smirks. "It almost looks like someone . . . kicked it in."

"Fuck off," I say.

Ian grins. "If you really wanted to do damage, you should've used a baseball bat. It's not nearly so hard on the body."

"Look," I say, facing him. "Why don't you go play fencing with Julia. I'm sure she'd really love that." I try to limp away, but Ian rolls his bike over the curb and across the sidewalk, blocking my path.

"I don't want to play with Jules," he says. "I want to play with you."

"Is that so?" I ask sarcastically. I want to slap him across the face. I want to tell him that I don't need to go out with a jerk like him. I could date any guy I want. Guys who actually invite me to their house, and take me to movies, and tell me how great I look. I want to say this right to his face, but my lip is trembling, so instead, I blurt, "Tell me, why are you so mean?"

Ian looks almost embarrassed for once. He says, "You sort of pissed me off."

"I was joking," I snap.

"I know. I lost it. Sorry. But fencing is kinda personal with me." He slouches forward on his bike. I can tell this isn't easy for him. He's not the type to apologize. He waits for me to say something.

I stare at his face, and he stares right back, serious and quiet, not messing around. Why is it that when a guy is sincere for about twenty seconds, you already feel your heart melting?

"Let me make it up to you," he says. "What are you doing Saturday night?"

"Icing my toe. And babysitting Buzz."

"Great. I'll keep you company," he says.

I look away. I drag out the moment, like saying yes would be doing him the biggest favor in the entire world. But now he's smirking, 'cause he knows I'm giving in. He reaches for me and pulls me close. He wraps his arms around my shoulders. I slide my hands under his jacket. Then we French-kiss, right on the sidewalk, and neither of us cares who sees.

"It Ain't Me Babe"

I learn everything I can about fencing from Mr. Gabor, not because Ian's interested in it, but because I am. I like the style of movement and the strategy of the fight. Mr. Gabor says that "fencing is like chess for athletes." It's a game for the mind as much as the body. When I walk to school, I play matches in my head. At home, I train every day. In class, I like to fight against the *J*s. I never spar with Ian anymore. Carla keeps him on a tight leash. Sometimes I feel him watching me, studying my progress and technique, and I'm flattered, but I keep away. Fencing is enough of a dangerous game.

At the end of October, as a kind of wrap-up, Mr. Gabor teaches us the first part of the duel sequence from *Hamlet*, act 5, scene 2. It's the climax, where Hamlet and Laertes fight to the death. Mr. Gabor's choreography is fast and exciting—lots of lunges and clashing swords. There's even a part where Laertes swipes at Hamlet's legs, and Hamlet has to jump over the blade.

Geoff ends up partnering with Ian. It's a terrible combination. Geoff leaps at Ian like Nureyev doing a grand jeté, and Ian snaps. "What are you? A ballerina?"

Mr. Gabor barks, "Slater, keep a lid on it." Then he turns to me and says, "Ms. Epstein, please switch places with Mr. Jones."

I have no choice. For the first time in weeks, I come face-to-face with Ian. He gives me a mocking bow and says, "Rapunzel, you've been avoiding me."

"No," I say defensively.

Ian smirks. "You're looking stronger."

"I practice."

"I noticed. Do you want to be Hamlet or Laertes?" he asks.

"Hamlet," I say. "I like Hamlet better."

"Then I'll be Laertes, but you'll have to work hard to hit me. Salute." He raises his sword.

"En garde," I say.

Ian smiles and we spring into action. We work through the sequence a couple of times with Ian offering comments and advice. "Keep your tip up," he says when my sword sags. "Relax," he says. "You can't fence if you're tense." I shake out my shoulders and take a deep breath. We vary the pace of the fight, drawing out the suspense, circling each other, then pushing hard and fast so the fight becomes dramatic and intense.

At the end of the session, Mr. Gabor stops the class and asks everyone to stand against the wall. He turns on the spotlights so they illuminate the center of the studio, and then asks Ian and me to demonstrate. "With dialogue," he instructs.

Ian and I move to opposite ends of the performance space, as if we are Hamlet and Laertes preparing for a "friendly" duel.

Of course, Hamlet doesn't yet realize that King Claudius and Laertes have poisoned the tip of Laertes's sword, so that Laertes has only to prick Hamlet's skin in order to cause his swift and painful death.

Mr. Gabor nods for us to begin.

I/Hamlet call out to Laertes in a bold voice, "*Come on, sir.*"

Ian/Laertes smiles malevolently and replies, "*Come, my lord.*"

We raise our swords, and in a flash, our bodies leap toward each other. Our swords whoosh through the air, and our blades smash, cut and strike. I'm in combat against a fierce opponent, and the duel feels almost real. Ian is fast—even faster than he was in practice—and I'm not faking it when I have to throw myself into the fight.

At first, Laertes pushes hard, forcing Hamlet backward, making me leap over his sword, but then I feint and twist away. Laertes raises his sword above his head and slashes downward, trying to hit Hamlet's arm, but I anticipate the move and lunge underneath his sword for a swift touch to his waist.

Hamlet calls out, "*One,*" meaning one point for me.

Laertes shouts, "*No.*"

"*Judgment,*" Hamlet demands.

Mr. Gabor, as Osric, the courtier who is judging the match, calls out, "*A hit, a very palpable hit.*"

Laertes swallows his anger and glares at me. "*Well, again.*" He raises his sword. We salute and hold our positions.

"And . . . scene!" Mr. Gabor says.

Ian and I break. The class cheers. I lean over, hands on knees, panting and exhilarated.

Mr. Gabor beams at us. "Yes! Wonderful! That's how it's done, people!"

Ian grins and extends his hand. "Well played, Rapunzel."

"Thanks," I gasp. "I could barely keep up!" He laughs, and rests his hand on my shoulder. We smile at each other, bonded by the blade. For one perfect moment, it's just the two of us under the lights.

Then Carla bulldozes her way over. She throws her arms around Ian's neck. "Oh my God, you were so amazing!" she shrieks. "You *have* to be Laertes in the play. You just have to!"

Jeremy says, "Yeah, man. You should definitely audition."

Ian smirks. "I don't do plays."

"Are you kidding?" Carla says. "I got goose bumps just watching you. You would make a fabulous Laertes." She turns to me with a fake smile. "Don't you agree, Julia?"

I look at Ian. "Yeah, I do."

Geoff bounds over and executes a mock lunge. "Jules, you were marvelous! You were like Errol Flynn in *Captain Blood.*"

Carla sneers, "Yeah, well, it's sort of a waste. I mean, it's not like there's lots of fencing roles for women. Like . . . none!"

Geoff rolls his eyes. Carla grabs Ian and leads him away. Geoff says, "Meow, meow."

"Carla hates me," I say.

"She doesn't like you messin' with her man," Geoff says.

"I wasn't messing. We were fencing." Geoff gives me one of those you-can't-fool-me looks. "What?" I say.

"Come on," he says. "I can tell you like him."

"Ian? Don't be silly," I say.

Geoff laughs. "Jules, I totally get it. Ian has that bad boy/ James Dean appeal. Sexy and dangerous. Who wouldn't fall for someone like that?"

"I wouldn't," I insist. "I'm not his type."

"Good thing," Geoff says. "He'd only hurt you in the end."

~~CARLA~~

"If You Really Love Me"

Debbie's Halloween party is three days away, and I still haven't decided what to wear, mostly because Ian won't commit to a costume. I think we should wear something matching, but Ian doesn't want to dress up at all. We're walking through the ravine and I say, "If you go as Batman, I could be Catwoman and wear my black jumpsuit and a cat mask, which would look incredibly sexy on me."

"I'm not dressing up like some queer," Ian says.

"Okay, you can be Zorro and I'll be a Spanish senorita," I say. I picture myself in a flamenco dress that shows a lot of cleavage, or maybe a pair of skintight capris, a bolero jacket and one of those flat-rimmed hats with the cute little bobbles.

"I hate costume parties," Ian says.

"Then obviously you've never been to a *good* costume party," I say.

We cross the bridge and spot Julia up ahead. Man, that girl gets on my nerves. Lately, in drama, she's been acting like some kind of fencing queen, slicing and dicing, trying really hard to impress Ian. She makes me sick.

When we reach Julia, Ian yanks her braid and says, "Hey, Rapunzel, what's up?"

I say, "Julia, where's your boyfriend today?" We all know who I'm talking about. She and Geoff are glued at the hip.

"We're just friends," Julia says.

Well, duh! I know Geoff isn't really her boyfriend because if anyone in the entire school is gay, it's him. Ian thinks so too. He says you can tell he's gay by the way he fences.

"You shouldn't hang out with him," Ian says. "People will call you a fag hag."

"I don't care what people say," Julia says, blushing.

We reach my back gate and I undo the latch. Ian says, "So, Jules, are you going to Debbie's Halloween party?"

I give him a look like *why are you asking her that*? Debbie and Julia are *not* friends. I say, "Ian, it's not up to you to invite people to Debbie's party."

"What's the big deal?" he says.

"It's Debbie's party," I say.

"So?"

Julia looks down at her feet and says, "It's okay. I already have plans."

"No, you don't," Ian says. "I bet you're just being polite."

"Ian, she *said* she has plans," I say. I open the gate and give him my *let's-go* look. For a second, he doesn't move. He just stares at me coldly, like he's not going to take orders from me. Then Julia says good-bye, and Ian follows me into the house.

In the kitchen, I say, "Ian, what the hell was that?"

"Why are you always such a bitch to her?" he asks.

"Why are you always talking to her?"

"She's different," Ian says, poking around in the fridge. "She's not what you'd expect."

I put my hands on my hips. I don't want to get into a fight with Ian, not when we have a costume party on the weekend, but sometimes he really pushes my buttons. "What's that supposed to mean?" I ask.

"Well, for one thing, except for me, she's the best fencer in the class."

"So? I'm the best actress in the class," I say. I wait for Ian to agree with me. He doesn't say anything. I say, "Ian?"

"What?"

"Don't you think I'm the best actress in the class?"

"I don't know. You do different things."

"What do you mean, 'different things'?" I sneer.

Ian helps himself to Ma's leftover lasagna. "Look, you're a comic actor; Jules is a dramatic actor."

"So, who's better, if you had to choose?"

"I don't know."

I grit my teeth. "Ian, if you had to give Julia or me an Oscar for Best Actress in a Grade Eleven Drama Class, which one would it be?"

Ian gives me a deadpan look. "Carla, this is really boring."

"No, it isn't," I say. Ian heads for the basement door. I block his path and glare at him. "Look, acting means a lot to me. It's the only course I care about. I get excited when I'm onstage. So actually, Ian, this isn't boring at all."

Ian walks around me and goes downstairs with his lasagna. I stand in the middle of the kitchen, livid. He actually thinks Julia is better than me! If he thought *I* was better, he'd come right out and say it, but no, he's sidestepping the issue, which means he thinks *she's* better. I can't believe it! What a jerk! Everyone else thinks I'm the best. Everyone except my own boyfriend! And here I am, inviting him to Debbie's party, trying to make his miserable, messed-up life a little more fun, and he thinks Julia's more talented than me?

Downstairs, I hear Ian turn on the TV. I pour myself a Coke and try to calm down. I wait to see if Ian will come upstairs and apologize for hurting my feelings, but he doesn't, so after about twenty minutes, I go downstairs and sit at the far end of the couch. Ian pulls a joint out of his pack of cigarettes. I don't like smoking pot in the afternoon, especially not on school days, so I only take one toke, and then I say, "Ma and Buzz could be home any second, you know."

Ian keeps smoking. I open a window and light a stick of sandalwood incense so the basement won't smell of weed. After a while, Ian turns off the TV and puts my *Who's Next* album on the stereo. He sings "Won't Get Fooled Again" with

Roger Daltrey and drums on my head like he's Keith Moon. I tell him to stop. He hops on the couch beside me and says, "Carla, I think you're really talented."

"You're just saying that because you're stoned and you want to fool around," I say.

Ian laughs. "You're a really talented kisser," he says.

"Great," I say sarcastically. "I hear there's good money in that."

"You're also the funniest girl I ever met," he says, passing me the joint.

"You're just saying that."

"I wouldn't lie to you," he says.

And that's true. Ian's not a liar. He won't say anything unless he means it, not even to be nice, not even to get what he wants. "So you think I'm funny," I say, taking another toke.

"And sexy," he says. He leans in and kisses me. Eventually, I kiss him back. Pot is such a love drug, and even without the weed, Ian is hard to resist. Soon we're making out on the couch. I'm sitting on his lap and my shirt is undone. I'm slowly rubbing against his jeans, and Ian's hands are all over me. And maybe it's the pot, or maybe we're just in another zone, but for some reason, I don't hear the door open, and suddenly footsteps are thumping down the stairs.

"Carla, it stinks down here," Papa says, walking into the basement. Ian and I spring apart. My fingers fly to my buttons—but too late. Papa's face boils red as a lobster. His shoulders bunch up, and he glares at Ian like he wants to rip him limb from limb. "Get out," he growls.

Ian grabs his smokes and beats it up the stairs, two at a time. Pa and I both wait till we hear the door slam. Then, World War III breaks out. I tell Papa that he has no right to barge in, but Papa roars and points to my shirt. The buttons aren't properly done up. I know I'm in trouble, but I don't back down. I yell, "I'm almost seventeen, and I have a right to some privacy around here."

Pa bellows, "You think that boy cares for you?"

"He does!" I say.

"He's using you," Pa snorts.

"You don't even know him!" I scream.

"I know what he wants. And you're acting like a tramp!"

"You have no right to talk to me like that," I say.

"I am your father," Papa shouts. "You live in my house; you obey my rules!" I scramble to my feet, but Papa's not done with me yet. He jabs his finger into the air. "Carla Antonella Lucia Cabrielli, you are grounded!"

I gasp. "But Debbie's having a party!" I shriek.

"Tough."

"I'm going."

"You're not going anywhere. The only place you're going is straight to your room!"

I burst into tears and rush upstairs. I slam my door, and then I slam it again just in case he didn't hear it the first time.

Later, Ma knocks on my door. She walks in wearing her boss-lady face. She says, "Your father is very upset with you."

"*He's* upset?" I say. "He's ruining my life. He embarrassed me in front of my boyfriend. And now he won't even let me go to Debbie's party." I beg her to please talk to Pa, but instead, I get a lecture about boys and their raging hormones, and how there's no point in closing the barn door after the cow is already out. "Why buy the milk when you can get the cow for free?" she says.

"I am not a cow; I am a person," I yell. "And what the hell is it with these stupid cow metaphors anyway? We're not living on a farm in the 1950s. It's not like I'm actually having sex with him or anything!"

Ma throws her hands up in the air. She storms out of my room muttering under her breath, *"Marito e figli, come Dio te li da, così te li pigli,"* which means *when God gives you a husband and children, that's who you're stuck with.*

Saturday night, I am held prisoner by my evil parents while everyone I know is at Debbie's party. I try calling Deb a couple of times to see how the party's going, but no one answers. They're probably having way too much fun to bother picking up the goddamn phone.

Sunday morning, Papa says that if I feel like getting out of the house today, I can always go to church with the family.

I pass. But as soon as the three of them drive off, I sneak out the back door and race over to Debbie's. Deb's mom answers the door. She says, "Debbie's still sleeping."

"That's okay," I say politely. "I'll just go upstairs and wake her up."

Debbie's huddled underneath her blankets. I throw myself onto the bed. "Tell me about the party," I say.

"Go away," she moans.

"Tell me," I insist.

Deb opens her slit eyes and wipes the drool off her face. She says, "You missed the best party ever." Gee, thanks, Deb! I am so bummed! Deb says, "Jason Titlebaum had the funniest costume. He wrapped himself in cotton wool and tied a string to the top of his head, so he looked like a giant tampon." Debbie grins. "And the sluttiest costume award goes to Sherrie Cumberland." Natch. "She dressed up as a French maid in fishnet stockings and a corset, probably so she could show off her boobs."

"Did Ian show up?" I ask.

"Yeah, but he didn't wear a costume," Deb says.

Figures. "Did you talk to him?"

"Not really."

"Did he dance with anyone?"

"No, but everyone else danced up a storm."

"Did he look at Sherrie Cumberland's boobs?"

Deb rolls her eyes. "Who wouldn't?"

"Did he talk about me?"

Debbie yawns. "He spent most of the evening smoking dope with Jim Malone, who wasn't even invited to the party but crashed anyway."

"But did he say anything about me?" I ask.

Deb sighs. "I said, 'Too bad about Carla being grounded,' and he said, 'Yeah.'"

"That's it?" I shout.

Deb covers her head with her pillow and says, "Carla, stop!"

I go home and wait all day for Ian to phone, but he doesn't. When I can't stand it anymore, I call him. His mom says he's out. I leave a message asking if she'd please tell him to call me as soon as he gets home. I wait and wait, but the call never comes. By the time I go to bed, I'm gnashing my teeth. I mean, don't you think that if your girlfriend got grounded because her father caught you feeling her up, you might want to phone and see how she's doing? Especially if she missed a party. A party she set up with you in mind! Wouldn't that be the nice thing to do? But no, Ian has no manners. It's always me chasing him, and I'm getting mighty tired of that.

JULES

"Went to See the Gypsy"

"I think it's time I met your mother," Geoff says just before
Halloween.

"Why?" I ask. "She's not interesting like your mother.
You're not missing anything."

Geoff shakes his head. "Maybe you don't really have a
mother," he says. "Maybe you and poor little Bobby are
orphans living off a family trust, pretending that your mother
is still alive so Social Services doesn't put you up for adop-
tion." I sigh. "Seriously," Geoff says. "It's almost like you don't
want me to meet her."

He's right; I don't. I don't want her to know that I've made
friends with a witty, charming, funny guy. If my mom sees that,
she'll think I'm "adjusting," and I want her to know how trau-
matized I am. I explain this to Geoff, but he just laughs, so
Friday after school, I finally relent. Geoff Jones meets Natalie
Epstein, and wouldn't you know, they hit it off like a house on
fire. Mom is delighted to meet my new friend, and Geoff
gushes over Mom like she's a movie star. He says, "Jules, you
never told me your mother looks exactly like Kim Novak!"

"Maybe that's 'cause I don't know who Kim Novak is," I say flatly.

Mom laughs. "I'm not nearly that pretty."

"But you are," Geoff says. "You have her blonde hair and almond-shaped eyes."

"Who's Kim Novak?" Bobby asks.

"A famous actress," Mom says.

"Her real name was Marilyn Novak," Geoff explains, "but Columbia made her change it to Kim because there already was a Marilyn—Monroe. Anyway, Kim made lots of movies and dated lots of men: Sammy Davis Jr., Frank Sinatra, Prince Aly Khan and Count Mario Bandini, Italy's tomato mogul."

I groan. Geoff is showing off, and Mom is lapping it up. She invites Geoff to stay for dinner. Over lamb chops, they talk about Kim Novak's performance in Hitchcock's *Vertigo*. I don't make any attempt to join in—not that I could. By the time dessert is served, they're practically best friends. So, when Geoff asks Mom if it would be all right if I spent Halloween with him and Clarissa, Mom is only too happy to oblige.

Sunday night, I'm expecting to hand out Halloween candies at Geoff's, but when I arrive at his apartment, the door is flung open by a man wearing a tuxedo and a black cape. He has thick eyebrows, slicked-back hair and fangs. "Velcome," he says in a Transylvanian accent.

"Ah, Count Dracula," I say.

Geoff bows politely and looks hungrily at my neck. "So glad you could come to my hummmble abode. But vhere is your costume?"

"Do I need one?" I ask.

Geoff calls out, "Mother, darlink, I think ve have a prawblem."

Clarissa appears in a white diaphanous gown that clings to her body. She wears gold serpent bands around her upper arms and head. Her green eyes are accented with eyeliner, like kohl, so that you can't help but think she's Cleopatra reincarnated.

"Cleopatra?" I ask.

"The goddess Isis," she says, angling her body sideways as if posing for an Egyptian frieze. "Didn't Geoff tell you we're going out?" I shake my head. "Never mind, I'm sure I have something wonderful for you in my closet."

Geoff and Clarissa leap to the challenge of finding me the perfect costume. Clarissa pulls out a little black dress with a scoop neck and says, "Audrey Hepburn?" I try it on in the bathroom. It's chic and fabulous. My mother would say it's way too sophisticated for me, but when I step back into the bedroom, Geoff and Clarissa applaud.

"She just needs gloaves," says Count Dracula.

"And a cigarette holder," says Isis.

"Like *Breakfast at Tiffany's*," says the count. "You *have* seen *Breakfast at Tiffany's*, I hope."

"No, but I saw Audrey Hepburn in *My Fair Lady*," I say proudly.

"Vell, it's the *Tiffany* Hepburn ve're going for here." Geoff arches an eyebrow. "Did you know her mother vas a Dutch baroness?"

Clarissa pins up my hair, while *Vogue* fashion photographer Geoff Jones snaps pictures of the entire makeover process, saying things like, "Chin up, darling, and a touch to the left."

Clarissa fills me in on the evening's plan. "We're going to see a psychic named Henry," she says. "He reads palms, and even the police use him. Last month, when a girl in Richmond Hill disappeared, Henry told the police to look in a watery ditch near power lines, and that's exactly where they found her body." Creepy!

At the stroke of seven, we sweep out of the apartment looking like characters in a Fellini film. Geoff drives Baby Blue downtown to a rickety house on Queen Street West, where Henry works with three other psychics. We walk up the creaky plank stairs and enter a hallway that smells of mildew and patchouli oil. A woman with long gray hair and a pointy chin directs us into a waiting room full of lumpy couches, Indian cotton throws and mirrored pillows.

"Ooh . . . the Wicked Witch of the West," Geoff whispers in my ear. "I wouldn't let her read my fortune."

Clarissa says, "Don't worry; Henry's a doll. Do you know, two weeks before Keith walked out, Henry told me that my marriage was a forked road. But I guess you didn't have to be clairvoyant to see that coming." Clarissa laughs, and then turns to me. "Anyway, I've met someone new."

"Who?" I ask. It never occurred to me that Clarissa might be dating.

"A theater director," she says. "Michael van Meers. I met him through some acting friends. He's very interested in promoting new Canadian playwrights."

"He sounds great," I say.

"If you like guys with John Lennon glasses and a ponytail," Geoff mumbles.

"You barely met him," Clarissa chides.

The witchy lady calls Clarissa's name. Clarissa gives Geoff a long cool stare, and then rises like a goddess from her throne and slowly ascends the stairs. Geoff and I are left alone in the gloomy room.

"So, why don't you like Michael van Meers?" I ask Geoff.

Geoff shrugs. "I don't know. He's okay. Not nearly as good-looking as my dad, though." He fiddles with a candle on the coffee table.

"How old were you when your father left?" I ask.

"Four."

"Do you remember anything?"

Geoff wraps his Dracula cloak around his body. "I remember little bits of things, like riding in my dad's convertible. Or this time in my parents' bedroom, when I was hiding in the nook between the dresser and the wall because the two of them were fighting and I didn't want to hear it." Geoff passes his finger back and forth through the flame. In his black cape, with his melancholy expression, he looks just like Hamlet. I can picture him wandering through the chilly, torch-lit passages of Elsinore Castle, casting long, flickering shadows on the stone walls and muttering, *"All is not well. / I doubt some foul play. Would the night were come! / Till then, sit still, my soul."*

"Do you ever see your dad?" I ask.

Geoff pokes his finger into the hot wax. "I tried once when I was in grade five. We were doing pen pals at school, and I got the bright idea that I could be pen pals with my dad. So I got his address off one of his checks to Clarissa, and I wrote him a letter with all the usual pen pal stuff: age, favorite subjects, hobbies, that kind of thing. At the end of the letter, I said that I'd like to see him again, and I included a black-and-white photo-booth shot of me so he'd recognize me when we finally met. I sent it off without telling Clarissa. Two weeks later, I got a reply. He thanked me for writing, but said he didn't think we should meet because he'd remarried and he had a new life now. He wished me good luck in school. And I never heard from him again."

I sit there, stunned. "How could he do that?" I ask. Geoff doesn't look up. I think about my own dad, his goofy impressions of Ed Sullivan and his terrible off-key singing. I remember how he used to take Bobby and me tobogganing at Beaver

Lake in the winter and on the roller coaster at Belmont Park in the summer, and how, at the lake, he'd always challenge us to swimming races and cheat, grabbing our legs and pulling us backward through the water till we sputtered with laughter and screamed, "Daddy, stop it!" I miss him.

Clarissa waltzes back into the room and announces, "Henry foresees a significant change in my life." She sinks into an overstuffed armchair, and a small cloud of dust rises up from the cushion. "He said, the man I'm seeing could be 'the one'!"

"The one for what?" Geoff asks.

"The one to spend my life with, of course."

"And you believe him?" Geoff asks icily. Clarissa and Geoff lock eyes.

"Next," the witchy lady calls out.

"You go," I say to Geoff.

"I don't want to," Geoff mutters.

I jump up. "All right then, I'll go. Let's see what Henry has to say about me." I try to sound light and breezy, but my words are swallowed up into the gloom.

Henry isn't what you'd expect from a psychic. He's a very ordinary-looking, middle-aged man in an oatmeal-colored sweater. We exchange hellos. I sit opposite him and he unfurls my palm, tilting it under the lamplight. He doesn't bother looking at my face; maybe for him, my hand tells the entire story. I wonder if he recognizes people by their palms the way dentists like my uncle Mort recognize people by their teeth: *Ah, yes, the lady with the large incisors . . .*

Henry starts off with a few general observations. He tells me that I'm smart, disciplined and stubborn—things that could apply to almost anyone. I don't say anything because I'm skeptical about this whole psychic business. I'm waiting to see if he can come up with something no one else knows.

Henry glances at me. His eyes are milky blue. He says, "This is a time of transition for you. Family issues. Change. Have you just moved to Toronto?"

"Yes," I say, surprised.

Henry stares back at my palm. He traces the web of intersecting lines. "Things are not what they appear to be," he says. "A man you love is going to disappoint you. But it's not about you. Remember that." Is he talking about Ian? What does this mean? He says, "Each of us is tested in life. Most people face their battles when they're older. In your case, the test is now."

Henry's voice is low and soothing, but I don't like what he's telling me. How will I be tested? I want a road map, not riddles. "I don't understand," I say. "What am I supposed to do?"

Henry smiles and pats my hand. "You're a warrior, my dear. Your power is always there for you to claim. But you won't win by the sword." A shiver runs through me. I wait for him to explain, but Henry just sits back in his chair. The session is done.

"Thanks," I say, feeling confused. "I'll send up my friend now."

"Your friend won't be coming," Henry says.

I head downstairs. Geoff and Clarissa are already at the door. How did Henry know? Geoff has the car keys in his hand, and he averts his eyes as he shoves the door open. Outside, the wind snaps at his cape. Baby Blue's windshield is etched with frost, and Geoff scrapes it off. Clarissa gets in the front seat and slams the door. Suddenly I feel like Cinderella at midnight, when all the magic disappears. Our beautiful clothes have turned to flimsy rags, and there's a blister on the back of my foot from walking in Clarissa's heels. On the drive home, no one speaks. I glance at Geoff's somber profile. This is a face I don't recognize. Sometimes, even between friends, there are dark corners where no one is welcome.

When they drop me off at my house, I notice a blue Cadillac in the driveway. In the living room, I find my mother and Dr. Katzenberg sitting on the couch. It's 10:05 on a Sunday night. What is he doing in our house? They stare at me in my Audrey Hepburn dress. Mom asks, "Whose clothes are you wearing?" I can tell she doesn't like the look.

"Geoff's mom's," I say.

"Have you been to a costume party?" Dr. Katzenberg asks in a hearty voice that I find false and offensive.

"No," I answer. He waits for me to elaborate, but I don't. Mom's eyes grow angry—she knows what I'm doing—but she forces out polite conversation. She says, "Les came over to help pass out the candy." I look at the two wine glasses and the empty wine bottle on the coffee table.

Dr. Katzenberg says, "You should've seen some of those trick-or-treaters."

"So cute," my mother says.

"That little bumblebee . . ." Dr. Katzenberg smiles at my mother. She smiles back. I want to throw up. Do they think I'm an idiot? Kids stop coming to the door by nine o'clock, so why the hell is he still hanging around?

I want to say something clever and cynical, but I can't think of anything. I just stare at them until Dr. Katzenberg says that it's getting late and he'd better go. In my bedroom, from behind Karen McDuff's ruffled pink curtains, I watch his Cadillac purr down the street. Seconds later, my mother blasts into my bedroom.

"How dare you be so rude," she hisses.

"What?" I say, pretending I don't know what she's talking about.

"I expect you to be polite," she says. "Would it hurt you to make a little conversation?"

"He wasn't here to see me," I say.

She grits her teeth. "Dr. Katzenberg is my boss, and my *friend*. And I want you to treat him with respect."

I look her straight in the eye. "Yeah, well, maybe you should introduce your *friend* to your husband sometime."

That's when she slaps me across the face. Hard enough to make my head snap sideways. I'm shocked, and so is she. Her lips tremble. My cheek stings, but I don't care. I hate her. Either she's flirting with the idea of having an affair or she's already having one. Either way, it's wrong. She swallows hard and whips out of my room.

I pick up a pen and write to Mollie. My hand is shaking. I tell her about Dr. Katzenberg and ask for advice. What should I do? Should I phone my dad? Should I tell him what I know? And what would he do if he found out? Maybe he'd move to Toronto to fight for her and save his marriage. Or maybe he'd be so hurt that he'd stay in Montreal and they'd get divorced.

When I write down the word *divorced*, my heart cramps up and tears drip onto the page. What a bleak, horrible, cruel word. A word like a scorched field. People in my family do *not* get divorced. And, yes, it's okay when you're young and single to "love the one you're with," like Stephen Stills says in that song, but *not* when you're married! That is *not* cool! And my mother has no right to trash her marriage because of the move to Toronto, or the FLQ, or whatever other excuse she has. They've been married for eighteen years. Marriage is supposed to be forever. Is she thinking about Bobby and me when she sips wine with Dr. Katzenberg?

All week, I don't speak to her. Friday evening, Dad calls. Mom is out with Dr. Katzenberg again. When Dad asks to talk to her, I think, *Why should I cover for her?* So I tell him, "Mom's having dinner with Dr. Katzenberg, that doctor she works for. I don't know what time she'll be back."

Talk about a big hint! I expect him to quiz me, but he doesn't. He says, "Okay, poopsie, tell her I called."

"But, Dad—" I hesitate. What should I say? "Did you know Dr. Katzenberg is a widower?"

"Yeah," he says. "That's a real shame. He sounds like a nice guy." He sends me a kiss across the telephone wires. I hang up. Poor Dad. He doesn't have a clue. I guess it's just beyond his imagination to even suspect that the woman he loves could cheat on him.

CARLA

"I'm Losing You"

On Monday, I catch up with Ian in the lunchroom. I sit down opposite him and fold my arms across my chest. "Did you get my message?" I ask coolly.

"Yeah, I told you, I don't like it when you call me at home," he says.

"Well, maybe if you had bothered to call *me*, I wouldn't have to call *you*," I say.

Ian looks at me like I'm getting on his nerves, but I'm the one who's mad here. I'm the one who was grounded all weekend, while he was out partying with *my* friends. I unwrap my sandwich. "My dad's the world's biggest jerk," I mutter.

"Your dad doesn't even come close to winning that prize."

"I bet your dad doesn't ground you," I say.

"No," Ian says quietly. "He doesn't do that."

I look up, waiting for Ian to explain, but when it comes to his family, he makes like a clam. "So what are we going to do?" I ask.

"About what?"

"About us." Ian shrugs. "Look, Papa and I are barely

speaking. And he's not exactly your biggest fan. So, maybe we can hang out at your place for a while."

"No," Ian says.

"Why not? Come on. I know you have family issues, but—"

"You don't know anything," Ian says, cutting me off.

"Then explain it to me," I say, annoyed. "Because this whole off-limits thing is really bugging me."

Ian shifts uncomfortably in his seat. "I don't get along with my parents, okay?"

I roll my eyes. "So, everybody hates their parents."

"No, Carla, not like that. I don't have anything to do with them. It's like we're guests at the same hotel. I don't talk to them. I don't take anything from them."

"Yeah, right," I scoff. "What about your motorcycle?"

"A gift from my grandfather."

"He must be loaded."

"No, my father's loaded," Ian says sharply. "My grandfather gave me the bike 'cause he knew I'd like it. My father doesn't do that. He gives people things *he* likes."

"Like what?" I ask. Ian turns away. He's getting steamed, but he can't always shut me out like this. "Ian!" I say.

He jerks his head back. "What? You want to know what he's like? Is that really so important to you?"

"Yeah, as a matter of fact, it is."

Ian frowns. "Fine," he says. "I'll tell you what kind of asshole he is." And suddenly words are flying out of his mouth like gravel spitting out from under the tires of a truck. "He's the kind of guy who buys his wife a pearl necklace so she'll wear it to the company party, 'cause he likes to show her off. Or he'll give her a Picasso print for her birthday, not 'cause she likes modern art—'cause neither of them knows fuck-all about art—but because it's a good investment. With him, it's all about owning things or owning people." He glowers at me. "You know what he gave me for my eighteenth birthday? A suit. A black suit. An expensive, tailor-made black suit. Like I'm ever going to wear a fucking black suit."

"Well, maybe you'll wear it to a family wedding," I say, trying to lighten things up.

"Or maybe I'll wear it to his funeral," Ian says.

I don't reply. I let it drop. Because now I feel like I'm walking through a minefield, and if I say even one wrong word, this whole place is going to explode.

Ian pushes his half-eaten sandwich away. "I'm going for a smoke."

"I'll come with you."

"Forget it," he says, getting to his feet. "Let's just chill."

Chill? "Wait," I say, "we're not finished yet."

"Yeah, we are," he says, and he walks away. I ditch my lunch and chase him into the hall. People stare. I feel a lump in my throat. I don't get it. Is he breaking up with me? I catch up to him at the doors of the smoking area. I grab his arm.

"Will you back off?" he says. He flings open the door and I follow him out.

"Why do you always do this?" I yell.

"What?"

"Act like you get to make all the rules. We're two people. We're going out. This isn't always just about you."

But Ian isn't listening anymore. He's sprinting to the parking lot. And I'm left standing outside in the cold as his bike blasts off down the road.

JULES

"A Hard Rain's A-Gonna Fall"

Most people lead quiet private lives, but Carla and Ian are larger than life. They play out their scenes on center stage, in public, like a Greek tragedy. As soon as Geoff and I walk into the drama studio, I can tell that today is going to be one of those days. The air crackles. Carla and Ian are sitting in their usual seats, but they're both twisted away from each other, and anger rolls off their bodies in waves.

Geoff raises an eyebrow and whispers, "A stormy day in paradise?"

"Duck and cover," I say, sinking into my seat.

Geoff and I take out our copies of *Hamlet*. Mr. Gabor has been assigning debate topics about *Hamlet* for class discussion, like *Is the ghost real? Does Hamlet believe in free will?* We're supposed to find quotes from the text to back up our opinions. Today, the topic is *Is Hamlet crazy?* Mr. Gabor asks for someone to lead off the discussion. Carla's hand shoots up. She likes debates. If there's one thing she's good at, it's arguing. Mr. Gabor nods at her. "Yes, Ms. Cabrielli. Do you think Hamlet is crazy?"

Carla says, "Well, for starters, anyone who decides to kill a person based on the advice of a ghost is obviously *not* in his right mind."

Geoff says, "Hamlet's friends saw the ghost too, which means that the ghost is real. And if the ghost is real, Hamlet isn't crazy."

"Maybe they're all hallucinating," Jason says. "Maybe the royal chef dropped some acid into the royal soup and they're tripping out, like . . . whoa, man, I think I see a ghost. And wow, he looks just like the king. Far out!"

The class laughs.

"I still think the ghost is real," Geoff says.

"Do you believe in ghosts, Geoffy?" Carla jeers.

Suddenly everyone is arguing about whether or not they believe in ghosts. Sherrie Cumberland says that her aunt stayed in a hotel in Manchester where doors slammed and furniture shifted, and her aunt saw a strange greenish light.

Benjamin, our class nerd, says, "There is a scientific explanation for every paranormal phenomenon, and only fools believe in the occult."

Mr. Gabor waves his hands in the air and says, "People, please, the topic is sanity. Is Hamlet insane or not?"

"He's *pretending* to be crazy," Geoff says, flipping through the play for a quote. "Hamlet tells his friends that he's going '*to put an antic disposition on*,' which means he's playacting. It's part of his scheme to find out if Claudius murdered his father."

"Yeah, well, he may *say* it's an act, but the truth is, he's clinically depressed and suicidal," Carla argues.

"Quote, please," Mr. Gabor says.

Carla scrambles through her text and reads from one of Hamlet's soliloquies: "'*O, that this too, too sullied flesh would melt, / Thaw, and resolve itself into a dew,*' which is another way of saying *I wish I were dead*," Carla says.

"That sounds pretty depressed to me," Sherrie says.

"He's strung out," Jason says.

"The prince needs a Valium," Jeremy says.

"He has a good reason to be strung out," I say, coming to Hamlet's defense. "Hamlet is having a normal reaction for someone whose father was murdered and whose mother married his evil uncle less than two months after the funeral. Wouldn't you be depressed?"

"I'd be pissed off, but I wouldn't want to kill myself," Carla sneers.

"He's not planning to kill himself," I say.

"He is so! He says it right here in the '*To be or not to be*' speech." She opens her book and reads

To die, to sleep —
No more — and by a sleep to say we end
The heartache and the thousand natural shocks
That flesh is heir to — 'tis a consummation
Devoutly to be wished.

Carla smirks. "He is definitely talking about offing himself."

Benjamin raises a finger in the air. "Isn't it true that according to Canadian law, if you seriously contemplate suicide, you are considered a danger to yourself and are therefore certifiably insane?"

"Thinking about suicide isn't the same as doing it," I insist. "Lots of people think about it."

"No, they don't!" Carla scoffs.

"Excuse me, but how would you know?" I say hotly. Carla's eyes flash open. I can tell she's shocked that I'm taking her on, but what does she know about suffering anyway? What horrible thing ever happened to her? "Hamlet is going through a crisis," I say, "so why wouldn't he have desperate thoughts. But it doesn't mean he's going to kill himself. He's just thinking about death, and war, and the way people are so cruel to each other, and the total lack of morality in the world. He's wondering if there's any point to it all."

Everyone stares at me. Mr. Gabor leans forward in his chair and says, "Yes, Epstein, there *is* a difference between thought and action, as Hamlet well knows. And I believe you're coming to the crux of the issue: We all grieve and suffer in this world, but has Hamlet driven himself crazy with grief?"

The class looks from Mr. Gabor back to me. "Hamlet isn't crazy," I say. "He's a sane man living in an insane world. That's the irony of the play, I think. Craziness is just his cover, but he's the only one who sees everything clearly. All the corruption, the greed, the betrayal. That's why he's so torn up inside."

"Well, it's partly his own damn fault," Carla snaps. "He could have chosen to marry Ophelia. He could've had a happy life with her. She loved him, and look how he treated her. Which is just more proof that he's insane."

Sherrie nods. "Yeah. First he's sending her love letters, and the next minute he's insulting her and shrieking, *Get thee to a nunnery*."

"Because he doesn't want her to turn out like his mother," I say.

"So he ditches her?" Carla exclaims. "That's his idea of loyalty?"

"She was the one who returned his love letters," Geoff points out.

"Only because her father made her do it," Carla says. "If Hamlet loved her so much, he should've stuck by her instead of ditching her. It's his fault she drowned herself."

"Yeah," Sherrie says. "He broke her heart."

I have to admit, I don't like the way Hamlet treats Ophelia either, so I'm not about to argue the point, but suddenly Ian speaks up. He says, "You can't blame Hamlet for Ophelia's death."

Carla swivels around in her chair. "What?" she says.

Ian shrugs. "It's not his fault. He made choices; she made choices."

"Are you kidding?" Carla gawks. "That jerk treated her like dirt. He was rude and mean. He humiliated her in public. I can't believe you're defending him!"

At this point, any other guy would've been backpedaling like mad, but not Ian. He laughs. It's the wrong thing to do. Carla's body goes rigid. Ian and Carla stare at each other like two cowboys facing off at high noon, and everyone knows that this is *not* about *Hamlet* anymore.

Ian says, "Look, Carla, you can't be responsible for what another person does. Yeah, Hamlet dumped her. But if she comes unglued because her boyfriend moves on, it's not his problem. Shit happens." At which point, Carla slugs Ian in the face, full force, right hook. Her fist smashes into the side of his nose. His head snaps sideways, and he howls in pain. Blood spurts out everywhere.

Mr. Gabor leaps across the room. He helps Ian to his feet and grabs Carla by the arm. He herds them both out the door. The rest of us sit there stunned.

"I believe we just witnessed the termination of that relationship," Benjamin says.

"That was better than the soaps," Geoff says.

"I'm surprised it lasted this long," Jeremy says.

"Aw, those two love fighting," Jason says. "That's what they do for fun."

"That wasn't fun," Sherrie says.

"It was fun to watch," Jeremy says.

"She has a good arm," Jason says.

"Do you think she broke his nose?" Geoff asks.

Jason shrugs. "I don't know. Either way, Carla's in deep shit."

CARLA

"Let It Bleed"

Mr. Gabor takes Ian to the school nurse, and I'm sent to the principal's office. When Principal McMillan asks me "what transpired," I tell him that Ian got exactly what he deserved. I explain that Ian insulted all women, and that as a feminist, I wasn't going to put up with any lip from some filthy, male chauvinist pig. Mr. McMillan stares at me like he can't believe I'm spouting this ridiculous feminist rhetoric in his office. I can't believe it either. I don't know where this stuff is coming from (TV?), but Papa always taught me that the best defense is a good offense, so I'm going with the feminist angle.

The secretary delivers two files to Mr. McMillan: mine and Ian's. Mr. McMillan looks them over. Mine is thin, but Ian's is thick with papers—probably from all those suspensions and expulsions he got in North Bay. I try to use this to my advantage. I tell Mr. McMillan that Ian is a bully and he shouldn't pick fights with girls. Unfortunately, Mr. Gabor storms in and tells Mr. McMillan that he has never, in his entire teaching career, seen such appalling behavior from a young woman, and that if I think the classroom is a public forum for working out private relationships, then I have another think coming!

Shit. I am in serious trouble.

Phone calls go out to the parents. Mrs. Slater arrives and whisks Ian off to Emergency. Ma flies into the office, all distraught, thinking that I'm the one who's been punched in the nose. When she realizes her mistake, she practically lunges for my throat. She apologizes for my inexcusable behavior and begs Mr. McMillan to throw the book at me and "teach that rotten child a lesson." I get suspended for a week. Ma hauls me out of my chair. As we leave the school, Jason and Jeremy call me Slugger and Ali. They fake-cringe when I walk past. Jason whimpers, "Don't hit me. Please, don't hit me!"

In the car, Ma won't even listen to my side of the story. She yells so loudly, she practically has a coronary. "What kind of girl goes and beats up boys!" she screams. "Wait till your father gets ahold of you."

Thinking about Pa makes me feel faint. On the phone, when I talk to Deb and Mar, they advise me to cry a lot and beg for mercy. Buzz stares at me like I've gone off the deep end. Ma walks around the kitchen slamming pots and pans. Finally, Pa's car pulls into the driveway. I hide in my room, chewing my nails.

After twenty minutes of talking with Ma in the kitchen, Papa calls me downstairs. "Get into the car," he says quietly.

I look at Ma, terrified. She looks at Papa, confused. She says, "Tony, where are you taking her?"

"We're going for a little drive," he says sternly. He buttons his coat, puts on his hat and gestures with his chin to the front door. Ma twists her hands nervously.

"Can't we talk here?" I ask.

"In the car," Pa growls. I'm not about to argue with him.

Buzz and Ma watch from the window as Pa and I drive off. I start to explain, but Pa silences me. We head south, across town. I think about all the Italian movies I've seen, the mob movies where someone gets driven out to a field and shot in the head, or tossed into the river with cement shoes. My cousin Frank told me that his dad and my dad were tough guys when they were younger. But isn't the mob supposed to look after their own? And anyway, Papa isn't a mobster. So what's the point of terrorizing me like this?

Pa parks on St. Clair just past Dufferin and leads me into a small Italian restaurant with steamed-up windows and rickety wooden tables. A mob hangout, for sure. The place smells like Nonna Cabrielli's kitchen when she has the entire family over for dinner. The waiters greet Pa with hugs and slaps on the back. Pa and I sit at a table in the corner. He looks at me with his dark, beady eyes and says, "Answer me honestly, Carla, and no bullshit. Did you really slug that boyfriend of yours in the nose?"

"Yes, Pa."

"On purpose?"

"Yes."

"Did you break it?"

I swallow. "I'm not sure. Maybe. There was a lot of blood."

Pa nods. He bites his lip. His shoulders start to shake. And then he laughs so hard that tears spill down his face and he can hardly breathe. Every time he tries to talk, he sputters, and wheezes, and starts laughing again. He slaps his thigh and shakes his head back and forth. Finally, he waves over the waiter and asks for a bottle of Chianti and plates of gnocchi and veal. "My daughter and I are very hungry," he says, tearing into a roll, "and if she doesn't like her food, I don't know what will happen." Pa laughs at his own bad joke. Then he makes me tell him, over and over, how I punched Ian in the nose.

He says, "You know, Carla, it isn't right, what you did." He pours us both glasses of wine. "Fists don't solve problems. On the other hand, when it comes to men, I'm glad to see you can take care of yourself." He raises his glass to me and smiles proudly. "Here's to my beautiful daughter, who doesn't take shit from anybody. *Cin-cin.*" He chuckles, and we clink glasses. The food arrives and it's fantastic. All through dinner, we talk and laugh and Papa tells stories about the trouble he got into when he was a young immigrant. The people around us smile and nod. I know I should be feeling shitty about Ian and my suspension, but Papa feels like celebrating, and in a way, I do too.

After dinner, in the car, Papa passes me a mint to disguise the smell of food on my breath. He says, "Not a word about this when we get home. I'm sending you straight upstairs to your room. *Capisci?*"

I nod my head. "What about Ma?"

"*Cane che abbaia non morde*," he says. The dog that barks doesn't bite. "Don't worry about it. Just be a good girl." Papa reaches over and squeezes my hand. "And about that boy, you forget about him. Remember, *tesorina*, you're the prize."

I tell myself that Papa's right. We smile at each other in the dark.

JULES

"See Me, Feel Me"

Geoff is in my kitchen holding a bottle of green and red sugar sprinkles in one hand and a cookie cutter shaped liked a Christmas tree in the other. "Today, we are making Christmas cookies," he announces to Buzz and Bobby.

"Cool," Bobby says.

"Can we eat the dough?" Buzz asks.

"Of course. Why else would we make cookies?" Geoff replies.

"Aren't you jumping the season?" I ask.

"It's December 1st," Geoff says. "In my calendar, Christmas lasts for an entire month. Lights, presents, fa-la-la-la-la . . . You should sign up to sell Christmas trees at the school. It's a fundraiser. I do it every year."

"No, thanks. I have a serious objection to killing trees for two weeks of decorative pleasure," I say.

"But it's tradition," Geoff says.

"Not my tradition," I reply.

"You have Hanukkah," Geoff says.

"Yes," I say, "but Hanukkah has nothing to do with

Christmas. Christmas is about the birth of Jesus. Hanukkah is a holiday about guerilla warfare, political oppression and the right to freedom of religion."

"That's not how I heard it," Geoff says.

I sigh. "The point is, Hanukkah and Christmas have nothing in common."

"But you light candles and we light Christmas lights."

"So?"

"So, we both light up the darkness."

I smile at Geoff. "If being an actor doesn't work out for you," I say, "you can always get a job as peace ambassador in the Middle East."

When Geoff hears that I've never decorated a Christmas tree, he insists that I come over and help him and Clarissa do theirs. So, on a cold Saturday afternoon, I arrive at the apartment expecting to find Geoff gushing nostalgically over tree ornaments and popping minced tarts into his mouth, but that's not how it plays out. Geoff opens the door wearing his red Christmas hat, but he looks like an elf who's had a bad day at the workbench. "What's up?" I ask.

Geoff grimaces and leads me into the living room. There, standing next to Clarissa, is a short man with John Lennon glasses, blue eyes and a ponytail. Clarissa says, "Jules, I'd like you to meet Michael van Meers."

"A pleasure," Michael says, shaking my hand. He gives me a toothy alligator grin. He's plump and rumpled in his old woolen sweater—not the type of guy I'd expect Clarissa to go for, but I can tell by the way they look at each other that they're hopelessly in love.

I smile at Geoff. He looks away. Clarissa passes me a glass of eggnog. I've never tried eggnog before. It's thick and frothy and tastes slightly medicinal, like something you'd take for an upset stomach.

"Shall we start on the tree?" Clarissa asks brightly.

We stare at the fir tree squished in beside the divan. Somehow, four people decorating this tiny tree feels like overkill, but Michael grins and says, "Put me to work." He unwinds a string of lights, and I open a bag of tinsel. Geoff plucks ornaments from a box and hooks them onto the tree, like someone clipping laundry to a line. He's behaving like a sullen child. Clarissa flashes me a desperate look.

I turn to Michael and try to make conversation, anything to ease the tension. "So, what's the best Christmas you've ever had?" I ask.

It's a dumb question, but Michael smiles gratefully. He recounts an amusing tale about being snowed in at Chicago's O'Hare airport on Christmas Eve with six drunken Italian opera singers performing impromptu arias in the airport lounge. He's a very funny storyteller, but Geoff doesn't even crack a smile.

By the time Geoff places the angel on top of the tree and Clarissa plugs in the lights, it's dark outside. The little, overloaded tree glows bravely. Clarissa sings "Silent night, Holy night." She slides her arm around Geoff's waist, and Geoff begrudgingly sings along. Michael and I join in, but the whole thing is awkward. Michael looks uncomfortable, and I, being Jewish, feel like an imposter on a Pat Boone TV Christmas special. Suddenly I wish I were back in Montreal, walking with Mollie along the slushy sidewalks of Saint Catherine Street, or skating outside on Beaver Lake, cutting my blades into the dark ice.

Finally, Michael looks at his watch and says they should go. He and Clarissa have a dinner date with some friends. It's a relief when they walk out the door. I flop down onto the couch and turn to Geoff. "Michael van Meers is a perfectly lovely man, and you were rude. You didn't even say a word to him!" I scold.

"She didn't tell me he was coming till the last minute," Geoff says. "It's *our* Christmas. He doesn't belong."

"You invited me," I say.

"Clarissa and I agreed on that. We didn't agree on Michael van Meers." Geoff scowls. I shake my head. "He always wears those lumpy sweaters," he mutters.

"A fashion indiscretion?" I ask. "Is that the worst you can come up with?"

"Yeah." Geoff sinks onto the floor and hugs his knees.

"They like each other," I say.

"I know," Geoff sighs. "She glows when he's in the room. He's funny and well-read. He shows up on time, and he always picks up the bill when they go out. But it doesn't mean he's going to stick around. Clarissa's done this before. She gets involved, and then something always goes wrong. So, why should Michael be any different?"

"I thought you were an optimist," I say.

Geoff shrugs and toys with the ornaments on the tree: a camel, a trumpet, origami cranes made from pretty Japanese papers. They bob and sparkle in the silken light, a colorful, dancing menagerie. "You know, she still keeps pictures of my father in her drawer, under her scarves, where she thinks I don't look," he says. "He was so handsome. Like a matinee idol. They met skating in Rockefeller Center."

"Sounds just like a movie," I say. Geoff throws me a sardonic smile. "But does she still love him, after all these years?" I ask. "Even though he walked out on her?"

"I don't know," Geoff says. "Maybe love is like a bad habit you can't break."

I think about that. I wonder if my mom still loves my dad. I wonder how many times a person can fall in love, and if it's ever as good as the first time. "Do you think love can last forever?" I ask Geoff.

"I hope so," Geoff says. "That's why I like the old movies. Either they're fearlessly romantic, or they make the sad things in life seem so beautiful, when really they're not." He spins a crystal icicle on the tree, and it sends arcs of rainbow light skittering around the room like lost wishes.

Geoff offers to drive me home, but I decide I need some fresh air. As soon as I step outside, the cold slams into my chest like a brick and the wind funnels down the street, rattling Christmas lights and shooting needles of ice into my face. There's no snow on the ground, just a stubbly crust of frost cemented to the grass like frozen dandruff. I pull up my hood and breathe through my scarf as I hurry down Cummer hill.

Halfway home, I stop at the plaza drugstore to warm up. A sappy Muzak version of "Rudolph the Red-Nosed Reindeer" plays too loudly, and I shuffle along the aisles, rubbing my frozen hands together, pretending to be interested in little pots of eye shadow by Mary Quant. A saleslady with penciled-on eyebrows and a beehive hairdo gives me the evil eye. The way she looks at me makes me want to pocket a lipstick or knock over a display of candy canes on the way out, but I don't.

I leave the drugstore, and I'm about halfway down the plaza, when a silver Mercedes pulls up beside me. I cut across the parking lot and the car follows. No one's around, and I'm starting to feel panicky, when the passenger window slides down and a male voice calls out, "Hey, Rapunzel, want a ride?" My heart *ca-lunks* in my chest. Ian is behind the wheel in the cavelike darkness of the car.

"What are you doing here?" I ask.

"Getting some smokes."

"Oh."

"Come on, get in. It's freezing." The automatic locks click open.

I slip inside and sink into the black leather bucket seat. "Thanks," I say, trying for a confident smile.

Ian puts the car into gear. "Where're you off to?"

"Home," I say, feeling like a loser. It's seven o'clock on a Saturday night. "What about you?" I ask.

Ian doesn't answer. He steers the Mercedes out of the plaza.

"I guess you know where I live," I say.

Ian nods. "I know where you live." His eyes are like slices of pale moonlight. He drives too fast, with one hand on the wheel, and it makes me nervous, but I try to look relaxed. The streetlamps sweep bands of light across his face, accenting the hollows of his cheeks and the curve of his mouth, making him look like a comic book superhero, or villain.

Ian takes a left turn where he should be going right. "Oops, you went the wrong way," I say.

"I know," he says. "There's something I want to show you." He stares straight ahead, and I, the nervous hostage, don't ask questions. A few minutes later, he turns onto Hawthorne Crescent and pulls into the driveway of an enormous dark house, his house. My stomach flip-flops. He gets out of the car, and I follow him along the side of the house, past a cedar hedge wrapped in burlap. The path slopes downward, so that in the back, the basement is at ground level. We cross a flagstone patio and pass the gaping turquoise shell of a pool. Ian tips up a stone urn, reaches underneath it to get his key and unlocks the French doors.

The basement den is done in blue and white, and everything matches. There's a blue leather sectional couch shaped like a giant *L* and a blue leather bar with three chrome swivel stools. The carpet is white, and you can see the neat, straight tracks of a vacuum cleaner on its thick pile. A painting of a sailboat hangs on the wall. Everything is new and expensive, like it was lifted straight out of *Architectural Digest* and plunked down in suburban Toronto, a showpiece of contemporary design. I can't imagine Ian living here. There's nothing of him in it.

Ian doesn't look at me. We take off our boots and toss our coats onto the couch. And then things get weird. I mean, he's the one who invited me over, but instead of showing me around, he just stands there in the middle of the room in his black Jimi Hendrix T-shirt and jeans. I don't know whether to sit or stand, so I make polite conversation, saying stupid things like "Well, this is a nice place," and "It's sort of a nautical theme, isn't it?" My words get sucked up into the dead air. Ian frowns.

"So, is anyone home?" I ask.

"No."

"Do you have any brothers or sisters?"

"No."

"Did your mother design this place?"

"My mother smokes, shops and gets her hair done," Ian says sarcastically. He shifts from foot to foot, looking like he already regrets asking me over.

Finally, I say, "So, what did you want to show me?"

Ian licks his lips and says, "You can't tell anybody." And suddenly I realize that he's nervous, and that whatever it is he wants to show me is important and personal, and Carla has never seen it. For some reason, he's chosen me.

"Okay," I say.

He nods. "Okay." It's a pact.

Ian leads me out of the den and down a hallway. At the end of the hall, he pushes open a set of double doors, and we walk into the strangest room I've ever seen. Mounted on the wall opposite the door is a massive, striped tiger skin, complete with head, teeth, claws, thick pink tongue and golden marble eyes. On either side of the tiger are antique rifles, hunting knives and scimitars.

The doors behind me click shut. I turn, and there, beside the entrance, is a towering bronze statue of a cross-legged Buddha sitting on a lotus flower. Smaller statues of Hindu gods and goddesses in stone, clay and bronze line the wall. The two walls are like yin and yang, darkness and light, violence and meditation. The air smells of decay and incense.

Even with the lamps lit, the space feels musty, like the cavernous inner sanctuary of an underground tomb.

"Wow," I say, gazing at the collection of exotic treasures.

"My grandfather's," Ian says. He walks to the corner and opens a battered trunk that looks like a pirate's chest. Inside are soft cloth bundles. Ian peels back the crimson fabric on the top bundle to reveal two long swords. Rapiers. Their polished steel blades are engraved with a snake design, and their hilts have been carved to look like coiled serpents. I don't know anything about swords, but these look ancient and dangerous, like relics from a raided treasure trove.

Ian picks up one of the rapiers and wraps his fingers around the grip. He extends the sword in front of him, and my eyes travel along the sinewy muscles of his arm to the gleaming tip of the blade. Nothing moves. Not him, not me, not the air in the room. His body is like a tensile wire. I can hear the rhythmic sound of his breath, in and out, like the wash of tides.

He lowers the sword, and his eyes meet mine. "Try it," he says. He offers me the sword, ceremoniously laying it across the palms of his hands. I slide my fingers around the grip and feel the weight of it. It's nothing like our tinny school swords. It has heft, power and history. What bloody battles have been fought with this weapon? I swish the blade through the air, moving it in arcs until it whispers back to me. It feels good in my hand. I walk around the room, admiring the balance of the weapon, swiping and stabbing at motes of dust that float in the yellow lamplight, while the tiger and the Buddha watch on.

When I turn around, Ian is waiting for me, holding the matching rapier in his hand. He salutes me with his sword. "En garde," he says, lifting it into the air.

I stare at him, thinking *He can't be serious. Surely he doesn't expect us to fight with real weapons and no protective gear.*

"Come," he commands, waving the tip of his rapier. "Don't you want to see how it feels?" He flicks his long black hair off his face.

I shake my head. "I'm not good enough."

"Don't worry, Rapunzel, we'll just practice," he says. His steely eyes pin me to the spot. And what can I say, here in this room, caught in this ghostly underworld? Ian has chosen me as his sparring partner—and really, haven't I been training for just this moment?

His rapier catches a glint of light. I bring my sword into the ready position. "En garde," I say. I swallow my fear and execute a simple cut, which Ian counters with a swift, sharp clang. The force of contact shoots through my arm. Ian grins. We beat our blades, testing the feel of them, listening to the metallic notes of their song. Then we run through the basic attack and parry exercises. Ian is fast, light on his feet but not aggressive, allowing me to get the feel of the weapon, to understand its strengths and demands.

Gradually, he begins to move me around the room, circling

me in a fluid dance. He forces my direction, pushing my pace. He challenges me to look for openings, to turn a defensive move into an offensive one. We hardly speak. He coaches by example. When I play well, he nods. When I don't, he guides me through the sequence again. When he lunges at me, I leap away, scared.

"Focus," he says calmly. We repeat. This time I parry, enveloping his sword and thrusting at his shoulder. "Harder," he commands. Our swords smash together. I throw the weight of my body against his. We lean into each other, holding hard. "Good balance," he says, smiling, then pushing me off. "Now, show me what you can do."

His eyes glitter, and he moves toward me like an animal stalking its prey. My head buzzes. Sweat trickles down my back. The gods and goddesses watch with impassive eyes as we face off.

"Defend," he shouts, attacking, and our swords arc through the air, flashing in a vortex of spinning steel. It takes everything I have to keep him away, but the harder I fight to protect myself, the harder Ian comes at me. We pant and grunt. Adrenaline rips through my body. I move on instinct, at the edge of panic.

"Stop," I say. But Ian won't stop. Terror wells up in my throat. "No more," I shout.

Ian laughs. Then he drives his sword straight at my chest. The steel tip quivers an inch from my heart. I yelp. My sword clatters to the floor.

"Touché," Ian gasps, lowering his weapon.

"You almost hit me!" I cry.

"I didn't."

"But you could have."

"I know what I'm doing," Ian says.

"Do you?" I ask. I'm shaking uncontrollably. My heart is crashing around in my chest.

Ian walks over to me, his eyes fixed intently on mine. His finger glides across my sweaty cheek and downward along the curve of my jaw. I see black splinters in his gray wolf eyes, and that tiny white scar at the corner of his lips. "You did well," he says. "I was right about you." Then he closes in and kisses me.

It happens slowly, as if in a dream. His long fingers slide into my hair. Our lips part, and I'm enfolded into the heat of his breath. I close my eyes. His tongue slips into my mouth. Our sweaty bodies press against each other. Soft and hot. Salty and damp. I'm dizzy with the taste of his mouth. I'm lost. Adrift. Floating. Gone. When he pulls away, I'm still in a daze.

"Again?" he whispers.

I blink at him. Is he asking if I want to kiss him again? I do. But then a smile flits across his lips, and he nods toward the rapier still in his hand. Oh. He wants another bout. But I have nothing left to give. Nothing. I shake my head.

Ian picks up my fallen sword and wraps the two rapiers in their crimson cloth. Silence folds over us like darkness engulfing an evening sky. My eyes travel around the room.

My head seems to be moving in slow motion, the way it does when you have a fever. I try not to think about kissing Ian, but it's all I can think about. I gaze up at the golden Buddha, whose plump petal-like fingers point upward and whose generous lips curve in bliss. The Buddha's eyes are half closed, looking inward, and his head almost touches the ceiling. I wonder what it would feel like to be so completely at peace.

Behind me, the heavy trunk clanks shut. The spell is broken. We leave the room. In the den, Ian pulls two Cokes out of the bar's mini-fridge. His hair is plastered to his forehead. My mouth feels swollen and gritty. We sit on the bar stools, not looking at each other, taking long cold gulps of Coke. Slowly, I surface through a sticky fog, back into the present moment. The swords, the tiger, the Buddha and the kiss seem like implausible figments of my imagination.

When I finally force myself to speak, it feels like I'm chewing my words. "Where did your grandfather get all that stuff?" I ask.

"India. He was with the British Army," Ian says.

"Doing what?"

"Intelligence, I think. He wouldn't say." Ian pushes his hair away from his face. "He spoke different dialects. My mother said he was away from home a lot. She was born in Kashmir, but my grandmother hated it there, so she took my mom and moved back to North Bay." Ian chugs his Coke.

"Did you ever visit him?"

"Sure," he says. "He's the one who taught me to fence."

"You learned to fence in India? That's so exotic."

Ian nods. "At his home in the countryside. Every morning we got up early, before the heat settled in, and practiced on the veranda. He worked me hard. It was great. Just us and the sounds of birds all around." Ian pauses and looks at me. "He shot that tiger, the one in the room. It was hiding in the fields for weeks. It killed a girl from the village, so he tracked it up a tree and shot it."

"Wow," I say. "Were you there?"

"No. But he showed me how to shoot the gun. And we took motorcycles everywhere. To villages, markets, temples, the jungle . . ."

"Are you going back?"

Ian looks away. "No. He died last year."

"Oh," I say. I feel so dumb. Of course he's dead. That's why his things are stored in that room. That's why Ian has his grandfather's rapiers. "I'm sorry," I say, but *sorry* doesn't cut it.

Ian's knees jiggle furiously. "I wanted to see him at the end," he says, "but they wouldn't let me go back. He said he wasn't afraid of dying. He wasn't afraid of anything." Ian's voice goes so quiet that the words almost disappear. I place my hand on his leg. For a few minutes we just sit there, and for once it isn't awkward or embarrassing.

Then, upstairs, a door opens and shuts. Instantly, Ian leaps off his stool. Footsteps cross the floor above us. Ian waves me urgently toward a room off the den. I don't get it, but I grab my Coke and duck inside just as the door at the top of the basement stairs opens and a man's deep voice calls down, "Ian?"

"Yeah," Ian says.

I peek out of the room. A long shadow glides down the stairwell. I edge back into the darkness. A bar of light streaks in from the den and I see a bed, a desk and a chair. I'm in Ian's bedroom.

"What are you doing?" the man asks.

"Nothing," Ian says.

"Your mother wants you to come up and say good-night."

"Okay."

"Are you alone?"

"Yeah."

"Why are you sweaty?"

"I was exercising."

I crouch low beside the bed.

"I trust you're keeping out of trouble, son."

"Yes, sir."

"Because your mother can't have that again."

"No, sir."

"All right then."

I hear the creak of footsteps going up the stairs. A minute later, Ian opens the door. I don't have to be told that my visit is over. I quickly put on my coat and boots. At the back door,

Ian whispers, "We should do this again. I need someone to spar with."

"I'm not in your league," I whisper back.

"But I like playing you," Ian says. "You're an interesting opponent. Most people wouldn't guess that about you. But I know you, Rapunzel." His lips slant into a wolfish grin. "I see you watching from your tower, plotting and waiting for an opening."

I step outside and a harsh wind hits my face. I look back at Ian. "You have me all wrong. I'm not plotting anything. I don't like danger, and I don't like taking risks."

"That's your weakness," Ian says. "Which is why I'll always win."

"And what's your weakness? Arrogance?" I ask, only half joking.

Ian smirks and slides the door shut. I hurry back along the side of the house where the cedars, in their burlap wrappings, look like a band of ragged soldiers returning from war.

I walk down the dark streets. The wind howls and the cold bites, but I have done battle and had its reward. Nothing can touch me tonight.

CARLA

"Ain't No Sunshine"

Deb and Mar do not say the words *I told you so* about Ian, but the thought hangs in the air like a bad smell, even a month after our breakup. Whenever they see Ian in the hall, Debbie and Marlene glare at him. When it comes to glaring, Deb and Mar are like professional snipers who can snuff out a target from a mile away with a single glance. Unfortunately, in Ian's case, it doesn't work because a glare is useless if the target doesn't give a shit, and Ian doesn't give a shit about anyone. He's bulletproof.

I tell Deb and Mar that breaking up with Ian was the best thing I could've done, but the truth is, I can't stop thinking about him. If he walks into a room, I know he's there. I can pick out his voice in a crowd. In drama, I can hardly concentrate. He's always on my radar, irritating me like a canker sore.

Marlene and Debbie think I need a distraction, so a week before the Christmas break, we decide to go see the new James Bond flick, *Diamonds Are Forever*, starring Sean Connery and Jill St. John. It's a busy night at the theater, and we're standing there with our popcorn and drinks, scanning the room for three good seats, when I spot Mrs. Epstein sitting beside a fat lady near the front. I point her out to Deb and Mar, and we end up sitting six rows behind her. She's wearing a royal blue silk scarf, and we all agree that it's a great color on her. Mrs. Epstein is an attractive woman.

Just before the movie starts, Debbie gives me a poke in the arm and I follow her gaze. A tall, distinguished man carrying a large popcorn and two drinks is moving into the empty seat beside Mrs. Epstein. She takes the drinks out of his hands while he settles down beside her.

"I thought she was with the fat lady," I say.

"Jules has good-looking parents," Marlene says.

The man turns to speak to Mrs. Epstein and—oh my God!— I clutch Deb's and Mar's arms. "That is *not* Mr. Epstein!" I hiss.

Mar and Deb gasp. "What?"

"Are you sure?" Marlene asks.

"Of course I'm sure. I've met Julia's dad. He has curly black hair, and this guy has straight brown hair. That guy is *not* Mr. Epstein."

"Then who is he?" Debbie asks.

We give each other a look.

"Do you think . . . ?" Mar asks.

"Oh my God," Debbie says.

Our heads swivel, and we eyeball Mrs. Epstein and Loverboy.

"Maybe they're just friends," Marlene says.

Debbie raises an eyebrow. "If he's her friend, I'm the queen of England."

The lights dim and the curtain opens, but all through the movie, I'm watching Mrs. Epstein and Loverboy. I'm dying to know if they're holding hands. When the show is over, Deb, Mar and I sink down in our seats and watch as Loverboy helps Mrs. Epstein with her coat. When he puts his hand on her back to guide her up the aisle, we grab onto each other and suck in our breath.

"Did you see that?" Debbie whispers.

"Yeah," Mar says. "He touched her."

"Guys don't touch you when you're 'just friends,'" Deb says.

"Wow," I say. "I can't believe it. She always seemed like such a lady."

"When the cat's away, the mice will play," Debbie says, like she's an expert on this stuff.

"Come on," I say. "Let's follow them."

"What if she sees us?" Marlene says.

"We're just walking out of a movie," I say. "There's no law against that, is there?"

We scurry out of our seats and trail them at a discreet distance. We follow them out of the theater and down the street. They're talking, but we're too far back to hear what they're saying.

"They're heading into the parking lot," Deb says.

"Quick, Batman, to the Batmobile!" I say, pointing to Deb's Buick. Marlene giggles. Loverboy holds open the passenger door of his blue Cadillac for Mrs. Epstein while Mar, Deb and I dash across the lot to Debbie's car and leap in. Debbie stabs her key into the ignition, and we track the Cadillac out of the lot and down the street, keeping two cars behind, just like James Bond.

"Don't lose them," I say.

"Don't worry, toots, I got that dame in my sights," Deb says in her mobster voice, and the three of us laugh so hard, we practically pee our pants. Debbie starts humming the *Mission: Impossible* theme music, and Mar and I join in. At Yonge and Eglinton, we almost get stuck when the light turns yellow, but Debbie guns it, and Mar and I cheer as we sail through the intersection with the Cadillac just ahead.

Loverboy continues east on Eglinton, makes a left at Leslie and then drives north until he comes to the medical/dental building where my dentist has his office. The Cadillac turns into the parking area. Debbie pulls over to the side of the street. "Should I follow them?" she asks.

"No. Too conspicuous," I say.

We sit tight in Deb's car, engine running, and a few minutes later, Mrs. Epstein's station wagon pulls out of the parking area and continues north on Leslie. The Cadillac turns south.

"I guess this is their little rendezvous spot," I say.

"'Cause she wouldn't want the neighbors to know," Deb snickers, looking at me.

Back at my house, we arrive just as Mrs. Epstein is getting out of her car. She sees us and waves a cheerful hello. We say hello back, and Mrs. Epstein walks into her house.

"I wonder if Julia knows," Mar says.

"I doubt it," Deb says. "Why do you think they're meeting in secret?"

"I'd like to see the look on her face when she finds out," I say.

Mar and Deb stare at me, intrigued. "Are you going to tell her?" Debbie asks.

"*Moi?*" I say, and we all laugh. "No, I'll just file this away." There's no need to bring it up now. Timing is everything.

JULES

"Winterlude"

I don't know what I was expecting. A conversation in the hall?
An invitation for a rematch? None of this happens. I don't
understand. Ian must like me if he kissed me the way he did,
but then again, he almost stabbed me in the heart. Was the kiss
just Ian's version of shaking hands after a fight? Ever since she
broke his nose, Carla and Ian don't talk, but he doesn't exactly
talk to me either. In drama, he sits with the two Js. Carla sits
with Sherrie Cumberland. We're a classroom of people who
don't look at each other, but we watch each other constantly.

I replay Ian's kiss in my mind a thousand times a day. I write
to Mollie about it. I tell her that kissing Ian was like dancing
with a dark angel, or like suddenly being able to see ultravio-
let light. I don't tell Geoff anything. He wouldn't approve,
and it might be hard for him to keep the secret.

On the last day of school before Christmas, I'm walking
out of math class when I see Ian loping down the hall. "Hey,
Rapunzel," he says with a smile.

"Hi," I say. I've been rehearsing a million things to say to
him, but suddenly nothing seems appropriate. "So, what are

you doing for the holidays?" I ask. Ian shrugs. "I'm going home, to Montreal," I say. "But I'll be back for New Year's." If that isn't a big hint, I don't know what is!

The buzzer goes. Ian says, "Have a nice trip."

That's it. He walks off. If I were Carla, I'd run after him and get his phone number, or arrange to see him when I'm back. But I'm not Carla. So, I go to my next class, where everyone shifts and squirms in their seats, itching to be gone.

School gets out early, and I meet Geoff in the parking lot. It's a raw, bleak day, but Geoff wants to go for a drive. I want to go home and pack, but Geoff says, "Come on, one more spin for 1971. After all, I'm not going to see you for almost two weeks."

I relent. I'm hoping to go somewhere close by, but Geoff insists that we drive to The Beaches. It takes forever. Baby Blue keeps stalling in the cold. The roads are a mess, and Geoff makes detours along side streets trying to avoid the knots of traffic.

By the time we park in front of the stone house, the temperature has dropped and a thin, pellet-like snow is falling. We trudge through the "inclement weather," as Geoff calls it. Today, Lake Ontario is the color of gunboat metal. The grass is crunchy with frost, and a sideways wind blows into our faces. Geoff marches glumly down the path and I trot alongside. When we reach the big oak tree where we usually turn around, the light is already fading. There is no horizon. Lake and sky have merged into a soggy, gray haze. It feels like we're standing at the edge of the earth. Anything could be on the other side. Anything, or nothing.

Geoff tightens his scarf. "God, I hate Christmas," he says.

"You love Christmas," I remind him.

"I always start by loving it, but it never lives up to its hype."

I stare at Geoff. "What's up?" I ask.

"It's just the time of year. Dark days. Long nights. The whole happy family thing. You know, a lot of people commit suicide on Christmas."

"Geoff, I hope you're not going to stick your finger into an electric socket while I'm in Montreal, 'cause you're the only real friend I have here," I say.

Geoff gives me a spare smile, but I was hoping for better, so I cajole. "You know, if Christmas is too depressing, you could always convert," I tell him. "Hanukkah is pretty low-key. No stress, no commercialism. All we do is light the menorah and exchange a couple of token presents, so the Jewish kids don't get jealous of the Christian kids. And of course, we eat latkes. Potato latkes with sour cream. Mmm. What Jewish holiday would be complete without a fattening food component?"

Geoff stares across the leaden water and doesn't reply. I link my arm through his and tug. "Come on. My toes are frozen," I say. We tuck our chins into our coats and hurry back along the path of black slippery leaves. All around us, skeletal trees rattle their bony limbs. In the playground, swings creak and sway as if ghost children are riding them.

Baby Blue's doors squeak with cold as we climb in, and Geoff cranks the heater to full blast. As we wait for the motor to warm up, a black Oldsmobile pulls up in front of us and four people get out: a man, his wife and their two children. They carry large parcels wrapped in Christmas paper, the kind that comes from fancy stores. The man has a handsome face, and his wife wears a black mink. The two kids, a boy and girl, race up the steps of the stone house, and they all hurry inside.

The indoor lights flick on, and for a moment, Geoff and I can see directly into their living room, with its tasteful oil paintings and classic Christmas tree. The children, in private-school uniforms, put their parcels under the tree. The man crosses the room toward the back of the house. His slender blonde wife, in a soft pink sweater, pulls the drapes shut. And that's it. *And . . . scene*, as Mr. Gabor would say.

Geoff and I stare at the multicolored Christmas lights strung across their wide veranda. "Isn't that the perfect family," he says in a hushed voice.

"Yeah," I say. "They're like a Christmas picture postcard. The only thing missing is snow. If we had snow, we could stuff them into a snow globe and shake it. That's how perfect those people are." Geoff doesn't laugh. I nudge his shoulder with my damp mitt. "Hey, they're probably having a big fight in there right now, yelling and flinging popcorn strings at each other."

Geoff shakes his head. "No, they're not. The children will be changing for dinner, their mother will be checking on the roast that the maid put in the oven this afternoon, and their father will be pouring himself a gin and tonic and popping in a tape of Rosemary Clooney singing 'White Christmas.'"

"You don't know that," I say. "Maybe it only looks good from the outside."

Geoff puts the car into gear and says, "Don't you ever wonder what it feels like to be normal?"

I bristle. I may not be the model of "normal," but I'm not one of Diane Arbus's circus freaks either. And why does normal have to be pot roasts and cashmere sweaters? Why should I be envious of that? "Do you really want to be like them?" I ask.

"Sometimes I do."

"Well, I don't. It looks pretty boring to me."

The wipers scrape across the windshield. Geoff says, "Maybe it's boring to you because you have a big family."

"So, you have Clarissa, who is much more fun than any parent I've ever met."

"Yeah, but sometimes I'd just like to know what it feels like to belong to brothers and sisters, cousins and grandparents, a mother and a father . . ." Geoff stares into the traffic, and I picture him and Clarissa on Christmas morning, opening each other's presents and then facing the long hours until they can get dressed and go to a restaurant to eat turkey dinner in the company of strangers.

I sigh. "Why is it that we always want what we don't have?"

"Because we don't have it," Geoff says wryly.

"Well, I'll tell you something," I say. "I don't aspire to that kind of normal. When I finish school, I'm going to go live in Paris or in a little whitewashed house on a Greek island, with olive trees and a view of the Mediterranean. You might want to come along."

"And what will we do when we get there?" Geoff asks.

"Drink wine and throw fabulous parties. You can be the new Richard Avedon and take portraits of the locals and the famous artists who visit us. And I will paint, and write novels, and have affairs with mysterious men who will probably break my heart."

"Maybe you'll break their hearts," Geoff says.

"Not likely," I say, thinking of Ian.

When we get to my house, Geoff parks. Then he reaches into the backseat and pulls out a present wrapped in azure foil. "Merry Christmas," he says.

I gawk. It hasn't even occurred to me to buy something for Geoff. Mollie and I never exchange presents for Hanukkah. "Geoff, I don't have anything for you," I say.

"That's okay," he says. "Go ahead and open it."

I peel back the wrapping paper and there, in a pewter frame, is a black-and-white photograph of me. It's from Halloween. I'm wearing Clarissa's Audrey Hepburn dress and black elbow-length gloves. My hair is pinned into a French knot. The expression on my face is wide-eyed and expectant, as if I've just spun around to catch a glimpse of something.

"Do you like it?" Geoff asks.

"It's beautiful," I say. "I look so . . ."

"Striking?"

"Did you airbrush this or something?"

Geoff smiles. "In most of the shots, you were mugging, but in this one, you're actually yourself."

"How unusual for me," I quip.

"I know," Geoff says. We lean together, peering at the photo. "I like the way you're glamorous and innocent at the same time. It's like I caught you in a moment of transition, where you're just about to discover something wonderful but you can't quite see what it is. Do you know what I mean?"

I nod. "I know exactly what you mean." I smile at Geoff. Most of the time, he's so funny that I forget that underneath his glitzy song-and-dance routine is the soul of a poet. "Too bad I don't look like that all the time," I say.

"Well, if you lost the turtleneck sweaters and the macramé vests, we might have something to work with," Geoff replies.

I give him a shot in the arm and then a hug. "Merry Christmas."

"Have fun in Montreal," he says. "And call me as soon as you're back."

CARLA

"Hot Love"

Two days into the holidays, I'm ready to tear out my hair. I am so *bored*! Debbie is in Mexico, Marlene is skiing with her family, and no one else is around, except for Nonna Cabrielli, who's visiting from St. Catharines for Christmas and sharing my bedroom. Nonna dresses in black and isn't exactly a barrel of laughs. Ma says that I should be more respectful of my grandmother. I tell her that maybe I'd be in a better mood if I didn't have to lie awake all night listening to Nonna snore and fart.

Over breakfast, Nonna looks at my long face. "*Cosa c'è?*" she asks me. What's the matter?

"Everything."

Nonna nods slowly. She pours sugar in her espresso. She says, "*Chi troppo vuole, nulla stringe*"—he who wants too much doesn't get anything. Great.

The whole week is like that. I don't know what to do with myself. I walk past Ian's house three times, but I never see anyone. I watch *White Christmas* on TV, and I feel totally bummed out because everyone in that movie ends up happy and in love and I'm stuck here with no friends and no boyfriend.

Finally, I'm so desperate, I phone Sherrie Cumberland and ask if she wants to do some last-minute Christmas shopping. We go to Yorkdale Mall, which is a zoo. Sherrie needs to pick up a present for her latest boyfriend, Paul McCormick, who is in grade thirteen at Vanier. Sherrie says he's going to U of T next year because he wants to be a dentist. I can't imagine wanting to be a dentist. Who would want to spend their entire life staring into people's mouths and torturing them with sharp metal objects? Of course, I don't tell Sherrie that. Instead, I say, "He must be smart."

"Yeah," Sherrie says, twirling her long blonde hair between her fingers. "And he's good in the sack."

"Really?" I ask, interested.

"Uh-huh." Sherrie gives me a sly smile, and I follow her into Eaton's, to the women's lingerie department. Sherrie flips through the 34D bras and picks out a lacy black one and a red satin one, with matching panties. They look like something a stripper would wear, minus the tassels.

I gulp. "You're getting him *that* for Christmas?"

Sherrie laughs. "Every guy's fantasy, right?" She leans over and whispers, "Paul's bedroom is in his parents' basement, and they never go down there, so we do it all the time. I'm on the pill."

"Wow," I say. "Where did you get it?"

"The women's health clinic downtown on Wellesley. My sister told me about it. She says all the girls at U of T go there because it's confidential. I told the doctor that I was already having sex using condoms—and they don't like that because they don't want you to get pregnant and have an abortion—so she wrote me a prescription for the pill. Sherrie opens her purse, and there, next to her wallet, is a green disk full of little white pills. "I keep them with me so my mom won't find them." She grins. "And now we fuck like bunnies. Last night, we did it three times, in three different positions."

"Wow," I say, truly amazed, mulling over the possibilities. I wonder how long it took, and if they had to take breathers between each time, or if they just did it—bam, bam, bam—all in a row. If Sherrie's trying to shock me, she's doing a really great job.

"Come on," Sherrie says. "I want your opinion on these bras." I wait outside the change room while Sherrie models bras and negligees. I have to admire the way she's so uninhibited. "You should try some on too," she says.

"What's the point?" I say. "Ian and I are history."

Sherrie pulls me into the change room and sits me down. "Do you still like him?" she asks. "I mean, I know you broke his nose and everything, but I see the way you watch him in drama."

I don't even try to lie. "He's such a jerk, but I can't stop thinking about him."

"Was he good in bed?" she asks. I squirm. Sherrie's eyes go wide. "Don't tell me you're still a virgin!" she gasps. "Carla! With a guy like that? Guys like that aren't going to wait around." She squishes onto the bench beside me. "Look, sleeping with your boyfriend doesn't make you a slut. It's just part of growing up. I mean, sooner or later we're all going to have sex, right? So why wait?"

"Well, that's what Ian says," I mumble.

"Of course he does. Because guys are totally obsessed with sex. Paul says that the average guy thinks about sex about every three minutes."

"Get out," I say.

"It's true," Sherrie says. "Paul is very open with me about stuff like that. He says that whenever a guy looks at a girl, no matter who she is, even if she's a real dog, he's thinking about what it would be like to fuck her."

"Get out!" I say.

"It's true," Sherrie says. "Even if he's already getting laid. Even if he's walking down the street with his girlfriend. It's just something they can't control. So, if you really like a guy, why fight it? I mean, it's fun. It gives you something to do together. And afterward, the guy is always sooo grateful."

"So, you think that if I was having sex with Ian—"

"He'd still be with you," Sherrie says. "The way I see it, life is give and take. If you keep your man happy, he'll keep you happy. And if he wants a bit of tits and ass," Sherrie wiggles her boobs, "I don't have a problem with that." The two of us burst out laughing. Sherrie buys the red satin bra and panties and asks the saleslady to wrap them up with a bow.

Later that week, I meet up with Sherrie at her house and Paul drops by. When he says hi to me, I wonder if he's thinking about what it would be like to fuck me. I look at Sherrie, and we both crack up because she knows exactly what I'm thinking.

"What?" Paul says.

"Nothing, sweetie," Sherrie says.

The three of us sit in the den listening to music, and within seconds, Paul's creeping me out. Yes, he's cute, in a Paul McCartney kind of way, but he's so conceited, and he can't keep his hands to himself. I mean, does he have to be pawing his girlfriend in public, playing with her hair and rubbing up against her like a dog in heat while I'm sitting there? What a pig! Can't he wait till I'm gone?

Finally, I tell them I have stuff to do. Sherrie walks me to the door. "Isn't he great?" she whispers.

"Great," I say. "I bet your present was a real hit."

Sherrie laughs. "You should call Ian." She winks at me. "Remember what I said."

JULES

"The Long and Winding Road"

As we pass through Belleville on Highway 401, fat lazy flakes begin to fall, and by the time we cross into Quebec, winter is as winter should be. Fresh snow softens the sharp edges of the world. We take the exit ramp off the highway into the Town of Mount Royal, and every house, hedge and tree is familiar to me. In front yards, kids are building snowmen with carrot noses and hockey-stick arms. Cars crawl along the white-matted roads. Finally, we pull up to our house, with the FOR SALE sign stuck in a snowbank.

The tires of my mother's station wagon squeak over the hardpacked snow on the driveway. Bobby leaps out of the car and is immediately pelted with snowballs from the Liebermans' yard. Next door, the ten-year-old Lieberman twins duck into the tunnels of their snow fort, cackling with glee. Bobby whoops a war cry and charges across the yard. The boys hurl snowballs back and forth, just as if we'd never left home.

I spend almost every day and night at Mollie's, so I don't really see how things are going between my parents. It isn't until the evening Dad comes to pick me up on the way to

Grandma and Grandpa Cohen's that I finally get a chance to be alone with him. If I'm going to bring up the topic of Dr. Katzenberg, this is the perfect opportunity. Mollie thinks I shouldn't do it. She says that even if my mother is having an affair—which she doesn't believe—there are some things parents have to sort out for themselves.

Dad turns on the radio in the car and says, "What's cookin', good-lookin'? I can hear the wheels of your brain grinding away."

It's an opening. I decide to test the waters. "I was just wondering what's going to happen if you can't sell the house."

"Don't worry. Everything will be fine," Dad says.

"How can you say that? Things don't work out just because you want them to."

Dad laughs. "Is that so?"

"Yes," I say. "I mean, sometimes you just don't see things coming."

"Like moving to Toronto?" he asks, mistaking my point.

"Or worse."

Dad shakes his head. "You know what, poopsie? The difference between you and me is that I'm an optimist and you're a pessimist. I'm having a good time, and you're always worrying about everything. I'm the grasshopper and you're the ant."

"You know what happens to the grasshopper," I say.

"Sure," Dad says. "The grasshopper dies with a smile on his face remembering all the good times he had singing and dancing with his buddies, while the uptight, miserly old ant dies of a massive heart attack and no one comes to his funeral." I roll my eyes, but Dad continues. "So, who had a better life? Eh?" he asks, poking me in the ribs. "You only get one shot, so you might as well enjoy it." He flashes me a big white smile. "California Dreamin'" plays on the radio, and he sings along with Mama Cass, full blast, off-key. I sigh. I could tell him about Dr. Katzenberg, but he probably wouldn't believe me anyway.

Dinner at Grandma and Grandpa Cohen's is like old times: flowers on the table, polished silver and gold-rimmed china. My mom's brother, Uncle Phil, has driven up from Boston with Aunt Dina and their three kids. Grandpa sits at the end of the table surrounded by his grandchildren. "How's school?" he asks me.

"Good."

"What did you get in chemistry this term?" He always asks about science classes because he wants me to be a doctor.

"Ninety-four."

"What happened to the other six points?" he jokes.

Grandma gives Grandpa a look. "What's your favorite subject this year?" she asks.

"Drama," I say.

"Drama?" Uncle Phil asks, making a face. "You want to be an actress? You can't make a living doing that."

"Let her do what she wants," says Aunt Dina.

"We're studying *Hamlet*," I say, trying to prove to them that it's not all artsy-fartsy.

"Ah, yes," Grandpa says. "'To be or not to be—that is the question,' isn't it? Or is it: To eat dessert or not to eat dessert . . ."

The cousins squeal, "Grandpaaa!"

After supper, Grandpa pulls us kids into the hall and whispers that the change in his pockets is weighing him down and if he doesn't get rid of it, he won't be able to walk (it's his shtick). He sprinkles coins into our cupped palms. When the others aren't looking, he slips me a few extra two-dollar bills and says, "Here, go to the movies, but don't eat popcorn kernels because they'll crack the enamel on your teeth."

The Epstein dinners are noisier and wilder than the Cohens'. We're a big group: Bubby and Zadie, their three married kids and ten grandchildren. When we arrive, Bubby hurries out of the kitchen, arms outstretched. Bobby submits to her squishy hugs and then races off to join the cousins. Bubby looks me over, her brown eyes floating behind her thick glasses like huge dark cherries. "Look at how tall you've gotten!" she gushes. "Irving, she could eat soup off my head!" she says to my dad.

Dad says, "Ma, everybody can eat soup off your head."

In the dining room, Aunt Connie and Aunt Rose, who is looking very tanned from the Florida sunshine, are arranging platters of food. In the kitchen, my little cousins are running around dressed up in Bubby's old high heels and veiled hats. They're practicing for a talent show they'll perform later tonight. In the living room, Zadie, Uncle Mort, Uncle Seymour and my dad stretch out on couches and exchange jokes. Uncle Seymour says, "Hey, Irv, have you heard the one about Trudeau going to heaven?"

My cousin Joe is in the den, and I'm surprised by how much he's changed in four months. His hair is down to his shoulders now, and he's wearing a puka shell necklace.

"You've turned into a hippie," I say.

"That's Florida for you," he says. "On campus, they call me a radical just for listening to music with the black kids. So, I guess I'm a radical." He grins.

Over dinner, the adults discuss Quebec politics: Will the Parti Québécois win the next election, and if they do, will Quebec really separate?

"Sun Life is moving their head office to Toronto," Uncle Mort says to my dad.

"When the big money leaves town, you know things are bad," Uncle Seymour says.

"I don't see why everyone has to panic," says Aunt Connie.

"Maybe because René Lévesque is the most popular man

in Quebec right now," Aunt Rose says. "And if he holds a referendum on separation, then—"

"Let him put it to a vote," my dad interrupts. "It will never pass."

"How can you be so sure?" Mom asks.

Everyone starts talking at once.

"Let's go," Joe whispers. We've heard enough. We head up the creaky spiral staircase to the unlit second floor. When we were little, we used to be scared to come up here because the furniture is covered in dusty white sheets, like a haunted house, but as teenagers, the upper floor became our refuge. Tonight, we stretch out on my dad's old lumpy bed. Joe lights a cigarette, and the smoke curls above our heads into the inky corners of the room.

Joe tells me about life in Gainesville. "The whole place is bizarre," he says. "For one thing, football is like a religion there. If you're not into football, you're un-American. And there's this huge right-wing culture: military guys in crew cuts, blonde sorority girls and these Holy Roller Christians with their pro-Jesus, pro-war, antiabortion, racist pamphlets." Joe takes a drag and slowly exhales. "It's enough to turn you into a commie." He grins.

I laugh. "I bet you wish you were going to McGill."

"I'll never become an American, that's for sure," Joe says. "What about you? How's life in Toronto?" From the way he glances at me, I can tell there's been talk.

"What have you heard?" I ask.

"That you're a pain in the ass."

I smirk. "Guilty as charged." I tell him about school, but I don't mention Dr. Katzenberg. Not that Joe would tell anyone. It's just a line I can't cross.

When it's time to go, Joe scribbles down his Gainesville phone number. "It's the floor phone in the dorm. Someone always answers it, and they'll come get me if you ever want to shoot the shit." When he passes me the paper, I get this bad feeling. It's like he's writing down the number of a crisis line, just in case something blows up in my face.

CARLA

"No Sugar Tonight"

There's nothing worse than spending New Year's Eve in front of the TV watching a bunch of drunk people in Times Square singing "Auld Lang Syne"—which is a dumb song because no one understands what the hell it means anyway. Unfortunately, the only party I know of is Sandy Kirkpatrick's, and Sandy is friends with Jim Malone, and if Jim's going, Ian will be there too.

"I don't want to be in the same house as that jerk," I say, nibbling on a slice of prosciutto. Deb, Mar and I are in the kitchen fixing hors d'oeuvres for Ma's annual New Year's Eve bash.

"Maybe Ian's out of town," Marlene says.

"We could always check it out," Debbie says. She wants to go to the party to show off her Mexican tan, even if it *is* peeling.

"Well, I'm not going, but feel free to go without me," I say flippantly. Deb and Mar look at each other, disappointed.

"I guess we don't have to," Mar says.

"I guess not," Deb sighs.

Ma marches into the kitchen carrying a jar of homemade antipasto. "And what's wrong with *my* party?" she says. "There's food, wine . . . and everyone's invited."

"Is Mrs. Epstein coming?" I ask, smirking at Deb and Mar behind Ma's back. The last time we saw Mrs. Epstein was at the movie with Loverboy.

"Of course she's coming," Ma says.

"Is she coming alone?" I ask, winking at Deb and Mar.

"I told her to bring Julia and Bobby," Ma says. I groan. Nonna shuffles into the room. Ma gives me a fierce look. "Carla, be nice to Julia," she says. "When you're the host of a party, it's your job to make everyone welcome. *Capisci?*"

"Yeah, yeah," I say.

Nonna wags a finger at me and says, *"Non sputare in aria; che ti ricade in testa."*

I translate for Deb and Mar. "Don't spit in the wind; it might land on your head."

For the party, I wear my absolutely favorite Christmas present of all: a pair of stunning, knee-high, brown suede lace-up boots. I love my new boots! It takes forever to do up the laces, but I don't care. The boots are so soft, they make me feel like Hiawatha, Indian princess.

When Marlene and Debbie arrive, I pour us all glasses of wine.

"Your parents don't mind?" Mar asks, taking a glass.

"We're Italian," I say. "Wine with food is no big deal."

"Anyway, it's New Year's Eve," Deb says.

"Yeah," I say. "So let's get drunk."

After two glasses of wine, I decide that the best way to get through the evening is to pretend I'm Queen Gertrude. *Hamlet* auditions are coming up, and I could use the practice. Mr. Gabor told us that in order to get into character, you have to understand how a person moves, so I stroll around the living room pretending I'm wearing a velvet gown loaded with pearls and jewels. I nod and smile, greeting the local peasants, saying, "Hello, so nice to see you," in a hoity-toity English accent. By the time the Epsteins show up, I'm on my third drink and I'm having fun. I sail over to Mrs. Epstein and say, "Ah, Mrs. Epstein, don't you look lovely this evening."

"Thank you," she says.

"And, Julia," I say in a smooth regal voice, "that black corduroy pantsuit really does show off your hair."

"Thanks," she says, clearly surprised by my compliment.

Ma gives me a proud smile. I bat my eyelashes at her. Ma sends me a don't-push-it look. I turn back to Julia. "How about some food?" I ask. I escort her into the dining room and heap crostini and shrimp onto her plate. "Try the asparagus wrapped in prosciutto," I insist. "It's one of Ma's specialties."

"Your mom's a really good cook," Julia says.

"Yeah, she is," I say, pouring us both some wine. "It's a wonder I'm not size-elephant." I crack up. Julia smiles politely. In the living room, Uncle Dominic cranks up the music and starts dancing to Nancy Sinatra's "These Boots Are Made for Walkin'," which is both embarrassing and hysterically funny. Mar and Deb are sitting on the couch flirting with my cousin Frank, who's a year older than me and looks like he's grown five inches in the last six months. I look at Julia. I could stand here and ask her about her holiday, but hell, I've been extremely nice already and a hostess must circulate, so when Uncle Dominic leads a conga line through the dining room, I use the diversion to make my escape. As it turns out, Frank has a couple of joints in his pocket. Marlene, Debbie and I whip upstairs for a smoke, and when I return to the party, Julia Epstein is nowhere in sight.

JULES

"One Toke over the Line"

I don't want to go to the Cabriellis' New Year's Eve party, but my mother insists that I "make an appearance." Surprisingly, Carla is actually friendly, in an overblown, maybe drunk, kind of way. She pours me a huge glass of wine and piles food onto my plate. I can't help but wonder if she's seen Ian over the holidays, but it's not something I can ask. After a while, Carla disappears. Bobby and Buzz hover near the dessert table, carefully picking the chocolate shavings off a large cake. A bald man leads a conga line across the room. I decide that this is my cue to leave, so, when my mom isn't looking, I gulp down my wine, grab my coat and duck out the back door.

Outside, a full moon hangs in the sky like a disco ball. Snow glitters like fairy dust. Everything is brushed with magic tonight, so I decide to go for a walk in the ravine. As I approach the bridge, I spot two figures huddled together passing a joint back and forth. Jim Malone and Ian Slater. My first urge is to turn back, but then, I think *Why should I be intimidated by them?* Besides, if Ian can pretend nothing happened between us, well, so can I.

Ian spots me as I get closer. "Well, if it isn't Rapunzel," he says. "Hey, Rapunzel, what're you doing out, alone, in the deep, dark forest on New Year's Eve?" Jim and Ian grin at me like a couple of lean hungry wolves on the prowl.

"I'm going for a walk," I say nonchalantly.

"Where's Geoff tonight?" Ian asks.

"He's out."

"Is Geoff your boyfriend?" Jim asks.

Ian shakes his head. "Nah, the guy's a fag. He's in our drama class. Geoffy Jones."

Jim holds his crotch and says, in a mocking voice, "Ooh, Geoffy Jones."

I don't like Jim. I've seen him around. He's the kind of guy who'll knock you into the lockers on purpose because he thinks it's funny. "Geoff is my friend," I say firmly.

"Is that so?" Ian sneers.

"Yes," I say. "And quit picking on him all the time."

"Ooh, she's taking you on, man," Jim says, puffing on the joint.

Ian laughs. "That's what I like about Jules. She knows how to fight back." He gives me a sly smile, and his eyes glint in the moonlight.

Jim passes the joint to Ian, who takes a drag and holds it out to me. He tilts his head and gives me a mocking grin. He obviously thinks I'm way too straight to smoke, which bugs me, so I reach for the joint, take a puff, hold it in and slowly exhale, as if I do this all the time. Fortunately, I don't choke. I pass the joint back to Jim, and Ian throws his head back and laughs. He slings an arm over my shoulder. "Jules, Jules, Jules," he chants. He looks at Jim. "Do you know, Jules is the smartest girl in grade eleven?"

"No kidding," Jim says.

"I don't think so," I say.

"That's what Carla told me," Ian says.

"Carla doesn't know my marks," I say. "Carla doesn't know anything about me."

Ian leans in, so that our faces are only inches apart. He says, "Tell me something: Why doesn't Carla like you?"

It's hard to concentrate with his face so close. "I guess you'd have to ask her," I say.

"I think she's jealous."

"Of what?"

"Of you," he says. When he says the word *you*, his lips pucker and his breath comes out in a white puff of air. I stare at the tiny scar at the corner of his mouth, and I want to put my tongue right there. The joint comes around again, and we all take tokes. Jim and Ian talk about a party they're going to. Sandy somebody. I lose track of the conversation. My teeth begin to chatter, but I don't feel like leaving. When the joint is down to a roach, Ian takes it between his thumb and fore-finger, inhales, squints against the smoke and then, instead of passing it to me, leans over and holds the roach to my lips.

I feel like I'm tottering on the edge of a crevasse. I bend my head forward and press my lips against Ian's icy fingers. I try to suck in the harsh smoke, but I can't breathe properly. This time I cough, and Jim and Ian laugh, but not in a bad way.

Ian passes the joint to Jim, who takes one last swift toke and tosses it over the bridge into the half-frozen stream. I listen to the gurgle and pop of the water as it swooshes over the rocks and forms channels below the ice. Everything is so calm and peaceful, and suddenly I realize that I'm stoned. Really stoned. Once, Mollie, Joe and I smoked a joint, and Mollie and I felt a bit light-headed, but this is quite different. This is mellow and pillowy, like falling backward into a snowbank in slow motion, frame by frame. I look around at the trees, the stream, the snow, and everything seems so beautiful.

"What?" Ian asks, looking at me quizzically.

"It's so pretty here," I say. "And I never noticed." The guys laugh. "No, really. And you know why?"

"No. Why?" Ian asks, smirking.

"Because tonight I'm seeing it differently."

"Because you're stoned," Jim says.

"No, not just that. It's like, when you let go of your mind, your whole perspective changes because . . . well . . . you *are* your mind!"

The guys burst out laughing. I try to think of another way of explaining myself—because, really, this is an amazing epiphany—but when I try to put it into words, I can't quite grasp the brilliance of my own insight, and so I just end up laughing.

Ian pulls a bottle from his leather jacket and offers it to me. "Daddy's good Irish whiskey," he says. I shake my head. I don't drink whiskey, but Ian says, "Come on. It will warm you up."

"Pass it over," Jim says.

"Ladies first. Where's your fuckin' manners," Ian says. He eases the cork out of the bottle and passes it over. I tip it back. The liquor oozes down my throat and radiates through my chest like a brush fire. We pass the bottle around and around. A little voice inside my brain says *Jules, what are you doing? You're in over your head.* But I don't listen. I want to be in over my head. I like it here. It's relaxing and fun, and people are nice, and anyway, why should I always be afraid that something bad is going to happen?

"Let's go to your house," Jim says to Ian.

"No," Ian says.

"But the bottle's almost empty, and this is good shit," Jim says.

"No," Ian says. "Let's go to the party."

I laugh because I can hardly follow this ridiculous ping-pong conversation, and the whole thing makes me giddy.

"Are you coming?" Ian asks.

"Where?"

"To the party."

"Sure," I say.

"Then, let's go," Ian says. He puts his arm around my waist, and I'm not sure if he's doing this because he likes me or because he thinks I might fall over, but it feels nice anyway.

We walk out of the ravine and down the street. A car pulls over out of nowhere. Sherrie Cumberland rolls down the passenger window and says that they're on their way to Sandy's party and do we want a lift. We do. We pile in, and I get wedged between Jim and Ian. The ride seems to last forever, but Sandy's place is really only a few blocks away. When we spill out of the car, I hear the thumping bass of rock and roll coming from a two-story brick house. Inside, the rooms are steamy, and people are drinking, smoking and shouting above the pounding rhythm of "Brown Sugar" coming from the basement. Jim starts playing air guitar, and in seconds, he's swallowed up by the crowd. And that's the last I see of him.

I dump my boots and coat on a pile near the door and look around. I don't recognize anyone, but this doesn't bother me. Everyone's having a great time, and I will too. Ian has disappeared, so I cruise the house by myself. In the basement, the lights are low and the room vibrates with hot, sweaty, dancing bodies. In a side room, people are smoking joints, and two girls are playing with a Ouija board. They keep saying, "Are you moving it?" "No, are you moving it?" "No, are you?" The Ouija board spells out someone's name, but I don't remember whose.

Upstairs, some of the bedroom doors are shut. Sandy's parents' bedroom door is open, and half a dozen kids are sitting on the queen-size bed watching TV. People in Times Square are waving and hooting. It's 11:22. Double numbers. Cool.

I find Ian in the kitchen, beside the stove. He says, "Do you want to hot knife?"

I have no idea what hot knifing is, but I say, "Sure." Tonight, I'll try anything. I watch as Ian heats a knife blade on the red-hot coil of an electric burner, while a guy with a huge Afro pinches off a crumb of hash and puts it on an unlit burner. Ian presses the hot knife onto the hash, and as it incinerates, he sucks up the smoke. White smoke curls and twists its way into his mouth like a dancing genie. I figure that if I can smoke pot, I can hot knife. So I do. The hash fills my head like smoke in a glass jar. Smoke signals. What does this mean?

Suddenly a freckle-faced girl appears out of nowhere, yelling, "Don't use the silverware, you moron!" Sandy, I guess. I sit down beside a bowl of salt and vinegar chips, and God, they taste good! Ian puts a cold beer in my hand, and icy water droplets trickle down the sides of the bottle. I shiver. I follow him into the basement.

I think hot knifing was a mistake. As we walk downstairs, the heat from the room swirls around me. I start to float, and time dissolves into ribbons. Music ripples through the pores of my skin, and when Ian takes my hand to lead me through the crowd, all I can think about are his fingers intertwined with mine and how my lips had pressed against the tips of his cold fingers on the bridge.

We slip through the dancers like otters diving through a sea of salty bodies and surface on the other side of the room, in the shadows. I'm parched and my cold beer tastes so good. I turn to find Ian watching me with those eerie wolf eyes. I want him to kiss me very badly. He says something. I can't hear the words, but when he leans over and puts his mouth to my ear, I feel the hot wave of his breath on my skin. "How are you, Rapunzel?" A whisper. An incantation. I close my eyes. His fingers trace patterns along my palm like he's reading my life, up and down the hills and valleys of my hand, sending me coded messages, kinetically, psychically, spiritually. I'm flooded.

Someone puts on the *Abraxas* album, the "Black Magic Woman" track, and we watch the dancers ride the arc and twang of Carlos Santana's Latin guitar. It occurs to me that if Ian leads me off to a bedroom, I'll go with him. I'll go all the way. I don't even care about condoms, about people in the house, about the fact that we aren't even going out. I want to be with him, even if it's only for one night. I just want to be free and spontaneous and to stop worrying all the time.

I lean against Ian's arm and let my mind drift across the swell of gyrating dancers. And then, like a terrible mirage, the specter of Carla Cabrielli rises up from the darkness. For a second, I think I'm hallucinating, but as she plunges across the room, I see that it really is her, in the flesh—and if fury has a face, I'm looking at it. Her Medusa eyes are deep black pits, and her face is a macabre mask of rage. If she had a knife, she'd shove it straight between my ribs. Ian and I drop our hands like stones. Ian says, "Carla."

Panic gurgles up my throat. Carla doesn't speak. She grabs Ian's arm and yanks him away. They vanish instantly. I blink, and when I open my eyes, Marlene and Debbie are bearing down on me from across the room, all fangs, poisoned claws and glittering eyes. I bolt. I duck into the Ouija room, back out again and stumble up the stairs. I grab my coat and boots and run out into the night, like Cinderella fleeing the ball. The clock strikes midnight, and people behind me scream, "Happy New Year!"

This is a nightmare. I careen through the maze of streets, lost and bewildered. Time warps. Minutes feel like hours. Every time I look into the night sky, the constellations have changed positions. Does everything always have to change? How can I possibly find my way?

Finally, I turn the corner and there's the McDuff house. Inside, it's dark and quiet, but as I creep up the stairs, my mother's voice calls out from her room. "Julia?"

Oh God. I can't face her like this. "Yeah."

"Where were you?" she asks.

"Sandy's."

"Who's Sandy?"

"A girl from school."

"You went to another party?"

"Yeah, but I'm really tired, so I'm going to bed." I dart into the bathroom and scrub my teeth over and over, trying to get the taste of smoke and booze out of my mouth. My tiny seed eyes stare at me from the mirror. The echo of party music thuds around my head. My body doesn't feel like my own.

I crawl into bed, and Carla's demon face rushes at me. Voices in my head scream down a thousand unmarked trails. I'm so confused. I'm so stoned. Sleep crashes into me like a tsunami, pulling me down, down, down, down.

CARLA

"I'll Be Your Baby Tonight"

It's Sherrie Cumberland who tips me off. Mar, Deb, Frank and I are in the kitchen, stoned, polishing off Ma's tiramisu cake, when the phone rings. I answer it. I hear party noise and loud music, and then I hear Sherrie's voice shouting, "Guess who Paul and I picked up on the way to Sandy's?"

"Who?"

"Ian and Julia."

I suddenly feel very alert. "Julia? Like with Ian?"

"He had his arm around her, and now they're hot knifing in the kitchen."

"You're joking!"

"Nope. Thought you might like to know." Click.

Two minutes later, Deb, Mar and I are blasting down the street in Deb's mom's Buick. I jump out of the car in front of Sandy's house and race inside, heading straight for the kitchen. No Ian. No Julia. I spot Sherrie in the living room necking with Paul. She nods at me and points downstairs. I dash to the basement. It's dark and smoky, and it takes a few minutes for my eyes to adjust, but then I see them across the room. They're holding hands, leaning together, and Julia has this blissed-out look on her face. I can't believe it. I want to smack her. I don't have a plan; I just ram through the crowd.

Ian's the one who spots me first. His eyes are glazed, and he's stoned out of his mind. Julia's stoned too, believe it or not. They drop their hands. She looks scared, and oh yes, she should be. I am not done with her yet. But first, Ian. I need to talk to him. Alone.

I drag him upstairs to an empty bedroom. Ian is laughing. I think I'm going to cry. I lock the door. All around us, people are shouting, "Happy New Year!" and firecrackers are banging and whizzing in the yard. I clench my fists and glare at him. "You're supposed to kiss me now, you idiot," I say.

He looks at me with those high-voltage eyes. "Happy New Year, baby," he whispers in my ear. Then he wraps me in his arms and kisses me, slowly, just like he did that first time in my kitchen. He makes me so mad, but I've missed him so much. I hold on tight and kiss him hard. He flicks off the light, and we're all over each other. I unbutton his shirt; he unbuttons mine. He strips off his jeans; I unzip my skirt. Our clothes drop in piles all over the floor. We rub against each other, skin against skin. His hand slides into my panties, and his dick pokes out of his underwear. I feel it pressing against my stomach. We peel off everything, except for my new suede boots.

"Nice boots," Ian whispers.

"You can undo them, if you want."

"No, I like 'em on," he says.

We grin and tumble onto a kid's single bed, and we both know *This is it, we're doing it.* And I want to. I don't hesitate—and he doesn't even stop to ask. We roll around naked, except for my boots, touching, kissing, going crazy for each other. Some guy starts banging on the door, but we just laugh and keep on going. Ian pulls a condom out of his wallet and puts it on. I glance down. It's kind of gross, like a sausage in Saran Wrap. I try not to think about how weird it looks. He climbs on top and slowly pushes in. For a second, I think this isn't going to work, and I tense up, but then I go with it. It's kind of tight, but not too bad. Ian rocks on top of me, faster and faster, closing his eyes and making moaning noises. And part of me thinks this is such a rush, and part of me thinks I'm just pretending, but really, it doesn't matter anymore. I chose this; this is what I want.

Suddenly Ian makes a grunting noise, arches up and collapses on top of me. What? Already? Yup, he's done. His breath whooshes out against my neck. I can feel his heartbeat through my skin. I wonder if he can feel mine. Eventually, I squirm, and Ian rolls off me. I shift, and Ian's leg flops over mine. My thighs feel gloopy, and I could use a Kleenex, but I don't want to ruin the mood, so we squish together on the single bed, just breathing, very quiet.

So, this is it. I'm no longer a virgin. I have lost my virginity on New Year's Eve, 1972. I guess I'll always remember that.

And, yeah, this isn't quite how I imagined it. Not that I need pink champagne, but a decent bed would've been nice. And candles, and romantic music. But still, I'm glad it finally happened. The earth didn't move, but hey, it was fun. Besides, according to Sherrie Cumberland, the first time is never the best. She says that, like everything else in life, sex gets better with practice.

Ian props himself up on one elbow and smiles at me. I smile back. His hair is mussed up, but that only makes him look sexier. I stare at his nose. It doesn't really look any worse than it did before I hit him. I think this is something we can get past. He arches his back like a long, lazy cat, then bends over and kisses me. "Hey, Carla, how's it going?"

"Fine," I say.

Ian grins. "I think 1972 is off to a good start."

"Yeah," I say, stroking his chest. Good for me, and good for Ian, but not good for Julia Epstein.

"The Thrill Is Gone"

I sleep right through the morning and wake up around one o'clock feeling like roadkill. My tongue is thick and dried up, like a dead slug. My head is an anvil on my pillow. My stomach gurgles like a witch's brew. I stare at Karen McDuff's vile pink walls, and through a semiconscious fog, the memory of last night plays through my head like a trashy movie. Oh my God! When Carla gets ahold of me, she's going to rip out my guts and hang my entrails over the balcony of the school atrium as a warning to the entire student body not to mess with her man. I am doomed.

I phone Geoff. "Put on the coffee," I say. I don't really want to tell him what happened, but school gossip travels at the speed of light, and it's probably better if he hears it from me.

Clarissa stayed over at Michael's house last night, so Geoff is alone when I arrive. "You look awful," Geoff says.

"Wait till you hear my story," I say. I sip my coffee and stick to the facts. When I get to the part about hot knifing, Geoff gasps. When I tell him about Carla appearing at the party, he covers his mouth and his eyes go wide. He says, "Jules! What were you thinking?"

"I wasn't thinking," I say. "I was stoned! I thought I was being free and daring for once in my stupid life."

"Oh Lordy!" Geoff says. He stares at me, dumbfounded. Then he sits up straight. "Well, it could have been worse."

"Not really," I say.

"But all you did was get stoned and hold hands. Big deal. Kids in grade seven do that. Technically, that's a two-minute penalty. Besides, Carla and Ian aren't going out anymore. They broke up. Ian's a free agent."

"Tell that to Carla," I whimper. "You should've seen the look on her face. Remember when she punched Ian?"

Geoff grimaces. "A flak jacket, personal bodyguards and joining the French Foreign Legion are all good options."

"It's not funny!"

"It will blow over. You just need to keep out of her way."

"Geoff, she lives right next door! We have drama together. Auditions are coming up."

"She doesn't stand a chance against you," Geoff says.

"She really wants to play Gertrude."

"So, who died and made her queen?" he scoffs. "Take a number, lady. She has to try out, like everyone else."

I sigh and put my head in my hands. "Oh God. I am so screwed."

Geoff puts his arm around me. "Don't worry, doll-face,"

he drawls. "If anybody wants to mess with you, they're gonna have to get through me first."

"Great. I feel so much better," I mumble.

"Hey, what are friends for?"

During the first two weeks of January, Geoff and I spend all our free time practicing for the auditions. Clarissa coaches us, which helps a lot. Meanwhile, I avoid Carla. She and Ian are together again. She got what she wants, and maybe that will be enough; although sometimes I feel her eyes tracking me like a heat-seeking missile.

In the middle of January, on a Wednesday after school, fifty-six noisy students swarm into the auditorium to audition for *Hamlet*. Geoff is a nervous wreck. We scribble our names on the tryout sheets. I sign up under Gertrude and Ophelia, a few names after Carla's. I'm surprised to see Ian's name under Laertes. I guess Carla convinced him to try out. The two of them sit together at the back, so Geoff and I take seats near the front.

Mr. Gabor calls on the Poloniuses first. Jeremy leads off. He does a hilarious version of a tottery, bug-eyed old man, and Jason cheers loudly for him. Then Jason does an equally funny version of Polonius as a nervous, officious bureaucrat, and Jeremy gives him a standing ovation. This makes us all laugh, and we applaud everyone after that, even those who flub their lines, because we're all trying to do our best, and this isn't easy. Mr. Gabor looks enormously pleased.

After the Poloniuses come the Claudiuses, and by the time we get to the Hamlets, Geoff is like an over-wound cartoon clock ready to *sproing*. Mr. Gabor announces that the Hamlet soliloquy will be *"Now I am alone. / O, what a rogue and peasant slave am I!"*

Geoff grabs my arm. "I know that one," he whispers.

"You know them all," I say dryly.

"What if I blow it?"

"Don't be ridiculous. You'll be fabulous."

I smile reassuringly, but Geoff's face is chalk-white. When Mr. Gabor calls out his name, Geoff walks onto the stage like a man headed for the gallows. His hands are shaking, his eyes are glassy and he stares at the monologue sheet as if the words are written in hieroglyphics. I've never seen him like this before. I watch, helplessly, as he licks his lips and begins. On the second line, he falters and stops. "Could I start again?" he asks nervously.

Mr. Gabor says, "Whenever you're ready."

The auditorium goes dead quiet. Geoff drops the monologue sheet. There's a murmur of concern as it flutters to the floor, but suddenly I know what he's doing. He doesn't need to look at the sheet; he knows the monologue by heart. He's playing without a safety net. All or nothing.

Geoff takes a deep breath and then speaks softly, as if he's staring into the murky depths of Hamlet's soul. "*Now I am alone. / O, what a rogue and peasant slave am I!*"

And he's off. He pulls us into Hamlet's bitter, lonely world. He recites the words as if they're his own. By the time he reaches the part where Hamlet berates himself for being a coward, he's so caught up in self-loathing that he cries out in anguish: "*Bloody, bawdy villain! / Remorseless, treacherous, lecherous, kindless / villain!*"

We sit there in awe. When Geoff finishes, we jump to our feet and applaud wildly. Mr. Gabor beams. Benjamin, who's up next, looks at the rest of us and says, "Would anyone like to change places with me?"

"You nailed it," I say when Geoff sits down. "You were unbelievable." I squeeze his arm. Geoff can't speak. I just wish Clarissa had been here to see this because he did exactly what she told us to do: He took that giant, waxy ball of fear and burned it up in the heat of performance.

There's a short break before the auditions for Gertrude, so I dash off to the washroom, while Geoff revels in a swirl of admirers. I tell myself that if Geoff can do this, so can I. I know I'm good; I just have to focus.

I lock myself into a stall, sit on the toilet seat and psych myself up. I tell myself that I am Gertrude, queen of Denmark, recently widowed and now married again. I'm worried about my son, Hamlet, but I'm also madly in love with Claudius. My lust blinds me to everything else. Truth whispers in the gloomy shadows, but I don't want to hear it. I live in dark and difficult times, and I must be strong. I straighten my back and compose my regal face. I push open the stall door—and then I stop cold.

CARLA

"War"

When Julia steps out of the stall, I'm leaning on the sink, and Marlene and Debbie are standing guard at the door. No one else is in the washroom. It takes Julia about two seconds for that to register before the shock hits her face like ice water. She makes a jerky move toward the door, like her body wants to run but her mind knows there's no point even trying. I smile, *not* a friendly smile. I say, "Julia, I think we should talk."

Julia stands like a deer in the headlights, but she knows what's coming. For weeks she's been hiding from me, sticking to Geoff like a Siamese twin, but there are always times when a person is alone. Debbie's the one who saw her go into the washroom. Really, the timing couldn't be better. *Karma*, I think. I've had to wait a long time for this chat, but as they say, revenge is a dish best served cold.

I saunter over to Julia, staring her down, making her sweat it out. Then I stand just a little too close, so her eyes have to flit back and forth across my face—very stagy, déjà vu, like a scene I've played out in my head a million times. I say, "You know, Julia, I never liked you, but I tried to be nice to you. I invited you to my house. I introduced you to my friends. I welcomed you at my New Year's party. But what did you do? You tried to steal my boyfriend. And that breaks all the rules."

"I didn't—" Julia sputters.

"What?" Is she trying to deny it? I jab my finger into her chest. "I saw you at that party. Do you think I'm blind? Did you think I wouldn't find out about you? You *knew* Ian was dating me. So what the hell were you doing with him?"

"Nothing," she whimpers.

"Liar," I yell. My voice bounces off the washroom tiles. Julia gulps, trying not to cry, but I don't feel one bit sorry for that bitch. I saw the way she was pushing up against Ian, holding his hand in that dark corner. And she calls that nothing? Is she fucking joking?

Julia starts to back away, but in two seconds, I'm on to her. I step on her toes and lean in hard. I pin her down with both my feet. She flails backward, like she's going to fall, but I grab her by the hair and pull her up sharply. I hold her there, so we're eye to eye. I give her hair a hard yank. "You're such a fucking phony," I say. "You always act like you're better than everyone, but I'd never do what you did to me, 'cause I don't hit on other people's boyfriends. I don't take what isn't mine. But I guess you're not such a good girl, *Rapunzel*. I guess you're just a cheap piece of trash, sneaking around town, like your mom."

Julia's eyes pop open. So she knows. Well, how's that for *touché*? And now she's crying, stupid girl. Serves her right. There's always a price to be paid.

"Let's go," Marlene says. She's taking my arm. Marlene and Debbie lead me out the door. Julia's sobbing and holding her face in her hands. I'm shaking all over, but I'm not sure why.

"You okay?" Deb asks when we're in the hall.

"Yeah," I say.

They stare at me. "You told her," Mar says.

"She deserved it," Deb says.

"I know," I say. "She had it coming." But this isn't how it's supposed to feel. And I shouldn't have to fight for Ian. He should be the one fighting for me.

Debbie and Marlene hustle me back to the auditorium. They've already started auditioning for Gertrude. Mr. Gabor has chosen the speech where Hamlet accuses Gertrude of behaving like a whore, and Gertrude suddenly realizes that she's fallen in love with the wrong guy.

O Hamlet, speak no more!
Thou turn'st my eyes into my very soul,
And there I see such black and grained spots . . .

Yeah, this is a part I can do. 'Cause what person doesn't have some inky-black spots lying at the bottom of their soul?

And what woman doesn't fall madly in love with a guy who's not the man she thought she knew?

Mr. Gabor calls my name. I grab a copy of the monologue sheet and stride onto the stage. I feel the spotlight on my face, and I'm front and center, where I belong. This is my shot, and I'm ready. I tap into my anger, and I rip into that role. Even Ian looks impressed. Oh yeah, I'm hot, and no one's going to stop me now.

A few minutes later, Mr. Gabor calls Julia's name, but of course, she isn't in the room. Geoff rushes off to look for her, but he can't find her anywhere. Well, that's her own damn fault.

"I wonder what happened to Jules," Ian says.

"I guess she got cold feet," I say, slipping my arm through his. "She's always been the nervous type."

JULES

"Tell Me Why"

I don't go back to the auditorium. I get my coat from my locker and walk home. Fortunately, Mom is at work, so I climb into bed with my clothes on and just lie there. My scalp feels raw to the touch. I'm defeated, but I'm not surprised. This was a cosmic inevitability. I felt it from the first day I met Carla; it was just a matter of time.

The telephone rings. I know it's Geoff. I don't want to talk to him, but soon my mom will be home, and I certainly don't want Geoff talking to her.

"Hello," I say.

"Jules. Thank God! What happened?" Geoff asks.

"I'm sick."

"Nerves?"

"No."

There's a pause. "Jules, listen, I'm still at school. If you come back right now, Mr. Gabor will squeeze you in."

"I don't want to. I've changed my mind."

"Are you crazy? After all that work? You're too good to quit! I'm coming to get you right now."

"No—"

"Be ready in two minutes—"

"I don't want to do it anymore."

"I don't believe you!" Geoff says. "What's wrong?"

But I can't tell him any of this. "I'm sorry; I have to go," I say.

I hang up and return to my room. Mollie was wrong about the possibility of transformation. Square pegs are square pegs. Caterpillars are not butterflies. Dreamers get slapped down. This is what happens when you transgress. High school has its hierarchy, and that's something I should have known. I'm just a very foolish girl who had to learn the hard way.

At school, everyone is talking about the auditions. Callbacks are this afternoon. I avoid Geoff; I can't face his disappointment. At lunch, I'm heading toward the library, past the drama studio, when Mr. Gabor steps into the hall. My stomach drops. I duck behind a group of grade twelves, but Mr. Gabor spots me in the crowd. "Epstein! My office," he barks. He doesn't wait for a response. He turns and I follow. Students glance over their shoulders, curious to see who the unlucky victim is.

Mr. Gabor orders me to shut the office door. He points to a chair. I sit. He stands. He towers over me and allows for a dramatic pause, as only Mr. Gabor can do. If there's one thing he's taught us, it's how to play the pauses. "Silence can be more powerful than words," he always says. Of course, I already know this, because silence is my favorite weapon.

Mr. Gabor leans against the edge of his desk. "Ms. Epstein," he begins in a mock friendly tone, "yesterday was audition day. You signed up for two parts, but then you vanished into thin air. Naturally, I was concerned." He folds his arms across his chest and waits.

"I had a change of heart," I mumble.

"Pardon me?"

"I'm not right for those roles."

"We're talking about acting, not typecasting," Mr. Gabor says.

I hesitate. What can I say? "Well, for one thing, I can't do Ophelia," I murmur.

"Why not?"

"I don't like her," I explain. "She's weak. She lets everyone walk all over her. She's so pathetic."

"Pathetic?" Mr. Gabor asks. He glares at me with black crow eyes. I shrink back into my chair. Mr. Gabor paces the room. "Epstein, why does Ophelia go mad?" It's like he's giving me a pop quiz.

I scramble for an answer. "Because Hamlet treats her badly. And because she loves him and she thought he loved her back."

"And . . ."

"And, she feels betrayed?"

"Yes. Betrayed, by a bunch of self-serving, ambitious men. Her own father exploits her in his sycophantic desire to please the king. Hamlet spurns her. Her heart is broken. She's an innocent girl trapped in an era where women are treated like chattel. Is that what you'd call pathetic, Epstein? You don't feel any compassion for Ophelia?"

I gulp. "Well, yeah. I do."

"Then . . ." He opens his palms, questioningly.

"She sings," I say. "I can't sing."

Mr. Gabor sighs, exasperated. "Then, Gertrude."

"She's despicable," I say.

Mr. Gabor laughs. "Despicable is good. Actors love despicable. It gives them something to work with. It's like getting cast as the Wicked Witch. No one wants Dorothy; the witch is the scene-stealer. The witch has balls! And so does Gertrude. Gertrude is a lady seduced by powerful men. Interesting type, wouldn't you say?"

I nod. I look at my feet. On any other day, I'd be thrilled to be sitting here discussing Shakespeare with Mr. Gabor, but today, I just don't see the point. If Mr. Gabor is trying to make me feel bad about passing up a chance to do *Hamlet* with him, he's doing a great job.

Mr. Gabor watches me. Finally, he says, "Epstein, I don't know what's going on with you, but I'm having callbacks this afternoon. Since you were 'struck down by illness' yesterday, I will allow you to audition today." He picks up his papers and straightens them. "You may leave now." He nods toward the door.

I sit on the chair like a lump of clay. His offer is generous. More than generous. He's giving me a chance to prove myself. He doesn't have to do that. I wish I could throw my arms around him and thank him, or tell him the truth about what's going on, but it's not just Carla, or Ian, or my mom. I'm in the wrong place. Someone put my card in the wrong file. My whole world is cracking up.

"I'm sorry, Mr. Gabor, I can't," I say. Mr. Gabor looks up, surprised. And then, in a stupid attempt at humor, I add, "So, who's your second choice for Gertrude? Carla?"

Mr. Gabor's face turns to stone. He says, "Ms. Cabrielli does have a callback today, and yes, she is a challenge to work with, but unlike you, Epstein, I like a challenge."

That stings. I lurch out of my chair. Mr. Gabor reaches the door first. "Epstein, talk to me," he says. I shake my head. He hunches over. He peers right into my face, forcing me to look at him. Softly, he says, "You're making a mistake, and not just about the audition. You're living too much up here," he taps his head, "like Hamlet. At some point, you're going to have to step into the light, whether it's the stage light or the light of day."

Tears well up in my eyes. "I can't," I say.

"Can't or won't?"

"Can't."

He sucks in a breath. "That's too bad. You could've learned a lot. And you could've had fun."

"I know," I say. I push open the door. I bolt out of his office and race down the hall, but there's nowhere to run to. I'm a fool and a coward. I'm a child in a fairy tale who's lost in the woods, and it's getting dark outside, and no one's coming to rescue me anymore.

CARLA

"Ain't No Mountain High Enough"

The morning after callbacks, the cast list is tacked to the studio door. I know I really aced the auditions, but still, my stomach is churning like a cement mixer. I muscle my way through the huddle of theater students, and there, beside Gertrude is . . . drum roll . . . *Carla Cabrielli*! My name! I scream my head off. And just below, for Laertes, *Ian Slater*!

"Yes! Yes!" I fling my arms around Ian's neck. I feel like I just won an Olympic gold medal. And now, stepping onto the podium for Canada, Carla Cabrielli! I jump into Ian's arms. Ian grins and does a little fencing jab. He's thrilled. And why not? He's the perfect Laertes. And to think I had to beg him to audition. I knew his fencing would give him the edge. Besides, he's so hot he could be a prop and still chew up the scenery.

I check the cast list to see who else got in. Geoff got Hamlet—no surprise—but it pisses Ian off because Geoff is such a crappy fencer, and now Ian will have to fence against him. Jeremy and Jason got the two comic friends, Rosencrantz and Guildenstern. The rest of the parts go to the grade twelves and thirteens. Ian can't wipe the smile off his face.

I swoop down the hall, waving students out of my path, shouting, "Make way for the queen. Make way for the queen."

After school, we have our first cast meeting, and Ian and I waltz into the studio together. It feels so great to have a lead—so much better than a chorus girl. Mr. Gabor gives us the old pep talk about hard work and commitment. Rehearsals begin in mid-February, "which will give everyone time to memorize their lines," he adds, looking directly at Ian. Yeah, we all know that Ian can fence, but can he actually learn his lines? Mr. Gabor is taking a chance on him. I hope Ian is up for it.

Ma and Papa are totally impressed that I actually scored a part in a Shakespeare play, but when I mention that Ian got a role too, Pa's forehead creases into angry little waves. "What kind of part did that *cafone* get?" he asks.

"A good part. Laertes. He fights a duel."

"Figures," Papa snorts.

"Papa, it's an important role. Lots of people tried out for it. Ian is very talented," I say.

"I thought you gave that boy the boot."

"Yeah, well, we made up," I say. "And now we're going to be rehearsing together, so could you please try to be nice to him?"

Papa glowers. "I don't trust him."

"Pa, please! This is for school," I plead. "And it's a really big deal for me."

Ma says, "Tony, *basta*! They're doing Shakespeare. Let

them be." I give Ma a grateful smile, and then I look at Pa with puppy-dog eyes.

Papa huffs, like I'm not fooling him for a second. He fixes me with his beady glare. "Don't give me anything to complain about," he growls.

"I won't," I say, hugging him. *"Ti voglio bene, Papà."*

Ian and I are going to be very, very careful.

The truth is, Ian and I are having sex all the time. So, the day after auditions, Debbie and Marlene escort me to the women's health clinic downtown so I can get the pill. Sherrie's right: It's a snap. You say you're having sex; you get a prescription. You go to a drugstore; they give you the pills. Deb and Mar are so impressed. And Ian is happy because he doesn't like using condoms. He likes doing it "au naturel." These days, he even asks me over to his house. Funny how it's suddenly okay to sneak me into his bedroom now that he's getting laid.

Deb and Mar are dying to know all about my sex life. We sit in my kitchen drinking coffee, and I tell them that I have no regrets.

"Losing your virginity is just part of growing up," I say. "And actually, having sex makes me feel more like a woman."

"As opposed to a man?" Deb asks sarcastically.

"Carla, you're such a drama queen," Marlene says.

"I'm just telling you how I feel," I say.

"Well, tell us what it's like," Debbie says. She always wants the play-by-play.

"Look, I can't divulge the nitty-gritty," I say, "but what I *can* tell you is, like they say in baseball, Ian has soft hands. And he knows what he's doing when his 'fingers do the walkin'.'"

Deb and Mar squeal with laughter. "Go on," Mar says.

"Well," I say, "he's very experienced. And he's not the kind of guy who's done in two seconds, if you catch my drift." At least not when he's drunk.

"Well, how long does it take?" Mar asks. "I mean, once he's in."

"I don't know," I say. "I don't have a stopwatch."

"Have you had an orgasm?" Deb asks.

"Of course," I say, although I'm not really sure.

"What does it feel like?" Mar asks.

"It's hard to describe," I say. I think about how Ian looks just before he comes. "It's like a wave, getting bigger and bigger, until it finally crashes onto the shore, and then sinks, exhausted, into the sand." I think that's pretty poetic.

Marlene looks unimpressed. "That's it?"

I do an imitation of Ian. "It's like *uhn, uhn, uhn . . . aaah*!"

Deb snorts. "It sounds like you're taking a big dump."

Mar giggles hysterically.

"Did you give him a blow job yet?" Deb asks.

"No!" I say. "I'm not doing that. I'm not putting that thing in my mouth. Who knows when he had a shower last. Ew! Get real!"

"He's going to want it," Deb warns. "And then you'll have to decide if you're going to swallow."

"Yech!" Mar says, making a face. "I will never do that! Ew. I think I'd gag. Ew."

"Yeah," I say. "If God wanted us to put men's dicks in our mouths, he would have made them taste like chocolate." At that, we collapse with laughter, and it occurs to me that talking about sex with Debbie and Marlene is almost as fun as doing it with Ian.

JULES

"Our House"

"The house is sold," Mom tells Bobby and me at the end of February. "The people move in on June 1st." I almost laugh. Things can't get much worse.

"Are we buying a new house?" Bobby asks excitedly. "Here? Near Buzz?"

"I don't know," Mom says.

"So when's Dad coming?" Bobby asks.

Mom sighs irritably. "I just don't know."

Dad calls at dinnertime. Mom takes the phone in her bedroom. After they talk, she doesn't come out. I don't know why she's so grumpy. This is exactly what she wanted.

At nine o'clock, Dr. Katzenberg's Cadillac pulls into the driveway. Mom walks out of her bedroom and heads straight to the front door. She says, "I'll be back later." And that's it: Off she goes. I wonder how Carla found out about them. Did she see them holding hands at a restaurant? And why is Mom running off to see Dr. Katzenberg tonight? Is she going to call off their affair because our house is sold and Dad is coming? Is that why she's so unhappy?

Outside, it begins to snow.

At midnight, Bobby is snoring softly, and Mom still isn't home. I read in bed, and then I go downstairs and peek out the front window. Snowflakes are falling thick and fast. A single lane of tire tracks runs down the center of the road. I wonder if the streets are slippery tonight. I picture Dr. Katzenberg driving his Cadillac down Cummer hill, skidding and losing control. The scene plays out in my head, in slow motion. He applies the brakes. The brakes lock. The two of them sit frozen in terror. The car hurtles down the hill, over the bridge, and crashes into the ravine below. Would they both die instantly, or would they suffer first? I imagine my mother's head at an odd angle, crunched against the shattered windshield, blood pooling onto the dashboard and slowly dripping into her lap.

At one-thirty, I begin to worry. Where is she? She's never this late. When I was little and Mom and Dad went on holiday, I used to worry that something terrible would happen to them—a plane crash, or a bomb in a hotel. I'd stand in my nightgown, staring out the window, making bargains with a storybook god for their safe return. And they always did return, relaxed and smiling, sweeping us into their tanned arms, and we'd be a happy family once again.

At two in the morning, there is no sound except the ticking clock on the mantel. Perhaps my mother and Dr. Katzenberg are on a plane to Spain, or Italy, or some other romantic

Mediterranean country. Will she cry knowing she's abandoning us to run away with her lover, or will she be happy to finally leave me behind because I'm so difficult to live with?

At two-fifteen, I make a deal with myself: If Mom comes back in the next five minutes, I will apologize for being moody and rude, and I will promise to try harder. I extend the deal to 2:25. At two-thirty, the deal expires.

Just after two-thirty, headlights bounce down the street, and Dr. Katzenberg's Cadillac pulls into the driveway. I dash upstairs and watch from the darkness of my bedroom. Mom doesn't get out right away. They sit there with the motor running. From my window, I can see their laps, but not their faces. He puts his hand on top of hers. Five minutes later, she unbuckles her seat belt. She leans over and they hug. Are they kissing? I can't see. I pull back from the window and lie on my bed.

I stare at the ceiling wishing Dad were here. I wish it was him in the car with Mom, squeezing her hand and calling her Natty-Tomaty, the way he does when he's teasing her. He hasn't called her that in a long time, but he always knows how to make her smile. I think about the time, when I was little, when Mom was at the sink doing the dishes and Dad snuck up behind her. He grabbed her by the waist and waltzed her around the kitchen, crooning some corny love song in her ear. They twirled and laughed, and dish soap dripped off her yellow rubber gloves, making soapy puddles on the linoleum floor.

So, how can she throw it all away? I hope she's telling Dr.

Katzenberg that it's over between them now, because she has two children and a husband who loves her. I hope she's doing the right thing.

On Sunday afternoon, Mom sets the dining room table, putting out a white tablecloth, wine glasses and the good china. She cooks our favorite meal: standing rib roast and potatoes, the meal we always used to have on Friday nights when Grandma and Grandpa Cohen came for dinner. At first, I assume she invited the Cabriellis, but then I notice that there are only four plates. "Who's coming?" I ask.

Mom answers, "Dr. Katzenberg."

I stare at her, shocked.

Sure enough, at six o'clock, Dr. Katzenberg shows up with a bottle of wine and a big smile on his face. He's wearing jeans and a sweater, trying for the casual look, like we're all just pals hanging out together. Mom, Bobby and I take our usual places, and Dr. Katzenberg sits at the head of table, in Dad's seat, which makes me think of the way Claudius took over Hamlet's father's throne. Usurper. Thief. Betrayer. Traitor. *"He that hath killed my king and whored my mother."*

Dr. Katzenberg offers me a glass of wine (poisoned, like Hamlet's wine that Gertrude drinks at the end of the play?), but I refuse. He compliments Mom on her delicious roast beef. Bobby tells him about our Friday night dinners in

Montreal, and how Mom always cooked a charred hamburger for Grandpa Cohen instead of the roast. "Because Grandpa likes his meat burnt," Bobby explains eagerly, "so we call the hamburger Grandpa's hockey puck, 'cause it's black and hard, but that's what he eats."

Dr. Katzenberg has a good laugh and Mom gives Bobby a warm smile, but I don't like the way Bobby is entertaining Dr. Katzenberg with our private family stories. Our family is none of his business. When Dr. Katzenberg asks me about school, I reply with curt one-word answers. I slice my food, but I can't bring it to my mouth. I push the meat around my plate, but in my mind, I'm leaping across the table and jabbing my steak knife into the jolly doctor's throat, like Hamlet slaying Claudius: *"Thou incestuous, murd'rous damned Dane."*

As soon as Dr. Katzenberg puts down his cutlery, I jump up to clear the table. Mom says, "There's no rush, Julia," but I ignore her and grab the plates. Dr. Katzenberg offers to help, but Mom says, "We're fine."

I walk into the kitchen and furiously scrape the bones into the garbage. Mom follows right on my heels. She hisses, "Will you please behave yourself."

I kick the kitchen door shut. "What do you think you're doing?" I ask.

Mom bristles. "I am trying to have a civilized dinner."

"With *him*?"

"I'm not having this conversation—"

"You're sleeping with him, aren't you?" I snap.

"Julia! We're just *friends*," she says.

"Oh yeah?" I sneer. "You don't stay out with 'friends' till two-thirty in the morning."

Mom gives a sharp laugh. "You don't know what you're talking about. This is a platonic relationship. Do you understand me?"

"No, I don't." I glare at her.

"Well, I'm sorry," she says. "I can't help you." She shrugs and turns away from me.

I feel Hamlet's words rise up in my throat, the words he spoke to his own mother, reminding her of the good husband she once had and of the conniver who stole his place. I say: *"This was your husband. Look you now what follows . . . / Have you eyes?. . . / O shame, where is thy blush?"*

Mom spins around. "What?"

But the dark prince is in my blood. No more deceit. No more lies. I will not stay in this foul house with that scheming villain for one more second. I dump the dishes and fly out of the room.

"Where are you going?" Mom calls.

"Out."

Geoff is surprised to see me. Things have been awkward between us since the auditions, but now all that is swept aside. I burst into the apartment and throw myself on the divan. "My mother is having an affair," I say.

Geoff blinks. "You're joking, right?"

"She says it's platonic."

"So, maybe it is."

"She's lying. I can tell by the way they look at each other."

"They, who?"

"My mom and her boss." I explain about Dr. Katzenberg. "I thought she was going to end it with him, but instead, she invited him over for dinner. He sat in my father's chair." I gulp. "I think she's going to leave my dad." It feels weird to say it out loud.

Geoff looks horrified. "What are you going to do?" he asks.

And suddenly it comes to me. It's like the answer has been there all along, just waiting for me to see it. "I'm going home, to Montreal," I say.

"You're not!" Geoff exclaims.

"I have to," I say. "When my dad finds out about this, he's going to be shattered. He'll need me."

"I need you," Geoff says. "You and me, we're like a team. Without you, I'd be like Tracey without Hepburn, Gilbert without Sullivan, Rogers without Hammerstein—"

"I get it," I interrupt.

"But who am I going to have lunch with?" Geoff asks. "And you're not going to miss *Hamlet*, are you? Jules! You promised you'd help me with the fencing! Ian hates me. He keeps trying to kill me."

"He's Laertes. It's his job to try and kill you."

"Well, he's very convincing," Geoff says. I laugh, but Geoff doesn't. He says, "Clarissa already bought the champagne. Who am I going to celebrate with?"

"You'll drink with your other friends," I say.

"I don't have other friends."

"Yes, you do. You're Hamlet. Everyone wants to hang out with you."

Geoff sighs dramatically. "They're just fair-weather friends, my dear. They'll drink my champagne, and then they'll be gone. You're only as good as your last show. One failure, and they won't come around anymore. Next thing you know, I'll be washed up and broke, like Frances Farmer. Where were her friends at the end?"

"Who is Frances Farmer?" I ask. Geoff rolls his eyes, and we both laugh. "Geoff, I have to do this," I say firmly. "I'm finally on the right path." I stare out the window at the sooty snow and the soulless streets of suburbia. Very soon I'll be leaving this place, and Toronto will be just a detour I took on the highway of my life. "It's a good thing I didn't get a role in *Hamlet*," I say. "Maybe this was meant to be."

I turn back to smile at Geoff, but there are tears in his eyes. And suddenly I feel selfish and mean. Why is it always like this: one person leaving and the other person left behind?

CARLA

"Eve of Destruction"

Deb and Mar are mad because they say I'm too busy to make time for them. Well, duh, it's true. I am too busy. They don't seem to understand that when you have rehearsals every day, a boyfriend with a strong sex drive and homework to do, there's not a lot of time left over. I'm exhausted! This play is a lot of work! I mean, sure, the first two weeks of rehearsals were fun, but it's one thing to block scenes with a script in your hand, and it's another thing to memorize the whole entire play. Especially Shakespeare. It's not like those words stick in your mind. And they certainly don't stick in *Ian's* mind. Mr. Gabor is furious with him.

On Saturday night, when Ian's parents go out, I sit in his basement and broach the subject. "Look," I say as he lights up a joint, "Mr. Gabor is losing patience with you. You really have to learn your lines." Ian ignores me. I sigh. "Ian, we're supposed to be off book. We only have three weeks left."

"Stop bugging me, okay?" he says. He sucks on the joint and holds it out to me.

I shake my head. "Why don't we run lines right now? We

278

can turn it into a game. Strip poker! It will be fun. For every line you get right, you get to take off a piece of my clothes. And at the end, we get to fuck like bunnies."

"Let's just fuck," Ian says.

After sex, Ian and I go to the Pickle Barrel for something to eat, because God forbid we should eat something at his house in case his parents walk in and actually meet me. They probably don't even know I exist. We order smoked-meat sandwiches and Coke. I say, "Wouldn't it be nice if we could spend the whole night together and not have to sneak around all the time?"

Ian says, "Yeah. We should leave town."

"Yeah." I laugh, but then I see he's not joking. "What do you mean?"

"We could take off on my bike and go somewhere warm, like Arizona, or Mexico."

"Like a little road trip?" I ask.

"Like leaving and never coming back."

"Oh," I say. We both bite into our smoked-meat sand-wiches. Suddenly I have a fluttery feeling in my stomach, because maybe he's actually serious about this. Is he asking me to run away with him? Does this mean he loves me? He's never actually said those words, but maybe he does. After all, you don't ask just anyone to run off to Mexico. I bet he never asked Kimmy to run away.

I sip my Coke and practically shiver with excitement. I picture Ian and me, like Peter Fonda and Dennis Hopper in

Easy Rider, biking across America with the open road ahead of us, meeting cool people, camping under the stars and making love in the moonlight. I imagine how great we'd look on his bike with our hair blowing in the wind as we tour the Grand Canyon and Yosemite National Park. So free, so romantic, so spontaneous, so alive.

But then I think about what happened to Peter Fonda and Dennis Hopper at the end of *Easy Rider*, when those rednecks shot them, and maybe this isn't such a fun idea after all. Maybe we'd end up driving for hours and hours across the burning desert, and I'd get sand in every crevice of my body. My bum would be sore from sitting on that bike all day, and I'd be absolutely bored to death. I'd get heatstroke, and Ian and I would have a stupid fight in some dumpy, run-down roadside café because, by that time, we'd be sick and tired of each other and grumpy from sleeping in campgrounds and fleabag motels. Ian would have one of his little temper tantrums, and he'd toss my bag into the dirt. Then he'd leave me sitting in a dusty booth in the middle of hick-town nowheresville. I'd be broke. So I'd have to get a job as a maid at Motel 6 in Death Valley. And the owner would be a fat, greasy, alcoholic pig who would jump me, get me pregnant and then fire me. I'd have to hitchhike with a trucker all the way to San Francisco to have an abortion, which I couldn't afford. In the end, I'd probably bleed to death in the back room of some flophouse, with no one to hear my dying words, which would be *Ian, you are such a selfish prick!*

I look across the table at Ian. He is a prick, but he's my prick. And I don't always like him, but I think I love him. I reach across the table and rub my finger along the worn cuff of his leather jacket. I tug at his sleeve. "Would you really like to run away with me?" I ask.

He looks across the table at me. "You'd never do it."

"Maybe I would."

He chews on his sandwich, watching me. Then he says, "Girls like you don't leave home."

"What do you mean, 'girls like me'?"

"Girls who are used to getting everything they want."

"Are you saying I'm spoiled?" I ask.

"I'm saying you don't have the guts to do it, that's all. You don't want it badly enough."

"How do you know what I want?" I say. "I happen to be a very complex person."

Ian reaches for our two glasses of Coke. He slides one glass in front of my plate, leaving a sloppy, wet trail across the vinyl tabletop. "Okay," he says. "This one is freedom." He slides the other glass beside it. "This is your family, friends, university, holidays, nice clothes, parents who pay for every- thing." He looks at me. "Drink one."

I look at the glasses and back at Ian. "Maybe I'll drink both," I say.

"You only get one. That's how it works."

"Then I'm not playing."

Ian smirks. "That's what I figured."

I feel set up. Why does it have to be either-or? He's always putting me on the spot. "Look," I say, "even if I wanted to go with you, I'm not quite seventeen, I have no money, and we're both doing *Hamlet*. You have to be realistic, even when it comes to love." I actually say that word out loud. For a second, it hangs between us like a thought bubble. Then Ian throws some money on the table, reaches for the freedom glass and downs it all in one long gulp.

In school, just when I think rehearsals cannot get any worse, they do. How? Well, as that poet says, *"Let me count the ways."* Number one, there's Ophelia. If I have to listen to her sing *"Hey, nonny, nonny"* one more time, in that grating, high-pitched psycho voice, I'm going to wring her scrawny neck.

Number two, there's the duel scene. Geoff fences like a gay pirate, and he makes the fight look ridiculous. And if we have a crappy duel scene, this whole play is going to sink like the *Titanic*. Yesterday, in the middle of the fight rehearsal, Ian lost it and sent Geoff sprawling across the floor. Mr. Gabor read Ian the riot act, and now Ian's walking around like a ticking time bomb.

Number three, there's my dress. Madame Grenier, the French teacher, is in charge of costumes, and you'd think that a person from Paris would understand a thing or two about fashion. But no. Today, she and her little troupe of sewing elves finally bring in the costumes, and when they pull out mine—it's hideous. First of all, it's olive green. Who looks good in olive green? Only an olive. I look good in lots of greens: lime green, kelly green, hunter green, even chartreuse—but *not* olive green. Couldn't Madame Grenier have noticed that? Out of all the fabulous colors in the world, couldn't she have picked something pretty?

Well, I take one look at that monstrosity and I say, "Mr. Gabor, I will not wear this dress."

He says, "Go try it on."

I say, "What's the point? I'm not going to wear it."

He gives me the Gabor glare, so I snatch up the dress and drag it into the girls' gym change room, where Ophelia is trying on her gown. Ophelia's gown is a soft, flowing, pink chiffon number with a low neck and a tightly fitted bodice. It's elegant and flattering. And I'm jealous. I'm green with envy—make that *olive* green—because she looks great, and as I climb into my heavy, bulky gown with the chin-high collar and the long trailing skirt, I know that I look like a big fat olive with a frilly white neckline. I want to scream.

Ophelia looks at me and says, "Whew!" And then, scrambling for words, "That's a lot of material. Can you move in that dress?"

"Can I move? Just watch me," I snarl. I grab fistfuls of leaden cloth, charge out of the change room and head straight for the auditorium. The guys are wearing tights and tunics, laughing and making fun of each other—except for Ian, who is refusing to put on his tights because he doesn't "want to look like a fag." Claudius's crown keeps falling off his head. Horatio's tunic is too big. Madame Grenier and the sewing elves are taking notes and snipping threads. Everyone is trying to get Mr. Gabor's attention.

Jeremy sees me and nearly chokes with laughter. I say, "One word, nerd face, and you're dog food." So he shuts his trap. I elbow my way to the front of the line. "Mr. Gabor!" He looks at my dress and frowns.

He says, "Turn around and let me see."

I try to turn, but some idiot is standing on the train of my dress, and I hear this little ripping sound. "Oops," says the girl behind me. "That can be fixed." She bends over and examines the dress. "It's just the hem."

"Fuck the hem," I say.

Mr. Gabor glares at me. "Carla! This is Mary." He gives me a warning look. "Mary is the student who sewed your dress."

Well, I whirl around and come face-to-face with the numskull who's ruining my life—a piggy-faced girl with bad acne and obviously no taste in clothes.

"*You* made this dress?" I say.

She nods proudly. "It's a French brocade."

"I don't care what the hell it is. There's too much of it, and it makes me look fat. I am *not* fat!"

Mary gulps. "I can take in the waist."

"And what about the neck?" I say. "It's choking me. It's too tight. And the dress weighs a bloody ton. It's like wearing a tank. I'm sweating bullets, and I'm not even onstage yet. And who chose this awful color? No one looks good in olive green!" At which point, I notice that Mary is wearing an olive green turtleneck sweater. And even she doesn't look good in it.

Mary squeaks. Madame Grenier steps in to defend her quivering protégé. "Mary worked hours on zat dress! How dare you speak to her like zis!" she says in her huffy French accent.

"I dare because I am Gertrude," I snap. "I'm the one who has to wear this dress. The dress has to work for *me*. I am the queen of Denmark. Not an old hag. Not a virgin. A powerful, lusty, sex-driven queen who's humping King Claudius like a lovesick rabbit. So wouldn't you think that a queen like that would wear a stylish, hot, red number with a bit of cleavage, instead of this ugly olive green piece of shit?"

Mary bursts into tears. Everyone in the room stares at me. I grab the collar of my dress and rip it right out of its seams. I fling it to the floor like a dead animal. I say, "I want another dress." In the change room, I claw my way out of that sticky, clammy gown, and when I walk back into the hall, Mr. Gabor is waiting for me.

He says, "The dress is ugly."

I smile, thinking I've won, but then I notice his face, which is darkening like a storm cloud.

"But it is not nearly as ugly as the way you treated that girl," he growls. His voice rumbles like a rockslide. "There are no prima donnas in my show. You are a student, you are *not* a queen, and unless you apologize to Mary right now, you are not getting up on that stage."

I feel my face turning red. I know he's mad, but I think he's bluffing. "I won't," I say.

Mr. Gabor turns and walks.

"No one can do my part," I call out. "You can't replace me a week before the show."

Without turning, he says softly, "Oh, I'll find someone."

And *bam*—I know exactly who he means. Julia. He'll ask Julia. It's like she's always there, lurking in the wings, trying to steal my boyfriend and now trying to steal my part. Well, forget that. I don't care if I have to crawl on my hands and knees across a field of cut glass and grovel in front of that stupid sewing elf—there is no way Julia Epstein is ever going to get my part!

So, I do it. I walk back into the auditorium and I apologize to Mary. I say I'm sorry, but I don't mean it. I just feel burned.

"Way Back Home"

Ironically, it's Dr. Katzenberg who provides me with the perfect opportunity to sneak out of town. He invites Mom, Bobby and me to his cottage for the Easter long weekend at the beginning of April. No one expects me to actually go. I tell Mom that I'll be busy helping Geoff with his fencing, and she believes me. *Hamlet* opens right after Easter. I buy us tickets for opening night, even though I won't be here. It's all part of the grand deception.

The only thing I feel bad about, other than missing Geoff in *Hamlet,* is leaving Bobby. The night before my escape, Bobby and I eat pizza in the kitchen. He thinks this is just another meal, but I know it's our last one. He's excited about the cottage. He talks about Dr. Katzenberg's sauna, and his fishing boat, and how the fishing season doesn't start till May. "What do the fish do in the winter?" Bobby asks.

"I don't know. Hibernate?"

Bobby laughs. "They're fish, not bears." He picks the mushrooms off his pizza. He says, "This summer, I'm going to bring my rod to the cottage, and Dr. Katzenberg is going to let me use his tackle box. We're going to fish for small-mouth bass. And maybe Dad can come too." Bobby gobbles his pizza, and we both leave the crusts. Afterward, we play Clue. I let him win. He gloats a lot. I really hope he doesn't hate me when he finds out I'm gone.

The cottagers leave Thursday evening. Bobby waves good-bye from the car. I wait for thirty minutes, just to be safe, then I grab one of Bobby's old hockey bags from the basement and pack up my stuff. I take only the essentials: clothes to see me through the winter, some jewelry and my favorite albums. I don't plan to come back here, so the rest will have to be shipped. It's liberating to pare down one's life like this. After all, how much stuff does a person really need?

After I'm packed, I write a note to my mother. I ask her to respect my decision to live with Dad. I tell her that it's best for everyone; Toronto was never my home.

At eleven-thirty, I'm wide awake. I decide that a little fresh air will do me good, one last stroll around the neighborhood. It's funny how I have to make excuses for myself, because really, I know exactly where I'm going.

There's a light on in the basement of Ian's house. I sneak along the side path to the backyard. When I tap softly on the French doors, Ian steps out of his bedroom. He's barefoot, in jeans and a T-shirt. He looks surprised to see me. "Rapunzel, Rapunzel," he says, quietly sliding the door open.

"I just came to say good-bye."

"Why good-bye?"

"I'm moving back to Montreal," I tell him. "I'm going to live with my dad. I'm finally taking control of my life."

Ian gives me a mocking smile. "So, you're leaving your lonely tower," he says.

"I'm going home, where I belong."

Ian nods. He gets it because he doesn't belong here either. "Good for you," he says. There isn't much more to say.

I look into his wolf eyes and glance at the tiny scar at the corner of his lips. I study the slope of his cheekbones and the cut of his jaw. I want to remember every part of him. I would like to tell him that he meant something to me, even if I didn't mean the same thing to him. I think that can happen between people; it doesn't always balance out.

"Well, I better go," I whisper.

"Keep up the fencing," he says. We both glance toward the sanctuary and smile. "Send me a postcard," he says. "Maybe, one day, I'll look you up."

He won't, and we both know it. So I kiss him on the lips, one last, soft, melting kiss, because that's what I came for.

Geoff insists that I take the train rather than the bus to Montreal. "If you must leave, then go in style," he says. "A train is so much more romantic than a bus. I will drive you to Union Station. I'll carry your bags and wear a brave smile, but inside, you'll know my heart will be breaking."

As promised, Geoff picks me up at six-forty-five Friday morning. It's dark and cold, but by the time we get downtown, a lemony sun is peeking between the office towers. Geoff parks Baby Blue on Front Street and carries my bag into the station. I smile to myself, thinking that even now, on my last day, Geoff is my personal tour guide to Toronto, trying to show me the best this city has to offer.

Union Station really is impressive. Even with all the people hurrying through, it feels holy and calm, like a cathedral. Geoff points out the high vaulted ceiling and the huge arched windows at either end of the great hall. Soft beams of honeyed light spill down onto the floor. Tall stone columns mark the entrance to the departure area.

"See, isn't this wonderful?" he whispers. "The grandeur. The scale."

"You were right," I say.

"No wonder Orson Welles loved train stations so much," Geoff sighs. "It's like the gods are watching us play out the entrances and exits of our lives."

Our footsteps click across the granite floor as we approach the ticket booth. I ask for a one-way ticket on the Rapido to Montreal. Geoff leans against the counter and speaks in his gangster voice. "Yeah, mister, you heard the lady. A one-way ticket outta here. She never wants to see this two-bit town again. It's good-bye to bad rubbish."

The uniformed man in the booth lifts a heavy eyelid, glances dolefully at Geoff, takes my money and slides my ticket across the counter.

We're early, so Geoff and I find a seat on a bench. Geoff fidgets. He says, "Can I buy you something? Mints? Coffee?"

"I wish I smoked cigarettes," I say.

"Yes, in an ivory cigarette holder," Geoff says, "wearing cerise lipstick and a pillbox hat—you know the kind, with the little black veil—and a three-quarter-length wraparound coat. If only you had a hatbox and a trunk." He frowns at my bag. "A hockey bag is so déclassé. If you had a trunk, we could call a porter. Would you like a porter? Wouldn't that be fun?"

I shake my head. We people-watch and invent stories about their lives: a middle-aged couple having a clandestine affair, an old man going to his estranged brother's funeral. Finally, we hear the *bing-bing-bong* tone and the announcement for the Rapido to Montreal. Geoff breaks into his Southern maid voice and says, "Ya'll better hurry along, missy, or you're gonna miss that train."

I smile at Geoff. "I'll be thinking about you on opening night. You're going to be amazing." We both get choked up and hug each other tightly. Then I pick up my hockey bag and walk between the towering columns to the blackened platform where the Rapido waits.

The train pulls out of the station, shuddering and heaving like a great iron beast. As we leave the city, I catch glimpses of Lake Ontario and clumpy, wet fields flattened by snow. Soon we're swaying and rocking down the track. I stare out the window and rehearse what I'm going to say to Dad. I line up my arguments like toy soldiers. He'll balk at first, and he'll want to speak to Mom, but he won't be able to reach her all weekend. And soon after that, he's going to find out about her affair.

When he does find out, it's going to be awful. But at least I'll be there to help. And then the two of us can make a fresh start. In June, we'll look for a smaller place—a duplex, or an apartment, like Geoff and Clarissa's. We don't even have to stay in T.M.R. We can live closer to downtown if he wants. We can shop together and share the cooking. I can bus to school and sign up for Eva von Gencsy's jazz class again. The point is, we'll have each other. Once he sees that, the rest will work out.

Five hours later, the train clunks and grinds into Montreal, past sooty factories and brick apartment blocks, where laundry hangs on clotheslines like limp, faded flags. Even before we jolt to a stop, I'm waiting at the door because I promised Geoff that I'd be the first to step onto the platform. "Like Cyd Charisse in *The Band Wagon*, when she strode off the train in her ultrasmart traveling suit where her tippet matched her muff." I don't even know what a tippet is, but I grin just remembering the way Geoff said it.

Outside, the afternoon sun is blinding. Cars speed past with license plates reading *La Belle Province*. Passersby chatter in French and English. People dart across the street, paying no attention at all to honking taxis and traffic signals because, unlike Toronto, this is a brazen city that walks, talks and plays whenever it feels like it.

I catch the number 65 bus, and we ramble past Mount Royal and swing left onto Queen Mary. At Victoria, I transfer to the 124, which takes me down the homestretch into the Town of Mount Royal. Finally, I get off at Lucerne and Algonquin, like I've done a thousand times before, and walk the two blocks to my street. I feel like bursting into song, like Julie Andrews in *The Sound of Music* when she bicycles down the lakeshore with the seven von Trapp children, singing at the top of her lungs. From the corner, I can see Dad's car parked in the driveway. He's home. I won't even have to use the hidden key.

Across the street, Mrs. Lazar is taking groceries out of her car. She looks up and her eyes widen in surprise. "Jules, how are you?"

"Great!" I say.

"We really miss you on the street."

"Me too," I say. I like Mrs. Lazar. At Halloween, she always gives out candy apples to the kids she knows. Her oldest son plays violin with Mollie in the school orchestra. I wish Mollie were here this weekend. She's in New York, auditioning for

Juilliard. But she'll be back Monday night, and Tuesday we'll walk to school together.

I wave good-bye to Mrs. Lazar and hurry past the SOLD sign on my lawn. The front door isn't locked, so I waltz right in. "Hi, I'm home," I call out.

Dad steps out of the living room. I fling myself into his arms. "Jules!" he gasps.

I squeeze him tight. "I wanted to surprise you."

He chuckles. "I'm surprised."

"Good," I say. "So, how're you doing?" I peel off my coat and kick off my boots. Dad looks down at my overstuffed hockey bag. Ah, yes, the bag's a giveaway. I realize this is going to require an immediate explanation. But that's okay. I'm prepared. "Guess what, Dad. Great news," I exclaim. "I've decided to move back here with you."

Dad stares at me like he hasn't heard right. "What?" I give him my most reassuring smile. "Julia, does your mother know you're here?"

"No," I say. "And I really don't care."

"Aw, Jules," he groans.

"Don't worry, Dad."

He rubs his forehead with the heel of his palm, the way he does when he has a big problem. "Poopsie—"

"Dad, listen to me. Mom and I aren't even speaking. I hate Toronto. And you're still here. It all makes sense. We can live together. It will be so good."

"Poopsie," he says. "It's not that simple." He sighs. "I already found an apartment—"

"Great," I say. "Two bedrooms?"

"Yeah, but—"

"Perfect."

"No." He shakes his head. "Poopsie, it's not like I don't want you to live with me—'cause maybe later, down the road, it's something we could talk about. But the timing's a little awkward right now . . ."

Something behind me catches his eye. A red Mustang is pulling into the driveway. A woman in a fur coat steps out of the car. She smiles at Dad, and he dashes outside. Her face is familiar. The real estate agent? I watch them talk in rapid-fire French. She's chic, petite, early twenties, pretty, and she's looking at me like she knows who I am. She smiles at me, so I smile back. Dad tries to coax her back to her car, but she shrugs him off and strides up the path, her boots crunching on the leftover patches of pebbly snow.

They step inside, and there's this awkward moment with the three of us crammed into the front hall. She looks at my dad and says, "Irv?" But she pronounces it "Erve," as if he's someone else entirely.

Dad sucks in a deep breath. She flicks him an annoyed look. He says, "Jules, this is Monique."

Monique extends a gloved hand. She says, "*Allo*, Julia, you remember me?"

And suddenly I do. She's the girl from Dad's store. "Yeah, hi," I say. "We met before."

"Jules is visiting for the weekend," Dad says.

"Not really," I say, looking pointedly at Dad.

Dad sighs. Monique raises an eyebrow. Dad scratches his head like a dog with fleas. Monique glares at him. Dad winces. And suddenly I can tell that something is off. There's something going on here that I'm not getting. And now Dad has a pained expression on his face. He's going to say something I don't want to hear, but I'm too stupid to figure it out. The dots are there, but I'm not connecting them. I mean, animals have instincts, but not me. I am the dumbest sheep in the flock. I just smile while my dad raises his ax in the air.

"You see, Jules," he says, "about the apartment . . . it's not going to work, because . . . the thing is . . . we're moving in together."

"Who?" I ask.

"Monique and me."

I almost laugh. I still don't get it. What is he saying? Dad and Monique? He's renting a place with the girl from his store? But he's her boss, and they have nothing in common. They won't even watch the same channel on TV.

Faintly, I hear the whoosh of the ax, but even now, it's like my mind cleaves in two. The intelligent half goes into shock, but the stupid sheep half keeps staring at Monique, thinking *I'm his daughter, and you're the clerk. Dad would never*

choose you over me. And I would be so much more fun as
a roommate.

And then, Monique's arm snakes around my dad's waist.
Freeze frame. Flash. Ka-boom. All my synapses fire at once.
Direct hit. Wave of shock. Ears ringing. Shrapnel. Blood.
Burnt flesh. Can't breathe. Can't move. Dad's mouth in slow
motion. Images burning up on the screen: ". . . was going to tell
you . . . didn't know . . . once we're settled . . . sofa bed . . ."

The ax slams deep into my chest. I hear a horrible groan,
and it's coming from me. Monique's smile fades and blurs.
Dad's arm reaches out for me. His hand squeezes my shoulder tightly, and this causes tears to spurt out of my eyes. His
head tilts. I can't hear what he's saying. It looks like his head's
going to roll off his neck, but I can't see clearly with all these
tears. I'm drowning. My breath gurgles. I'm backing away.
Baby steps. The way you retreat from a rabid dog.

"Jules . . ."

"No." I'm zipping my boots, but my hand keeps banging
against my leg. Thud-thud, thud-thud. Body convulsing. My
legs are wax. I can't breathe. I reach for my bag. Dad tries to
take it. "Let go!" I shriek. I yank it away. I swing my bag hard
at his knees. "Get away!" I screech like an old crow. "Leave
me alone!" A long, low howl.

He drops his arms. I stagger outside. I run down the street,
bag thumping, turn the corner, cross the road, stumble into
the field of my childhood school, drag my bag to the

kindergarten entrance, crumple onto the cement steps. This cannot be happening to me. Not my dad! No! No! I curl up into a tiny ball. I'm inside out. I'm a hollow gourd. I cry so hard, I almost puke. I cry until my bones ache.

Time passes. My head throbs. My head is a bowling ball. My lips are puffy, like the Pillsbury Doughboy. A thin line of drool hangs from my chin. It stretches all the way to my sleeve, like a glistening, silver spider's thread. This isn't real. I want to wake up. I stare at the big double doors of the kindergarten. I want to start my life over.

Kindergarten. I am six years old, all dressed for school: pleated navy tunic, crisp white blouse, navy knee socks, new shoes. The socks itch. I grip Mom's hand. She smiles at me. She promises she'll be right there, waiting, when I come out.

Inside, there are colored tables: red, yellow, green and blue. The teacher tells us to sit up straight, hands folded, like good children. Later, we paint. I wear a smock and stand in front of a big easel. The paint is floury and frothy on top. It smells sharp and sour, and it streaks across the paper in bright, grainy, runny lines. I paint a house with a pointy roof, a yellow sun in a blue sky, Mom, Dad, baby Bobby and me. Little stick figures, all smiling.

After, we play instruments in a band. I like the triangle because it makes a *ping* when I strike it with my silver stick. The vibrations shiver to my fingertips. *Ping!* I'm a good girl. *Ping! Ping!* Good things happen to good girls.

So what happened? I don't understand. How did I end up here? How can the person you love the most turn into the person who hurts you the most?

I stand up on stiff, unsteady legs and wander down the long street, my bag scraping against my jeans. Across the road is Dakin Park. I sit on a glossy red wooden swing. The heavy chains creak and clank. Mollie and I used to swing here for hours, higher and higher, leaning way back, so the world turned into a dizzying blur of blue sky and bright light.

The shadows lengthen. It's cold now. A couple of teenage boys appear. They smoke cigarettes, talk in loud voices and jump on the platform of the merry-go-round. They spin and laugh, and then they leave. The sun dips down behind the houses. The sky flares pink and crimson. Evening rolls in, the color of a bruise. I can't stay here, but where will I go? Not Aunt Connie's because she's my dad's sister. Maybe she already knows about him. Do they all know? Does Joe know? Is that why he gave me his dorm number? Do Bubby and Zadie Epstein know? Somehow, I don't think they do. I decide I'll stay at their house tonight. Tomorrow, I'll take the train back to Toronto. Mom won't even have to know I've been gone.

Zadie is the one who answers the door. He's wearing his usual brown pants, white shirt, black suspenders and cracked, faded leather slippers. He stares at my face for a long moment, then down at my hockey bag, then back to my face. "Jules," he says. "What a nice surprise." He hugs me gently and calls out, "Bubby! You'll never guess who's here." He pats my cheeks and leads me inside.

Bubby squawks with delight to see me. "No one told me you were coming!" she exclaims. She clutches me tightly to her shriveled, bony chest and then steps back to admire me, as if I'm a living saint, a walking, breathing miracle. "Look how tall she is," she says to Zadie. "But you've lost weight. You're too thin." She ushers me directly into the dining room, to the heart of the house, to fatten me up. If she notices my blotchy face and red eyes, she doesn't say anything.

Bubby and Zadie have already eaten, so she busily sets the table for one: a blue-and-white Wedgwood plate, a crystal goblet and heavy silver cutlery. Everything in the house comes from estate sales and auctions. The ten Epstein grand-children have all been taught to flip the plates and read the imprints of Bubby's eclectic, mismatched collection: Spode, Royal Bavarian, Crown Staffordshire, Royal Doulton. The ceiling paint is yellowed and lifting. There are cracks on the walls and dusty spiderwebs laced into the chandelier, but we all focus on Bubby's treasures: the vases, teacups, Venetian paintings and Quebec landscapes.

Bubby wobbles in from the kitchen carrying a plate bear-ing half a grapefruit, sliced into segments, topped with a maraschino cherry. A silver serrated grapefruit spoon rests on the rim. She places it before me.

"Bubby, I'm not that hungry," I say.

"You ate?" she asks, horrified.

"No, but—"

"So eat," she insists.

I push a cool wedge of grapefruit into my dry mouth. Zadie asks about school. Bubby shuffles back and forth between the kitchen and the dining room, bringing in platters of food. I offer to help, but she waves me to my seat, clucking her tongue and shaking her head. Finally, when all the food is arranged in front of me, she sits down and asks if I've seen my father yet.

"I dropped by the house, but he wasn't there," I lie. "Maybe I could stay here tonight."

Bubby looks puzzled, but she says she'd be "deee-lighted." She says, "Your father's always busy these days." She puckers her lips, as if she's bitten into a sour apple. "He comes over to the house once a week for dinner. He reads the paper, and then he leaves." Zadie reaches for the *Gazette* and retreats to the den. I guess he's heard enough griping on this subject.

"I don't understand your parents," Bubby says, her eyes magnified behind her thick glasses. "They should not be living in two separate cities. A family needs to be together. Either your mother should move back here, or he should move there. This is ridiculous!"

So, she doesn't know about Dad. I'm not the only one who's been left in the dark.

"I know I'm old-fashioned," Bubby continues, "but I say, when there's children involved, the children come first." She wags a crooked finger in the air. "And I understand about the politics. But still. I never see you anymore. And it's the same with Seymour's family in Florida. The whole family's breaking apart." She takes a dusty, wrinkled Kleenex from her sleeve and dabs at her eyes. I know exactly how she feels. And worse is yet to come.

I sleep in my dad's musty ghost room. Bubby puts fresh sheets on the saggy bed. In the dark, I cry. My head feels slushy. My mind races on its hamster wheel. Why didn't my mother tell me the truth? How could Dad trade her in? For his store clerk? A girl half his age? She's closer in age to me than him. And when does he think he'll see me again? For holidays? With Monique? My Kleenexes pile up into a soggy, white pyramid. I can't think. I can't stop thinking. I don't sleep till early morning, and then I have violent, labyrinthine dreams.

In the morning, Bubby is in the kitchen cooking blintzes in her blackened cast-iron pan. I force a smile, but inside, I shudder: another painful trial by eating. Bubby urges me into a chair. She brings out bagels, cream cheese, lox, fresh fruit and gooseberry jam. Fortunately, I don't have to talk because she launches into a lecture about raw fish. "The Japanese eat their fish raw," she says, her face contorting into a grimace. "And raw fish have worms." She opens a drawer crammed with yellowing newspaper clippings. Her fingers flutter through the deep pile until she finds the fish article. "Read this. Worms. A boy died!" I skim the article. I promise that raw fish will never touch my lips, except for lox, which, being smoked and Jewish, is okay.

The buzzer rings. Bubby's eyes widen like Mr. Magoo's from the cartoons. "Who could that be?" She shuffles to the door, but I already know who it is.

Dad walks in, all smiles. "Hey, poopsie, how're you doing?" he asks. He slides into the chair opposite me.

"Do you want some blintzes?" Bubby asks him.

"Could I say no?" Dad winks at me. Yesterday, I might have winked back, but not today. Those days are done. As soon as Bubby leaves the room, Dad drops his smile and leans across the table. "Did you tell her anything?" he whispers.

"No."

He exhales, relieved. Obviously, the idea of his parents knowing about Monique has been gnawing at him. "I don't want to upset her," he explains.

What about upsetting me? I think. "So you'd rather lie," I mumble.

Dad sighs. "Jules, I didn't want you to find out like that."

"How *did* you want me to find out?"

Bubby calls out, "Irv, coffee?"

"Sure, Ma." He turns back to me. "After breakfast, I'll take you to the house, and we'll have a talk."

"About what?" I ask. "Why you're dumping my mother? Or why you're screwing your store clerk?"

"Don't you speak to me like that, young lady," he hisses. "I am still your father."

"Funny, you don't act like it."

We hear the sound of a coffee cup rattling on its saucer as Bubby totters into the room. Zadie walks down the hall. He says, "I thought I heard Irv's voice."

I can't bear to look at my dad. Bubby heaps blintzes on my plate. Dad chats with Zadie about the store. I glance at his receding hairline and his paisley shirt, which suddenly seems too young for him. It's embarrassing; he's going to be the joke of the family. *Did you see Irv with his French-Canadian shiksa? Hoo-ha, what a babe. She's young enough to be his daughter. Next thing you know, he'll be driving a red Camaro and going to the disco.*

Dad looks across the table at me and says, "So, how's Bobby doing in school?" Is he actually trying to make small talk with me? "He had a good hockey season, eh?"

I don't respond. I don't care who's in the room; I am not playing this game.

"Is your mom enjoying her job?" he asks.

I want to throw hot coffee in his face. Bubby looks from Dad to me. I get up. "I have to check the train schedule," I say.

As I leave the room, Bubby asks Dad, "What's going on?" I don't know what lie he tells her, but by the time I come back downstairs, Dad and Zadie are reading the paper, and Bubby is clearing the table.

"I'm catching the noon train," I say.

"You're going back today?" Bubby asks. "You just got here!"

"I have things to do." Dad offers to drive me to the station. I say, "I'll take the bus."

Zadie says, "Don't be silly. Your father will drive you. Especially with your heavy bag." Zadie looks me right in the eye. He doesn't say much, but he's nobody's fool.

Bubby packs me a lunch. Zadie gives me a chocolate bar from his stash in the sideboard. I kiss them both. Bubby presses her soft, papery face against my cheek and whispers, "I love you, darling. Remember that. No matter what, I love you." She looks at me with tears in her eyes, and I can't decide if she knows something or if these are just the tears of parting.

In the car, Dad and I stare straight ahead. He drums his fingers on the steering wheel. Finally, he says, "I know you're upset. I don't blame you." He glances at me. "Your mother wanted me to tell you in person. I was going to come down and tell you soon."

"And the rest of the family? Do they know?"

Dad nods. "They know."

"Oh." I bite down hard. I can feel my jawbone right up to my ears.

Dad sighs. "Look, Jules, it's not like I went looking for this. Monique and me . . . we fell in love. It's just something that happened, okay?" I can't believe he's saying this—like having an affair isn't a choice. Like it's an act of God, an earthquake, a volcanic eruption, something totally out of his control. He says, "You know, your mother and I had a lot of good years together, but sometimes people drift apart."

"You cheated on her," I say. "That's not drifting."

"Jules, come on . . ."

"When did this start?"

"It doesn't matter."

"It matters to *me*!"

Dad shrugs. "Almost two years."

"Two years?" I stare at him. "Dad, that girl is half your age! It's like you're dating our babysitter."

"Stop it!" he barks. "The marriage is over. I know it's sad, but we have to move on. And the fact is, you're older now. You don't need me that much anymore. We're all starting a new chapter."

"You're abandoning us!"

"I'm not abandoning you!" he shouts. "I love you. You're my children. You're the most important thing in the world to me."

"Could've fooled me," I mutter.

Dad slams his fist on the steering wheel. "You think this is easy for me? You think I didn't struggle with this? The whole family is against me. Nobody's giving Monique a chance. And it's not her fault. She's a gem. Smart. Funny. We're good for each other. And she wants to get to know you kids. Next time you come, we'll all go out for dinner."

Is he kidding? I almost laugh. I picture us at the House of Wong eating pineapple chicken and fried wonton with all the other Jewish families craning their necks to stare at us. Bobby, me, Dad and the nubile Monique, who will stick out like a sore thumb. The husbands will take a long hard look at her, and the wives will sneer and order extra plum sauce. I almost pity her. Does she realize what she's getting into? Aunt Rose will call her the bimbo. And what will she do at Passover dinners? Will anyone even speak to her? Does Dad actually think that just because he's smitten with her, everyone else should line up and accept this? Well, he's an idiot if he believes that. Because I'm going to hate her for the rest of my life.

"I just want to know one thing," I say. "When we moved, did you know you were never coming?"

Dad hesitates. "I wasn't sure. Your mom thought we should try again . . . but . . . well . . ."

He's not even a good liar. "You knew," I say. "You knew the whole time. You just didn't have the courage to try."

Dad pulls up to Windsor Station. He turns off the motor and looks at me. "I know this is hard on you," he says, "but you'll adjust. And you can visit us anytime. I'll buy you a ticket. Just name the date. Poopsie? Okay?" He looks at me with pleading eyes.

I shove my door open. Dad lumbers to the trunk and grabs my hockey bag. "I'm sorry," he says as he passes it to me. "When you're older, you'll understand." What a stupid thing to say. I'll never understand this. He tries to hug me, but I push past him. He calls out, "You're still my favorite girl." I just keep on walking.

On the train, I get a window seat. The whistle shrieks. The engine hisses. The train clanks and lurches ahead. Hamlet whispers into my ear: *"How weary, stale, flat, and unprofitable / Seem to me all the uses of this world!"* We pass through the shadowed alleys of the city. It's hard to believe that, only yesterday, I saw everything in reverse.

The city gives way to open fields flecked with scraps of hardened snow. Lakes, like mirrors, shine with silvery light. The sky is a pearly blue. The train rocks me in its steely arms. A lady beside me passes me tissues. She says, "All things pass in time, dear." But I have no use for platitudes. I will never live in Montreal again, and I will never love my father again, at least not the way I used to.

At Union Station, I step off the train, light-headed and hollowed out. I feel like a stranger returning from a long journey, like I've been away for two years instead of two days. I take the subway and bus back to the McDuff house. In the early evening light, the houses shimmer in a pink glow. The air is soft, and the neighborhood is quiet. The street is empty—deserted, or maybe enchanted. It's as if, while I was away, everyone was put under a magical sleeping spell, but now, when I put my key back into the lock, life will resume as if no time has passed at all.

It's only when I reach the front door that I realize I don't have my house key. I left it on my mother's pillow, a symbolic token of my departure. Mom and Bobby aren't back till Monday. The only spare key is at the Cabriellis'. They're away for the long weekend, but Ian's motorcycle is in the driveway, so I guess Carla must be home.

I knock on the door. Carla answers. She's the last person I want to see right now, and I can tell the feeling is mutual. I explain about the key. She doesn't invite me in. "I'll check the kitchen drawer," she says, disappearing into the house.

Ian steps into the hall. He's surprised to see me. Yeah, how humiliating. He says, "I thought you were moving away."

I shrug. Carla can't find the key. In the kitchen, I try to phone Geoff, but there's no answer. Carla and Ian stare at me. I guess I must look pretty beat. And, obviously, I have nowhere to go.

Ian says, "You can hang out here. We're having a party tonight."

"What?" Carla says.

"I invited people," Ian says.

"Well, uninvite them!" Carla orders.

"Carla, chill. Your parents are away."

Carla glares at him. "I don't care. This is my house. I don't want a party. We have plans." Ian shrugs. He takes three beers out of the fridge. He passes one to me, and I go downstairs. Carla and Ian yell at each other in the kitchen. I curl up on the couch and cover my ears. I drink a beer. I close my eyes, but sleep won't come.

CARLA

"You Can't Always Get What You Want"

At eleven o'clock, Ma's house is littered with beer bottles, cigarettes and garbage. Ian, Jim and a bunch of band groupies are in the basement with the music cranked up. The entire cast and crew of *Hamlet* is here. Julia Epstein is here. Even Mary, the frumpy little sewing elf is here. Yup, Ian invited everyone. My home is a bloody three-ring circus. And me, I'm sitting in the kitchen, eating my way through an entire frozen Pepperidge Farm chocolate layer cake. So far, I've eaten a third of it, and I'm not sharing it with anyone.

Marlene and Debbie stare at me, disgusted.

Mar says, "You're going to be sick."

"If I am, I'll be sure to puke all over Ian," I say. Deb and Mar exchange looks. "I'm breaking up with him. I've had it."

Marlene laughs. "You always say that."

"This time I mean it."

"That's what you said the last time," Deb says, smirking.

I stab my fork into my cake. Debbie and Marlene light cigarettes. One of the band groupies stumbles into the room. "Is it somebody's birthday today?" she asks.

"Get lost, Barbie," I say, scowling.

"I'm not Barbie," the girl says, confused. I roll my eyes, and Marlene snickers.

The girl puts her hand on her hip. "Well, you don't have to be so rude, you know."

I glare at her. "For your information, this is my house, and I am not in a party mood. I have an important show to do next week. So, why don't you make like a bee and buzz off?" The girl grabs a beer and prances downstairs. No one in this joint is listening to me.

By midnight, the whole house is vibrating. I wander around checking for damage. I stub out cigarettes and put coasters under beer bottles. I find a greasy half-eaten chicken leg on the carpet. Has nobody here ever heard of a plate? And where is the rest of the goddamn chicken? Sherrie Cumberland and Paul are making out on the couch. The basement is dark and stinks of weed. In the upstairs bathroom, four kids I don't even know are leaning over the sink doing lines of coke.

"Get out," I say. They ignore me. I pick up my hair dryer and crank it up, full blast. "If you're not out in five seconds," I tell them, "you'll be sucking coke and pubic hairs off the floor." That gets their attention. They swear at me and leave.

I retreat to my bedroom and close the door. I take off my jeans and crawl under the covers. I light up a ciggie and smoke in bed. I'm wearing my new black lace underwear. It was going to be a surprise for Ian. This was supposed to be *our* weekend. No parents, no Buzz, just him and me. I have a bottle of Black Tower wine in the fridge—well, somebody probably drank that by now—and I was going to make us a romantic dinner. And it's not like he didn't know about it. And yeah, I know he really likes me. When we're good, we're really great. But half the time, it's no good at all, and I'm so tired of pretending.

I chain-smoke in bed, and sure enough, Ian shows up eventually, like he always does when he wants something. He's like a wild animal; he only comes when he's hungry. And when he's hungry, there he is at my door, rubbing up against me like a cat in heat. He has a joint in one hand and what's left of Papa's cognac in the other. He shuts the door with a bump of his hip. He looks at me with those bedroom eyes. And yeah, he has a gift for sex, the way some people have a gift for music. I think about how easy it would be to whip off the covers and show him my black lace underwear. He'd jump my bones and stay all night. Tomorrow, we'd wake up in each other's arms. And then we'd have sex all over again. But that's just some bullshit love story.

I don't even bother yelling at him. "Go away," I say. "I don't want to see you anymore."

"Carla, let's make love, not war," he says. He gives me the peace sign and tries to climb into bed. I shove him off, and he pretends to look offended. He says, "Hey, baby, you're not going to slug me again, are you?" He laughs, like he's some hilarious stand-up comedian. He leans on my desk and grins at me. "Come on, don't be mad," he says. "Life's too short not to party."

"And who's going to clean up this dump tomorrow?" I ask.

"I'll help you," he says.

"Yeah, right. You'll take off, like you always do. You only stick around for the fun."

"Hey, that's not fair."

"I know you, Ian."

Ian laughs. He takes a swig of cognac. "Carla, you don't *really* know me. No one really knows anybody."

Oh, so now he's Mr. Mysterious? Mr. Drunken Philosopher? Does he think I don't know what goes on in his little pea brain? Okay, I'll bite. I sit up in bed. "You want me to tell you who you are?" I list his traits on my fingers, one by one. "You're selfish, you're a loner, you're mean, you're irresponsible, you think you're hot shit, you'd rather fight than talk, you don't have a clue about how to treat women, and you act like you don't care about anyone. But everybody cares about someone, even you."

Ian smirks and starts to undo his belt. "And who do I care about, hmm?"

He expects me to say *me*. But instead, I say, "Your mother. Your flaky alcoholic mother."

The smile drops off Ian's face. "You don't know fuck-all," he says.

"Yeah? Well, I know when I'm playing a losing game. And I know when to fold."

"Meaning what?" Ian snarls.

"Meaning I don't want to see you anymore." I take a shaky drag of my cigarette. I look straight ahead, avoiding his eyes. I pinch my thigh hard under the covers. I will not cry. I will not cry.

Ian walks over to the bed and stares at me. "Why are you always trying to change me?" he sneers. "You and all your stupid rules. You want me to fit into this nice little package, but I don't fit in. Never did. And you can't fix it." His voice is raw, like it hurts to talk. He shifts on his feet. "So, you want to break up? Fine. Works for me. I've had enough of this shit." He waits for a second, then he walks out the door.

And even though I hate his guts, I throw the covers over my head and sob, 'cause *"L'amore domina senza regole"*— love rules without rules. And I love him, even if he's bad for me. He's my drug of choice. He's the fix I need. But I'm not going back anymore. I'm cutting him loose, and I'm not changing my mind.

"Walk on the Wild Side"

I wonder if it's the crying that makes me thirsty. Maybe losing all that water out of my eyes makes my mouth go dry, and maybe that's why the beer tastes so good. And the next beer. And the next. By the time I reach Geoff on the phone, I am drunk, which is good because the pain in my heart isn't nearly so, well, painful. It's numb. Like in a deep freeze. A cryogenic chamber. Yes, my heart is being kept alive, but at a very, very cold temperature so it can't get upset about what a schmuck my dad is. I try to explain this to Geoff on the phone. I'm yelling into the phone about that little slut, Monique, but it's hard to hear with all this party noise.

"Where are you?" he asks.

"At Carla's party," I say.

"I'm coming right over," Geoff says.

Ten minutes later, here he is. I hug him. I'm about to crack open another beer, but Geoff says this is a bad idea. He says that a fourth beer will be followed by the throwing-up stage of drinking, which, in his experience, is horribly unpleasant and bound to ruin any of the upside I'm feeling now. Okeydokey. Geoff is my friend. He's looking out for me. Geoff is someone I can count on.

"Let's go," Geoff says.

"What's the rush?" I ask. "I'm going to reinvent myself tonight. I'm going to become a new person."

"An alcoholic person?" Geoff asks.

"Maybe," I say.

"I was quite fond of the old person," Geoff says. He looks at me with a sad smile, and if he's sad, then I'm sad. And I don't want to be sad anymore. "I'm sorry about your father," he says.

"Don't worry," I say, waving that ugly thought away with my hand.

"Come on," he says. "Clarissa and Michael are away for the weekend. You can sleep in her bed tonight. You look like you could use some sleep."

"Soon." I link my arm through his. "Come on, let's check out the party."

In the dining room, Jeremy, Jason and a bunch of kids from *Hamlet* are playing Monopoly. They cheer when they see Geoff and call out greetings from the play: "*Stand ho! Who is there?*" and "*Hail to your lordship.*"

Geoff replies, as Hamlet, "*I am glad to see you well.*" They all start talking in quotes to each other, the way actors do when they're in a play together. I leave Geoff and follow the music downstairs. *Muse*-ic, like *Follow your muse.*

That's a-*muse*-ing. I smile to myself. Sometimes I'm just a barrel of laughs.

In the basement, Led Zeppelin II is blasting from the stereo. Jimmy Page's electric guitar dive-bombs through the air, and Robert Plant's high-pitched voice wails "Whole Lotta Love." A girl sprawled across Carla's beanbag chair tries to stand up and spills her beer all over the carpet. She screeches and giggles as her friends help her onto her feet. The beer soaks into the orange shag rug and no one cleans it up.

People are dancing and I dance too. I don't need a partner to have fun. I can have fun all by myself. It's hot, and I'm queasy, but I love dancing. I shimmy and shake. When I twirl around, Ian is there. "What happened in Montreal?" he yells over the music.

"Didn't work out," I say, spinning off in the other direction. I really don't want to talk to him. But a few minutes later, he sneaks up behind me again. He leans his chin on my collarbone. "Nice moves, Rapunzel," he whispers in my ear. His whiskery face scratches against my cheek. He presses a bottle into my hand, but I'm not making that mistake again. I'm not the same person I used to be. "Always poaching someone's booze," I mutter.

"Only the good stuff." His eyes shimmer. His fingers press against my neck. What makes him think he can touch me like that? He shouldn't mess with people the way he does. I squirm away. I've had enough of this party. I want to go to Geoff's place and climb into bed. I weave through the dancers and up the stairs, but I can feel Ian's wolf eyes watching me.

Geoff is still in the dining room playing Monopoly. "Let's go," I say.

"But, darling, I just bought Park Place," he drawls. The other players laugh. Geoff tap-dances his silver shoe token across the Monopoly board.

I whisper, "Hamlet, this is your conscience calling. It's time for your beauty sleep."

"I know, I know. Five minutes, lovey," he says in an uptown voice. "I'm just heading over to Fifth Avenue. Maybe I'll nip into Tiffany's."

Geoff is on a roll. I shake my head. Someone picks up a Chance card and everyone yells, "Go directly to jail."

"I need some fresh air," I say to Geoff. I wander into Carla's kitchen. Someone's cigarettes are on the table, and I help myself to the open pack. I am definitely taking up smoking tonight. I light up. Woah. Yuck. Maybe smoking is an acquired taste. As I leave through the French doors, I hear Geoff singing, à la Frank Sinatra, "Luck Be a Lady."

A couple of kids are hanging out in Carla's backyard, but I want to be alone, so I cut through the hedge and sit in the darkness on my back deck. The deck is cold, and my throat is dry. I could use another beer. Or maybe not. When I think about drinking, I feel nauseous. I take small, elegant puffs on my cigarette.

Music drifts over from Carla's basement. Laughter splashes into the night and seeps away. Inside the house, kids are falling in love, or wishing they were in love, or thinking they are in love. But what is love anyway? I think about *Brief Encounter*. Wasn't I the one insisting—yes, *insisting*—that Celia Johnson dump her husband and children, and run away with Trevor Howard because they were so much in love? Because love is always so beautiful in the movies. And affairs are so romantic. Unless you're the family being left behind.

Elephants mate for life. What do elephants know that my dad doesn't? I flick my cigarette into the air and look up at the stars.

Starlight, star bright,
First star I see tonight,
I wish I may, I wish I might
Have the wish I wish tonight.

I wish I were a kid again. When you're a kid, life is simple. You eat, you play and you read funny stories like *The Cat in the Hat*. I always liked that book. I always wanted to be like the cat, but really, I knew I was more like the fish in the pot. That pink fish flopping around in the blue teapot, with the stern look on his fishy face. Yup, that's me: the anxious, uptight fish. But why can't I be a cat who knows how to have a good time? A cat who always lands on his feet.

A cool cat. A snob cat. A cat who doesn't give a shit about anyone else. Ian, Carla, Dad . . . they're all cats. I didn't choose to be a fish. I don't like being a fish. But some people are born fish, and you can't change yourself into a cat if you're a fish, can you?

I take a deep breath and begin to recite *The Cat in the Hat* out loud. I know it by heart, and I can see all the drawings in my head. I picture Sally and her brother, whatever his name is, sitting side by side on their cute little red chairs, staring out the window at the rain, wishing they had something fun to do.

Ah, be careful what you wish for . . . because something always goes *bump*!

My stomach churns and my head feels sweaty. Someone stumbles out Carla's back door. I continue with my story about the cat on the ball with the rake and the cake.

Ian's face peeks through the hedge. "Hey," he says, pushing through the bushes. He drops down beside me on the deck, in the shadows. "Are you talking to yourself?"

"No, I'm reciting poetry," I say in my fishy voice.

Ian laughs. "Out here in the cold?"

"I'm not in a party mood," I say. My stomach gurgles.

"What's with everyone tonight?" he says. He looks over at me, and even in the dark, I can see the silvery flash of his eyes. He says, "I'm finished with Carla."

I laugh. "For tonight," I say.

"I am," he says. "She's so demanding. We drive each other crazy."

"That's because you're both cats, like *The Cat in the Hat*," I explain. "You yowl and howl, and you go a little wild, and you always have to have things your own way."

"And what are you? A puppy?" he asks, smirking.

"No! I'm a good little fish," I say.

Ian grins. "Cats eat fish." He takes my wrist and licks my palm, like a hungry cat. I pull at my hand, but he holds it tight, and his tongue trails a slippery path all the way to the tip of my forefinger, which he bites between sharp, white teeth.

I yank my finger away. "Don't." I don't like the way he moves from Carla to me without missing a beat. Cats are dangerous animals. "I'm going to find Geoff," I say.

"Geoffy," Ian calls in a high, drunk voice. "Geoffy."

"Quit it," I say. "You're so mean."

"Hey, I'm the one who has to fence with that loser. He makes the duel scene look like shit." Ian scowls. He leans toward me, swaying drunkenly. "Too bad it's not you, Jules," he whispers. "You and me, we could make that scene hot." He grins. "Do you want to fence with me, Jules?"

"No." I stand up.

"Come on, we could spar right now."

"We don't have swords."

"I have mine," he sniggers. "And you don't need one. I'll teach you a new technique." He leers at me. "I'll show you this, and I'll show you that. We'll have some fun, said the Cat in the Hat . . . Hey, that's pretty good." He laughs at his own rhyme and leans over to kiss me. I wriggle away.

Ian throws back his head and laughs louder. He calls out, "'Rapunzel, Rapunzel, let down your hair, / so that I may climb the golden stair.'"

Someone next door yells, "Shut up."

I walk toward Carla's yard, but Ian grabs my arm and spins me around. He mashes his mouth against my lips and forces his tongue into my mouth. "Stop it," I gasp.

"Come on," he says, smirking. "Don't be shy. I saw you watching through the window that night." I shudder. His eyes spin in the darkness. "I saw you, Rapunzel, and you saw me." He holds me tight. He licks the corner of his mouth like a wolf who's tasted blood. I yank away and trip on the deck. I land on my back and he's on top of me in seconds, pinning me with his bony knees, unzipping my jacket, his mouth on my neck.

"No!" I shout. I shove him away. "Stop." His fingers claw at me. "Get off!" I shriek.

"Fuck! What's your problem?" he snaps.

"Jules?" Geoff's voice comes from Carla's yard. "Jules? Hey!"

I'm going to be sick. I stagger to my feet. I lurch to the side of the house and throw up. I lean my forehead against the brick wall and puke again. My head spins. I wipe my mouth on a handful of gritty snow.

Oh God, I feel so sick. I want to leave now. I have to lie down. I need to find Geoff. I don't want to pass out. I stagger back across my yard and stumble through the prickly hedge. Someone is lying on their back, on the ground. It takes me a second to realize it's Geoff.

CARLA

"Riders on the Storm"

There's nothing like a fight to clear out a party. Within seconds of hearing that some guy is sprawled out in my backyard, bloody and unconscious, kids are jumping into their cars and taking off like firecrackers. I leap out of bed and race outside, where Debbie, Marlene and the cast and crew of *Hamlet* are circled around Geoff's body like mourners at a funeral.

"Shit!" I say. "Is he dead?"

"Knocked out," Jason says.

"Maybe he's just passed out," I say, but then I see the blood on his face. Nobody knows what to do. Ice? Water? A blanket? A pillow? Jeremy says we should call an ambulance, but the last thing I need is a siren screaming down my street. Fortunately, Geoff moans and opens his eyes. Everyone breathes a sigh of relief. Julia tries to help him up, but Geoff buckles and clutches his side.

"Ribs," Jeremy says, putting his arm under Geoff's for support.

"Damn," Jason says, getting Geoff's other side.

"There goes the play," Jeremy says.

"You don't know that yet," Jason says. "They tape ribs in hockey."

"Where's Ian?" Debbie asks, naming names.

Everybody looks at me. "How the hell should I know?" I snap. "I broke up with him."

"Again?" Jason says sarcastically. But no one laughs. We're all thinking the same thing. You don't have to be a brain surgeon to figure out what happened here.

I'm the one who drives Geoff and Julia to the hospital, not because I want to, but because Debbie doesn't want blood on her mom's car seat, and no one else is sober enough to drive. The Js help Geoff into the backseat beside Julia, who doesn't say a word to anyone.

I know my way around the North York General Hospital Emergency because of my toe incident, which, of course, was also Ian's fault. I drop off Geoff and Julia at the Emergency door, and by the time I park and walk into the hospital, Geoff has been moved to one of those cubicles. Julia's answering questions at the front desk. She tells the nurse that Geoff's mom is away for the evening, and she doesn't have a number for Geoff's dad. "They're divorced. His name is Keith Jones. He's a doctor. That's all I know."

"There's a Dr. Keith Jones at St. Mike's," another nurse says.

They send us into the waiting room. I figure that if I had to wait two hours for a sprained toe, it's going to take all night long to deal with Geoff's injuries. "I'm not staying," I tell Julia.

She nods. "Thanks for driving."

"Yeah," I say. I glance at her, and man, is she ever a mess. Blood and dirt smeared on her jacket, eyes like two holes in a white sheet and even her breath smells gross. "Julia," I say, "you look like shit."

"I know," she says.

"Where's your purse? You should buy some mints. Your breath stinks." Julia looks around for her purse. No purse. Well, what the hell. No purse, no key, no money, no brains. "You know, for someone who's so smart, you're really disorganized," I say.

"Yeah," she says. But she's not listening to me. And now she's kind of freaking me out 'cause she looks all waxy and slumped over, like a zombie in *Night of the Living Dead*. Maybe she's in shock, or maybe she's drunk. Either way, if Ma were here, she wouldn't leave Julia all alone because Ma takes care of everyone. And maybe I'm not Ma, and I'm dead tired, and I have a whole bloody house to clean, but still, I know how to do the right thing. So, I plunk myself into that uncomfortable chair and I force myself to say something nice. "Julia, Geoff's going to be fine," I tell her.

Julia sinks lower in her seat. "He only came to the party because of me."

"Oh, I see. So this is your fault? That's what you're saying?"

Julia nods. "If it wasn't for me, he would've been at home running lines."

"Well, that's just stupid, Julia," I say, "because if it wasn't for me, Ian would've been having hot sex instead of losing his temper and beating the crap out of Geoff, but that kind of thinking doesn't get you anywhere, does it."

Julia sighs. "Everything has consequences," she says. "Everything is connected." I roll my eyes. "If Pierre Laporte hadn't been murdered, I wouldn't be here talking to you."

"Yeah. So what's your point?" I say.

She shrugs. "It's like Newton's third law in science. For every action there's an equal and opposite reaction. So maybe we're all part of a chain reaction, just complex packages of molecules acting and reacting to each other, like tiny metal balls pinging around a giant pinball game."

I stare into Julia's spacey face. Is she really spouting philosophy at me, at one o'clock in the fucking morning? Well, two can play the philosophy game. I say, *"O mangiar questa minestra o saltar questa finestra."* Julia looks at me, baffled. I translate. "Either eat this soup, or jump out the window."

"I don't understand," she says.

"I learned it from a wise old woman," I say. "It means take it or leave it. Look, Julia, whether you're a pinball or a molecule, the world doesn't revolve around you. So why don't you just stop blaming yourself for everything, and let's go home and get some sleep."

But she won't come, so what can I do? I buy her a coffee from the vending machine and lend her money for cab fare.

I tell her that I'll leave my back door unlocked, so she has a place to go to, if she wants. I ask her to let me know about Geoff. Then I drive home through the dark empty streets, wondering how so much can go wrong in one night.

JULES

"Slippin' into Darkness"

Hanging out in a hospital waiting room is like living in time-lapse photography; no one seems to move, yet every time I look around, someone is gone, or someone new is sitting there, or the hands on the clock have jumped half an hour. Finally, after Geoff has been taken for X-rays, I'm allowed to see him. He's in one of those narrow, curtained-off cubicles, wearing a hospital gown, lying under a thin pale-blue sheet. The blood has been cleaned off his face, so the damage is more visible now: swollen left eye, a cut on the brow, a scrape on the chin. His face is puffy and bruising. "How're you doing?" I ask.

"It only hurts when I breathe," Geoff says. He tries for a smile, but it's more like a grimace.

I stand by the bed. "Can I get you something?"

"A new body?"

"Steve McQueen or Kris Kristofferson?"

Geoff chuckles, but the pain grabs him. "No jokes," he says.

"But if I can't make you laugh, life's not worth living."

Geoff blows out a breath. "I'll be fine when the drugs kick in. They think it's just cracked ribs."

"Just?" I say. "And the shiner?"

"Nothing a little pancake makeup won't take care of."

"You can't be serious."

But he is. "I did not spend my whole year practicing for *Hamlet* just to watch it go down the drain."

"Geoff, you can't move without hurting."

"That's why some genius invented drugs," he says. "Drugs and tape. If Sarah Bernhardt could perform after one of her legs was amputated, certainly I can get onstage with a little crack in my ribs." He takes a shallow, painful breath. "I have four days to recover."

"Three and a half. But even if you could do it, Mr. Gabor will never let Ian onstage after this."

"Why not?"

"Because he beat you up," I say pointedly.

"Says who?"

"What are you talking about?"

"Jules, it was too dark to see." I stare at Geoff like he's out of his mind. He says, "That's my story and I'm sticking to it. Without Ian, there's no play. I need Ian, and Ian needs me. I'm not telling anyone. Not even Clarissa, okay?"

"No, it's not okay," I say sharply. "It's just a play."

"Not to me."

"Well, I'm not going along with this."

Geoff reaches for my hand and stares at me with his one good eye. "Yes, you are. You won't say a word. 'Cause you're my best friend."

The X-rays show two fractured ribs on his right side, which wouldn't normally keep a person in the hospital, but because of the concussion, the doctor wants him to stay overnight. Geoff is wheeled to another floor, to a shared room. An elderly man is in the other bed. It's quieter here than in Emergency. Geoff is drugged, and he drifts off.

The nurse says I should go home now, but *home* has become a confusing word. My house is sold. Monique sleeps in my parents' bed. *Home* is fragmented and realigned. Even tiny words like *us* suddenly have new meanings. Small adjustments in vocabulary, like shifting tectonic plates, have seismic consequences.

I take a seat under the florescent lights outside Geoff's room. My eyes feel scratchy. Time creeps along the edges of the wall. The black hands on the clock jerk spasmodically. Hamlet whispers:

> *'Tis now the very witching time of night,*
> *When churchyards yawn and hell itself breathes out*
> *Contagion to this world.*

I flip through stacks of outdated magazines. I pick up an old *National Geographic* and look at pictures of camel trains in the Rajasthan desert. Camel trains. Isn't that an oxymoron? Isn't travel by camel the antithesis of travel by train? Animal, iron. Ancient world, modern world.

Oxymoron. What a strange word. It's like someone was a moron for thinking it up. I turn the page, and a camel's goofy, loutish face stares back at me with its black languid eyes, long lashes and grinning lips. What an odd creature. On the opposite page is a pullout photograph of a line of camels plodding across golden dunes beneath a relentless cobalt-blue sky. I wish I could be there, so far away: desert, dust, heat, the tinny clank of metal cups and the creak of heavy packs. I blink.

Ding. I open my eyes. It's 3:25 and at the end of the hall, the elevator doors slide open. A tall slim man strides out. He's in his mid-forties and has a handsome movie star face. He walks over to the nurses' station, talks with the nurse and then walks down the hall in my direction. There's something familiar about him. I rub my eyes. For a moment, I can't place him, but then I recognize him. He's the man from the stone house in The Beaches. The man with the perfect family. Funny how people's lives intersect. I wonder if someone in his family has had an accident too.

The man walks into Geoff's room. Ah, he must be the elderly man's son. After a few moments, he comes back out and looks down at me. "Hello," he says.

"Hello," I say.

"And you are . . . ?"

"Jules. I'm a friend of that boy in there. Geoff Jones."

The man nods. "Where's Clarissa?"

I scrunch up my forehead. "What?"

"Do you know where Clarissa is?" he repeats.

I shake my head. "She's not here." How does this man know Clarissa?

The man sighs impatiently. I look up into his hazel eyes. His eyes are exactly the same color as Geoff's. He could practically be Geoff's dad. And then I realize he *is* Geoff's dad. The nurses phoned him. That's why he's here. That's why Geoff parks in front of his house. He's been spying on his own father. Oh God! Why didn't he tell me?

I stare at Keith Jones's handsome face. "You look so much like Geoff," I say.

"Apparently so," Dr. Jones replies.

"He was beaten up."

"I read the chart. Look," he says, "can you give Clarissa a message? Just tell her that Keith came by. If she needs to get in touch with me, call my office. *Not* my home. Okay?"

"Okay."

"Thank you," he says. He turns away.

"Wait," I say. "You're not staying?"

"No," he says. He strides down the hall.

"But don't you want to talk to him?" I call out. Keith Jones doesn't look back. His footsteps echo off the tile. My voice comes out shrill and loud. "He would want to talk to you!"

The nurse steps out into the hall. She glances from me to Dr. Jones. The elevator swallows him up. It's 3:37. He was here for all of twelve minutes.

I blink. I look back down the empty hall. Did I dream this? Can this be real? What heartless, cruel man was that? My head pounds. My body is a pillar of steel. Lights hum and flicker above me. Ghosts rise up from the dead. And there is Hamlet, huddled in the corner in his black cloak, churning, grieving, soul raging at the injustice of it, while his father's ghost calls out for revenge: *O horrible, O horrible, most horrible!*

And Hamlet's words come to me: *"O, from this time forth / My thoughts be bloody or be nothing worth!"*

CARLA

"Everybody Plays the Fool"

All day Sunday, I make like Cinderella in the house: scrubbing, washing, vacuuming, dusting. I use every cleaning solution I can find. When I attack the grease stain on the living room carpet, I pretend it's Ian's face, and I scrub really, really hard. How dare he ruin this for everyone! Even himself. After all the rehearsals and all that work. So what if Geoff's a crappy fencer? Hamlet carries the whole damn play, and Geoff is an amazing Hamlet. So who gives a shit if he's gay?

Around mid-morning, a blue Cadillac pulls up next door—Loverboy!—and Mrs. Epstein and Bobby are dropped off. Ten minutes later, they're at my front door. Mrs. Epstein is clutching a piece of paper in her fist. She asks if I have any idea where Julia is.

I sigh. "Yeah, as a matter of fact I do." I give her the pared-down version of the fight. I don't mention Ian by name. As soon as she hears about Julia staying at the hospital with Geoff, Mrs. Epstein tears off in her car, leaving Bobby with me. Well, things are getting "curiouser and curiouser," but Deb and Mar don't call me the Queen of the Interrogation Room for nothing.

"So tell me about your weekend," I say to Bobby. And before you know it, the whole story spills out. Apparently, "Doctor Loverboy" is Mrs. Epstein's boss, and he invited them up to his cottage for the weekend, but something must have gone terribly wrong because suddenly, this morning, she was packed and ready to go. Bobby didn't even get to try out the sauna, and no one talked on the drive home. Then his mom found a note on her pillow, and she phoned Bobby's dad in Montreal. There was a lot of yelling and crying. And now Bobby doesn't know what the heck is going on. He wants to know when Buzz is coming back.

"Tomorrow," I tell him. Bobby looks bummed.

An hour later, Mrs. Epstein and Julia drive up. I walk Bobby back to his house, hoping for the inside scoop. Mrs. Epstein tells me that Geoff has two broken ribs. Damn! I ask to see Julia, but Mrs. Epstein says she needs to rest.

Meanwhile, my phone is ringing off the hook. Everyone wants to know what's going on. Debbie says she heard that Ian spent the night at Jim's place. Jim swears that the two of them left the party before Geoff got beat up. Jason says he heard that one of the guys at the party belongs to the Hells Angels, and maybe *he* beat Geoff up. People are saying Ian is going to be expelled; *Hamlet* is going to be canceled; Geoff is in a coma; Geoff is paralyzed for life. Where the hell do they get this stuff? After a while, I stop answering the phone. Only Julia knows what's going on, and so far, she's not talking.

JULES

"Let It Be"

What do I remember of the days before the show?

I remember the hospital. When I wake up in the hospital chair and see my mother's face peering down at me, I'm not surprised because nothing surprises me. She found my note and spoke to Dad. She's so sorry. She says she really wanted Dad back even after she knew about Monique, because love isn't a switch you can turn on and off. Dr. Katzenberg, she explains, is a kind man, but he wants more than she can give right now. I can't look at her. She should have told me the truth a long time ago. Now it's just *"Words, words, words,"* as Hamlet says. They land around me like bullets in the sand, making soft popping sounds somewhere in the part of my brain that's still listening.

Does she say, like Gertrude: *"O Hamlet, thou hast cleft my heart in twain!"*?

Shall I reply, like Hamlet: *"O, throw away the worser part of it, / And live the purer with the other half!"*?

When Clarissa arrives at the hospital, Mom takes me home. I sleep in the pink room for a long time, day into night into day, and I have strange dreams crunched together like cars in a highway pileup. I cannot remember any of them, but each time I wake up, I see Hamlet sitting on the end of my bed, waiting and fingering the scabbard of his sword.

Sometime on Monday, Bobby runs into my room and says that Dad's coming next weekend. He thinks this will cheer me up. He tells me not to worry about Geoff because someone on his hockey team had a broken arm, and then it was in a sling, and now it's all better.

On Tuesday and Wednesday, Mom lets me stay home from school. She and Clarissa talk all the time now. I never imagined the two of them could be friends, but they have more in common than I would've guessed. Meanwhile, I visit Geoff briefly each day. His eye looks like a rotten plum. He walks stiffly and pops painkillers like candies, but he assures everyone that he's improving by the hour. Maybe he is, and maybe he's not. I run lines with him, but we make a mess of it. The painkillers make him groggy, and I can't concentrate on anything. My thoughts keep drifting to Dad and Monique, the two of them standing in the front hall. The scene loops through my head like a scratchy Super 8 film. I can practically hear the clicking of metal sprockets as Monique's hand snakes around Dad's waist, over and over and over.

At night, I lie in bed and revisit events of the past two years: Dad's canceled visits to Toronto, his week in New York that he said was for business, the many late nights at the store. Lies upon lies. Did my mother think, like the ghost in *Hamlet*:

What a falling off was there!
From me, whose love was of that dignity
That it went hand in hand even with the vow
I made to her in marriage, and to decline
Upon a wretch whose natural gifts were poor
To those of mine.

The words of the play haunt me. Hamlet wraps his black cloak around my shoulders. He keeps me company, whispering soliloquies in my ear. Our worlds blur, one no more real than the other.

At Geoff's place, Clarissa makes pots of chamomile tea. Geoff and I sip, but we have no appetite. Michael van Meers shows up with chocolates. Mr. Gabor drops by and tells Geoff that Benjamin is standing in at rehearsals, but Geoff insists that he will perform; he's just saving his strength for opening night. As for me, I don't say much anymore. Everything will unfold as it must. As Hamlet says before the duel, *"If it be / now, 'tis not to come; if it be not to come, it will be / now; if it be not now, yet it will come. The / readiness is all."* I finally understand that speech. It's not that Hamlet is surrendering; it's that he finally has the courage to meet his destiny.

Wednesday is opening night, the night we have all been waiting for. At five-thirty, Clarissa and Geoff pick me up in Baby

Blue. Clarissa grips the steering wheel, white-knuckled. Geoff's ribs are taped up, and he claims it makes all the difference. Curtain is at seven. Clarissa will sit in the audience with my mother and Bobby. In the school parking lot, she kisses Geoff on the cheek and says, "Darling, I'd tell you to break a leg, but I think you've damaged enough bones already."

I carry Geoff's bag into the school. He has dubbed me his "personal valet." The gym change rooms are being used as group dressing rooms, but Mr. Gabor has arranged for Geoff to be alone in a classroom down the hall, away from all the flurry and commotion. The cast, except for Ian, drops by with hugs and best wishes. Benjamin pumps Geoff's hand. "I am immensely relieved to see you," he says, grinning. "Even at your very worst, you're a thousand times better than I am." They joke around, but as soon as Benjamin leaves, Geoff's shoulders sag and he pops a pill.

"Didn't you already take one?" I ask.

"I need another," Geoff mumbles. He does voice warmups and runs lines, but his timing is sluggish, and his words are garbled. Is it the pills, or is it nerves? "Hey," he says brightly, "why don't you help me with my makeup. If I do it myself, I'll look like a clown."

I sit facing him, our knees touching. His eye has turned ghastly shades of purple, ocher and mustard. I dab on the creamy pancake as gently as I can, but Geoff winces with each touch.

"Sorry," I say.

"It's okay," Geoff says. "Stage makeup is a wonderful thing. It covers all sins and hides all scars. Soon I will be without fault or blemish." He smiles dreamily. I look into his eyes—the same hazel eyes as his father, except Geoff's eyes are glazed with a medicated dullness, and behind them is a skulking pain. I see it now.

"What?" Geoff asks.

"Are you going to be okay out there?" I ask.

"Of course," Geoff scoffs. "Are you kidding? I could do Hamlet in my sleep."

I stare at Geoff. His fingers are gripping the edge of his chair, and his arms are locked against his ribs like steel bars. His torso is a block of stone. The emperor is wearing no clothes.

I try to make my voice sound calm. "So, how bad does it feel when you fence?" I ask.

Geoff hesitates. "I don't know. I haven't actually tried that yet."

"You haven't tried? Not even once?" Geoff shakes his head. I lean back and my hands twitch in my lap. "But, Geoff, you have to fight against Ian—"

"Did Clarissa put you up to this?" Geoff snaps.

"No," I say.

Geoff glares at me. "I'm not afraid of Ian," he says. "What more can he possibly do to me?"

But we both know what Ian can do. I glance at Hamlet's sword lying on the desk.

Geoff lurches out of his chair. "You think I can't do it?" he spits out. He glowers at me. "*Give us the foils. Come on,*" he says roughly, calling out Hamlet's lines. "I'll prove it to you. *I'll play this bout.*" He grabs his weapon and wrenches the sword out of its scabbard. Pain crackles across his face.

"Don't," I say.

But Geoff won't surrender. He's like a warrior king in the final throes of battle. He hoists his sword above his head, and with a hoarse cry, he lunges forward. But even this single thrust is too much. He buckles and cracks, like a felled tree. He drops the sword and grabs his ribs, bleating like a wounded animal. I reach for him. What was he thinking? Was he hoping for a miracle? Did he really believe he could step onto the stage and become a legend like Sarah Bernhardt?

Geoff sinks into his chair. He covers his face with his hands and weeps. He butts his head into my shoulder. I ache for him, but I have no tears. I think about Ian, and my chest burns. Where is he now? Primping in the mirror? Flirting with the makeup girls backstage, while everyone knows what he did, but no one says anything?

Geoff picks up the sword and stares at it. My watch reads 6:08. "I should go find Mr. Gabor," I say. "Benjamin will need to get changed soon."

Geoff looks at me with a withering smile. "Benjamin is no Hamlet," he says. He pushes the sword from his lap to mine. "Take it," he says. "You do it, Jules."

We stare at each other. I feel a lump in my throat. I know what it costs him to give this up. He nods at me. "You know the lines. And you know how to fight." He squeezes my hand.

I do know *Hamlet*. It's in my blood. And I'm not afraid. I'm not even surprised. It's almost as if this were preordained. As if everything in my life has been converging on this one terrible event.

"*Revenge should have no bounds*," Hamlet whispers Claudius's line.

I look up, and there he is. The dark prince. He beckons me. I glide my fingers along the length of the sword. I feel the chill of the blade across the tops of my legs. I curl my fingers around the grip. "*There's a divinity that shapes our ends*," Hamlet says. And yes, I know what I have to do.

It takes me ten minutes to run from the school to Hawthorne Crescent. I move swiftly, as if in a dream, on long legs, in smooth strides. I never tire. I am fleet-footed, like those long-distance runners of ancient Greece who carry messages into battle. When I reach Ian's house, I merge into the shadows, cut down the side path and slink into the backyard. I find Ian's key under the urn. It's so easy to slip inside. I hear Mr. and Mrs. Slater's voices upstairs. They must be getting ready for the show. I move silently. I know what I'm after, and I take only what I need.

Ten minutes later, I'm in the girls' washroom, the one near the math area at the far end of the school. It's quiet here. No one's around. I stand in front of the mirror, pale and thin, staring at the ghost of my former self. My face is sallow and older than my years. My chestnut hair tumbles down my back. I think about Mollie, who loves my hair, but she's so far away and she wouldn't understand. I brush my hair in steady strokes, and then I take out the scissors. *Snip, snip.* I start at the front, just below the ear. I'm going for a pageboy look. It's difficult to get it right, especially at the back where I can't see properly. *Snip, snip.* A ritual offering. Long cords of hair drift down around me, encircling my feet in a feathery halo.

As I cut, I think about Rapunzel, and Ian. "Rapunzel, Rapunzel, let down your hair . . ." Then the witch climbed the golden stair. Rapunzel cried when the witch hacked off her long thick braid, but I shed no tears when I cut my own.

When the job is done, I almost look like a boy. My head feels light and my neck is cold. Hamlet smiles at me from the mirror. *"Come on, sir."* It seems I am transformed after all.

When I show up in the dressing room, Geoff is aghast. "Jules! Your hair!" But there's no time for talk. It's ten minutes to curtain. I quickly change into Hamlet's clothes. Being tall, thin and flat-chested has its advantages tonight. Geoff's shirt is big, but once I tuck it under the tunic, it's fine. The rest of the costume fits perfectly. Geoff smiles sadly to see me in his clothes. "You even look the part," he says bitterly.

I place my hands on his shoulders. "I might be a change-ling prince," I say, "but you watch, I promise I'm going to make you proud."

By the time I appear backstage as Hamlet, it's too late to stop the show. The cast stares at me, appalled.

"Hamlet can't be a girl!" Ophelia gasps.

"She could easily pass for a prince," Benjamin insists. "I say, better Jules than me."

"A cross-dressing prince?" Carla scoffs. "I can't do the bedroom scene with her!"

"She knows how to fence," Ian says, appearing from the shadows. "Let Jules do it. It will be a good match."

I haven't seen Ian since the night of the party. He's regal and handsome in his royal blue vest. It picks up the color of his eyes. He'll cut a striking figure onstage.

"*The devil hath power / T' assume a pleasing shape,*" Hamlet whispers.

I look Ian hard in the eye, and he has the nerve to grin back at me.

"*That one may smile and smile and be a villain,*" Hamlet sneers.

Oh, I *will* be Hamlet to his Laertes.

Mr. Gabor peers at me. "Can you do this, Epstein?" he asks. I nod. "All right then," he says. He speaks Claudius's line: "*Come, Hamlet, come and take this hand from me.*" He

his drowned sister. He leaps on me, bellowing with grief and
rage, and we wrestle, rolling across the floor. I fight hard, but
Laertes pins me down. He grabs my throat and tries to strangle me. Hamlet shouts at him, warning him off:

> *I prithee take thy fingers from my throat,*
> *For though I am not splenitive and rash,*
> *Yet have I in me something dangerous,*
> *Which let thy wisdom fear. Hold off thy hand.*

Does Ian hear the edge in my voice? Does he sense the
danger then? I think he enjoys it. My anger spurs him on. It
gives him something to play against.

The scenes move swiftly after that. King Claudius preys on
Laertes's lust for revenge, and the scheme for Hamlet's demise
is set in motion. Which brings us, finally, to act 5, scene 2. The
duel scene. The climax. The trumpets sound, the drums roll and
the royal court of Denmark assembles on the stage: King
Claudius, Queen Gertrude, Osric, Horatio, Laertes and Hamlet.

Laertes and I prepare for the duel. We strap on our white,
padded fencing gear. King Claudius jauntily takes our hands
and clasps them together in a show of sportsmanship. As we
shake, I glance into Ian's eyes. I see the cold thrill of anticipation there; he is so hungry for the fight. He meets my gaze
and squeezes back hard. In that instant, we connect—two
sides of the same blade. Yin and yang. Darkness and light.

For a second, I almost lose my nerve, but then we break, and the play moves on.

I deliver my soliloquy on madness to Laertes, and as I do, Osric wheels the trolley onto the stage. He's staring at the swords bewildered. I boldly call out my line, *"Give us the foils."*

There are four swords displayed on the cart: two stage swords and two rapiers, the ones I've taken from Ian's sanctuary. I see the shock register on Ian's face. He immediately recognizes his grandfather's swords gleaming brightly under the stage lights. He almost falters on Laertes's next line: *"Come, one for me."*

Hamlet replies, *"I'll be your foil, Laertes."*

Ian catches the challenge in my voice, and his eyes light up as he puts it together. He knows that only I could have made the switch, but he still thinks this is just a game. He smirks as he says, *"You mock me, sir."*

"No, by this hand," Hamlet replies.

Ian and I lock eyes. Every line we speak is straight from the play, but everything is double-edged.

Claudius discusses his wager on our duel. Laertes replaces his flimsy stage sword on the cart. He says, *"This is too heavy. Let me see another."* Ian reaches for one of his grandfather's rapiers. He cuts it through the air with a fierce swoosh. The audience sucks in a breath. Carla looks nervously from Ian to me. Her eyes bug out, but what can she do? By now, the entire cast and crew understand that things have taken a dangerous turn. At the back of the auditorium, way up in the lighting booth, Mr. Gabor must know that we're headed for trouble.

I snatch up the other rapier and feel the weight of it in my hand. It hisses wickedly as I slice it through the air. Hamlet says, *"This likes me well."*

Claudius toasts to Hamlet and drinks. Ian and I don our fencing masks. We strike our positions: salute, en garde.

The first bout is fast and neat. Ian and I perform it flawlessly. After a burst of rapid exchanges, Laertes forces Hamlet back. He slashes low, at Hamlet's legs, and I deftly jump over his sword. Laertes thrusts his rapier at my shoulder, but Hamlet spins around and lunges. I jab underneath Laertes's arm for a quick touch to his waist. Hamlet calls out triumphantly: *"One."*

Laertes: *"No."*

Hamlet: *"Judgement!"*

Osric: *"A hit, a very palpable hit."*

Laertes sneers: *"Well, again."*

We move apart and take up our positions. In the second round, the choreography is more acrobatic. Laertes slices his rapier at my head and I duck, narrowly escaping the blow. The air whistles; the audience gasps. I think about Geoff and how he hated this part; how he always cringed, terrified of Ian. My anger swells as I hunt Laertes across the stage. Our swords blaze beneath the lights. I jab and strike with a hit to his side. My blade grazes Ian's vest. His eyes widen at the closeness of my attack.

Hamlet: "*Another hit. What say you?*"

Laertes: "*A touch, a touch. I do confess 't.*"

Two points for Hamlet. None for Laertes. I catch my breath. Laertes seethes with rage. He is desperate to hit Hamlet now. Just one nick of the poisoned sword and Hamlet will die. We separate again.

Meanwhile, Queen Gertrude picks up Hamlet's goblet and innocently sips from the poisoned wine.

Hamlet calls out, "*Come, for the third, Laertes. You do but dally. / I pray you pass with your best violence.*"

Laertes scoffs at my challenge. "*Say you so. Come on.*"

We play the third bout, pressing each other back and forth across the stage. Finally, we smash our swords together and hold tight, leaning our bodies full into it. Osric cries out, "*Nothing neither way.*" He pushes us apart; no points scored.

Laertes scowls. Hamlet turns away to wipe the sweat from his brow. And this is Ian's cue to leap out and attack. Laertes shouts, "*Have at you now!*" He lunges at Hamlet, going for the hit. Ian's rapier passes so close to my arm that I almost feel the kiss of the blade.

I gasp, as if Hamlet's arm has been cut. Quickly, I crush a fake blood capsule against my skin. Hamlet wheels around, wounded and furious. He will not suffer this unprovoked assault. If Laertes does not play by gentlemanly rules, nor will he. The fight is on.

Hamlet charges at Laertes. Laertes thrusts his sword at my stomach. I grab his blade with my free hand while he wrestles my sword away from me. In the scuffle, we exchange rapiers; his sword is now mine, and mine is his. We leap apart, swords poised, all according to the choreography.

It isn't until I hear Carla gasp that I see the blood dripping from my fingers. I've sliced my palm on the razor-sharp edge of Ian's blade, and blood gushes from my wounded hand. The audience murmurs sounds of distress. Can they tell the difference between real and fake blood? Or do they think this is all part of the show?

Now I feel the flaming pain, but I don't care anymore because I am done with this play! I am off the page. I am unleashed! I, Jules, leap at Ian Slater, shouting out my unbearable rage. *"O villainy! Ho! Let the door be locked. / Treachery! Seek it out."*

The cast gawks. They're confused. They think I've blown my line. Wasn't I supposed to hit Laertes in the arm? Shouldn't Claudius be speaking now? Carla scrambles to get us back on track. She blurts out, *"The drink, the drink! I am poisoned."* She swoons, dying, collapsing on the floor, but no one watches because the play is over and I am attacking Ian for real.

He flings off his mask. I rip off mine. He howls, and his wolf eyes glitter as he charges. Our rapiers fly up into the air. I will have justice! I will have my revenge!

At first, we're almost evenly matched, my polished anger against his superior strength and skill, but soon the advantage of my surprise attack is gone. Ian is by far the better player. He forces me back, and I stumble against the trolley, sending it crashing to the floor. Ian drives his sword at my chest, but I swing my rapier up to meet his. *Smack!*

My lungs are on fire. I can't keep this up. I'm flagging badly. Blood spurts from my open wound, speckling the stage with a crimson spray.

Ian feints left. I flick at his hip. He reads my attack, parries and cuts. I ward off the blow, but he surges against me. I stagger backward as his sword swoops down. I raise my weapon, but I am too slow. My wrist snaps back as his sword connects. *Crack!* My rapier flies out of my hand. It spins wildly across the stage, like the flashing spokes of a silver wheel. Claudius ducks and tumbles over his throne. Carla shrieks. Ian laughs. I stand on the stage, frozen and disarmed. Ian and I stare at each other.

Ian points his sword at my chest. Will I feel the blade? Will he actually do it? I see the cold gleam in his eye, but I do not flinch. I am prepared to meet my destiny.

Ian springs forward across the stage, but he is so arrogant in victory that he doesn't see Carla's foot kicking out. As he runs, his foot snags on hers. He trips and falls. The rapier goes flying. It twirls upward like a ribbon of light, and I snatch it by the hilt in midair. Ian hits the ground and rolls onto his back. But before he can move, there I am, leaning over his flattened body, the tip of my blade upon his throat.

I hold the sword to his bare white neck. And now, everything slows down. I hear the buzz of the stage lights, the rasp of my breath, the splat of my blood as it hits the floor. And even though my chest heaves and my hand pulsates in a rhythm of pain, inside, I am serenely calm, like a golden Buddha on a lotus flower.

My rapier wobbles in my trembling hand, the sharp tip nudging against Ian's throat. His skin dimples, and a little pucker of flesh oozes a drop of glossy red. Not because I press, no, but because Ian gives a shudder. Fear, or just the instinctive urge to move away from the blade? A nick. I don't intend to cut him. I don't move. I hold my position. Even when the blood blooms at the tip of my sword and trickles gently down his neck, I remain very still.

We all stand in our Shakespearean frieze, in poses of shock and disbelief. In the gap between the beats of time. I have all the time in the world. I am a warrior. This is my time. The choices are mine to make now. The threads of fate lie in my hand, and everyone must wait to be released. What will I do? *That is the question*. I look down the length of steel into Ian's shocked face. What is Hamlet supposed to do? What can we hope for in this sad, strange, imperfect world?

I listen, and from the shadows, Hamlet whispers, *"Let be."*

Let be. What wisdom in that? What justice served? What dignity there? Hamlet gives me a melancholy smile. *"There is a / special providence in the fall of a sparrow."* Let it go. *"Let be."*

Around me, the dust dances in the cold white beams of light, like the dust clouds from a sand mandala, like the sand from the Rajasthan desert. Even ordinary dust sparkles in the stage light. It is all a play, a play within a play, tragedy or comedy, just an illusion.

I drop the sword and walk offstage.

From the wings, Fortinbras stumbles onto the broken set. He speaks in a shaky voice, *"Where is this sight?"*

Horatio replies, *"What is it you would see? / If aught of woe or wonder, cease your search."*

In the wings, Mr. Gabor reaches for me. Around me I see sparks of light.

My mother appears and takes me in her arms. Everything is shining bright.

CARLA

"It's All Over Now, Baby Blue"

I think it's common knowledge that without my fast footwork, Julia Epstein would've had more than twenty stitches in her hand to worry about. Mar and Deb still can't believe I had the guts to trip Ian.

"That was so amazing," Mar says.

"What made you do it?" Debbie asks.

I shrug and give them my most humble smile, but the truth is, I didn't even plan it. I just stuck out my foot. Maybe I have great instincts. Anyway, it did put an end to the fight. And now, everyone's treating me like a hero! Ma and Pa can't stop bragging to the family, and Papa says the school should give me a gold medal for bravery because if it wasn't for me, someone could've been really hurt. Not that Ian was going to skewer Julia or anything—he's a fencer, not a killer—but still, the whole fight was totally out of control. And the thing is, Julia started it.

That's the kicker. I mean, shit! Julia Epstein, of all people. I still can't figure out what the hell was going on in her head! She had to know she had no chance against Ian, so what did she think she was doing out there? What kind of idiot goes around stealing weapons from somebody's house, picking a fight with an expert fencer and holding a sword to a guy's neck in front of over two hundred people? Talk about stupid! And yeah, I know she was upset about Geoff, but what exactly was she trying to prove? If she wanted to get back at Ian, there are better ways than doing it in public.

And the saddest thing about the play is that up until the point where Julia lost it, everyone was so fantastic. I mean, every single one of us. And if I was good—which I was—Julia was great! Even in the bedroom scene, where Hamlet grabs Gertrude by the shoulders and tells her what a whore she is, I was totally convinced that Julia was Hamlet. I actually stopped thinking about her as a girl. She was so intense and so real. Suddenly we weren't pretending anymore. We took that play to another level. I actually *became* the queen. Gertrude's words flew out of my mouth, like Carla and Gertrude were mind-melded. I never knew that was possible. I mean, shit, that really blew my mind! And even the people in the audience who usually hate Shakespeare and were only there because their kid was in the show (my parents) were totally hooked. It was incredible. Better than drugs. Better than sex. Yeah, it was magic.

So, with all that adrenaline and talent, it's a shame the play closed after opening night. Geoff was injured, Julia got suspended, and Ian ran away from home. I found out from

Mr. Gabor the next morning. He called me into his office at recess and asked if I knew where Ian was.

"At home?" I asked, getting this sick feeling in the pit of my stomach.

"No, Ian is not at home. This morning, when Mr. and Mrs. Slater woke up, Ian was gone, and so was his motorcycle." Mr. Gabor never calls him Ian, and it sent goose bumps up my arms.

"Maybe he went to Jim Malone's," I said, but even as I said it, I knew it wasn't true.

"He took clothing and some items from the house," Mr. Gabor said. "His parents phoned the school. They're very concerned."

Concerned? Right. Furious, more like it. I wonder what "items" Ian stole. Money? Pearls? The Picasso print? Something he could sell for quick cash?

"Cabrielli, did he speak to you last night?" Mr. Gabor asked.

I shook my head. "Not a word." After *Hamlet* ended, backstage was a madhouse: Julia fainting, parents plunging onto the stage, everybody upset and confused. And in the middle of that, the Slaters barged in. I saw Mr. Slater grab Ian in the wings and rattle him like a bag of marbles. The man is a beast. And she's an alcoholic. It's just like we suspected. The whole family is screwed up.

So, I told Mr. Gabor everything: the party, Geoff, the Slaters, the works. 'Cause there's no point in covering it up anymore. Ian is gone, and he's not coming back. He's probably past the border by now, zooming south, racing into the sun, flying free and solo on his bike. It's what he wanted. And maybe he'll be happier now. Anyway, he had nothing left to do but run.

And yeah, like Marlene and Debbie always tell me, Ian is trouble. I know that. He's wild and selfish. He doesn't care about school. He smokes way too much pot. He drives too fast. But they don't know how we sang songs in bed and drew messages in ink on each other's skin. And that boy kissed like there was no tomorrow. They don't know that side of him.

JULES

"I Shall Be Released"

"Do you know why you're here?" he asks.

I force myself to answer calmly. Do not be irreverent. This isn't an existential question. He's not asking about my purpose in life. He's asking why I'm here, in this office, sitting on the couch across from him.

He sits in a swivel chair. There's an oak coffee table between us, with a ceramic bowl in the center and the requisite box of Kleenex. The bowl is pale blue, fading to white at the rim. Pretty. Maybe his wife bought it. There's a picture of her and the kids on his desk. They're smiling, heads leaning together. Two girls, a boy, a mom and a dad.

Instantly, I'm ambushed. All threads lead to my father. Nothing is innocent anymore. Not the corny family photo on this desk, not my dad's old sweater left behind in the closet, not the cashier saying, "Have a nice day"—as if nice days are possible. The casual things are always the worst, the things other people take for granted. Even listening to music is difficult now—so many songs about undying love, or spurned love, or broken hearts. These things sting, like paper cuts.

Dr. Martin is waiting for my answer. He's about the same age as my dad, but he has thinning hair and the kind of eyes that watch you all the time, even when he's not looking directly at you. He wears a shirt, but no tie. Is that supposed to put me at ease? I'm sure he's a nice man, but still, this is a waste of time.

The answer to his question is simple: I'm here because the principal said that, as a condition of returning to school, I'd have to see a psychiatrist. It's really not an unreasonable request, considering what I did. If it wasn't for my marks, the support of teachers like Mr. Gabor and the "extenuating circumstances," as Mom explained at their meeting, I would have been expelled. Instead, I got a three-week suspension. I'm relieved. I need the rest, and I can't face school anyway. I'm tired, but I can't sleep. I have trouble concentrating. My mind tends to drift, just like it's drifting now.

I focus on Dr. Martin. "I'm here because the school requires it," I say.

"Do you see this as a formality?"

Yes, but that's not what he wants to hear. So I say, "I know what I did was wrong. I'm really not a crazy person. I'm very sorry for the trouble I caused." I try to look contrite, but Dr. Martin doesn't seem impressed. I guess my acting skills have slipped. He should have seen my Hamlet. Now *there* was a performance. I remember it like a dream. If I look in the shadows, will Hamlet still be there?

Dr. Martin flips open a file. Probably a report from the

principal, or Mr. Squash, or Mr. Gabor, or maybe even the police. Mr. Slater threatened to lay charges against me for theft, break and enter, and assault with a dangerous weapon, but after Ian ran away, everything was dropped.

Dr. Martin cuts right to the chase. Full points for not messing around. "It says here that you attacked a fellow student. Maybe we could start with that."

"It was the duel scene in *Hamlet*," I explain. "I sort of got carried away."

"Did you initiate the fight?" he asks.

"Yes, but Ian's the better fencer."

"The report says you drew blood."

"I didn't really hurt him," I say.

Dr. Martin looks at my bandaged hand. "You got hurt."

"That was a mistake."

"It says you fought with real swords."

"Yeah."

"Isn't that dangerous?"

"Yeah."

"Did you hold a sword to his throat?"

"Look, if I'd wanted to kill him, he'd be dead," I say dryly.

Dr. Martin raises an eyebrow. Oops. I must avoid sarcasm. You cannot joke about killing people, especially not with a shrink. It makes you look like a psychopath. And I don't want to make these appointments a habit.

"Julia—"

"Jules."

"Jules," he says, "if Ian's the better fencer, and you chose to pick a fight with him, did you expect to lose?"

"Winning or losing wasn't the point."

"What was the point, Jules?"

"I just wanted to fight back."

"Against Ian?"

I nod. "For starters."

"Who else?"

"I have a list."

Dr. Martin laughs out loud. At least he has a sense of humor. He tells me we have an hour. "Start wherever you like," he says.

Days pass. Time is elastic. Mom quits her job with Dr. Katzenberg, so she's around the house a lot. She says she'll look for another job after I go back to school. Thing are better between us now that she's not pretending. We talk about practical things, like finding a house to rent next fall, or signing me up for driving lessons. She looks at me differently these days, like I'm someone she'd like to get to know better. I look at her differently too, now that I understand.

On the weekend, Dad comes to Toronto. I refuse to see him. He stays at the Howard Johnson Hotel and takes Bobby out for a burger and fries. He tells Bobby about Monique, and Bobby cries for days after that. Mrs. Cabrielli sends over casseroles that pile up, uneaten, in the fridge.

Sometimes, when Bobby can't sleep, he sneaks into bed with me, and then he asks those terrible questions, like "Why did Dad stop loving Mom?" and "Does this mean Dad's never coming to my hockey games anymore?" and "How can he be my dad if he's living in another city?" On nights like these, I lie in bed and pretend I'm in a sanatorium, the kind you see in the movies where they send tuberculosis patients to recover. I imagine that I'm in a cold, clean room, looking out on an English country garden where birds sing, the air is crisp, and everything is washed with rain.

Sometimes I just feel disembodied, like pieces of me have been stored in canopic jars, like I'm a dead pharaoh waiting to be stitched together in the afterlife.

Or I see people doing ordinary things, like walking dogs or mowing lawns, and I wonder how they can be so content when there's so much damage in the world.

I know this isn't normal. Dr. Martin says it's part of grieving and that divorce is like a death in the family. He tells me to keep a journal. I write in it every day. I tape Diane Arbus's monkey photo to the cover. I list the annoying things people say when they're trying to make me feel better:

1. Time heals all wounds.
2. You have your whole life ahead of you.

3. This too shall pass.
4. Be grateful for the things you have.
5. You'll always be our family (the Epsteins).
6. You're a strong girl and you'll get through this (the Cohens).
7. One door closes and another door opens.
8. This is the first day of the rest of your life.

These banalities don't help. I wonder if people said this stuff to Pierre Laporte's children after he was murdered. I think about those children from time to time, and I wonder how they're getting on. The FLQ is yesterday's news, but some of us haven't forgotten.

Mollie phones often. She doesn't mess with platitudes. She says, "Jules, your father is an idiot, and he's going to live to regret this. When she's thirty, he'll be fifty, and then she'll dump his sorry ass. And he'll beg your mom to take him back, but it will be too late for that. I think I'm going to egg his car."

"Maybe you could also egg *her* car," I say. "It's the red Mustang parked in the driveway."

"I could spray-paint a few choice words on the doors."

"And let the air out of the tires," I add.

Our conversations are full of plots—elaborate, devious, gruesome, adolescent fantasies. We know we won't carry them out, but it feels good to plan them.

Geoff and Benjamin bring me homework. Geoff's ribs

are healing well. My hand is still swollen and sore. I'm going to have an ugly scar. Sometimes the three of us take walks in the ravine. I ask Benjamin what people are saying about me at school, and he says, "I do not hold currency with gossip-mongers and mudslingers, and neither should you." But I dread going back.

The day before my suspension is over, the season turns, and the flat heat of summer arrives. Geoff decides it's perfect weather for an excursion. He picks me up in Baby Blue and we head to The Beaches for the first time since Christmas. I haven't told him about my encounter with his father, but as we park in front of the stone house, I know I can't avoid it. I don't want any secrets between us, even the painful ones.

"You know when you were in the hospital . . . ," I say. Geoff looks over at me. "When they couldn't reach Clarissa, they phoned your father. He came. And I met him."

"Oh," Geoff says. He glances at the house.

"Yeah," I say. "You look a lot like him."

"Ironic, isn't it," Geoff says softly. "Did you talk to him?"

"Not much," I say. "He didn't stay long."

Geoff looks at his feet. "I guess I'm surprised he came at all."

"Men can be so stupid," I say. "Present company excluded, of course."

Geoff smiles. We walk in silence down the street and across the park to the water's edge. Today, the lake is cerulean blue and a million sun-sparks play on the waves. Geoff stares up at the cloudless sky. I toss a stone into the water.

"You know, you could have told me," I say.

"I know," Geoff says. "I should've, but I didn't."

"Are you going to be okay?" I ask.

Geoff nods. "I'll learn to be."

CARLA

"New Morning"

About a week after the *Hamlet* fiasco, I'm sitting on my bed painting my toenails, when Ma and Pa walk into the room, and right away, I can tell something's wrong. "What?" I ask. "Is it Nonna Cabrielli?"

"No, nothing like that," Papa says.

"We have something to tell you," Ma says, "but you can't tell anyone, not even Debbie and Marlene, *capisci?*"

"All right," I say. "What's the big secret?"

"It's the Epsteins," Pa says. "They're getting a divorce."

"Wow!" I say, picturing Mrs. Epstein and Loverboy. "How could she do that to her family?"

Ma huffs. "It's not *her*, it's *him*."

"What?" I gasp.

"It's *Mr.* Epstein. He's been having an affair in Montreal. He's dumping Natalie for a twenty-year-old!"

"Holy shit!" I say.

Ma's nostrils flare. "*Puttana*," she spits.

"What do you know about her?" I ask Ma.

"I know she went after a married man, and that's all I need to know," Ma snorts.

I am shocked. I only met Mr. Epstein twice, but he always seemed like such a nice guy. "Why would he ditch his family like that?" I ask.

"Age," Ma sneers. "He's chasing his youth. Men are afraid of getting old. They get flattered by these skinny young girls, and the next thing you know, they flush their lives down the toilet."

Papa gives me the male point of view. "Some men just can't keep it in their pants," he says.

"Tony!" Ma says.

"It's the truth," Papa says.

"But not all men are like that," Ma assures me.

Papa grins. "You're right, *cara*. Some men fall in love for a lifetime. And lucky for you, I'm one of those." He gives Ma a big fat smooch on the lips.

"Ew, can you please stop that?" I say.

But Ma is lucky, and so is Pa. And when I get married, the guy better know where his own bed is, 'cause if he cheats on me, I'm going to cut off his balls. I can't imagine how Julia feels. "Does Julia know?"

Ma nods. "She found out over the Easter weekend. She went back to Montreal and caught them in her own house. What a slap in the face." Ma wipes away a tear. "No wonder the poor girl went bananas."

And suddenly it all makes sense: the way Julia got totally

smashed at my party, her zombie look at the hospital, the way she flipped out onstage with Ian . . .

Ma says I should go over and talk to her, but what am I supposed to say? Sorry your dad is a stupid prick? Sorry you had a nervous breakdown? It's not like we were friends before. And nobody likes a pity visit. It would just be awkward, so I do nothing.

It's May by the time Julia shows up at school again, and her first day back is a real bummer. She's like Moses parting the Red Sea; when she walks down the hall, people step back and gawk, like she's some kind of three-legged circus freak. Even the grade tens snicker.

"Hey, isn't that the crazy girl from *Hamlet*?"

"Yeah, she's the one who attacked that cute guy."

"I heard she went totally psycho."

"Is she, like, a transvestite or something?"

They say these things really loudly, and they don't give a shit that she hears. But most of them never even saw *Hamlet*. They don't know how talented she is.

At lunch, I sit in the caf with Deb and Mar, in our usual spot. Julia sits in the corner reading. Everyone stares, 'cause she looks like shit with her hair hacked off and those dark circles under her eyes. She's way too bony in the face. Ma would want to fatten her up.

"God, her hair looks terrible," Deb says. "And really, that was her only good feature."

"I bet it sucks to be her," Mar says.

"I heard she got electric shock therapy," Deb whispers.

"Really? Like Frankenstein?" Marlene giggles. "Maybe that's why she looks so fried." They laugh and crane their necks for a better view. And yeah, maybe I'd be dishing the dirt too if I didn't know what was really going on. But I do know, so it pisses me off.

"Why don't you stick your eyeballs back in your head," I snap. I snatch up my lunch and push away from the table.

"Where're you going?" Debbie asks.

But I don't need to explain anything to anyone. I march straight over to Julia's table.

JULES

"If Dogs Run Free"

"Is anyone sitting here?"

I look up from my book, and there's Carla Cabrielli. She has a lunch bag in her hand and a fake smile on her face. At nearby tables, people watch us like they expect a confrontation.

"I guess this seat isn't taken," Carla says, "'cause half the people in this room think you're going to pull a knife on them." She laughs to let me know it's a joke.

"Carla, what do you want?" I ask. "In case you haven't noticed, I'm not exactly the flavor of the month."

"Oh, I noticed," she says, sitting down opposite me. "And yeah, some people can be so rude!" She pulls out her lunch and spreads it on the table: a sandwich, an orange, chocolate milk and cookies. She arranges the items in a neat little row. Then she stares across at my untouched sandwich.

"Aren't you going to eat that?" she asks. "'Cause according to *Cosmo*, you don't want to get *too* thin. I mean, it's better to be too thin than too fat, but you're on the verge of overdoing it. Especially with your new short hair. You know, if you got a decent cut, it actually wouldn't look so bad. I go to Mario in the Bayview mall. He could give you a Twiggy cut. Short and feathery. It works for her, and Mia Farrow. And you're super skinny, just like them." She stuffs a straw into her chocolate milk and sucks on it.

"Do you ever say anything nice to anyone?" I ask.

Carla smirks. "I don't think so," she says. "But just 'cause I'm a bitch doesn't mean I'm a bad person." She grins. I shake my head. "Well, it's true," she says. "I know I'm blunt, but at least I'm honest, and honesty is something I admire in people." She bites into her sandwich. "Ian was like that too, wasn't he?"

I look away. Is that why she's here? To talk about Ian? I don't say anything. I wonder if she knows where he went. I'd like to ask, but instead, that's what she asks me.

"Have you heard from Ian lately?" she says.

"No," I say. "Why would he contact me?"

"Because he liked you," Carla says.

"No, he didn't."

"Yes, he did." Carla stares at me. "Come on, Julia. I know you two had a thing going on."

"You're wrong," I say.

"Oh, really," she says sarcastically. "Then tell me, when you stole his swords, how did you know where to find them, hmm?" I hesitate. Carla leans across the table. "I've been to his place plenty of times, and I never saw any swords around. But you knew exactly where to look. You knew because you'd been there before. Which is also how you knew about his key." She tosses her hair and gives me a self-satisfied smile.

"You'd make a good detective," I say.

"Yeah, I figured it out." She shrugs.

"But you have it all wrong," I say. "He only invited me over once. And he only wanted to fence with me."

"Yeah, well, he only wanted to fuck with me," she says dryly.

"I'd say you got the better deal," I reply.

Carla blurts out a laugh. "Touché."

"Salute."

"Well, at least I didn't stab him with a sword," she teases.

"At least I didn't break his nose," I retort.

We're both smirking now, enjoying the verbal jousting. We're fencing with words, and we're well matched. This is not what I expected. Not from someone who's been torment-ing me all year. But strangely enough, she doesn't scare me anymore. In fact, if anyone's trying to be nice here, it's her.

"So, why did we fall in love with that jerk?" Carla asks.

"You call that love?" I ask. "In the end, I hated him."

Carla looks me straight in the eye. "You know, for someone who's so smart, you don't know very much about love." She juts out her chin. "You know what my nonna Cabrielli says? 'Love and hate are two sides of the same coin.' I think with Ian it was kind of like that. And not just for you. For both of us."

I consider this. Perhaps she's right. There is no halfway place with love. That's why it hurts so much when they leave.

Like with my dad. I glance up at Carla, and suddenly I understand why she's here.

"You know about my dad," I say quietly.

She nods. She looks embarrassed and annoyed. "Yeah. I heard. That really sucks. Men can be such idiots. Always thinking with their dicks. I mean, what the fuck does he think he's doing? A twenty-year-old? Give me a break! That is not love. That's some sick porno fantasy. You don't dump your family for that kind of shit! What an asshole!" She grinds to a halt, like perhaps she's being a little insensitive? After all, I am the asshole's daughter. She hesitates, but then, in her typical Carla way, she sees the line and steps right over it. "Marriage should be a holy thing," she says, "not that I'm religious or anything, but I have my rules, and the first rule is: Married men don't fuck around." Carla sighs. "Look," she says. "I'm not saying your dad's a pig. I don't know the man personally. But he sure knows how to roll around in the shit."

I stare at her. And then I crack up. It's not really that funny, but I can't help it. All day long, I've been walking a tightrope, expecting someone to push me over, and suddenly I'm free-falling and laughing with Carla Cabrielli. How bizarre. And perfectly hilarious. People stare, but we couldn't care less. We're a couple of fuckups in the love department, and all we can do is laugh our heads off.

"Hey, what's so funny?" Geoff says. He slides in beside me. Benjamin sits beside Carla.

ACKNOWLEDGMENTS

Does it take a village to complete a novel? Writing is a solitary affair, but much gratitude and appreciation goes to those who encouraged, read drafts and offered wise counsel along the way. Many thanks to Max, Sarah, my parents and the extended Leznoff clan, who endured hours of mumbling and groaning (on those rainy cottage days) as I read chapters aloud and muttered, "Not now!" to their questions. Thanks to fellow writers and test readers, young and old, who offered their generous feedback. Hugs to Jane McBride for providing the Maui refuge and to Janice McDonald for escapes abroad (how lucky can a girl get?). Carolyn Bateman offered her valuable insights. Douglas College gave me a term away from teaching to write: Thank you! Super-agent Ali McDonald magically plucked the manuscript out of the ether, and my wonderful and wise editor, Sue Tate, coaxed me down the final stretch. Finally, I want to thank my smart, funny, lifelong friends, some of whom date back to those childhood and teenage years in Montreal and Toronto: You were there then, and you're still here in my heart now.

"Oh, nothing," I say, wiping my eyes.

"Men," Carla says. "Right, Jules?"

I glance at her. Is it *Jules* now? It's not like we're actually going to be friends. Not after everything she said and did. Those mean things could fill a book.

Carla's orange rolls across the table. Geoff catches it and tosses it into the air. An orange. My sandwich. Benjamin's apple. He's juggling, and he's a bad juggler.

"Hey, I want to *eat* that apple," Benjamin says.

We laugh.

Carla unwraps her mom's cookies. She pushes them into the center of the table. I pick one up and take a bite.